CITY OF EXILE

Published by The Kraken Collective
krakencollectivebooks.com

Edited by S.L. Dove Cooper.
Cover by Gabrielle Arseneault.
Interior design by Key of Heart Designs.

claudiearseneault.com

ISBN: 978-1-7778464-2-8

City of Exile

An Isandor Novel

Claudie Arseneault

FOR ALL THE RELATIONSHIP MISFITS,

You will find your people.

Previously

in the City of Spires Series

The scene:

Isandor, the City of Spires. A nexus of eccentric towers in which bickering merchant families vie for power through overbearing shows of wealth and endless trade wars. At its edge is an enclave from the Myrian Empire, a conquering mageocracy of dubious ethics and an economic powerhouse meddling in local politics.

A few key players:

Diel Dathirii, Head of Isandor's only elven noble house, an eternal idealist.

Master Avenazar, Leader of the Myrian Enclave, ruthless and powerful mage.

Nevian Ollu, young Myrian apprentice, stubbornly trying to learn magic despite Avenazar's abuse.

Varden Daramond, High Priest of Keroth. Talented artist, loving soul, powerful fire-wielder.

Branwen Dathirii, Dathirii spymaster, master of disguise and owner of the greatest wardrobe.

City of Strife

Our story begins on a cold late autumn day, on a plaza surrounded by a great many shops. **Avenazar** has caught his apprentice, **Nevian**, there, and he intends to show his discontent in the traditional means: by shooting pain through his forearm until it overwhelms his mind. For **Diel Dathirii**, a witness to the event, this is one-too-many horrible acts from the Myrian. He interrupts, and tells Master Avenazar know that the Myrian Enclave will no longer be tolerated, and he will do all in his power to eradicate them from Isandor's politics.

Thus begins the hostilities that underpin our tale. Diel Dathirii returns home and musters his forces: cousins, nieces and nephews, lover and steward. The plan is two-pronged: to protect his network of local merchants, and to convince other Houses of Isandor to rally against the Myrian Enclave. Master Avenazar is, however, much more direct: he instructs the enclave's High Priest to walk into a Dathirii-affiliated shop and burn it to the ground.

Varden Daramond knows better than to refuse. His position is ever-precarious; in Myria, his people are more frequently slaves than titled priests. When he finds **Branwen Dathirii** inside, he knows he is expected to kill her. Instead, he whisks her away to his quarters, hiding her until she can escape. Winter solstice is coming, and most of the Enclave will be attending an all-night ritual to mark it, providing a perfect opportunity. In the meantime, their rocky start turns into mutual respect, then quiet friendship.

Little do they know, Varden will not make it through winter solstice unscathed. You see, all this time Nevian has been sneaking out of the enclave to meet with a mentor, and Varden, feeling kinship with another rebellious soul, has known and helped this. But when Nevian is spotted leaving—in the distance, unidentified—it is Varden, the outsider and easy scapegoat, who is accused.

Master Avenazar is all too happy to confirm the accusations by invading Varden's mind—and in the process, he learns of Branwen's ongoing escape and Nevian's outing in Isandor. He ditches the High Priest and teleports to his apprentice. While Master Avenazar carefully and painfully erases all of Nevian's knowledge of magic, Branwen interrupts him with a well-placed dagger throw then makes a narrow escape afterwards. Helpful, but not quite enough to save Nevian, who falls of the bridge.

And here we must interrupt, for there is another story unfolding in Isandor, one far from the high towers of nobles and the troubles of the Myrian Enclave. This second tale started in a Shelter, little more than a hovel squeezed between two towers, where those of meagre fortunes can find a roof and a meal for free. We should, perhaps, introduce **some new key players.**

Arathiel Brasten, drifter from the past, returned after 130 years in a magical trap, all senses drained.

Calleran Masset (Cal), servant of Ren, luckiest and most generous soul.

Hasryan Fel'ethier, secret assassin for the Crescent Moon Mercenary, open sass master.

Larryn, owner and cook of the Shelter, a bubbling stew of anger and spite.

Drake Allastam, firstborn son of House Allastam, uses the power and privilege to harass those less lucky.

Sora Sharpe, investigator for Isandor's Sapphire Guards. Quick of wits and pigheaded.

Lady Camilla Dathirii, centuries-old elven lady, dispenser of tea, cookies, and wisdom.

Now that we have that settled, let's rewind a moment, to **Arathiel**'s arrival in the docks of Isandor, wet and out of luck, a stranger in his own city, a ghost uncertain of his future. He finds his way to the Shelter, where through luck and **Cal**'s insistence, he integrates three friends'—Larryn, Hasryan, and Cal—regular card games. In particular, he bonds with **Hasryan**, with whom he shares an easy understanding; two outsiders struggling to let others in.

It is during one of these card games, up in a fancier tavern of the Middle City, that the group is interrupted by **Drake Allastam,** who has an antagonistic history with **Larryn.** It takes less than a minute for it to devolve into a fight, and while Hasryan gets a solid headbutt in, the fight lasts long enough for guards to walk in, and Hasryan is arrested.

Nothing would've come out of it if not for **Sora Sharpe**'s eagle eye. She ties Hasryan's dagger—an unique weapon with a jagged blade and the ability to produce electricity—to several unsolved murders, and pins him down for them, prolonging his stay in prison. One of these, the death of Lady Allastam, remains the highest profile assassination of Isandor's history. No big deal, Hasryan tells himself. He didn't do it. A bribe and a lie, and his boss will get him out of there.

Except she doesn't. The head of the Crescent Moon organization leaves him out to hang, confirming the dagger is his—a dagger she gave him, shortly *after* Lady Allastam's death. After a decade of working together, the person Hasryan trusted most, the woman who'd picked him off the streets and taught him to survive has scapegoated him through a ploy she had set up over a decade ago.

That knowledge shatters Hasryan as surely as his trust and, dejected, he is ready to give up and wait for his execution—but his friends certainly aren't. Unaware of their friend's real job and angered that he is being scapegoated, Larryn and Cal plan to use the winter solstice as cover to sneak into the prisons, pretending to be two priests.

And this brings us back to winter solstice, and to poor Nevian falling off a bridge—only to crash right in front of Cal. Cal, with his very limited healing skills and big heart, with his absolute faith in the randomness of life and his own, ridiculous luck. Cal, who is awaited for a prison infiltration but stops, knowing this teenager's life is in his hands. He can only interpret this happenstance as the will of his deity.

He patches what he can, and is running back to the Shelter to gather help bringing Nevian back when he finds Arathiel. Flustered, desperate to save Nevian, filled with guilt over his absence from the prison heist, Cal unburdens all of his worries on calm, patient Arathiel.

It is worth noting that Arathiel, who was alive in the city a hundred and thirty years ago, held a noble title at the time. He has been recognized by **Lady Camilla Dathirii**, with whom he has shared tea multiple times since, and to whose door he runs that night. She had offered help—any help he wished—and it is direly needed now. To send healers to Nevian, certainly, but that is not all he intends to ask. Arathiel has no intention of letting Hasryan's execution go through, but he'll need help to stop it and to hide afterwards.

Larryn is not one to be deterred by Cal's absence (although he is certainly one to be angered by it). He makes his way to Hasryan's cell and prepares to free him—until Hasryan, desperate for someone, *anyone*, to accept him without any lies left, tells him about his true job. Shocked, already primed for anger, Larryn tells him off, and is forced to flee before he can get over himself and fix his initial reaction.

When he reaches his Shelter once again, all of his anger is bottled tied and ready to blow at the one friend who should have been there. Cal's attempts to defend himself only infuriates him further, and in the heat of the yelling match, his fist flies faster than his brain, knocking Cal to the ground with a solid punch.

And thus the winter solstice night comes to an end. Branwen has returned to the Dathirii Tower and into her family's loving arms, but few others have had such luck. Varden is imprisoned in the Enclave, at Avenazar's mercy, and Nevian clings to life only through sheer stubbornness, his memory of magic erased. The long-standing friendship between Cal, Larryn, and Hasryan has shattered, existing fissures finally cracking.

But not all is lost, as they say, and in the following days, as Branwen and Lord Dathirii struggle to convince Isandor nobles to ally against the Myrian Enclave, Arathiel's plans solidify and come to fruition. On the morning of Hasryan's execution, he is ready.

So we come to our last scene, a park commemorating one of the city's founders with the delightful habit of hanging criminals above it. On bridges above, the high-born have gathered to celebrate the capture and execution of Isandor's most infamous criminal. Below, Lower City residents fume at one of their own once more sacrificed on the altar of politics.

Moving through the crowd towards the investigator responsible for it all is Camilla Dathirii, an old elven lady—perfectly innocent and respectable, here only for congratulations, of course. And when, in the process of doing so, she drops her purse and provokes a small commotion of guards trying to help pick it up before everything rolls off the bridges, it is also without malice, and not at all the distraction Arathiel has been waiting for. *Of course.* (It is.)

Nevertheless, Arathiel uses the opportunity to drop into their midst, blades drawn, and sprints for Hasryan. He is outnumbered, but he possesses one advantage no other has: he does not feel pain any more than he does cold or touch. Wounds that would stagger other fighters leave him unfazed, and so despite his profuse bleeding, he pushes through the Sapphire Guard surrounding Hasryan and they escape by leaping into the park below.

The landing is hard—impossible for one who does not feel the pressure of ground under his feet. Arathiel's ankle snaps when they hit the park, destroying any chance he has of walking away from his spectacular rescue and the chaos that will ensue. Only Hasryan slips away, clinging to the written address offered by Arathiel and the certainty he still has at least one friend in Isandor willing to risk it all for him.

He does not expect the safehouse to be Lady Camilla's quarters, nor does he anticipate the delicious butterscotch cookies awaiting him and the crash of emotions they will bring. He sits in the living room, cookies in hand, unexpected acceptance washing over him while on a balcony nearby—a few stories above, really—Diel Dathirii considers his few remaining options.

The nobles of Isandor refuse to help him, the Myrian threat is growing, and they hold a man to whom his niece owes her life. But today he saw a man who does not know pain—a man he knew, over a century ago, as caring and courageous. Arathiel's aid would destroy the political goodwill he has left, but what good is that, when all of his allies rebuked him? The choice is simple and dangerous, and he is ready to make it.

Here ends *City of Strife*, but certainly not their adventure.

All of Isandor is searching for Hasryan, some for revenge, others to save their friend. Only Arathiel knows where he hid, however, and he is recovering from the dangerous escape, cuffed to a bed in the Sapphire Guards Headquarters. What time he has awake, he spends with Investigator Sora Sharpe, who is desperate to understand why this stranger—this unknown noble from a time long passed—has risked everything for the city's most infamous criminal. Arathiel has no answers to give: the bond he shares with Hasryan is not easily explained with words and his sense of rightfulness goes beyond the city's laws.

What could (and should) have been a prolonged stay in prison is interrupted by Lord Dathirii, who brings his political influence to bear in order to cut a deal with Arathiel: temporary freedom if the man is willing to lend him his aid against the Myrian Enclave.

The time eventually comes for his mission, and Arathiel has been allowed to call for help—a favour Cal is more than happy to grant him. They are to assemble in Lord Dathirii's office. However, on the same day, through circumstances and quick deduction, **Kellian Dathirii**, the family's guard captain, figures out that Lady Camilla is involved in hiding Hasryan and confronts her about it. She refuses to give in, and instead challenges him to arrest her for her crime and brings her to the Sapphire Guard headquarters—a challenge Kellian readily accepts.

Hasryan, a witness to the confrontation, refuses to let Camilla face prison on his behalf. As soon as possible, he sneaks his way up the Dathirii tower, to Lord Dathirii's office, and warns Diel Dathirii of his aunt's arrest, risking his own fate in the process. Instead of bringing him to the guards, Diel ropes Hasryan into his Myrian Enclave mission, adding invaluable assassin skills to the infiltration team.

And thus Hasryan finds himself part of a small team with Arathiel, who has saved him when he thought everything lost, and Cal, who had never given up on him and is thrilled to prove it through spontaneous hugs and squeals of joy. Their last member is none other than Branwen, the driving heart of the mission, who will gladly take any help if it lets them extract Varden from his terrible situation.

They set off as night falls, and their infiltration starts without a hitch—in no small part thanks to Cal's subtle luck-bending magic. Only, Varden is no longer in his cell. Master Avenazar has dragged him out of it, to the great brazier in Keroth's Temple, to try a brand new spell of his own devising. With it, he slams into Varden's mind, forcing him to channel Keroth's power through the flames, and uses the magic to further nourish his spell and wipe Varden's spirit out of his own body and mind.

Branwen's team arrives just in time to interrupt the ritual, but the confrontation is not without pain. They must also face not only Avenazar's deadly green whips of magic, but also Varden's streams of fire, as the High Priest has not regained control of himself. Hasryan's successful stealth-and-stab breaks the spell, but by that time Arathiel has been flung directly into the brazier's great flames.

And here, several things happen at once.

First, the ritual's accumulated power goes haywire, causing an explosion which collapses the temple, and which the ragtag team only escapes with a magical bubble shielding them. Second, Arathiel's contact with the fire causes him brutal and entirely unexpected pain. His scream is what causes the third event: Varden, in possession of himself once again, pulls fire away from Arathiel and uses every inch of his power to keep them both safe. Although no one is left unscathed, the entire team is alive when the dust falls, and they are ready to head home.

Here we must pause again, for there are many agents whose story has unfolded in the sidelines, more quietly perhaps, but in a way no less essential to our tapestry, in House Dathirii and in the Enclave both. These **key players** are:

Vellien Dathirii, youngest Dathirii cousin, anxious singer and expert healer.

Hellion Dathirii, arrogance and drama incarnate. Convinced of his own cunning and the supremacy of elves.

Lord Allastam, Head of House Allastam, father to Drake. Arrogant and choleric. His wife was assassinated a decade ago.

Master Jilssan Wich, second in command at the Myrian Enclave, transmutation specialist, irremediable pragmatic.

While his infiltration team made its way into the Enclave, Diel Dathirii attends a meeting of Isandor's ruling instance, the Golden

Table. Here, nobles from the most prominent houses gather to decide of the city's future—or, in this case, that of House Dathirii's. **Lord Allastam** leads the charge against Diel, angered that he dared free Arathiel, the man who'd stopped the execution of his wife's killer. The price to pay for rescuing Varden is steeper than Diel Dathirii had expected, however: by the end of the Table's meeting, House Dathirii has lost all of its seats around it, and thus its claim at nobility.

The political downfall is only the first of Diel's problems tonight. Without titles, he and his family are unprotected, and he returns to his home to find it invaded by Allastam soldiers. Worse, he is brought to the elf who betrayed him and, with Allastam's help, claimed his place. **Hellion Dathirii** awaits him in Diel's own office, smug and convinced he can force Diel to yield his place publicly, but Lord Allastam has other plans. He has struck another deal, this one with Master Avenazar, and promised to send him Diel as a prize. In the dark of night, Diel Dathirii is shipped towards the Myrian Enclave, shackled and shattered.

He is received by **Master Jilssan Wich,** but their brief chat is interrupted by the temple's explosion. Jilssan immediately heads out, and on her way there she intercepts Branwen's team. Jilssan has been known for her ambition and ruthlessness, but over the course of this conflict, she has witnessed the depths of Avenazar's cruelty and, more importantly, his fickleness. By now, she knows neither she nor her apprentice are safe around him, and the only people foolish enough to openly fight him are Diel Dathirii and his people.

So she tells them Diel is here, at the Enclave, allowing Branwen and the others to save him. When it becomes clear none of them can return to the Dathirii Tower, now under Allastam control, Cal offers his home as temporary shelter.

This should, by all means, have marked the end of their troubles for the night. Unfortunately not, but to understand what comes next, we must return to the lower levels of Isandor.

While political players make their moves, Nevian continues his slow recovery at the Shelter. He is aided by young **Vellien Dathirii**, who through frequent visits helps him restore his missing memories and slowly heal both body and mind. The rest of his time is spent relearning his spells, a fact not unnoticed by Larryn, who has been feeding and housing him. In exchange for these, Nevian accepts to work on a spell to try and track down Hasryan.

The scrying spell is cast on the night of the infiltration, with Larryn looking in, and they find Hasryan as he infiltrates the enclave, at a time where he is alone with Branwen. Larryn concludes House Dathirii is secretly holding him, and he takes it upon himself to arrange a hostage exchange: when young Vellien steps into the Shelter that night, he kidnaps them.

The ransom letter for Vellien is, shall we say, not well-received. It is, however, received in the presence of Hasryan, who offers to sneak to the Shelter and talk some sense into his old friend. It is their first meeting since the attempted prison break and it turns into a rocky one, but Hasryan is firm and clear: the Dathirii are helping him, and Larryn needs to get his shit together and his anger under control, both for his friendship with Cal and for his own sake. Vellien is freed and returns with Hasryan to Cal's house, where their healing talent will be welcome at Varden's bedside.

Here ends *City of Betrayal*. Master Avenazar is grievously wounded but House Dathirii is in disarray, its members split throughout the city—some in Cal's home, others trapped in the Dathirii Tower.

CITY OF DECEIT

In which new <u>**key players**</u> come to the limelight:

Brune, Leader of the Crescent Moon Mercenaries, Hasryan's old boss

Lady Amake Brasten, Head of House Brasten, ambition and ethics combined.

Lady Mia Allastam, the caged bird, preparing her escape.

Now that she's helped Diel Dathirii once, Jilssan knows she either keeps going, or lose alongside them. She uses the chaos at the Enclave to cover her tracks, then buys everyone some time by poisoning Master Avenazar behind the healers' back. Lord Dathirii might have failed to kill him, but with an assassin at his employ, she reasons it's only a matter of time before Hasryan returns to finish the job.

That is, of course, without counting on Diel's rigid ethics. Unaware of Jilssan's hopes, he uses the time to rest in Cal's home, his presence kept secret while Branwen (sonder) her spy network and he formulates a new plan. Helped by Vellien's magic and under Arathiel's very attentive care, Varden slowly recovers from his ordeal. But time is ticking, and Diel needs allies urgently.

He can think of only one: **Lady Brasten**, who has voted in his favour during the Golden Table and recognized Arathiel Brasten as one of their own despite his very public rescue of Hasryan. Accompanied by Branwen and Arathiel, he petitions her for support and is welcomed with open arms. She offers them quarters as well as official backing and her considerable political acumen in the coming battles. They pen a missive to officialise her support and recognize him as the true leader of House Dathirii.

His return makes quite the splash, and among others, the ripples affect three important figures caught inside the Dathirii Tower, who vowed to fight Hellion together.

Yultes Dathirii, once liaison with House Allastam, now Hellion's steward. Uncertain of his loyalties.

Jaeger Larethian, once the stalwart steward and nerves of the House, always Diel's lover.

Garith Dathirii, Dathirii coinmaster and incorrigible flirt. Branwen's cousin.

The trio has been hard at work tricking the Dathirii books to thwart Hellion's designs and spare most of the household staff from a brutal culling. Frustrated by it, Hellion has been playing hot-and-cold with **Yultes**, switching from best friend of decades to dismissive boss on a whim. When Hellion receives Diel's challenge, he is furious and threatens **Jaeger** again, but Yultes successfully steers him away from violence by proposing a grand reception with the remaining members of House Dathirii instead.

The Dathirii Tower is not the only one to hear of Diel's presence within House Brasten and, frustrated by his lack of initiative, Jilssan seeks him out in the cover of night and gets him to agree to her version of events—one in which Lord Allastam never sent him to the Enclave, and thus betrayed the Myrian Enclave. A lie she repeats to Master Avenazar, who promptly orders Drake Allastam killed in retaliation.

Unfortunately, Drake is not alone when the Myrian mages come for him. They find him in a scuffle with Sora Sharpe, who'd just defended Larryn from his harassment, and decide not to be particular about their targets. In the brief fight that ensues, Larryn only keeps his life in extremis, managing to kill both Myrians, and Sora is grievously injured. At a loss about what to do, Larryn brings her to the closest safe place he can think of: Cal's home.

The reunion is awkward, to say the least. Larryn is shaken to the core by the lives he took, but when Cal tries to comfort him, he pushes him away—not out of anger, he says, but because he's yet to deserve it. It's Hasryan's impromptu arrival that helps him work through the worst of his panic. The assassin also elects to stay and reveal his presence to Sora, forcing her to choose her side once and for all.

Once Sora has promised not to arrest him, they hit it off, a long conversation that sprawls for hours and over the course of which Sora invites him for breakfast at her place. There is, she has realised, one Dathirii who has been missing since the day of the Golden Table: Kellian Dathirii. She needs help finding him. Present at the breakfast are also Camilla, who has been staying at Sora's place, along with Branwen. Together, they narrow the possible location of Kellian to two: the Allastam Tower or **Brune**'s headquarters.

Meanwhile, Jilssan has moved to phase two of her plan: rile Lord Allastam against Master Avenazar. She attends an audience with him with the intent of accusing *him* of betraying *them* and prompting a retaliation—and it works. Only, he retaliates immediately, on her, and locks up her in the cells at the heart of the Allastam Tower.

Without Jilssan to poison Master Avenazar, the dangerous wizard finally recovers. He inquires after her to the last of our key characters, **Isra Enezi**, Jilssan's apprentice—Isra who unfortunately holds two very important secrets: that Jilssan has betrayed him, and that Nevian is still alive. When he painfully crashes through her mind, she is able to hide the first, but not the second, and Master Avenazar is all too thrilled to learn his apprentice has somehow survived. He releases Isra, eager to return to a favourite toy.

He shows up at the Shelter and is gleefully plowing through Larryn's courageous but futile resistance when Nevian—hearing the familiar dreaded cackles and the cries of people he's come to care about—emerges from his room and surrenders himself. Master Avenazar takes him back and invades his mind.

Nevian discovers his careful healing with Vellien has granted him unprecedented knowledge of his own mind, and that with it he can dodge Avenazar's assault … for a time. Luckily, Avenazar has not fully recovered from his poisoning, and his recent burst of magic exhausted him. He quickly leaves Nevian alone.

In the brief interlude, Isra comes with apologies, spills out Jilssan's secret betrayal as well as her research into spells to protect themselves from Avenazar's attacks. Nevian, who for the first time has managed to defend himself, demands to see it all—and soon combines his lived experience with theory into the sketches of a spell.

Meanwhile, Varden has joined forces with Vellien and Larryn to mount a rescue mission. They travel through the Shelter's fire and into the Enclave, and through fire and luck, extricate Nevian from his room. This leaves Isra behind, and she decides to buy everyone time. She coats a letter opener with poison, stabs Avenazar with it, and barely escapes with her life, to take refuge in House Brasten.

Unaware of the sudden escalation outside, the Dathirii Tower has completed preparations for Hellion's great reception. Yultes has rigged it to fail: lacklustre food, inconvenient accident, and a Dathirii banner set to fall on Hellion. While all the Dathirii nobles are gathered and enduring the less-than-stellar reunion, Branwen makes her way through the tower, to Jaeger, hoping to sneak him out. They are caught, and Hellion brings them to the main hall where he makes an unexpected offer: anyone who has no wish to follow his leadership can leave unarmed, and House Dathirii will continue without them.

Jaeger laughs at his face. He claims the Tower as his home and refuses to abandon it to Hellion, no matter the threat. Before Hellion can retaliate, Yultes signals for the banner to fall on him, humiliating him in front of everyone. Jaeger slips back to his quarters in the chaos that ensues, and Yultes is soon left to deal with an infuriated an inebriated Hellion. His attempts to placate his friend earn him a brutal slap, the first time Hellion's rebuttals have become physical, and Yultes retreats with sharp words for Hellion, an open defiance of his leadership he had never dared before.

While this is where we have left the Dathirii Tower, its equilibrium whittled to a thin breaking point, there is one last piece of the story to bring forth; one last foolish decision to be recounted. When Hasryan learns of the assault on the Shelter and Larryn's brush with death, he decides he's had enough. He sneaks into the Allastam Tower, officially to find Kellian Dathirii within, but intent on putting his assassination skills to good use and taking Lord Allastam off the board in the process—and, perhaps, to move to Master Avenazar next. Lord Allastam thwarts his plan with emergency healing and a cane swipe that breaks his arm, turning a messy assassination into a disaster. Hasryan's consciousness quickly slips away, and the last thing he hears is Lord Allastam's promise of the pain to come.

And that is where we find him now as we begin the last stretch of his long adventure. Happy reading, everyone!

CHAPTER ONE

PAIN welcomed Hasryan back into the world.

It clung to his body like a sizzling web, its burning lines crisscrossing his skin and tightening around his arm until the entire limb threatened to burst. Maybe it had. Maybe that was why it felt like a hundred tiny pieces that were held together only by the pain, connected to him by one agonizing nerve. Hasryan indulged in a long moan, and as the sound passed his cracked lips, it anchored him deeper to his unfortunate reality.

He'd been captured by Lord Allastam. The asshole had shattered his arm.

"Don't worry. We know how to treat the scum of the earth here."

The echoes of Lord Allastam's voice buried the constant throb of blood rushing against his temples. Hasryan's eyes fluttered open, and he stared into darkness so complete he couldn't parse it. The stone floor under his back was cold—freezing, even, untouched by any hearth or warmth—and the familiar stink of human refuse filled the air.

A cell. Colder than most he'd known, and no doubts deadlier, too, in the long run.

To think he had meant to find these very cells when he'd first sneaked into the Allastam Tower. He should have stuck to the initial goal: to break someone out of there, not to get thrown behind bars alongside them. What a mess. But if Hasryan was honest, he'd never truly planned to do that. 'Finding Kellian' was an excuse, a thin lie he'd told himself to hide his intention to kill Lord Allastam. For once, he would've done it not because he 'd been hired to, not even to defend himself, but because he'd wanted to. Gods, he wanted to. This Myrian war had gone on too long and come too close to killing his friends, new and old, and Hasryan had had enough of it. His entire life had taught him a hyper-specific set of skills—one that got him shunned more often than not—and he'dfinally wanted to use it for good.

Except he had been careless. Couldn't help but taunt his target, and he hadn't been ready for Allastam to jab himself with some emergency healing. He should've been ready.

"Brutal awakening?"

A voice snaked out of the surrounding darkness. If the accented lilt and sultry tone belonged to Kellian, Captain of the Dathirii Guard, then the man was very different from what Hasryan had expected.

"You could say that, yes."

It wouldn't be the most brutal portion of his day. Lord Allastam's last words had been a promise the bastard would inevitably fulfill. Part of Hasryan wanted to curl up and wait for it, his broken arm tucked tight against his chest, a last shield for his dimming hope. The other part, however, perked up in curiosity at his companion.

"Been here long?"

A bitter laugh floated through the darkness. "Every minute in this cold hell is an eternity." They shuffled about with a groan, and Hasryan turned his head in the general direction. Some distant light glinted off the cell bars, but beyond that, he couldn't see anything. "You'll excuse me if I'm pleased with the sudden company."

Hasryan laughed—and sharp stabs of pain in his ribs transformed that into a hiss. "Won't hold it against you," he promised. "So you're alone?"

"Don't sound so disappointed."

Did he? It would have been nice, to have at least found Kellian, even if he couldn't do anything about it from here. One good thing to outweigh the rest of his failures. But more than anything, Hasryan was glad he wasn't alone. And this person … the voice was familiar. He tried to place it, to imagine it less weighed by fatigue, but it still eluded him.

"So what beautiful crimes have you committed to anger our great Allastam overlord?"

They laughed again, the sound even thinner than before. "He is frustrated by our failed attempt to kill his son and I am being held responsible. Which is accurate, mind you, but the point was to have him blame my boss instead of me."

"You chose the wrong target, then. Lord Allastam is very good at killing the messenger."

"No kidding." The tinkling sound of nails on metal bars echoed through the jail corridor. "It's Jilssan, by the way."

Through the fog of pain and cold, it finally clicked. The familiar voice, the attempt on Drake Allastam, the mention of a boss to blame: Jilssan, the Myrian Enclave's second-in-command, with whom Diel Dathirii had established a reluctant alliance to sow chaos between Lord Allastam and Master Avenazar. It clearly hadn't worked as planned.

"We've met!" They had run into one another in the enclave when Hasryan had saved Varden with the Dathirii team. If not for her magic-enhanced speed, he'd have killed her, but she'd treated that as a fact of life rather than a personal affront—and she'd helped them free Diel. He brought a hand to his forehead and saluted the darkness above him. "Hasryan Fel'ethier, at your service."

Her breath caught, and hope threaded her voice when she spoke again. "Did Diel Dathirii finally get over himself and send you here?"

She didn't need to spell out what he'd be sent to do—and even though assassination *had* been his primary plan, that hurt. He wanted to be known for something other than death.

"Our pooled intelligence led us to believe Kellian Dathirii was held here, and I was supposed to retrieve him. I may have taken liberties with the mission goals when I ran across Lord Allastam. Someone had to do *something*. Your shit boss almost killed my best friend."

Horrified silence followed his reply, so tense Hasryan knew Jilssan had stopped moving, as frozen as the stone under him. When she spoke, her voice held the weight of a death sentence.

"He's up again, then. Master Avenazar."

"You bet."

He had found out his apprentice was alive and raided the Shelter where Nevian had been hiding, shattering half the furniture within along with most of Larryn's bones. Varden had healed those before rescuing Nevian, and in the end everyone had made it through, but they wouldn't be so lucky next time, and Hasryan hadn't wanted a next time to be possible at all.

Jilssan shuffled in her nearby cell, leaning against the bars. "Are we, perchance, fortunate enough that you've been caught *after* killing Lord Allastam?"

Hasryan didn't respond. The failure burned his tongue, a thick, bitter layer.

"No, I suppose not." She thunked her head against the bar, and the echo felt as heavy as their gloom. "I grew one of his beautiful trees right through him, and it wasn't enough either. Oh well. At least you're alive, and people knew you'd be snooping around the Tower, right?"

She meant Lord Dathirii and everyone surrounding him, but Hasryan hadn't exactly informed any of them of his plans. He'd used Branwen's intelligence as a pretext and only confided in Larryn. "I, uh … may have chosen the worst person to warn of this?"

Larryn had promised to keep breakfast warm for him, and he'd go on a crusade once his best friend didn't show up to claim his plate. Which was exactly the problem. Larryn would create the most reckless and impulsive plan conceivable and fling himself into it.

"So they're not coming," Jilssan said, and he could hear her hopes die with every word.

"Oh, he's coming," Hasryan said, guilt gnawing at him. Larryn was no one, not even worth the prolonged revenge Lord Allastam had planned for him. If they caught him, he was dead. "Maybe the gods will shine on us and for once in his life, he'll keep his cool instead trying to barge in through the front doors."

CHAPTER TWO

ARRYN dumped his cold breakfast plate on Sora's desk, spilling caramel sauce and apple chunks all over her desk. She sprung to her feet, snatching parchments and ink bottles away from the disaster, the cuff of her sleeves dipping in it. They glared at each other, Sora cradling the bundle of ruined work as she struggled to remain calm.

"What's your problem?" she demanded, her voice a harsh whisper. "Did we part on terms too friendly for your taste?"

A lump blocked Larryn's throat, anger and fear knotted so tight his words struggled to worm through. His last encounter with Sora was the reason he'd come—an impulse, a leap of faith. She'd helped him against Drake Allastam, parrying a blow that would have been fatal and spurning the entitled little shit. Not only that, but she'd spoken with Hasryan after, sided with him.

And now he needed help, and Larryn didn't trust himself to

succeed alone. His track record of Hasryan rescues wasn't exactly promising—Vellien could attest to that.

"I promised Hasryan to keep breakfast ready for him." His halting words betrayed the fear pounding within him. He reached deep inside his pocket and wrapped his fingers around Cal's holy symbol, drawing courage from it. "He never claimed it."

Sora's angry scowl turned into concern. She set her pile of parchments and quills on her chair before motioning at the one in front of the desk. "Sit down. I'll need a better explanation."

Larryn eyed the creamy apple sauce that had dripped on the chair and instead gripped its back. He hadn't slept a lick again, not even the fitful spurts that had marked his last nights. His head pounded, and it made gathering his thoughts a fight all of its own.

"Last night, Hasryan sneaked into the Allastam Tower to find Kellian Dathirii." *And* kill Lord Allastam, but Larryn had no intention of sharing that particular fact and ruin the chances of Sora helping him. If she didn't, who would? Cal's absence during their first prison break still bruised him, and the Dathirii, for all their claims of allyship, would never sully their names for Hasryan. "He never came out."

Sora paled. "He got caught. He got caught in the Allastam Tower."

Hearing it aloud was a hammer to his chest, and for a moment it was all Larryn could do to breathe. When air came, however, it rekindled his anger.

"Yeah! They got him, and they won't tell. You know how this goes!" He flung his arms up, pushing all his building anger into the wide gesture. "Nobles vanish those they hate every day and none of you lift a finger about it. But if we don't do anything—if I don't get in there—then this old fart gets to fulfill whatever revenge fantasy he's had brewing in that skull of his. And I—I couldn't think of anyone else to go to for help."

Larryn's voice cracked at the end, and he tore his gaze away from Sora, heat flushing his cheeks. He hated how scared and overwhelmed he felt, how his world unravelled a little more with every passing day.

"Curse it all, why did he go alone? He didn't need to infiltrate on his own." Sora huffed and crossed her arms—or started to. A dangerous spark lit her eyes, and she snapped her attention to Larryn. "He didn't go in there to kill Lord Allastam, did he?"

Did she have to be so astute? Lies burned Larryn's tongue, but he didn't deny it upfront. "I don't give a rat's ass what he meant to do. If Hasryan saw a way to end this war game everyone is playing, then I'll cheer him on. I almost died, you know? Avenazar ripped my Shelter to pieces, along with my body. Everyone present when Mister High and Mighty Wizard of the Green Tentacles showed up is lucky to be alive." His knuckles hurt from gripping the chair so hard, and he half-expected either it or his bones to break. After a deep breath to steady his flaring anger, he met Sora's gaze. "You wanna give him morality lessons on murder, then be my guest. I'll laugh and make faces behind your back. But he has to be alive for that, so consider stuffing it for now."

Anger, sadness, and horror danced across Sora's face, her mouth twisting or parting with the flow until it settled into a resolute mask. She granted him a quick nod, so slim Larryn might have dreamed it.

"All right."

She strode around her desk, past Larryn, and out of her office. Larryn stared at his cold breakfast plate, confused. All right? All right *what*? All right, I'll help? All right, I've had enough of your very true rants? All right didn't mean much by itself! He spun around and glowered at the door she'd left through, the surge of energy from his tirade draining away, leaving him a shell of fear. Larryn pulled the chair and collapsed into it despite the sauce puddle.

He summoned what little patience he had to wait, but his stomach soon grumbled. Larryn's gaze drifted to the plate. He hadn't eaten yet—he'd wanted to wait for Hasryan. If Sora was going to leave him unattended… He grabbed the plate, swiped the minuscule pancake in caramel sauce, popped an apple slice on top and shoved it down his mouth. It tasted like ash, but it settled his stomach to some extent, so he kept going.

By the time Sora returned, he was licking the sauce off his sticky fingers and acting like he hadn't spilled a fair bit of it on her beautiful wooden desk. She scowled and flung clothes at him. Hard leather gloves smacked him in the face then flopped to the ground, but Larryn managed to grab the rest of it. A Sapphire Guard uniform.

"What the—"

"Change. We need to go."

"You want *me*…" He pointed at himself. "… to wear *this*."

"And once you have it on, we'll fit the breastplate and tie a shiny sword around your waist."

Larryn wished she was kidding, but when had Sora Sharpe ever joked about work? As much as he hated the idea of putting on a uniform, he had been ready to do much worse—even to talk to Lord Dathirii—for a chance to save Hasryan. He grumbled, shucked off his winter coat, and started to pull up his shirt—and stopped, cheeks flushing deep, as Sora continued to stare. "Do you have to look? There's nothing to see!"

Her eyebrows shot up, but she turned to face the wall without arguing. Larryn hurried through the motions, desperate not to dwell on the awkwardness of standing in Sharpe's office with nothing but frayed underwear and thick socks. He grasped the pants, made of a sturdy cotton of higher quality than anything he owned, but a quick knock at the door froze him. His heart climbed into his throat as the doorknob turned. Sora, still close to the door, whirled around and caught it.

"Apologies, but I can't see anyone at the moment."

"You sure? 'Cause I got some juicy information."

Larryn frowned, tilting his head to hear better, trying to place the familiar voice. He'd heard it before, but where? Something in the cheeky confidence, the musicality of her tone—and then it struck him. One of his countless expeditions into House Dathirii had ended with him crouched in an oversized wardrobe, listening to her pointless banter with the quarters' owner. They were cousins or something, and neither of them ever shut up.

Branwen Dathirii, elven spymaster, and one of the last people in this cursed city he wanted to meet face-to-face. What if she recognized Yultes' characteristic cheekbones? Even with darker skin and brown hair, he resembled his father too much.

"Sora…" he whispered.

She glanced his way at her name, and Larryn shoved the pants between them, covering what he could of his rail-thin body. His cheeks burned. It was silly, but years of poverty had left scars over him—badly healed rashes and splotches, skin drawn tight over bones, and a sense that his body would crumple at a glance—and he hated letting others see it. Sora's gaze absorbed it all in a fraction of second, before she met his eyes. He mouthed "don't open".

"I'm on my way to arrest Lord Allastam. Whatever you meant to share can wait."

"*What?*" The pants slipped from Larryn's fingers as he blurted out the question.

"Who's in there?" Branwen asked.

"A source. Anonymous. Which is why you cannot enter."

"But—"

"You of all people understand the importance of preserving a network."

Larryn hoped she meant that. If she arrested Lord Allastam and put his name down in some paperwork, he could kiss the Shelter goodbye. But Sora had to be exaggerating, right? Just words to placate the Dathirii on the other side. There was a price to pay for arresting a powerful noble in Isandor.

"Be careful, Sora," Branwen Dathirii said. "*My* informant reported that the house is in something of an uproar."

They both knew what had caused that.

"Duly noted. Now, if you'd please leave? Any help or connection with a Dathirii could strip my arrest of any credibility. Your very presence here endangers it."

A frustrated huff answered Sora. "Right. I suppose we best prepare."

They listened to her receding footsteps in silence, but Larryn's incredulity built with every passing second until he could no longer contain it.

"Arresting Lord Allastam?"

"You heard that right. Hurry up." She gestured at the clothes, and Larryn finally shoved the pants and everything else on. By the time he'd passed the shirt over his head, Sora was holding a decorated breastplate. He grimaced, and he'd swear she smirked at him for a moment. "You've informed me Lord Allastam is illegally detaining Hasryan and I have reasons to fear for the latter's security. I'm well within my rights to bust his door."

"Even if Hasryan tried to kill him?"

"The law makes no provision for personal vengeance in such circumstances. Others may choose to turn a blind eye, but I will not."

Larryn wondered if it was as much a thinly veiled excuse as it sounded, but she forced the armour on him before he could protest. He grunted as the heavy metal rested on his shoulders. Sora tightened the straps, then placed a hand on his lower back and another on his shoulder.

"Straighten up. You're not some street skunk now. You're a

proud member of Isandor's guards and your posture will reflect that."

"As if." The armour and its lie clung to his skin, cutting deeper than even his awful noble disguise. "Your proud guards keep beating up my people and dragging them into dank cells for no reasons. I hate everything this armour represents."

Sora slapped the front of it with a scowl. "It's an act, Larryn! Channel your personal hate into fake pride and act the part. I don't want to go in there without backup, and I wouldn't trust anyone here."

Her admission caught Larryn off guard, flattening his spike of rage. He wasn't exactly good backup, especially if she anticipated a fight, but at least he wouldn't stab her in the back like a power-hungry colleague. "Good. That's wiser than I expected."

Her eyes rolled with such force you could have seen them all the way from the Lower City. "How wonderful to receive the seal of approval from Larryn the Angry, Purveyor of Shelter and Mistakes in equal parts. I am truly blessed."

A twinge of insult tugged at Larryn's heart, yet he couldn't deny the title fit him like a glove, and the smile growing on Sora's lips doused his urge to retort. A soft laugh escaped him, and he squared his shoulders in mock arrogance. "Glad you appreciate my worth."

"There!" Sora exclaimed. "That's better."

He grinned back at her, warmed by her praise. "All I gotta do is throw in some unyielding sneerage and everyone will be fooled."

Sora stepped forward to tie belt and scabbard at his waist, and all his bravado vanished at her proximity. He didn't let other people dress him. Hadn't had anyone do that since he'd been a child, and though there was no motherly tenderness in Sora's movements, the echoes of his memories cut him deep, leaving his throat dry and his heart pounding. He covered it all with a scoff the moment she retreated.

"Still glad you have no looking glass. Don't want more memories of this than necessary."

"You cut a fine figure."

Larryn grunted. He didn't care to. All he wanted was to get this over with, Hasryan safely at his side. He bent over to rummage through his clothes, the scabbard scraping across the floor as he moved. Before long, he'd retrieved Cal's coin again and stuffed it in these oversized new pockets. "For luck."

"Right. I'll explain the plan on the way."

She offered the last piece of disguise, a full-face helmet to hide him. Larryn shoved it on, gritting his teeth at the thinness of the inside padding. He felt like his head was floating in a bucket, and he hated how it limited his vision. Larryn felt himself slumping, readjusted his position, then cast a last look at his empty plate. He much preferred to be the Lower City's cook than a city guard, and soon he could go back to it. But they were all a part of this mess now, and he'd be damned if he left Hasryan alone in it. He fell into step behind his unlikely ally, a thin smile emerging at the idea he'd work with Sora.

"Can't wait to hear your mighty plan."

CHAPTER THREE

A COLD wind billowed through Isandor's bridges, whipping up dancing curtains of light snow, but nothing could douse the fire burning within Sora as they climbed towards the Upper City.

Never in her lifetime had she taken such an impulsive decision. Even Larryn was baffled at her recklessness. He'd underscored how her 'plan' was not worthy of such a term—that as Larryn the Angry, Purveyor of Mistakes, he could judge the size of her current mistake better than most. She'd grinned at him and corrected one important detail: it wasn't *her* mistake, it was *theirs*. He'd laughed, sharp voice muffled by the helmet, and the sound had expanded her chest threefold.

Sora grew giddier and lighter on her feet with every step bringing her closer to the Allastam Tower. No one had ever dared to walk into the Allastams' stronghold and arrest Isandor's most powerful political figure with no evidence but the word of a nobody. It thrilled her to break every unspoken rule of law enforcement and its shadow hierarchy, bought with bags of gold and accelerated promotions. In theory, the Sapphire Guard operated independently from the nobles' authority, a balance to their power. In practice, the Golden Table chose its Commander and could begin or interrupt any investigation, so it never paid to defy Isandor's most influential Houses, which held more sway in the decision-making. They'd punish her for stepping out of line, tear down her career and reputation both, but she found she didn't care. She would be free and Hasryan would be safe.

That was, of course, if she made it out alive.

Two weeks ago, she'd never have questioned her safety upon arresting Lord Allastam, but two weeks ago, he hadn't invaded the Dathirii Tower and sold their leader to the Myrians, all without major pushbacks from the other Houses. The signs of this brash violence had already existed, however, seeded in the Freitz' downfall—tragic accidents happening to key figures, mysterious departures from others on years-long merchant trips ... the coordinated attacks hadn't stopped at important trade deals. All of it had been sufficiently covered for plausible deniability, unlike the brazen march of soldiers into House Dathirii. No one who mattered had been killed then, though—unless they never found Kellian, a possibility she'd rather not dwell on—so the political community in Isandor had chosen to hold its breath.

She was about to punch it into the stomach and force the release.

Larryn kept pace with her, easing her concern for him. He'd

been all skin and bones under those clothes, with nearly no muscles, and she'd wondered how he would handle himself with the weight of armour on his shoulders and so many stairs to climb. No laboured breathing escaped his helmet, however, so she had to conclude he was made of raw anger, and it kept him going.

They approached the tower at last, and instead of slowing down, Sora imbued every stride with purpose. The two soldiers guarding the massive entrance stepped forward to block her way. No going back now, she thought, raising her chin and throwing her voice with authority.

"I must speak with Lord Allastam immediately. His life could depend on it."

Both guards looked at each other, hesitant. "Our orders—"

"Are to protect him and his family at all cost, yes. Myrians might appear within your walls at any moment and you want to keep me out?" She stepped closer to glare down at him. Despite being a few inches taller, the guard shrunk back. Sora jumped on his hesitation. "Pray tell me, how will Lord Allastam react once he learns you delayed vital information? What happens if these Myrians kill the family? An assault is coming. Lord Drake Allastam and Lady Mia Allastam are not safe. They weren't very particular about which family members they meant to murder last time—I'd know, I was there."

As the first guard fumbled for an answer, his companion whistled appreciatively.

"Go," she said. "They must want to cover for last night."

Sora struggled to keep any emotion out of her face at the

mention of last night. They must mean Hasryan. She hoped it wasn't too late for him, that they hadn't killed him on sight. Fear clawed at her chest, and she grounded herself in Larryn's presence behind her, miraculously calm *and* calming.

The first guard motioned for Sora to follow then led her across the floor, ignoring the two wide staircases around the centre of the Allastam Tower. Sora caught a glimpse of the room beneath them, a wide training grounds with at least a half a dozen soldiers sparring. How many more would be scattered throughout the building, ready to rush at the first sign of alarm? House Allastam possessed the largest squad of guards in the entire city and even with a significant chunk of their forces guarding the Dathirii Tower, she couldn't possibly fight the ones left here. If Lord Allastam refused to follow, she would be hard-pressed to coerce him.

They travelled around the training ground, down a narrow and curved corridor she'd have thought dedicated to the staff. At the end of it, barely perceptible, stood a black door in a black hole. Her heart stumbled as she found her bearings within the tower's structure. From the outside, the spire looked like three helixes intertwined—one grey, one white, one black. The black one, however, had always seemed too narrow to house any rooms. Sora had always figured it was decorative, or perhaps contained the occasional cupboard. Yet this door clearly led into it. Its base, hidden by the other two helixes, must have widened enough to allow proper rooms—rooms one wouldn't expect or search for unless they had prior knowledge of them.

The guard opened the door and Sora spied an antechamber and

a staircase curling up. She could take it from here; it'd be a small enough section of the Allastam Tower to comb through. She'd rather not encumber herself with a potential enemy longer than necessary.

"Thank you, soldier." She smashed the pommel of her sword on the back of his head, and he crumpled with a surprised cry. "Lock the door, Larryn."

At first, he only stared at her, stunned grey eyes visible through the helmet's visor. She snapped his name, and he finally jumped into action, shutting the door and locking it. He even dragged the guard to the side.

"Let's move. We've no more than a few precious minutes before they realize I was lying and come looking." She started up the stairs, fingers wrapped around the pommel of her sword. Larryn clanked behind her. "Do you have a fake name I could use?"

"Fleece."

He provided it without the slightest pause, and Sora turned to frown at him, troubled by his ease. If she searched their records for a Fleece, would she find even more crimes to his name? Part of her wished there was a more innocuous reason.

"Is that your last name?"

Larry tensed and ground out his answer through his teeth. "I don't have a last name."

She recognized the anger just below the surface and decided not to press the issue. She'd have to satisfy her burning curiosity another day. Now was not the time to risk an argument with Larryn.

"Fleece it is, then."

She launched herself up the stairs, but was forced to slow down when she caught hints of Lord Allastam's voice to avoid detection. Behind her, Larryn's clanking steps had vanished. She needed to focus to hear his boots land, and despite being encased in unfamiliar metal bits, he managed silence. As if the readied fake name hadn't already been suspicious enough… She itched to dig out the truth, but whatever Larryn had been up to, it'd never compare to Allastam's crimes. She had to focus.

They passed a landing, but Lord Allastam's voice still drifted from above, so Sora kept going, taking each steep stair with care. On the next floor, a corridor spun towards the right, hugging the staircase in a tight spiral. Cell bars glittered in the light of a flickering torch, but none held Hasryan. Lord Allastam said something else, snide and grating, and this time a second voice replied. A chuckle, a quick retort; words impossible to decipher, but Sora would have recognized Hasryan's voice anywhere—especially the characteristic mockery laced with despair he'd so often used on her, in the Sapphire Guard's headquarters. She gripped her hilt and lengthened her strides.

Hasryan's comeback ended in a scream of pain. Her head ringing with it, her sword brandished, Sora followed the sound to the right door and kicked it open.

TODAY, more than ever, Hasryan needed humour as an escape. What else could he do but laugh as goons dragged him into a barely lit room, a single pair of chains and shackles hanging from the ceiling in the middle, bloodstains under it and a simple table by the wall, with nothing but his own dagger on it? He needed to cover the plunge of his stomach with a snort, to comment on his missing half-inch when they hoisted him up and his toes barely touched the ground. Sure, he struggled to get each word past the jolting, burning pain in his arm, now forced to support his entire weight, but a wise crack still sounded better than a sob. Even so, by the time Allastam's two brutes had cut through his bloodstained cotton clothes, tears had been streaming down his cheeks. His smirk hadn't vanished, though.

Then he realized he'd been wearing Branwen's gift, the tight red underwear she'd jokingly bought for him, and his façade cracked. Memories rushed to the forefront of his mind—Camilla swooping him into a hug, Branwen laughing as she teased him, Sora gently scolding her very deadly cat. He had gained so much over the last weeks and it became brutally impossible to cope with the idea of losing it all.

Hasryan squeezed his eyes shut and clung to that fleeting joy as Lord Allastam talked at him—some long-winded ramble about his life's woes, how he had loved his wife and how unfair her loss had been to the children. Hasryan didn't care. At one point under it all, however, he caught the scrape of metal on wood—Allastam picking up his enchanted dagger.

"Many would leave the dirty work to their underlings, and in general I agree with them. But this isn't *work* at all. This is pleasure. A gift to myself."

Even behind his eyelids, Hasryan saw the flash of sparks, and the flimsy threads of good memories slid between his fingers, recoiling from the inevitable pain. He opened his eyes to meet Lord Allastam's.

"Now now. Don't you think that's a little fast for a first da—"

Lord Allastam slapped the dagger on his side. Lightning jumped from it and into Hasryan. He screamed, his mind flaring red as his skin burned under the blade, and jerked away. The swing multiplied the pain from his broken arm and the world around vanished, reduced to two hot spots of agony.

A loud noise pierced through the ringing in his ears, startling him.

"Drop that dagger now!"

Sora's commanding voice washed over him, a thunderous wave of elation, and he watched her step inside through a blur of tears, sword at the ready, a single guard trailing behind. Just. One. Hasryan's brief hope came crashing down. What did she plan to do with so little backup? What was she even here for? … Him?

He stared at her, his heart hammering, his brain rendered mush by the agony travelling up and down his arm, a current that wouldn't stop looping. Sora Sharpe, who had gone to great lengths to track him down and put a noose around his neck, had come to *rescue* him? Sure, they'd found a truce, even had a great talk together, but this was a different sort of dedication. One that felt an awful lot like friendship.

Lord Allastam removed the dagger from Hasryan's side, and breathing became brutally easier. Hasryan gasped, dazed by the sudden release. If he hadn't been hanging, he would have collapsed to the ground.

"I'm sorry… Miss Sharpe, isn't it? What in the name of all unholy gods do you think you're doing?"

A question even the poor guard by her side must be asking themself. They stood still, staring straight at Hasryan with exemplary cool, as if there was nothing peculiar about his current position. Sora, on the other hand, hadn't glanced at his way. She met Allastam's gaze, as serious as ever.

"Lord Allastam, you are under arrest for the illegal detention and torture of Hasryan Fel'ethier." She reached for her manacles and stepped forward. "Please drop the dagger."

Allastam was unimpressed. "Under arrest? He tried to assassinate me yesterday! I bear the mark of his crime on my stomach."

This time, Sora did turn to him. Hasryan shrugged, and the tiny movement from his shoulders sent new waves of pain down his arm. He hissed, but despite the renewed agony and his dried throat, he couldn't help but force a few words out. "I dunno, m'lord. Aren't those scars from the *other* prisoner in your cells? She was real proud of stabbing you there with the beautiful trees of your audience hall."

Surprise flashed through Sora's expression, and she turned to Lord Allastam. "You know full well that lords of this city are only allowed to detain prisoners with the full knowledge and approval of the Sapphire Guard, Lord Allastam. *You* are not the law of this city."

"Didn't you hear what I said?" Lord Allastam asked, his mild amusement quickly transforming into irritation.

"Of course I did." She turned her deadly glare to Hasryan and held his eyes as she continued. "We'll add attempted murder to his already long list of crimes, and within a few days he'll receive the rightful punishment he deserves for them. By *our* hands."

Hasryan's chest squeezed, her words a torture far different than Lord Allastam's. She had to be lying. Placating him. They'd shared breakfast and laughed together, damn it! Yet it wouldn't be the first time Hasryan had wrongly convinced himself someone cared, only to discover that was only true within certain parameters. Perhaps Sora only valued him if he played nicely. If he redeemed himself or whatever. He didn't want to believe it, but the possibility was poison, spreading from still-open wounds into his soul. And if that was true—if what little they'd had was already broken—then he had only one defence. He smirked.

"Oh, good! I always liked your cells better."

Sora rolled her eyes, but he caught the brief hint of a smile on her lips, panacea against his creeping doubts.

"Now, Lord Allastam, kindly drop the dagger before I add to *your* list of accusations. You know very well the object you hold is key evidence in your wife's murder. It, along with Hasryan, should've been brought back to us immediately."

"You're not kidding." His incredulity amused Hasryan. This was the mark of a man used to being unchallenged and obeyed. "This isn't how it works, Miss Sharpe. Laws are made by people like me, respected by people like you, and enforced upon scum like him." He gestured at Hasryan then flung the dagger over his shoulder like the most vulgar of weapons. Hasryan cringed as it hit the wall and clanged to the floor. "I do what I want in my tower."

"I'm afraid Isandor's laws apply here, too. To everyone."

Allastam laughed. "Why would I come with you? What's the

point? More sensible people will release me within an hour."

Sora's shoulders stiffened—not a lot, but after hours in interrogation chambers with her, Hasryan had learned her tells. She knew he was right. This entire arrest was a joke, and no one in Isandor would find it amusing.

"Then it seems to me that there are no good reasons not to come." Sora's voice betrayed no hesitation. "I even daresay it would be … safer."

"Are you threatening me?"

Even Sora's companion startled, his strangled noise almost as comical as Lord Allastam's surprise. She had more courage than they'd given her credit for, and perhaps something of a death wish. Sora smiled, exhilarated pride shining through her face, then raised her sword, and he could barely breathe from how striking she was.

"We are taught not to take kindly to those resisting arrests. The Lower City's residents have often witnessed the meaning of this."

Lord Allastam stared at her as if he couldn't decide whether to rip her head off or congratulate her, and long seconds trickled past, tension growing thicker with each of them. Sora stood her ground, unflinching. She had to know he still had the upper hand. They were at the heart of his tower and Lord Allastam was right: he could do whatever he wanted here. At least if he refused, Hasryan would get to see Sora kick his old ass into oblivion first.

"You know what?" Lord Allastam said. "I'll play your little game. There's nothing quite like crushing an over-righteous and pathetic opponent to brighten my day. I'd know!" The reference to Lord Dathirii wasn't lost on anyone in the room. Sora scowled and brought the sword ever-so-slightly higher while her companion shuffled about, clearly uncomfortable. Lord Allastam smirked. "I'll even come along peacefully."

"Great!" she declared. "Let's get everyone in handcuffs, then. Fleece … untie and cuff Hasryan, please." Sora's neutral tone rippled with tension, but to Hasryan's ears, it was celestial music. Keeping his wits about, hanging like that on his broken arm, was proving a trial.

The guard next to her stiffened and turned their head to her. Sora glared back. "Fleece!"

"Yes, ma'am."

Hasryan's heart stopped. He'd know Larryn's voice amongst thousands, and suddenly he could barely keep the grin out of his face. *Larryn and Sora.* Could he have asked for a more unexpected rescue party? He kept his gaze to the ground, following 'Fleece's' boots as they approached. His friend snatched the key from the nearby table but needed the little wooden stool to reach the shackles and unlock them. Hasryan fell the instant they released him, legs too weak to support him, and he caught himself on Larryn. His head spun, the ground tilting under him as he struggled with the sudden relief from brutal pain in his arm. It still throbbed, and an insidious nausea rose to replace the acute pain, but still. Improvement! Hasryan squeezed Larryn's forearm briefly before untangling himself, as if ashamed of his legs' weakness.

He'd just stepped aside when he caught movement at the corner of his eyes—his dagger, once laying on the floor, vanishing from the ground. Hasryan's heart clenched. Brune's gift had more than its electrical properties imbued within. When wielded long enough by someone, the weapon returned to its attuned owner of its own accord if left unattended. How often had Hasryan flung it ahead of him, embedding it into a poor soul's chest before he ran up to them? Over the last decade, the timing of his dagger's return had become a second nature.

It was returning, *now*, into the hands of its last wielder—and Lord Allastam stood right by his side, a spin and stab away from slicing Hasryan open and spilling his guts. Instincts and experience told him he'd never dodge in time. Hasryan jumped back anyway. Lord Allastam's gnarly fingers tightened on the handle as it materialized and he slashed with a snarl.

The blade stopped a hair's breadth away from Hasryan's burned skin.

Larryn had stepped forward and grabbed the lord's thin wrist, blocking the movement. For the space of a breath, they glared at each other, then Larryn twisted Allastam's arm, spinning him around to slam him into the wall. The dagger fell to the ground once more, and Hasryan's mental countdown began anew.

"I advise against such tactics, sir."

Hasryan had never heard Larryn use any honorific before, and it dripped with such intense sarcasm it hardly deserved the name. One could taste the visceral satisfaction emanating from him, and Hasryan had no doubt his friend would enshrine this moment in memory for a long time. Larryn unclipped the cuffs from his belt and snapped them around Lord Allastam's wrists, tighter than needed.

"Take the dagger or it'll return to him again."

Larryn followed his advice while Sora strode up to Hasryan. Her fingers reached out, and for an instant Hasryan thought she'd brush them against his side, still throbbing from the burn. The world grew hot, her silent reproach searing as badly as any weapon. She snatched her hand back, her expression hardening, and retrieved her own handcuffs.

"Ah, Sora. I almost missed this," he quipped. She rolled her eyes and motioned for him to turn around and offer his hands. He raised his eyebrows. "I'm not even dressed!"

"To our collective dismay, yes," she retorted, her tone chiller than any air on his bare skin. Was this really an act? He'd never known Sora to be that good a liar, and her brusqueness felt like the cold metal of handcuffs had clamped around his heart, not his wrists.

"You might want to find a third pair, or use my old ceiling friends," he told Sora. "Lord Allastam is also holding Master Jilssan in his cell. Y'know, from the Myrian Enclave? She doesn't sound like someone you should to abandon to a freezing death."

"Stellar. Truly, Ren must have forsaken me." Her hand firmly on Hasryan's shoulder, she led him to a corner across from Allastam. "Sit down, Fleece, keep an eye on them. Don't let either get the dagger, and shut them up if they start flinging insults. No special treatment for Lord Allastam. Of *any* kind."

Hasryan snickered. Larryn was liable to punch the old cur into unconsciousness at the slightest provocation, and they all knew it. Larryn huffed and shoved the lord into a sitting position before resting a hand on his sword and squaring his shoulders. The posture seemed incredibly wrong, but Hasryan doubted anyone except him could tell.

Hasryan plumped down to the ground, hissing at the pressure of the cuffs on his broken arm. He tried to set it against the stone wall. Its cold numbed the pain somewhat—a meagre consolation, when his whole body had been battered so badly, but he could only endure. He closed his eyes, certain Larryn would protect him, and dreamed of Cal's healing, a bed, and a free day filled with Larryn's best cuisine.

Chapter Four

IA Allastam sank into her bath water, submerging her head as if dulling the sounds of the outside world could dull the pain inside. It never did, not for long, but very little did. At least it was quiet here, nothing but the muted vibration in her ears and the sharp pinpoints of pain at her temples that heralded a headache—or worse. Hopefully not. Her day had started too well, and she'd like it not to go downhill from there.

She had awoken almost two hours ago, before the sun had truly risen above the city, and she'd stayed in bed as it made its way, taking stock of her state. Anxiety hadn't eaten away most of her night for once, so she'd emerged more rested than average, with naught but a manageable throb in her muscles to contend with. Good. She'd asked for a bath drawn, moved herself through a few, careful exercises, then soaked in deep as a reward.

Of all the luxuries in her quarters, the massive bath was her favourite. It had been built with two sections of varying height, allowing her to either sit comfortably or sink several feet in. Runes ran along its edge, keeping the temperature pitch perfect for however long she wanted. Mia rarely missed a chance to be alone in the vastness of her tub, honey-scented water easing the pressure on her bones and muscles, the days' endless work kept at bay.

Mostly kept at bay, she corrected as she emerged to find Alton leaning on the wall.

Warmth spread through her at his familiar pear-shaped figure, full and reliable. Her gaze snagged on the long elven ears, so prominent since he'd shorn his hair to leave only dark curls. The new haircut still did a number on her; in all their shared years, he had rarely looked this sexy, setting fire to nerves far different than pain.

The smirk on his lips might fool most into thinking him at ease, but Mia noted his crossed arms and the shoes still at his feet. Normally he'd have removed those—and much more than that, in better, quieter times. She missed their days of conspiring, both naked in her bath, foreheads touching, whispers and schemes traded between them as often as kisses and caresses. There hadn't been time these last weeks—months, even—and the recent stress had strained her energy and health.

Mia arched her eyebrows at him. Her thin blonde hair pooled about her as she remained in the water up to her neck.

"Emergency?" she asked.

"Of the worst kind," he said. "Events are unravelling, but they're not what we expected, and I'm unsure we can steer their course."

Mia laughed at the direness of his tone. Her feet found the bottom of the tub and she let her fingers curl in the soft lining before she pushed herself forward, to lean her arms on the edge of the bath. "We'll improvise."

She was rewarded by an amused headshake. "Of course this pleases you," he said. "Well, milady, here is your prompt: Investigator Sora Sharpe gained entry to the Allastam Tower this morning and has barricaded herself in the cell area. Her purpose is unclear, but your father is in there, too."

Sora Sharpe, huh? Unexpected indeed. "You did inform Branwen about the extra meals our cooks have reported sending there, didn't you? And instead of a Dathirii agent, a high-profile Sapphire Guard investigator showed up?"

"Oh, but there's more," Alton said, his self-satisfied smirk warning Mia to brace for the twist. "Mister Ijun, who was tasked with keeping fires warm overnight, had quite the tale for me. Your father roaming the corridors at night, an assassin emerging from the shadows, skin dark as the night, a heroic scuffle, and the murderer dragged to our cells." Alton spread his arms out. "Honestly, Ijun is quite the improvisation master himself, and he might have made up half the story after spying guards hauling off our would-be assassin's body. Regardless, I am inclined to believe that last night, your mother's killer infiltrated the tower and tried to complete the pair."

A chill coursed down Mia's spine, and the bath's water no longer seemed warm. She could still hear Drake's cries bouncing through the twisting corridors, the way he'd come running and flung himself in her arms, blabbering incoherently about their mom. It was her only clear memory of the day: her brother's anguish and a crystalline sense of dread lodging itself in her stomach. She had known, even then, that her life would take a turn for the worse.

From that day, she became the Allastam princess, the frail, precious girl to protect at all cost. The consideration afforded to her illness multiplied, and where her complaints about pain had been mostly ignored before, they suddenly became reason to keep her inside and watched at all times. At first, she'd been glad; she'd needed the love, had revelled in her father giving her even half the attention normally reserved for her brother. Until she grew older and they continued to treat her like a child, too young and impulsive to know her limits, too precious to be allowed to test them. While Drake rushed out to meet his ever-expanding circle of friends, she stayed inside in her quarters, learning paper craft to distract herself and have one thing that was entirely her own. With a few notable exceptions, only the house staff asked her about the hobby, or herself, and before long she counted more friends among them than any noble group.

Then there was Alton, who was a friend and lover and a co-conspirator, whom she'd helped find himself and adored in such a visceral way that words could not possibly cover it, who for all the casual mirth with which he'd presented his news now watched her like a hawk, knowing the echoes of her mother's death still rippled through her life. Mia smiled at him, hoping to reassure.

"Who knows about this? About Hasryan?"

"To my knowledge, only the two of us and the soldiers Lord Allastam called upon. It's only a matter of time before they or Ijun talk, though. Unfortunately, Drake has caught wind of Sora

Sharpe's actions and was, let's say, very heated about it."

"Great. We needed that."

Alton laughed at her open bitterness and spread his arms out. "As I said, events are unravelling, as is our control over them."

All right, perhaps she did regret her cheekiness about it now. Things were always more complicated once Drake was involved, and she was struggling to untangle the implications of Alton's news. Two different intruders, neither of which had ties to Branwen Dathirii to their knowledge, in the day following their passing of information about a secret prisoner? At least one of these was not a coincidence, but which and why? There *had* been a report of Camilla Dathirii in Sora's company, the day of the Golden Table.

She had always known this conflict would sweep her house, but where many in Isandor saw her father as unassailable, she held no such illusion. She saw his failings every day—the impulsiveness, the anger, the arrogance—and she knew he'd lose sooner or later. When that happened, she would be ready.

Mia steeled herself against the outside cold with a steadying breath then pulled herself out of the bath. The air prickled against her pale skin as she walked towards Alton, who waited towel at the ready.

"Help me dress," she said. "It's time to improvise."

MIA found her brother in the armoury, his arms spread out as Allastam soldiers fit the armour to him. It was strangely similar to her own posture a few minutes ago as Alton and Felicia laced her dress, and she supposed they each had their preferred weapons.

"Brother," she said, her voice pitched loud enough to overcome the din of their guards preparing for battle. "What is happening?"

Drake turned to her, and the sudden spin made one of his helpers drop the leather straps. A curse formed on their lips, only to be immediately swallowed.

"You shouldn't be here, Mia."

"But I am," she said, her tone hardening. It'd have been pointless to argue against Father, but Drake couldn't resist her. She smiled at him at stepped closer, lifting the hem of her dress to keep it from the dirty floor. "Please tell me. The tower is awash with rumours, and I have no desire to wait patiently in my quarters, worry devouring my heart."

He grimaced and gestured for someone to bring him his rapier. The jewelled hilt caught the room's magical light as he tied it around his waist. "I'm gonna fight this Sharpe fraud. She's got something against us—told me straight to my face the other day— and now she's invading our home under false pretense? It'll be a pleasure to teach her a lesson."

Fear tightened Mia's heart. Drake had been taught to fight, but she suspected Sora Sharpe had seen more action than him. Of the two, she was not so certain who would receive the lesson. "Have you spoken with her? Do we know what she wants?"

Drake scoffed. "I don't care what she wants, sis. She's not getting it."

Which meant, of course, that he had no idea at all. Frustration boiled within Mia, but she forced it to stay inside, to stay quiet.

Thousands of protests wanted to burst—you can't just rush in, you're being foolish, acting the hero will only get you killed—but they'd only rile him up, especially if voiced in front of others. Instead, she settled on "I worry for your safety."

It was true. Despite Drake's propensity to dismiss her, despite his rashness and fast-growing arrogance, despite his mistreatment of the staff she counted as friends, she loved him. They had grown up together, shared countless games and laughter, and shared their grief when no one else would. Drake still came to her every anniversary of their mother's death, still relied on her to sort through his mind when he got upset. Even as they drifted ever further apart—even as she acknowledged she'd one day have to take House leadership from him, and he'd never forgive her—she had trouble letting go.

The soldiers finished tying his breastplate and released him. He walked to her, then, and brushed her shoulder ever-so-slightly instead of squeezing it, to avoid triggering the worst of her pain in case her skin was particularly raw.

"I won't be alone. Wait for me in your rooms if you want to hear of my exploits." He pressed a kiss to her forehead, then gestured to the soldiers now lined up in the room, ready to move. "Let's go, boys."

Drake walked out, and as the troops made to follow, Mia had to pull her dress close to her and press herself against the doorway, making space for them to pass. He didn't look back, and none of their guards spared her a glance. Mia seethed more with every one passing her. She did *not* want to wait, gentle and quiet, but following him would only put her at risk, too.

She had other options, however. If the key leadership of House Allastam was busy with unexpected intruders, she might have a unique opportunity to get her foot into the political action. Mia doubted her father's schedule had been clear of appointments today. Perhaps her best bet for now was to ignore Alton's prompt altogether, and create her own improvisation stage.

CHAPTER FIVE

JILSSAN watched her temporary jail companion vanish with undeniable sadness. He'd been fun while it lasted, but she doubted she'd hear more than distant screams from him anytime soon. At least it wasn't her. She'd already had her turn in Lord Allastam's interrogation chamber, although he'd been careful not to 'irremediably damage her'. He must still have a healthy fear of what Master Avenazar might do in response.

More than once, he'd implied Myrians were hiding Hasryan from his best scryers, and Jilssan had played coy around the notion, never denying it. It fit the ill-conceived ploy she'd proposed to Diel Dathirii too well to shatter, even if Lord Allastam only grew angrier at her non-answers. Not exactly a pleasant phenomenon to watch when you were the most likely recipient of that rage. Now he could vent it out on Hasryan, at least, and she was glad for the reprieve.

When the first of his screams came, Jilssan gritted her teeth and hunched over. Reprieve or not, this would be unpleasant to listen to. Yet before it even died out, a slamming door echoed up the stairs leading to their cells. Jilssan's head shot up, hope flaring at the authoritative voice following. Distance blurred any words from the ensuing reaction, but they were arguing. She crawled to the bars, straining to parse more, to no avail. She managed to distinguish four voices, including Hasryan's and Lord Allastam's. Could these newcomers be no more than a pair? If this was Hasryan's infamous rescuer, he truly *was* as reckless as predicted.

The voices calmed, and her meagre hope began to dwindle. Maybe they wouldn't even come for her. On the surface, they were enemies. Hasryan might not even know she'd struck a deal with Diel Dathirii. As time passed, her stomach sank and she started to accept this ice-cold cell would remain her home a while longer—until boots echoed across the steps and torchlight streamed under the doorway. The door creaked open, and Jilssan eased out a sigh of relief.

She struggled to her feet, and with every movement her magic-dampening manacles clinked reminders that this wasn't over, not yet. Jilssan squinted against the blinding light to get a better view of her saviour. She had broad shoulders, straight dark hair, and intense eyes. Hard ones, though, from someone you didn't mess with—an impression reinforced by the full Sapphire Guard regalia. Jilssan clutched the bars, holding herself upright. A few seconds on her feet and she was already getting dizzy, damnit. The flickering light glinted off manacles, giving them an eerie orange glow.

"Are you all right in there?" the Sapphire Guard asked.

"I'd be better out of it." Jilssan edged closer to the bars and the torch's glorious warmth. It tickled the tip of her fingers, full of promises. Unlike her rescuer, who studied her in silence, clearly in no hurry to free her.

"What earned you a stay in these cells?"

Jilssan tilted her head to the side, rifling through possible answers. The full explanation would require time and energy she'd rather not waste, even though her inclination was to trust this stranger to some extent. She had the kind of solid, determined aura Jilssan loved in women, and she *had* come for Hasryan. Nevertheless, she had no time to unravel the complicated mess she'd landed herself into.

"Lord Allastam does not take kindly to bad news."

"Could you, perhaps, be a little vaguer?"

Was that a challenge? Jilssan laughed, her voice thinned by thirst, and spread one arm out, keeping the other on the bars for support. "A relationship soured," she offered. She was immediately rewarded by a groan, and her grin widened. The imminent release from this cell was making her giddy. "Glad to see Hasryan was wrong and you came to—"

"Arrest him," the guard interrupted. "He's an assassin and I placed him under arrest."

Jilssan froze. That didn't bode well for her. Maybe they weren't Hasryan's friends after all? Besides, hadn't he been rather clear his expected rescuer was a man? Jilssan let her momentary panic flow through her then reasserted her calm. Hasryan wasn't her responsibility.

"I am thankfully no such thing. Can I leave?" She lifted her hands to exhibit the magic-dampening manacles. "Lord Allastam has no right to detain me."

"Indeed, and we're also bringing him back in handcuffs. I arrested him on the grounds of illegal detention."

"You—" She was either the boldest guard in the entire city, or had the weirdest sense of humour. "Can you do that? Will it last?"

"I can try." She lifted a key ring and started trying them in Jilssan's door. "Given time, I could prove over a dozen crimes without breaking a sweat, I'm sure, but they'll never let me get that far. You don't touch a lord in this city unless the others hate him enough to protect you. Unfortunately, Myrians already tried to assassinate Drake Allastam, so your presence here is no more than self-defence to them, and Hasryan…" She huffed, and although she tried to keep the sound derisive, Jilssan caught a whiff of disappointment and anger in her tone. So she wasn't *any* guard after all; this was personal. Jilssan made a careful note in case there was something there to exploit farther down the line.

"For people constantly dragging the Myrian Empire, you're not exactly exemplars of morality and lawfulness," she said. "We'll turn a blind eye unless we hate your face is hardly a pure model."

"You misunderstand the city. *It* is not concerned with your people's morality." She paused long enough to flip to another key and try again. "Few in Isandor dared to shine a light on the depths of Myrian awfulness besides House Dathirii, and look what they did to it."

"I know! Isn't it gloriously ruthless? Lord Allastam sold poor Diel like vulgar merchandise, and none of them cared!" The disinterest had been so brazen, so unapologetic, Jilssan couldn't help but be impressed. "Lord Allastam could have melted him into gold and shared the newly minted pieces, and they would celebrate."

Keys stopped clinking, and the Sapphire Guard's expression shifted from disgusted to thoughtful to … confident? She met Jilssan's gaze, then shoved a new key in the hole and turned. It clicked open, and she grinned.

"Master Jilssan, isn't it? I'm Investigator Sora Sharpe." She pulled the door open and lifted her torch high. "I need to ask you questions regarding this 'deal' between House Allastam and the Myrian Enclave, and the precise timing of it."

Jilssan hung at the edge of the cell's entrance, flooded by sudden wariness. What would these questions entail, exactly? How safe was it to play along with Sharpe's plan, and where did this woman's alliance truly lie? Avenazar would skewer her, but what did it matter, at this point? She'd already given him plenty of reasons to kill her.

"Do I have a choice?" she asked, hoping to fish more information out of Sora. "If you have means to force it, say so. Because if you need my consent, you'll have to be more precise before I agree. I have little but information to my name now."

Sora hesitated. Jilssan's hands tightened over the cold bars and she watched the dancing shadows on the other woman's face. So much was at stake here—for Isra and her, even for Varden. But she had no idea if she could trust Sora, or what would happen should she reveal key information. Jilssan didn't want to spill her secrets only to be discarded without protection. She needed leverage, yet in order to get there, Sora first needed to trust her.

"The last time I got involved in a ploy against Lord Allastam, I wound up here. I'm not keen on repeating the experience, or on transferring from one cell to another." She stepped out and set her freezing fingers on Sora's hand, holding the torch with her. The guard stiffened at the touch but didn't withdraw, even though Jilssan was inches from her. She tilted her chin up to meet her gaze. "At this point, I want to be safe, and I want my apprentice to be safe. Everything else…"

She waved at the thin air at the edge of their vision. Jilssan had grown too exhausted to care. Her entire body threatened to give in, and only willpower kept her this close to Sora without support from the bars. She started shaking, and Sora put a steadying hand on her shoulder. When she spoke again, her voice had become kinder, calmer.

"I've worked as an investigator in Isandor long enough to know where nobles trace the line between acceptable infringement upon the law and unspeakable offence. If the victim has no title or no backing from a noble, they'll look the other way. If the victim is a noble yet the crime has been disguised sufficiently to be deniable, then their line shifts according to potential political gain."

She paused to punctuate her explanation with a disgusted noise, as though the latter wasn't a perfectly reasonable and shrewd tactic. It was almost cute, how offended this line of decision-making made her.

"Lord Allastam has never answered for his crimes because he was always careful to toe the line. Many would benefit from his downfall, however, especially with the recent growth in his power and influence. With a witness high in the Myrian hierarchy vouching he'd sold Lord Dathirii *before* the title was lost, I could convince allies to call another Golden Table. No one is above the Golden Table. They could even give me an actual investigation into all of Lord Allastam's actions!" Sora raised the torch high and squeezed Jilssan's shoulder harder, her excitement rising. "Listen, if you help me, Allastam's arrest today might be more than a pretext!"

"Oh, so it *is* a pretext." Sora's smile vanished, wiped out by a wave of horror. Jilssan laughed. The poor woman was far too easy to read. "Don't worry. Your secret is safe with me. I'll even help you … *if* you can extract my apprentice, Isra, from the enclave and protect her. Truly, I'd love to participate in Lord Allastam's woes and be your infamous witness. It sounds fun!"

Perhaps Sora wasn't the only one too easy to read. Jilssan should keep her feelings closer to her heart, weigh every word more carefully. That demanded so much energy, however, and although every minute out of the cell and in the torch's warmth revived some long-numbed part of Jilssan, exhaustion still dragged down her mind and wits. Self-control could wait for more serious threats than Sora Sharpe.

"How do I know I can trust you?" Sora asked, perhaps finally wizening up to the sort of woman she'd freed.

Jilssan shrugged. "Talk to Lord Dathirii about that one. I'm not here to ease your worries."

"Diel Dathirii could teach me to trust Lord Allastam with my life."

"My point exactly!" She grinned, and Sora smiled back. "So how did you pull this off? Did you knock the asshole out? I managed to run a tree through his belly. I mean, not an entire tree, but some parts. Clearly not enough to be rid of him."

"He's still conscious. I would rather not knock him out, but we might have to." Sora turned on her heels and started back towards the entrance. "I think he's waiting for his troops to gather to mess with us again."

Jilssan fell into steps behind her. "And your plan for that is …?"

Sora did not answer. She had no plan. Had Sora walked in there with nothing but a pretend arrest just to get Hasryan out? Maybe he'd been right about his friends. At least Jilssan had had a proper scheme going before she'd beenshoved into this cell.

"Great. It'll have been a fun walk, and I guess I'll at least have more company."

"I do not intend to finish the day in a cold cell." The slump in her shoulders contradicted her determined tone. "I'll find a way. I counted twenty guards close at hand, with more likely scattered throughout the tower. Suggestions to fight them off are welcome."

Fight them off? This lady overestimated her skills, no doubt. "Don't. Remove my manacles." She lifted her wrists with a wide smile. "I'm exhausted, but if I need to burn through what little strength I have left to get out of this hole, I will. While my expertise lies in body enhancements, I can transmute other materials."

"What are you suggesting? A shield?"

"It'll depend on where we are and how much energy I can

summon."

She gave the manacles a quick shake. Sora sighed, slid the key in, and freed her. She clipped the anti-magic cuffs to her belt right away—no doubt she'd make good use of them one day. Jilssan hoped it'd never be on her.

As they headed back towards the stairs down and the torture room, she rubbed her wrists and stretched, trying to get rid of the stifling pain in her back. Every muscle screamed at her, and the world seemed a little too distant, as if filtered through a fog. She might need an endurance spell to carry her through the day, especially if she intended to draw on her reserves and cast a lot. Whatever. She refused to go back into that cell. Her life had just taken an unexpected turn, but if her new allies were willing to take such risks for one another, she could do worse. And if she could get them out of here, they would be indebted to her.

That, as always, sounded like music to her ears.

LARRYN shoved his back against the wall as they reached the end of their slim corridor, his heart hammering with panicked irregularity. The training grounds would be right around that corner, and there'd been loads of people in it earlier, and every single one of them knew how to fight better than he did. Especially with this armour. The cursed thing weighed heavily, hampering vision and movement, and he hated it.

"Hear anything?" Sora asked, her mouth drawn into a grim line.

He grimaced. "I'm half deaf. Ear infection." He'd hear better if they'd switched placed, but he doubted it'd matter. The rapid *schtack* of wooden swords and shields should have echoed across the wide hall, an unmistakable cacophony. The dull silence that had replaced it was a threat of its own.

"They're waiting for us," Sora said, and her sharp tone made him turn back. Despair and defiance wrapped into one another, like she could see the abyss below them but would still leap into it.

"This is where the whole thing turns into a shitslide, isn't it?"

"Every attempt to stop us is an infraction of its own and will be held against Lord Allastam."

Larryn fought himself to contain the bitter laugh that wanted to spill. None of them gave a shit about that. Sora had asked Lord Allastam to make his troops stand down earlier, and he'd laughed in her face. It had taken Larryn everything not to punch him. Sora better name him Larryn the Angry, Master of Acting and Self-Control after all this, because this asshole embodied all Larryn hated. He still stared at them, smug despite the rag in his mouth and the manacles on his wrists.

Behind him, Jilssan was going through routine stretches as if she'd just awoken from a long night. She could be humming and it wouldn't surprise Larryn one bit, and even though they'd need all the help they could get, part of him wished she'd remained in shackles. He'd experienced the dangers of Myrian transmuters too closely, and the very thought of her abilities made the armour around his neck stifling.

In between all of them, under 'arrest' for appearances' sake,

Hasryan leaned against a wall, eyes closed. He looked like shit, one arm dangling as if broken, a deep burn across his stomach, and renewed exhaustion weighing his shoulders. A single glance at him set Larryn's blood to boiling. They'd found him. No way he'd let anything stop him now.

Besides, he had his own secret weapon, didn't he? Larryn touched the armour on his chest, under which he'd tucked Cal's holy symbol. He'd seen its subtle power when rescuing Nevian, and what did Cal always say? Fortune favours the bold.

If there was one thing he knew, it was how to be bold.

Larryn shoved himself off the wall, and with no more than a "get going while I distract them", he rushed into the room.

Two rows of guards waited, one with a knee on the ground, the other standing. All of them with a crossbow at the ready. The sharp *thwang* of crossbow release buried Sora's horrified "Fleece!". Distantly, as if his mind refused to register the twenty-something bolts flying in his general direction, Larryn commended her for using his thieves' name.

What his brain refused, however, his body knew. He flung himself to the side, drawing the sword in a clumsy movement to cut at the air before him. Dimly, he registered the golden glow below his eyes, the tinkling of coins in his ear. His blade deflected a bolt. Another smashed into the ground and only shards smacked against his armour. A third skidded on his helmet and the metal rang hard, stunning him. Yet through all the missed shots—the unfortunate, impossible misses—one bolt sliced through his left leg, a trail of blazing pain. He gasped and reached for it, but fingers clamped on his own and yanked him up then back into the corridor. Sora held him against the wall, anger and fear warring in her scowl.

"What were you thinking?"

A commanding voice cut him off before he could answer. "After them! Stay ready."

"Retreat?" Jilssan asked, irritatingly calm.

"Retreat."

Sora half-dragged Larryn along, and any impulse to protest vanished when he first put the slightest weight on his wounded leg. It burned, the surge of pain blanketing his vision with black dots. Larryn blinked them away, gritting his teeth as he stumbled inside the room. Sora slammed it shut, and Jilssan stepped next to it.

"Let me handle this one."

She pressed her palms against the wall nearby and closed her eyes, leaning in as if to listen. The stone under her fingers softened and melted, the effect spreading all along the door before it stretched, the very wall slowly covering the door. Jilssan's breath grew shallower, but soon she had the entire exit covered with half an inch of stone. She released the wall and smirked at Sora.

"Should keep them out a bit."

"Let's find the exit, then." He pushed himself off the wall and forced a first step, bracing against the pain. They needed to get moving, and he'd already messed up. If they kept moving, he wouldn't need to think about his blunder.

Lord Allastam's chuckles pierced his gag. They all turned to him, and one by one their expressions darkened. Larryn's heart sank. They'd been pretty central inside the tower. What if there *were* no exit?

"We move," Sora said, her firm tone betraying no despair.

Her hand gripped Lord Allastam's forearm and pulled him along. He didn't protest, even seemed to find the whole routine amusing. Larryn wished he could kick his feet from under him, or knock the smugness out of him. He instead focused his growing anger into every step, fighting the pain in his leg and ignoring the blood sticking to his pants. An elbow prodded him.

"Might wanna hold your prisoner, so he doesn't run off," Hasryan whispered.

Larryn slapped his hand over his shoulder, tightening his grip, and using Hasryan to support his weight. Holding him helped with more than the walk; it anchored him to the stakes, fuelling his determination to see this through. Larryn clung to that fire as they climbed one set of stairs, then another, reaching yet another corridor with damp, cold cells. Below them, soldiers hammered at the blocked door, every bang a warning of impending violence that sent Larryn's heart stumbling. How long did they have? They were trapped in here, with no real plan, and it was only a matter of time before the Allastam soldiers broke through.

A bigger, more violent bang boomed from downstairs and Larryn shuddered as if the tower's walls were his own bones, frail and easy to break. Or maybe that was his hope, cracking with every slam of their battering ram.

"Shall we make our escape?" Jilssan's chirpy tone jarred Larryn from his rising gloom.

"Something up your sleeve?" Hasryan asked. "Or even actual

sleeves of any kind. I'm sure everyone present greatly appreciates the view, but it is getting very cold to walk around in my beautiful bare chest."

"You're quite correct, the view is delightful. A shame we didn't have any light yesterday."

Hasryan laughed—genuine mirth, not the awkward chuckles of the uncomfortable target—and that was the only thing that kept Larryn from snapping at the Myrian wizard. That was his best friend, not some piece of meat.

Jilssan scanned the room and slipped into one of the cells to pick up an old, moth-eaten blanket. With a smirk, she gave it a quick snap—and it turned into a hideous fur vest of an impossible bright red speckled with black. She flung it at Hasryan, who'd have no way of putting it on with the manacles on.

"Here you go, cellmate. Now, I do have better to do with my talents." She walked to the back of the cell and set her palm against the wall. "Either this leads elsewhere in the tower, or it leads outside. We're going through it regardless."

She slid her fingers along the stones as she crouched down, her hands eventually resting on the juncture with the ground. A tiny glow emanated from her fingertips, and if he turned his head just right, Larryn caught her low chant. He glanced at Sora and saw his grim hope reflected in her expression. The echoes of Allastam soldiers battering at their reinforced door filled the silence as they watched Jilssan work. Seconds trickled by, punctuated by the ramming. The pale radiance surrounding Jilssan's hands spread into the wall, rising up. As Jilssan's light coursed along the wall and into the ceiling, Allastam started to muffle into the gag. Larryn patted his back.

"No one cares what you have to say."

The outraged glare he received would brighten Larryn's memories for weeks, if not years. No doubt Allastam was mentally threatening to break this random guard's career into thousands of tiny pieces and piss on them. Except he'd never find a Fleece. The small victory made him giddy.

A wintry gust snapped him out of his internal celebrations and his gaze latched onto Jilssan's handiwork.

The wall extended outward, the strip she'd illuminated slowly unfurling. The material changed texture, too, turning into a darkened crystal as it stretched, catching the sunlight outside. Larryn whistled. No wonder mages played at being overlords in so many parts of the world. She was remodeling an entire wall! Just bending it to her will, no big deal. The sheer amount of power involved left him uneasy. Could Nevian do any of this? Would Efua one day be able to, too? How much could they do for the Shelter with even a fraction of Jilssan's power?

"You must have made some terrible decisions to wind up in a cell despite such abilities," Hasryan commented.

Jilssan's reply was cut short by din of the door crashing several floors below them. They all jumped, and Allastam grunted in satisfaction.

"Hurry," Sora said. "Fleece, you lead the way. I'll cover our backs."

Larryn wanted to argue, but he'd already got his leg shot and his knowledge of fights was limited to those happening in taverns. His heart tightened at the idea of leaving Sora behind, no matter how close she'd follow. He nodded anyway. "Yes boss."

She grimaced at him. "And keep a close eye on Hasryan."

In their skeleton plan, she would handle Allastam while he took Hasryan away, supposedly to the guards' headquarters. They'd fake an unfortunate escape on the way, and Fleece would vanish with the assassin. If they could make it out of the Allastam Tower, their thrilling and ill-planned rescue could finally come to an end. Larryn crowded closer to Jilssan, pushing Lord Allastam along, while Sora fell behind with her sword drawn. The first echoes of booted feet reached them.

"Master Jilssan," Sora said, "make sure Lord Allastam stays with you."

A vague grunt was her only acknowledgment. All of Jilssan's energy remained on the wall, its black stone unfurling across empty space, a long finger reaching for a street passing on a slightly lower level. She morphed their path as she worked, forming long crystalline steps to ease the descent, raising the occasional rod for them to grip should the wind push them. It'd be a wild dash across a narrow walkway, but Larryn would still rather that than face the mass of soldiers rushing up the stairs, their boots drumming a promise of violence.

He set his hand on Hasryan's shoulder and roughened his voice into pretend gruffness. "You stay next to me."

"Whatever you say, buddy." Hasryan smirked at him, as if he was mocking the guard's authority. "But you ought to look into laws to regulate Jilssan's horrendous sense of fashion. It's a crime in and of itself."

Jilssan withdrew her hands from the wall, its other end now fused to the closest of Isandor's bridges. She remained crouched for a second, her skin pale and her shoulders slumped, but soon pushed herself up. When she turned to them, her smile matched Hasryan's.

"Can I be blamed if I had to create something that would match the wonderful and minimal outfit you already sported?"

"You didn't even pick the same red!" Hasryan threw his arms up and the clink of his chains covered Jilssan's chuckle. "At least Bran—"

"Cut it off and get moving!" Sora interrupted. The onslaught of soldiers couldn't be more than a floor away. "What are you, teenagers? Run!"

Her order provoked a slew of angry shouts from bootlickers eager to save their lord. Jilssan traced a quick symbol midair, snapped a word distorted with the power of her magic, then closed her fingers into a fist, as if grabbing invisible lines. Larryn's earlier fear spiked back … until she lifted Lord Allastam and slung him over her shoulder like a sack of potatoes—another memory he'd cherish for a long time. They ran out as a group, the howling winter wind burying Allastam's muffled protests.

Emptiness and a deadly fall flanked Larryn on each side as he advanced on Jilssan's thin magical bridge, and between the buffeting gusts, the reaping pain in his leg, and his cumbersome armour, he slowed his pace to long strides rather than an all-out sprint, one hand always ready to grab the spaced-out poles. Hasryan wound up a step before him, and Jilssan closed the march with her squirming package. Larryn forced himself to focus on his feet and balance. Sora could handle herself. He had to trust she'd follow.

Then he heard Drake's voice, its snide pitch striking torrents of fury within him. "Take aim! Don't let this rabble get away with my father!"

He spun about, self-control annihilated by the presence of this slime, and his heart stopped in sync with his feet. Sora stood alone on the thin bridge, sword raised, facing the Allastam troops. They crowded around Drake, forming three lines of two—one lying down, one kneeling, and a last standing—all with crossbows pointed at her.

At Sora, their only competent fighter, whose light chainmail wouldn't protect her against the heavy bolts. Sora, who had devised this ridiculous rescue, without whom Hasryan would still be tortured. Sora, who was everything city guards should be, rather than what they were.

Sora, whom he had grown quite fond of.

Larryn started back, his stomach clenching as soldiers adjusted their aim. She was so close, yet so impossibly far away.

"Sora!" he called.

She glanced over her shoulder and scowled. "Keep running, Fleece!"

Larryn knew she meant *fleeing*, but he decided to take her order literally. He sped up, bracing his body against the agonizing flare each step sent through his wounded leg, hoping to reach her in time and yet knowing the moment Drake raised his arms to give the signal that he never would, that he would still be missing a few, crucial steps in order to use his armour and Ren's blessings to shield her. She would die on this bridge, for a pointless heroic stand while others fled, and a bitter bile rose in Larryn's throat as the certainty settled within him.

The soldier's arm swung down; Larryn's heart plummeted with it.

The sharp *schtak* of crossbows promised death, yet his eyes betrayed what his ears told him. In the single instant that half a dozen bolts flew towards Sora, a pillar of earth slammed onto the bridge from above, walling them off. The bolts crashed into it, and Larryn breathed again. He spun to stare at Jilssan, but she stopped even as he turned, astonishment plain on her face. But if not her, then who?

The pillar disintegrated into dust, and the wind scattered it away, leaving a single fighter behind.

Shoulder-length golden hair had been pulled into a ponytail, revealing long elven ears, and he held his sword high, shoulders squared with pride—exactly the posture Sora had wanted him to adopt. The dust hadn't even completely dissipated and he was already sprinting at the Allastam soldiers. A loud crack echoed every time his boots hit the bridge, and Jilssan's crystalline structure crumbled behind him, leaving a widening gap behind and cutting them off from the Allastam Tower.

"Kellian?" Sora's exclamation was strangled, but she recovered quickly and ran to the edge of the leftover bridge, its jagged stone somehow still holding. "Kellian! What are you doing?"

Wind carried his answer to them. "Keep going—I'll take care of them."

A storm brewed in his voice, and it sent Larryn's heart skittering. Not for the Allastam goons—they could suck it—but as an echo of all his close escapes from within the Dathirii Tower, that same voice cursing as it asked his guards to arrest the thief who'd once more sneaked into their home. Larryn grabbed Sora's wrist and pulled.

"You heard him."

She didn't budge—didn't even acknowledge him. Her eyes wouldn't leave the golden-haired prince who'd just saved her.

Kellian brought his sword down in an overhead arc, smashing it into the bridge at his feet as if wielding a hammer. Brown stone erupted from Jilssan's crystalline structure, running down its length and into the Allastam Tower. It rose, wrapping itself around the soldiers' bodies—legs, hip, chest, and arms, all the way until in had crawled into and hover their helmets and encased them completely, leaving statues behind.

Only Drake remained partly freed, his hands trapped but his upper torso spared. Kellian strode up to him with deadly calm; an attitude Drake was far from sharing.

"You think you can get away with this? We'll have your head, you worthless shit. You've got no titles, no homes—you're nothing! All of you, just nothings, and I'll—"

Drake stopped with a gasp as Kellian raised his left hand and closed the fingers in part, the gesture similar to Jilssan's earlier. Larryn squinted. He thought he'd seen the stone near Drake's chest bend inward, pressing against his lungs.

"If I am nothing or no longer my own, then so be it," Kellian said, his growled voice carried by the wind. "It leaves me nothing to lose."

His fingers turned into a fist, and the resounding snap of Drake's ribs sent a chill through Larryn. Kellian turned away as the young man struggled for his breath and slid his sword back into the scabbard. Stone still curled around his wrists like bracers.

"He'll live if your healers arrive fast enough," he said over his shoulder before freeing a single man with a dismissive gesture. The soldier scampered off without hesitation.

"Kellian." Sora pronounced his name with equal parts horror and awe. "Are you all right? Where were you? Since when can you do all this?"

In response, Kellian strode back towards them, and the bridge reformed under his feet, grey-brown stone simply erupting from his boots to form the path as he needed. He never did answer the questions. A few dozen feet behind Larryn, Hasryan did for him.

"It's not him, not really." The flatness of his tone sank Larryn's heart. "Brune is here."

CHAPTER SIX

ASRYAN didn't bother searching for Brune. He would not find her unless she wanted him to, and why give her the satisfaction? His fingers twitched for a blade to defend himself with, pointless as it was against a fighter of Kellian Dathirii's calibre. Even had the elf's deadliness not been well known throughout Isandor's bridges, the predatory grace of his run across the bridge would have given it away. Not to mention these new abilities…

Quietly, as Kellian advanced, he began to wonder how long he and Brune had cooperated, and whether or not his insistence to bring Camilla to the headquarters for housing Hasryan had been pure stick-up-his-ass, or if there was more to it. Brune might have gotten to him long ago, bidding her time until she needed to pull his strings. But what for? What in all the gods did she want now?

Kellian stopped several strides away and brought his sword to bear. The slender blade caught sunlight, reflecting it so brightly it seemed to shine from within. Hasryan managed one step back, as if belatedly realizing he should have been fleeing all along. Behind Kellian, Larryn sprinted in an awkward gait, flinching with every step on his wounded leg, his own weapon forgotten in a charge he must intend to turn into a full-blown tackle—one that might send them both over the edge. His heart squeezing, Hasryan signalled for him to stop, and to his great surprise, his friend obeyed, skidding to stop before he could smash into Kellian.

The elven captain sliced at the ground before him, and as the tip brushed against the crystalline bridge, the earth spiked all around Hasryan's feet, grasping fingers capturing his ankles and clenching tight. Panic rose in waves within Hasryan, heaving through his stomach and lungs, wrestling with him for control over his body. He forced a smirk to his lips and instantly felt better.

Kellian stopped a few feet away, his sword back in a ready position. Did he expect Hasryan to break out from the stone anchor wrapped around his feet and legs?

"I have a message from your boss," he said.

Hasryan snorted. "She's not my boss." He cast the words out like a spell, enunciating them with force, as if they could protect him from the desire to hear Brune rooting itself within him.

Kellian's lips quirked. "Perhaps not. But we're all pawns in her games, aren't we?"

He wished he could tell Kellian off, but the truth of it formed a tight lump in his throat. "What does she want?"

"To talk. But she wants you to come willingly."

Talk. Hasryan would have laughed if he didn't fear hysteria would overtake him. Brune's talks could turn as dangerous as any assault. It didn't matter. Hasryan was done with these games. She had something to say or do, and she would get to it sooner or later, whether or not he complied. He wasn't going to spend the next days or weeks worrying over it.

"Let's get it over with." He bent over to tap the stone encasing his legs. "Come on, Brune. I know you're listening."

He hadn't even finished and already the stone at his feet shifted. It started as a soft wave, as if the solid material had gone wobbly, then it erupted upward, stretching towards the sky before closing in. Hasryan glimpsed the city's spires reaching for the sky, bridges stretching between them, then the earth fused in one smooth ceiling. Compared to the windy outside, it was warm here, the steady temperatures he'd grown used to in the Crescent Moon headquarters. It calmed him, slowing the frantic beat of his heart as he waited in this stone egg that'd carry him to whatever fate awaited.

Pressure on his chest shifted as the egg moved—plummeting down, he realized. He might have floated up from the speed had his feet not been rooted to the ground, and as his furs lifted, he found himself wishing he was wearing something better than Jilssan's ugly red furs and the tight underwear beneath.

The egg stopped moving and the walls collapsed around him, releasing his feet. He was somewhere in Brune's headquarters, or she'd gone through great pains to make it look similar. Familiar patterns lined the walls, encoding directions for the initiated, and ceilings arched smoothly above his head. The walls' soft innate glow bathed the modest furniture: a small table with a kettle and tea, along with two chairs.

Brune stood behind the farthest of the two. She had braided her long brown hair backward, and instead of her usual pragmatic pants-and-shirt, she wore a long, multilayered dress, each fabric a shade of ochre lighter than the one below, forming an impressive strata-like pattern. Hasryan stared, mouth agape. She even had subtle make-up and crystal earrings for the occasion, and he couldn't fathom her intentions. He had expected a smug and brutal murder, not … whatever this was.

"Please take a seat." She motioned for the second chair as if nothing in the whole world was amiss with this situation.

"What?"

"Take a seat," Brune repeated. "I heard you've developed a recent liking for tea?"

Anger surged through Hasryan. Brune knew him better than anyone. She'd been the first to bypass his walls and get close to him, the first he'd opened to about his past, his fears, his goals. She'd mentored him on everything—street dangers and politics and assassination, yes, but writing and negotiating and formal dances, too. She had given him a purpose and a home, had asked nothing more than loyalty for so many years. More than a decade of close relationship, all shattered in a single betrayal. And now that he was rebuilding without her, filling the abyss she had left behind, she was mocking him, toying with him.

"I did." The strange calm in his voice startled him. It was so detached from the whirlwind inside of him, so at odds with the clash of longing and betrayal Brune's very presence called forth. "Once I moved from pungent teas whose earthy aftertaste overpowered everything, I discovered a whole range of potential combination. Soft with unexpected lemongrass hints at the end, sweet and underplayed lilacs that fill you with warmth, even strong and bitter taste I thought would never agree with me. It's wonderful, really, what an open heart can bring you."

He smirked, lips curving on their own, the defensive expression so natural he barely noticed. Brune had wanted to rattle him, and he'd thrown up every wall he could, encasing himself in the armour of pithy humour and ill-thought metaphors. He wouldn't let her see his pain. She could too easily guess at it, and he wanted to preserve what illusions he could.

"I'm … glad," she replied, and the hint of regret in her tone was a hammer into his defences, cracking the walls instantly. He could hardly breathe. "But please, allow yourself one last drink of earthy aftertaste. Some things deserve proper goodbyes, don't you think?"

"Was a noose around my neck not proper enough for you?"

He didn't walk towards the chairs, *couldn't* walk. Hasryan held himself very still, convinced the slightest movement would shatter his tenuous control. The scar at his neck throbbed, phantom pain from his first betrayal, years of struggles flooding back in. His fingers twitched and he forced himself to keep staring at Brune, to whom he owed so much, whom he had loved so deeply. She had been the solid rock on which he'd climbed to escape the swift and deadly currents of his pain. And while it turned out he'd climbed on unsteady, treacherous ground, he still loved it more than he cared to admit.

"Oh, Hasryan."

She strode to him, and his panic rose with every step closer. Then she reached for his cheek, and briefly cupped it, and he froze. She was touching him. She never—

Hasryan jerked away, gritting his teeth at the surge of pain in his arm as he put himself out of her reach. She had to be toying with him, tugging at just the right strings to play him as she wanted. This wasn't tenderness or regrets. He couldn't allow that possibility within his mind or it would shatter him.

She dropped her hand, her lips pinched in disappointment, and Hasryan's heart pounded harder. Was she faking? Had she expected him to stay there, to listen to her without hostility? Brune had always shown her affection through small and practical favours, acknowledging she enjoyed his company without ever doting on him or expressing anything clearly. He was her best assassin, her most trusted mercenary, loyal to the end. Now nothing tied them but this shared past and the shattered illusion about *her* loyalty. He didn't understand why she allowed vulnerability to show, what her goal was. Could she want him back? Did she think for a moment she could rebuild their relationship?

"What do you want?" he hissed.

"To apologize."

Hasryan barked a quick and strangled laugh. His legs were threatening to give in. He was going to snap, to just fall to the ground in a thousand pieces. He squeezed out a joke, forcing amusement into his voice. "Allastam knocked my head harder than I thought."

This time, Brune rolled her eyes. "Don't be a fool. Even I make mistakes, but I prefer not to dig myself deeper into holes I've created." She reached for her crystal earring and twisted it. "I had a more formal invitation planned for you but may have precipitated this encounter due to your propensity to get in trouble. I do wish you'd had the opportunity to change into better clothes."

She raised a single eyebrow, and he scowled back. Brune didn't give a damn about what he was wearing. She was trying to lessen the tension and make him more comfortable. He shoved his hands into the pockets of his furs. "I rather like these. They're gifts. If all you want is to say you're sorry for shattering my life, get on with it and send me back out. I'm not taking tea with you."

Brune glanced back at the table and raised a hand. The stone ground welled up around the small set-up and sealed it in a half-sphere and sank into the ground. Once the floor had regained its smoothness, she returned her attention to Hasryan. "No tea, then."

"Great. Now get on with it."

Hasryan wished it didn't sound like a plea, but he needed Brune to be quick while he still held himself together, even if barely. He had no idea how to deal with her apology, and a part of him hoped she had no intention of making one. Every minute of Brune's presence complicated his feelings, making it harder to bury decades of companionship under anger and hatred. Why couldn't she be like Avenazar or Allastam? Wanton cruelty, a complete lack of self-awareness, and unbridled arrogance would help him a lot right now. But Brune had protected him from scrying since his escape, and he could no longer convince himself it was entirely out of a self-serving, convoluted plot. She captured his gaze, unflinching, and Hasryan's breath caught as he braced for the impact.

"I'm sorry," she said. "You deserved to be protected, and I failed you."

Hasryan had expected a rush of emotion and the tears or nausea or dizziness that so often followed. Instead, he felt… empty. His head buzzed, but he found himself breathing easily, unaffected. It should have meant something to hear her acknowledge her harm so plainly, yet it rang hollow. Slowly, the cracks that had snaked through him since Brune's betrayal filled up, fusing into one solid certainty: he was better off without her, and he owed her *nothing*.

"You did. I don't accept this apology." Surprise and hurt flashed through her expression, and he didn't allow her to recover. "I don't care to, and I don't need to. It's done now, but you'll have to contend yourself with the fact I will *never* forgive what you did. Release me."

Hasryan couldn't remember being this forceful with Brune. He'd just given her an order, and while she didn't flinch, he knew from her slight frown that she was re-evaluating the situation. Measuring, calculating, planning. Always layering schemes and manipulations, placing even the pieces she cared about in her game.

"I had an offer, too, to go along with the apology."

He snorted. Irritation was slowly replacing the emptiness as he recognized her patterns. "Of course you do. Is this a both or neither kind of deal? That's not very sincere."

"It's not." She remained calm, as if unaffected by his refusal but he heard the knots into her voice, straining her usual façade. "The issue of this war between the Dathirii and the Myrians is without consequence to your situation as Isandor's most noteworthy and researched assassin. If you wish to escape and rebuild elsewhere, however… I have the resources and network for such endeavours. Wherever you'd want to go, I can help. It's up to you."

As if to emphasize her point, she tapped his shackles. Stone spiked out of the lock, breaking it, and they fell to the ground. Hasryan brought his wounded arm closer to himself and stepped back, scowling. "I'm not leaving unless I'm forced to. This is my home, and I'm tired of moving around and starting from scratch. You can shove your offer up where it belongs."

Her mouth quirked, and she spread her hands out. "Suit yourself, but you may be forced out sooner than you'd like. I will not waste my life shielding you from divination spells. Once this conflict is over, you're on your own, Hasryan."

He'd known that the instant refusal had crossed his lips, yet hearing it spelled out squeezed the air out of his lungs. After today, House Allastam would not readily forget about him and they had all the resources they'd need to track him down. They might even hire Brune herself. It didn't matter. Whatever came next, he'd find a solution—but not with Brune, never again. He had others to rely on.

"I'm not," he said, "and I never will be again."

She smiled with such obvious fondness his longing squirmed back in. "May Gresh protect you, then. You'll need it."

The stone egg sprung to life around him, enclosing him once more. Hasryan squeezed his eyes shut and let it transport him, its movements churning his stomach in sync with the jolts of nostalgia and hurt. When the egg deposited him at last, he was standing in front of a beautiful wooden door, painted blue and partly buried under snow: one of the Crescent Moon's many hideouts. A parting gift, then. Hasryan was of a mind to refuse, but his arm throbbed, he'd slept like shit, and he desperately needed somewhere to lose his shit. He slipped inside, latched the door, and slid against it, collapsing on the ground right there and then.

CHAPTER SEVEN

SORA watched, numb to the core, as the stone egg encasing Hasryan detached from Jilssan's transmuted bridge and plummeted down, vanishing between bridges and taking her heart with it. She had risked everything to save him, and now he was gone. Taken by Brune, and there was nothing she could do—nothing at *all*, not even scream or curse or dash after it, a fool desperate to save a friend. She could only stare, the stoic Sapphire Guard who'd come to arrest Lord Allastam, the investigator who didn't care for a criminal.

Her hand shot out, catching Larryn's, squeezing it. To stop him from throwing himself at Kellian in anger, but for herself, too. The tiny emotional contact she could afford, even though she desperately needed more. Everything was crumbling between her fingers, and her mind spun wildly, trying to place reality and lies, to know what needed to come next.

Larryn jerked to a halt at her touch, his reinitiated dash interrupted. Briefly, he squeezed back. Then his fingers slipped away and he met her gaze. Under all the expected fury in his grey eyes, Sora read some amusement, too.

"Boss, he broke the assassin free! Needs some arresting, don't it?"

"What?" The question was out of her mouth before she could check herself. Arrest Kellian? Sora felt at wit's end, unable to reconcile the ruses and her goals, and now all the attention had spun to her. She could have cursed Larryn. But bless him, too, because he was right, this was the best path forward. "He does."

In one practised motion, her fingers fell to the anti-magic cuffs she'd taken off Jilssan. She stomped the short distance towards Kellian, who hadn't moved since Hasryan's disappearance, safe for sheathing his sword. He didn't turn at her approach, either, only spoke to the wind.

"I won't resist."

The dead tone stoked her anger. Was that it, then? He'd landed in the middle of their chaos only to send Hasryan to his doom, and now he didn't care about his fate? Didn't even care enough to turn around and face her? She grabbed his hands and cuffed them behind his back with more force than necessary.

"I thought you were dead," she spat near his ears. When he didn't answer, she nudged him forward. "Let's move."

At least Jilssan hadn't used the chaos as an opportunity to ditch her. She stood at the connection between her transmuted path and Isandor's regular bridges, one hand firmly on Lord Allastam's shoulder. If she still had that magical strength, he was going nowhere without her permission. Sora glanced back at the many soldiers still encased in stone. Healers would arrive for Drake soon—healers and reinforcements, no doubt. She wanted to get somewhere safe, if possible.

She started off, their mismatched group following behind her. Sora guided them upward, choosing her bridges to put a few towers between her and the Allastam one before climbing up. They'd gone up two flights before she realized Larryn had started to trail behind. Her gaze fell on his bloodied pants and the occasional red stains across the snowed pathways.

If anything had gone according to plan, Larryn would've been with Hasryan by now, not trudging with them towards the Upper City. She doubted he wanted to follow her as she petitioned Lady Brasten for help. He'd given her an out with Kellian. Least she could do was give him his.

"Fleece, you're bleeding all over the place," she said. "We got this handled. Get your ass to the Headquarters and see to that leg."

"Right. Of course."

She couldn't read the tightness in his voice. Fatigue from the day's ordeal? Anger at being dismissed? Relief, perhaps, even? Sora stared several seconds too long, as if that could help her unravel what boiled under the full-face helmet. Then Larryn spun around and left them, leaving her questions unanswered. It surprised Sora just how much she craved that particular knowledge, but that was another thing she didn't have time to pause and consider.

Shoving all those finicky emotions deeper in, Sora turned to the rest of the party and removed the gag in Lord Allastam's mouth with a polite 'milord' empty of all real deference. They were far enough now that he couldn't call for his tower's guards. He could, however, treat them to a string of threats and promptly obliged. He'd destroy their careers (she'd known that), destroy her life (a distinct worry), destroy those they loved (if he touched Kirio she'd destroy *him*)—nothing she hadn't expected or heard. When that didn't faze them, he switched to a subtler kind of menace.

"A Dathirii in league with my wife's killer," he mused aloud, very obviously aiming for Kellian to hear him. "Who would've thought I'd receive such a gift on this otherwise outrageous morning?"

Kellian's entire posture went rigid. "There's no leagues."

"I'd have you arrested for that, dear Kellian, but well…" He gave a quick shake to his own shackles and smirked as Kellian growled at him.

"Your list of criminal offences is too long to make, *milord*."

"And making that is *my* job," Sora interrupted. "You'll have ample opportunities to share your recriminations with me."

It shut Kellian up, but Lord Allastam was not a man to wait for his turn. He complained for the remainder of their trip—about the manacles chaffing his wrists, about his insufficient clothing for such a cold day, even about the fresh scar on his belly hurting anew because of their brutal transportation. That last one made Jilssan smirk, and she began humming a pleasant song. For all her good humour, however, the Myrian wizard dragged her feet and began stumbling, her feet catching on stairs or slipping on ice.

Then they finally stood in front of the Brasten Tower, the

imposing double doors looming above them, and both Lord Allastam's recriminations and Jilssan's song died down. Sora hoped Lady Brasten would shelter her. By law, a Sapphire Guard could request the use of any tower's rooms to temporarily house prisoners, a provision created specifically to safeguard them from political corruption. To accept, however, implied House Brasten considered her accusations legitimate. Had Sora walked up without Jilssan, she would've fully expected to be turned away. Now, however…

Two women stood guard at the door, with only a sword at their side and no armour or extensive livery, as the Allastam ones had— more a filter for visitors than protection against intruders, really. Yet nervous energy wormed itself through Sora's stomach, more unsettling than facing the rows of crossbows and certain death had been. Too much hinged on how her words would be received in the next hour. She squared her shoulders and walked up to them. Behind her: Isandor's most influential noble, the missing Dathirii Guard Captain, and the Myrian Enclave's second in command. The Brasten guards shifted uncomfortably at her approach.

"By virtue of Isandor's laws, I require the use of Lady Brasten's cells," Sora declared. "Please warn her Investigator Sora Sharpe would like an audience."

The shock delayed their reaction, but one of them soon dashed off with a mumbled "right away". The other led everyone inside, through a high-ceiling entrance hall. Warmth greeted Sora, and as the great doors closed behind her, some of her tension slid off. Whatever happened now, they had at least made it to the Brasten Tower. Lord Allastam protested every step of the way, exposing in a great many words to the guard how absurd this charade was, how they all knew Lady Brasten would have the sense to see through it, and why waste any time on "a wench fit for the shitslides". That last part had all of them flinch, even the Brasten guard, and Jilssan chirped a little "charming." Sora did her best to ignore him. Only Lady Brasten's opinion mattered now.

Sunlight streamed through tall east-facing windows, their heavy dark blue curtains pulled to the side. A handful of wooden-backed chairs and a sofa had been arranged around a low table in a half-circle, and the lit fireplace warmed the area. Jilssan ignored the central zone entirely as they walked in, instead draping herself on a lounge chair against the farthest wall. Kellian let himself fall into the least comfortable-looking chair, sitting at the edge and staring at the fire, while Lord Allastam remained standing in dignified protest. Sora was too drained to imitate him and settled for the sofa, which let her view both doors leading in. She stayed at the edge, too, trying to keep the stains of Larryn's blood on her pants from ruining the seat.

The fire's crackling filled the silence, and the last hour began to unfurl again in Sora's mind, sinking in. They'd failed. Ultimately, they'd failed to get Hasryan to safety, moving him from Allastam's clutches to Brune's, and not even the prospect of wringing a path forward for House Dathirii could fill the hollow growing inside her. She'd try, of course, but it felt almost secondary. Sora combed her hair with her fingers and smoothed her uniform, as if she could fix it all by fixing herself. When she looked up, she caught Jilssan watching her with a smile. The wizard raised a thumbs up for her.

Sora stopped fidgeting.

The door leading deeper in the Brasten Tower opened, and Lady Brasten stepped in with purposeful strides. She wore an elegant sleeveless tunic over pants, its rich cream colour soft against her dark skin. Gloves in the same fabric espoused her thick arms, a silver pattern threaded into them. Sora pushed herself up, standing to greet the lady, but she couldn't say a word before Lord Allastam rammed himself into the conversation.

"Lady Brasten! I demand that you put an end to this charade immediately." His voice contained just the right amount of indignation and command. Even with shackles on, his very presence could be imposing. "I have been mistreated as if I were some vulgar criminal. Someone of my stature—"

"What are the charges, Miss Sharpe?"

Amake Brasten had dismissed Lord Allastam with a single glance, cutting him off in favour of Sora, and in that precise instant, Sora had never loved anyone more. Lady Brasten's smooth and serious tone inspired trust and her steady, open gaze reignited Sora's dwindling courage. At the very least, Lady Brasten had consented to consider her claims.

"Milady," Sora said with a deferential nod. "Illegal detention, torture, resisting arrest, and attempted murder, as of now. On a political scale, however, those are inconsequential." She needed to convince Lady Brasten not only that the accusations were viable, but that she, Sora Sharpe, her would-be partner in pursuing this path, understood the realities of power in Isandor. "No one will support an attack on Lord Allastam for the actions he took, for the most part, against Hasryan Fel'ethier, who appeared to be in his tower with deadly intents."

"As I said—" Lord Allastam started.

"However," Sora continued, levelling a whipping glare at him, "I have conclusive proof that Lord Allastam had plans to send Lord Dathirii to be tortured and killed long before the latter's titles were removed by the Golden Table. I had hoped we could discuss those in private—along with Master Jilssan here, and Diel Dathirii—once I knew my prisoner was safe."

Lady Brasten set her hands on the back of a chair, spreading them out in an even, composed fashion. Something itched at the back of Sora's mind at the movement, however—little details in her posture, tensions she'd expect from pain points instead of stress. She didn't grip the chair, but Sora wondered if she wasn't subtly using it for support nonetheless. The lady's gaze hovered between Jilssan, Lord Allastam, and Sora before finally turning to Kellian Dathirii.

"Your cousin will be glad to hear you're safe, as am I," she said. "The handcuffs do raise questions."

Kellian shoulders rose with his deep inhale. "I helped Hasryan Fel'ethier escape his latest arrest. I would rather not discuss the reasons here."

"He will also need a cell here," Sora added, "and I'd like his visits from family limited until I've had a chance to question him myself."

Lady Brasten's fingers drummed on her chair, a tap-tap that marked the flow of her thoughts. Sora's chest tightened until breathing turned into a struggle. If Lady Brasten refused, that was it. Sora had no means to enforce this arrest on her own—her superiors would never back her.

Lady Brasten's fingers settled, and she turned to the guard who'd led her here. "Taneka, please lead Lord Allastam and Kellian Dathirii to our locked quarters. See to it that they receive water, lunch, and several sets of clean clothes, as well as a visit from Umaho to ensure they're not wounded. And please, treat Lord Allastam with the respect warranted by his rank."

A hint of humour tinged her voice, just at the edge of deniability should Lord Allastam take offence.

"You cannot be serious," he protested.

"I am always serious," she said.

Taneka moved forward and set a firm hand on his elbow. "Please, milord."

Sora watched it unfold, numbed by the waves of incredulous relief rising and crashing through her. It was happening. Her request had been granted. She barely registered Lord Allastam's indignant huff, or how he turned to her.

"This isn't over. You'll regret this farce."

He stomped out without waiting for a response, and both Taneka and Kellian followed. With all of them out of the room, staying focused became harder. Sora gripped her knees with her hands to keep them from shaking.

"Thank you," she said, and her voice croaked.

"You must have gone to great lengths to arrest him," she said. "Your reputation as an investigator of skill precedes you. Word is that Sora Sharpe isn't the type to risk her life on an impulse or push accusations without solid grounds. I don't want to waste your hard work before I know what's going on."

Sora struggled to keep a straight face. She *had* done all of this on a whim. She'd run in there with a skeleton of a plan, intending to drop almost meaningless charges on him and buy herself enough time to free Hasryan. Luck had placed Jilssan in those cells, and Sora had seized her chance.

"I'm grateful for your trust. I understand, also, that you are eager to hear the details, but if we could have time to clean up, it would be appreciated. We barely escaped alive, and Master Jilssan has spent a considerable amount of time in a cold cell. A pause would be welcomed."

"Granted."

Lady Brasten turned to Jilssan and her smile stiffened. They stared at one another, and the intensity of it stifled the room. What was going on? Did they have a history Sora wasn't aware of? Or was this only the result of House Brasten more openly siding with Diel Dathirii against the Myrians?

"I think," Lady Brasten started, still fully turned towards Jilssan, "that in addition to the three of us and Diel Dathirii, I'd like to invite a fifth person. Someone with enough prior knowledge of Master Jilssan and the enclave to evaluate the veracity of her claims."

"Milady is wise, then." Jilssan stretched out onto the lounging chair as if she owned the place. Dirt and blood caked her blouse and skirt, and Sora belatedly realized that while Jilssan had provided Hasryan with furs, she'd gone outside with very little to cover herself. She looked every ounce the prisoner in need of help: hair dishevelled, wounds half-healed, outfit torn and sullied. All except for her playful smirk and obvious ease. "I lie, manipulate, and trick whenever it suits my needs. Ask Diel Dathirii."

Lady Brasten lifted her chin, unimpressed. "I certainly will."

Great. Now Lady Brasten was wary of Sora's key witness, all because Jilssan couldn't resist playing the manipulative bad girl. Couldn't she have kept that for herself? It baffled Sora she even wanted others to know she enjoyed lies. What was she trying to do? Put others on edge and play with their minds? Lady Brasten's House and family were at stake here, and if she refused to help because she didn't trust Jilssan, then Sora would drag the Myrian wizard back into the Allastam cells herself.

"I assure you her needs suit ours, too," Sora said, hoping to alleviate some of Lady Brasten's suspicions.

Jilssan laughed and pushed herself upright. "Isn't it wonderful? The stars rarely align like this."

Sora glared at her, but Lady Brasten acted as though she hadn't even noticed she was speaking—not unlike how she'd pointedly ignored Lord Allastam's threats earlier. Sora wished she had the self-control to avoid dignifying insignificant interactions like this.

"My steward will be along shortly," the lady promised. "He will show you to your rooms, where you will have time to clean up, eat, and rest. I will arrange our meeting in two hours, so don't dawdle too much."

"Food," Jilssan whispered, and her own voice seemed to surprise her. When Lady Brasten's eyebrows shot up, she had the decency to look sheepish. "I'm quite convinced your House's cuisine will beat House Allastam's repugnant offer. The prospect of a delicious meal has briefly robbed me of self-control, I'm afraid."

"If it takes so little, we may get along after all." Lady Brasten smiled at her, and there was something of a challenge in her expression. "I will signal to my cooks they should bring you something extra special, so that you can properly celebrate your return into more hospitable walls, and I'll eagerly await your critique."

"It will be my pleasure," Jilssan replied, and she bent forward as if offering a seated bow. Her gaze met Lady Brasten's, and they held each other locked for a time. Sora could already feel that tension building again, a silent conversation building invisible pressure in the room.

"Milady is most gracious," she said, louder than strictly necessary. Her interruptions broke the spell ensnaring both women and they turned to her. "We're grateful for your help in this matter and the hospitality."

Lady Brasten's smile widened. "Don't misunderstand me, Investigator Sharpe. I accepted your request for a cell, but I've yet to decide whether I should give this arrest my prolonged support. Please make the most of your meal to prepare. I am quite eager to hear what you have to say."

Sora's heart hammered against her chest. Over the last weeks, it'd seemed like all the certainties of her life had fallen apart, eroded by the world's injustice, by her own confused morals and feelings. Yet in a single morning, all the pieces had returned to their rightful place. All but one, an assassin with an easy smirk and gentle laugh that could send her heart spinning. She balked at staying here, bathing, while he was in danger, but she'd never find him if Brune wanted him hidden. Here, leading the charge against Lord Allastam, Sora could have an impact. She could make the city better. She had to give it her best shot.

"You won't be disappointed."

Chapter Eight

IEL Dathirii set down his quill and stared at the still-blank parchment before him. The sun had fully risen now, but he hadn't managed more than standard salutations for Lord Balthazar. Words that had once flowed from his mind to the paper under his hand had become near impossible since Branwen had returned from the Dathirii Tower, alone, and broken down into his arms. He'd held her tight, wishing he could weave the miracles she'd once expected of him and fix the world for her.

That power had slipped away from him, however, and any confidence he'd had in regaining it diminished with every day without Jaeger. He felt so adrift, so powerless. Words and ideas had always been his weapons, yet these days they came in short supply, his well drier than the ink he'd set down hours ago, when the sky had barely lightened for the coming day. He would have to try again later. Re-establishing contact with the noble leaders of

Isandor, petitioning them to recognize his House Dathirii as the true one, and remaining an active and impossible to ignore player was of the utmost importance. He wished he received more than carefully worded responses of neutrality or vague promises of support should he win, at best, and, at worst, reproaches for bothering the lords of Isandor with matters below the concerns of the Golden Table. He couldn't give up. Lord Balthazar, in particular, had seen his House rise quickly in power and had skirmished with Lord Allastam on quite a few occasions over the last year. The words Diel chose could make the difference between an ally and an enemy.

That was the theory, at any rate. More and more, Diel felt like they had all already accepted the change in Dathirii leadership and looked forward to his dismissal into the dust of history. Elves lived a long time, however. It made them harder to forget, and Diel had no intention of vanishing for their convenience.

He grasped at the spike of frustration and spite rising within him, pushing the desperation weighing his every thought away, and found a basin of water to splash his face. His hair hung loose, unbraided, but he refused to touch it beyond a quick brush. No one but Jaeger had braided it for well over a century, and Diel couldn't bear the thought of anyone replacing him. It had been a ritual between them, a space they'd shared in the middle of the night or early at dawn, when the Dathirii Tower grew quieter and it felt like the whole world vanished, leaving nothing but their voices and Jaeger's nimble fingers. The memories flooded through him, tightening his throat. Diel missed him in so many small ways that

Jaeger's absence felt like having his insides scooped away. Even Jaeger simply standing there, silent and smiling, had been an integral and essential part of his life.

Jaeger had chosen to stay in the Dathirii Tower, to flaunt Hellion's offer to leave back in his face, claim the space as his own, and accept the risks involved. No matter how much Diel craved his presence, he needed to honour that decision. He needed to find his words and charm again, to be the irresistible idealist who'd upturned so many odds before and who could force the nobles of Isandor to not only acknowledge him, but help him rid the city of Master Avenazar. A tall order.

Knocks at his door interrupted his inner pep talk, and he reflexively glanced up and to the right, where Jaeger's desk would have been in his office—where the steward would've mouthed the name of his visitor, recognizing them by sound alone if they were a regular. His stomach pinched, eroding his frail confidence, but he called for his visitor to enter.

Amake Brasten strode into his room, catching him off guard. They usually scheduled meetings, or he'd climb to her office to discuss an idea or a particular wording. By the grim line of her mouth, an emergency had come up.

"Our lucky break may have knocked at the door this morning," she said.

Diel needed a moment to absorb her meaning, so at odds were the good news with her attitude. "I sense a catch?" he asked, his voice rising to a questioning lilt at the end.

"Not quite." She made her way to the double seat by the wall and sat into it. No, not sat, Diel realized. Slumped, insofar as he had ever seen Lady Brasten slump. Her posture had always stayed impeccable and controlled, and he suspected allowing him to witness anything else was a mark of trust few were afforded. "First, however, you should know Kellian Dathirii is alive and here."

Diel's heart leaped into his throat. Branwen had promised she was making headway, that they had narrowed down his location to two possibilities and she'd recently received important intel that pointed in a single direction.

"Is he all right?"

"He is under arrest for helping Hasryan Fel'ethier escape." Her voice turned sharp, and she stopped any reply with a raised hand. Diel swallowed down the hundred questions pressing at his lips. "Unfortunately, he's done so in full view of Lord Allastam, Master Jilssan, and Investigator Sora Sharpe, who proceeded with the arrest and requested the use of our rooms." She paused, and it lasted long enough that Diel thought his turn had come. Yet as he opened his mouth, she gestured for him to wait once again. "I'm not out of surprises, believe me. The cell petition was not primarily for Kellian Dathirii. Lord Allastam is also under arrest, and quite unhappy about it."

"W-what for?"

He blurted it out as if Lord Allastam didn't have plenty of potential crimes to his name. But which fit this outlandish puzzle? What could be so important that Sora Sharpe would put her entire life on the line?

Amake Brasten met his gaze, then, eyebrows arched and lips

curved into an amused smile. He'd learned that particular expression over the last days, a sort of cheeky and cunning enthusiasm entirely unique to her. "His crimes against you, Diel."

Diel blinked, very slowly absorbing the information. Perhaps he should have seen it coming, but he still felt out of touch and sluggish. If Sora Sharpe had made such a request, then she must have proof to back it up. Recent proof, or he'd have heard of it through Branwen.

"I will venture a guess and say no cells were requested for Master Jilssan."

"Only a bath and a meal," Lady Brasten confirmed. "She will be present when we discuss the exact nature of Investigator Sharpe's proof … as, I suspect, the primary witness."

"That ought to be interesting. She is not known for the goodness of her heart."

"Or her honesty, yes." Lady Brasten's mischievous smile widened and she leaned conspiratorially. "She was very prompt to inform me of this herself, in fact. I think she enjoys playing with others' expectations and putting them on edge."

From the hints of fondness in her voice, Amake Brasten quite liked being put on edge. She did get more alert and involved when he himself challenged her ideas and plans, forcing her to justify her political instincts or work around flaws in her designs. So did he, really. Debating which lords to write to and how to approach them had brought him a sliver of his usual back-and-forth with Jaeger, and at times he managed to forget the hole in his soul in the midst of an argument. Perhaps this turn of events would do him a lot of good, too, but he needed to see to his family first.

"I have time to visit Kellian before this meeting, don't I?"

"I advise you do so, in fact." She rose to her feet, fingers gripping the armrest for support, and her mask slipped once again, a grimace of fatigue briefly twisting her lips before she erased it. Her shoulders straightened and she swept towards the door, all confidence once more. She stopped at the threshold and looked back at him. "One last thing, Diel. You *cannot* afford to be directly associated with Hasryan Fel'ethier. Tread carefully."

Cold fear ran all the way to Diel's fingertips as she left, years of listening for double meanings setting off every alarm within him. She could have been referring to Kellian's actions, helping the assassin escape, but the sharpness of her tone led him to believe otherwise. She knew, and in this matter, he could not challenge her conclusion at all: if his partnership with Hasryan became known, his chances at regaining Isandor's favour—of returning home with Jaeger—were gone.

THEY made him wait for Sora Sharpe—long excruciating minutes, with his cousin on the other side, safe and sound and with a story to tell. It didn't help that one of the nearby doors also hid a man who'd happily sold him out to his enemy and unravelled his house from the inside. Part of Diel wanted to stride in and demand why, even though he knew. His House's alliance with the Allastams had been tenuous for years, held together more by tradition than any real political alignment. Certainly nothing strong enough to survive Diel's decision to free Arathiel despite his ties to Hasryan.

You cannot afford to be directly associated with Hasryan Fel'ethier.

It gnawed at him, this forced secrecy. The respect he'd gained for Hasryan when the young man had risked his freedom to tell him of Camilla's arrest had only multiplied after sharing living quarters with him. An assassin he might be, but Hasryan's love for his friends and care for the city were truer than most nobles of Isandor.

"I apologize if I kept you waiting, milord."

Sora's voice startled him out of his thoughts. She stood a few feet away, the usual white-and-grey livery of the Sapphire Guard entirely discarded, sky-blue cape included. Instead, Sora had wrapped herself in cotton pants and a long-sleeved shirt of thick pale brown wool, with large buttons sealing it. Her hair hung loose and wet, unbraided still. Her only concession to formality was the brooch pinned at her breast, marking her as a guard despite the casual outfit.

"Accepted," he said, and from the depths of his exhaustion, he conjured his most charming smile.

Sora laughed and turned to the Brasten guard watching the door. "We'll need privacy."

The woman there arched an eyebrow, but eventually nodded, unlocked the door, and moved farther down the corridor, well within shouting range. Sora opened the door, then motioned Diel inward with a sharp gesture—a very simple wave of the hand so packed with anger and tension it set him on edge.

Inside stood a familiar small elf, barely over five feet, still clad in the full dark green Dathirii livery. Diel's gaze swept through

Kellian's sharp eyes and square jaw, the ponytail of golden hair partially undone, the fingers gripping empty air where his pommel would have been, and the air left his lungs in a sudden rush of relief. His chest expanded, the tightly held vice of grief and hope brutally released as his mind finally accepted what Lady Brasten had promised. Kellian was alive.

"Kellian!"

Emotion roughened the name as it burst from his lips, and Diel hurried into the room—only to stop short as Kellian set a knee on the ground and bent his head down in shame.

"Milord," he said, every inch the serious, contrite captain. "Once, you named yourself House Dathirii's greatest challenge, and you were right. You were mine, too, and I failed you."

His guilty admission hit Diel like a sledgehammer, knocking all strength from his knees. He slumped down by his cousin's side, reeling. No one had called him lord since his title had vanished, and Kellian's decorum threw in sharp relief what lack of easy deference he'd grown so accustomed to, and which few afforded him now. Family and allies had stopped looking to him for leadership, and he'd forgotten to rise up and convince them to renew their trust.

Slowly, slotting the confused mess of feelings roiling through him, Diel grabbed Kellian's shoulders and forced him to look up.

"It was my challenge, too. I hold more than my share of responsibility in what happened and continues to happen." He rose to his feet, pulling Kellian with him. "But all of this is meaningless compared to my joy at seeing you alive."

"But the Tower—"

Diel interrupted him with a raised hand. "It was lost the moment

I set Lord Allastam against us. Please, Kellian, enough of this. We have other matters to discuss."

He stepped away and aside, physically allowing Sora Sharpe into the conversation. The guilty pinch of Kellian's eyebrows only deepened as he saw her. "Hasryan."

"What did she want with him?"

If Sora could have pierced the man with her question, Kellian would be dead. Branwen had warned him Sora had pieced together the Dathirii involvement in helping Hasryan hide from the law and she'd hinted that despite being in charge of Hasryan's case, Sora herself seemed to care a great deal about the assassin. Those hints cast a very unique light on her current anger.

"To 'talk' was all she'd told me."

Sora's scoff came out strangled, and she bit back her initial reply, squeezing her eyes shut as she wrangled her feelings into something calmer. When she spoke again, her tone had evened out, but the way she raked her fingers through her loose hair her betrayed her fury.

"Let's put our cards on the table. We might as well, considering all three of us have now protected or aided Hasryan."

She directed the full force of her glare at Diel then and, scary as it was, he could not help his smile as he remembered standing in the great Dathirii hall, telling Sora he would cooperate fully with her investigation after the Golden Table, knowing the assassin she sought had been hiding in his very own office. They had all come a long way since, Sora perhaps most of all. What calm she had regained with her last pause vanished with every new word.

"I put everything I had on the line to reach Lord Allastam and arrest him, and I did it first and foremost because I wanted Hasryan to be free. Not with Brune. *Free.* And now he might very well be dead."

She spun back towards Kellian as the last word dropped, her fear and anger and grief all tightly packed into it, a weapon more cutting than her sword. He flinched but did not look away.

"You would have died without my help. Riddled with crossbow bolts and condemned to a long fall. She invited me to watch the escape—every excruciating second of it—and made her terms clear. I could accept her powers and save you, or I could sit in my little stone-egg prison and watch it unfold. So I took the deal."

He had begun pacing as he spoke, the familiarity of his long and graceful strides calming Diel even as his words tightened his chest.

"Kellian," Diel said, "what did she want from you?"

"That's what worries me. I don't know."

"You said she wanted Hasryan to come willingly." Sora crossed her arms. "Right after you trapped him to the bridge with that stone of yours. Remember?"

Kellian turned fully back to her, exasperation and despair warring in his voice. "Aren't you listening? She has always known where he was. She all but told Camilla and me the day she swept me off the bridges. Please, Sora, you have to see she could have nabbed him at any time." He grabbed her hands, then, pressing them together as he closed the distance between them and captured her eyes. "You could be saved, if not him. How was I to refuse?"

A red undertone darkened Sora's cheeks and she promptly yanked her hands out of Kellian's, stepping back. Diel had the distinct impression of witnessing moments not meant for him and was relieved when Sora changed topic.

"So … what now?"

They turned to him, and the deference steadied his thoughts. "For now? The truth, I think. He was coerced by Brune into helping Hasryan escape but has saved the life of one of Isandor's most daring and astute investigators. Deflect what blame we can on Brune, for as long as we can. I'm sorry you'll have moved from one cell to another, Kellian, but I suspect the company will be better here. Branwen and Vellien won't wait long to drop in."

A smile finally touched Kellian's lips, the first since Diel had stepped inside, and its deep longing echoed within Diel. He craved a chance to sit at a long table full of Dathirii elves, discussing the latest concert in the city or initiating narrative games that could last deep within the night, any worries far from their minds.

"Miss Sharpe, if we could have a moment?" Diel said. "Family business."

"I'll let the guard know to give you five more minutes. No more."

She stared back at Kellian, her lips split as if she meant to add more, then she tore her gaze away and strode out, the stomp of her boots too loud to be entirely natural. Kellian pressed his lips tight, his smile gone, and Diel could not help but wonder what had been between these two, once upon a time. The days when they'd collaborated to find the thief constantly sneaking into the Dathirii Tower seemed forever ago.

"Kellian … nothing horrible may have come of it and we have more pressing concern, but when I'm Lord Dathirii again—" No *if.* He did not want to allow himself or anyone room for doubt anymore. If he acted the part, others would follow. "—I never want to hear that you arrested another family member without my permission. Always come to me first."

Kellian closed his eyes and released a long sigh. "Of course," he said, without a trace of protest or derision in his voice. "I've had ample time to consider that particular decision while in my prison. I'm sorry, Diel, and I fully intend to apologize to Camilla once I see her again, too. But…" His face twisted in a grimace. "Why did you help him, Diel? First Aunt Camilla, then you, and now Sora… I don't understand."

"There are more ways to hold someone responsible for his crimes than to drag them to the noose, Kellian," Diel said. "I cannot speak for others, but Hasryan came to me of his own volition to warn me you'd arrested Camilla. He was willing to risk execution if it spared her prison time, and I felt this spoke at length about his true character. He has not proven me wrong so far, and I doubt either High Priest Varden or I would be alive without his help."

"I see." Kellian's grimace softened as he slowly digested the information, accepted it. "Perhaps, given the opportunity, I would owe him an apology too."

"There is no perhaps there, Kellian."

"What about Brune?" Kellian asked, and while the change of topic could not be clumsier, Diel let it slide. "She is powerful, moreso than we or anyone had ever accounted for. She could have killed me with ease, and I'm not entirely sure why she didn't, but I do not trust these new powers she insisted on giving me." He flicked his fingers, and little bits of earth grew at their tips before falling to dust. "Whatever strings she's attached, I cannot see them."

Diel disliked this new development as much as his captain. He'd promised Hasryan he would look into Brune once this war with the Myrians—and now Lord Allastam—was over, and he wondered how big a target he'd picked. Every new information led him to the conclusion she did nothing by accident and knew how to plant fail-safe years ahead of time. If she'd planted something within Kellian…

"If she knows I helped Hasryan, she might understand I have no intention of letting her manipulate the city unfettered forever. Whatever else this is, it's a message, too. Blackmail and a show of strength, telling me to stay quiet and out of her way."

Kellian's expression darkened. "So I played straight into her hand."

Diel couldn't hold back his bitter laugh. "Does it matter? Kellian, with everything you know about me, do you think threats will cow me into silence? Inaction?"

A hint of a smile played on his lips. "One might expect our current predicament to be a lesson for you, Diel."

"I've always been a terrible student."

He grinned, and Kellian answered in kind. It was grounding, a return to normal. He'd let himself grow listless, but he couldn't afford to continue in this fashion—with or without Jaeger, with or without titles, he needed to be Lord Dathirii. He pushed the long strands of air in his face back, wishing he had something to tie them with.

"I suspect our five minutes is up, and I have a meeting to prepare for. Rest, Kellian. I doubt your strength will go unneeded for long."

Chapter Nine

HE first meeting in her father's schedule had been late in the morning, and by the time it arrived, what excess energy Mia had had upon awakening had vanished, sapped away by the widespread chaos in her home.

The group of soldiers rushing to stop Sora Sharpe had failed. They had destroyed the investigator's makeshift barricade and pursued, only to discover the group inside had used magic to create their own escape route, carving out the wall and stretching it out in a thin bridge that spanned over a brutal fall. Drake had led the charge, but as their well-trained troop had unleashed a deadly volley, a sheer wall of stone had slammed down before them, and the bolts had crashed into it. The man responsible, Kellian Dathirii, had then proceeded to trap them all into solid earth before crushing Drake's ribcage inward.

Or so the captain of the guard told the tale. He had not wanted to, at first, pressuring Mia to return to her room and assuring her that the danger had passed, all fake concern and condescension. She had broken out the *prestige* voice, haughtiness carrying her tone as she reminded him that with Drake unconscious and her father arrested, of all things, House Allastam fell under her care and she would tolerate no dismissal from an underling.

Using that voice, in and of itself, had drained her. She hated having to demand respect out of others, to force them to see her as more than a doll to preserve, lest they risk her father's anger. The shocking tale itself had not helped, nor had the hour by Drake's bedside, staring at his bruised chest while the healers worked their magic. He would live, they assured her, and it filled her with relief and disappointment, the conflicting emotions spiralling endlessly within her. She sat with it, bile at her throat, quiet pain lurking within her bones, until the time came to attend her father's meeting.

Lord Allastam had been arrested. His son and heir was wounded, unable to replace him. Uncle Byrd, Uncle Lucius, and Aunt Alva had not yet heard of this disaster and could not set her aside. The House was hers, even if only for a few hours, even if only a little. She would not waste her opportunity to move the needle.

What sense of filial duty still fought with her ambition could not erase a simple truth: if House Dathirii emerged victorious—if they unravelled her father's stranglehold of power—she stood a much better chance of claiming House Allastam as hers, or escaping its grasp entirely. Mia pieced herself together, hanging a gentle and cold smile to her lips, and made her way to her father's audience chamber.

It had been a long time since she'd come to the magical forest, its transmuted blue leaves rustling above her head as she swept down the aisle, wide dress trailing. The great silver trees flanked her like so many soldiers, and better days rushed Mia's memories as she passed beneath—playing hide and seek with her mother, climbing into taller branches with Drake's help, sitting against a root, reading books while her father received nobles for audiences. Most ignored her, but never Yultes, and never Amake. They stopped and asked about her book and her day, and as time passed and Mia grew older, they shared tea with her and treated her as they would any other adult. It was kindness without pity, and Mia had treasured it all her life.

It helped, to think of those times, knowing that in their eyes she was more than her father's daughter, that she existed as a full human being outside of Lord Allastam, that should she tear herself from the name and heritage, they would still *see* her. Or something close to it, anyway. No one but Alton truly knew her—no one could until she was ready.

That might be sooner than expected, depending on how the next days unfolded. Sitting on her father's throne at the end of the great garden, hands on her knees and shoulders held straight and tight against the pain, Mia Allastam waited for her guest to arrive.

Hellion Dathirii strode down the aisle as if he owned the place, long golden hair flowing behind him, framing a delicate face as if eternally bathing it in sunlight. He was resplendent and gracious, the embodiment of the elves' reputation for grace and haughtiness. At least from a distance. As he neared, Mia noticed the hints of magical threads woven into his hair, diffusing that golden light, and the twitch of his mouth betrayed his displeasure. He stopped as the tree line of their garden dispersed, the trunks growing farther apart to shift the space from corridor to audience hall.

"Mia," he said, her name acid on the tip of his tongue.

"Hellion," she replied, far more successful at infusing her voice with warmth. "It has been a long time."

So long, in fact, that she couldn't say when they'd last talked. At a reception, no doubt, two guests with no affinities brought together by little more than the circumstances. Yultes had always had high praise for his friend, yet the stories he told left her ill at ease, pondering if the imbalance she perceived was the result of her projecting the jagged edges of her own relationships. Those doubts had all but vanished, and Hellion brushed away their ashes in one, razor-sharp sneer.

"I have a meeting with Lord Allastam. Would you alert him to my arrival?"

The thin politeness could not cushion the intensity of his dismissal. Mia Allastam tilted her chin up but did not bother to rise from the seat.

"I'm afraid that is not possible, *sir*." She honed her anger into a piercing point, channelling it all into the honorific now his, the charred remains of his lost title. Hellion huffed, but Mia raised her voice, burying his first words of protest. "My father has been taken into custody by the Sapphire Guard."

Shock deflated the rest of Hellion's pompous protest. His jaw worked, mouth agape, until he stammered, "D-Drake—"

"Wounded," she cut in. "He'll recover, worry not. This is all I am at a liberty to disclose, however, and none of your concern, truly. So perhaps you could pick up your jaw from the floor and proceed with the matters that brought you here?"

He bristled, reading in her words the slight she had meant to offer.

"My *matters,* as you just put them, were meant for the ears of Lord Allastam alone. They require political cunning one does not learn folding paper into flowers."

Mia laughed, allowing her voice to carry the frustration of more than a decade of similar dismissal. She leaned back, drawing upon the arrogance her family so easily carried to mask hurt—emotional and physical both—and project control.

"Perhaps you'd like to offer advice? I do wonder how one loses control of their house to such an extent that banners bearing their sigil fall upon them, and enemies prefer to remain within rather than take a chance to flee. It is truly a unique achievement."

She savoured the horror and anger swirling in his perfect elven face, twisting otherwise beautiful features into an ugly mask. When Hellion tried to speak, she raised a hand, palm open, and he stopped short. Giddiness bubbled within her and she struggled to control it. Never before had she had this commanding effect on others.

"I'm not interested, if we're honest," she said, brushing away any chance he'd had to speak. This was her stage. "I am Lord Allastam's daughter, I sit here in his stead, and your petty dismissals will be met in kind. Consider today a warning, Hellion Dathirii." She let the words hang, full of menace, before leaning forward with a near-benevolent smile. He slid back a step, involuntarily. "Now, I believe you'd come to petition for more soldiers."

"How did you—"

"Political cunning I learned while folding pretty little flowers." She gifted him with her most beautiful smile—and truly, there was joy in watching him fume. "Unfortunately, we cannot spare the troops. Events from today prove we need them more than ever. In fact, as this is the second incident in a short number of days, we'll be recalling our soldiers home. All of them."

Hellion stared at her, blank horror stealing his words. The stunned, gaping fish attitude proved her suspicions she'd held ever since the Dathirii coup: her father had chosen him because he made an easy puppet, not for any other inherent qualities. Still, he eventually recovered from the shock, and even dared to step closer, indignation cresting in his voice.

"If you think that because Lord Allastam is not presiding over this meeting you can simply void our agreement, you are sorely mistaken. We are allies, and—"

"And it's time you do your part," she interrupted. "Surely a close ally of ours would not wish harm to the family because we lacked the full presence of our inner guard? And surely, one of such political acumen can fly of his own wings. Get your house under control, Hellion. Not only are we bringing our soldiers home, but we'll have a look at your books. You owe us a debt, I believe."

This was, perhaps, the most important and most risky part of this move. Her father had not granted Allastam soldiers to Hellion for free, but he'd left *when* the payment should come entirely up to his desires—something Hellion had not been wise enough to correct. She could exploit this and weaken his position, but she knew Yultes had been squirrelling away gold, too. If her own people found out, she'd be hard-pressed to hide it without tipping her hand.

"You have a week," she declared.

"But—"

"Enough." She snapped the word, her voice high and commanding, but her fatigue frayed it, the toll of repeatedly asserting herself heavier with every passing minute. Mia hoped Hellion could not hear it as clearly as she did. "I was very clear. If you think I am *playing*, feel free to pass this sentiment to my father. I'm sure he'll be pleased to hear you doubted me. Until then, I suggest you do not waste our respective time with pointless protests. I am informing you of this decision, not asking for your agreement."

She rose, then, and pain shot up all along her spine, sharp jabs bouncing and springing up her back and into the base of her skulls. Mia set every inch of willpower she owned into burying her gasps deep within and keeping her shoulders straight, her back rigid. Her vision unfocused as the tide of agony passed over her, and when it vanished, it washed the rest of her strength with it. She needed to leave.

"Dismissed," she added, and strode away herself, fingers tight on her cane, each step more difficult than the last. She never looked back, praying to Kaisa for the strength of showmanship and a lie well told.

CHAPTER TEN

HOUSE Brasten must have quite the reputation for hospitality if they treated all their guests as they did Jilssan. A hot bath waited in her assigned rooms, scented with cedar oil and complemented by a selection of soap and oils. Steam filled the room, enveloping her, filling her lungs with the promise of safety, and she undressed without pause. Her muscles hurt, the throb growing into sharp lancing pain around her back, and a dull buzz slowed her thoughts. Now that the excitement of their escape had evaporated, Jilssan felt ready to collapse. What would it cost, she wondered, to let the pieces of herself dissolve into the hot water?

She sank into the bath, closing her eyes as the warmth soaked into her long-chilled bones, erasing days in a freezing cell, underdressed and shivering. She couldn't vanish from all scheming and plotting, no matter how weary of it—not while Isra's safety was on the line. She'd tough it out long enough to cut the perfect deal, and then, perhaps, she would finally rest.

Thankfully, Lady Brasten had provided with the perfect pick-me-up to help Jilssan last until then: a bottle of a rich red wine from the southern lands of Myria—conquered Isbari lands, in fact. She leaned over the bath's edge and poured herself a glass, filling it up to the brim. Under most circumstances, Jilssan was not a heavy drinker. It dulled her wits, and she did not find the taste to be as spectacular as many claimed it to be. But the first sip of this revealed it to be a good, simple bottle, and it promised to dull her pain and worries along with everything else.

The first sip was followed by another, then a third, and soon enough she was humming Myrian rhymes while scrubbing herself. The hot water was glorious, enveloping her body in a reassuring cocoon, and Jilssan relaxed into it, her mind light from wine and exhaustion alike. She dreamed of hands massaging the hurt out of her muscles, moving slowly across her body, firm and gentle all at once. Safe hands from someone she trusted, perhaps even someone she was intimate with. How long had that even been? Isandor had been such an isolating period of her life, nothing but her and Isra and the urgent need to shield them from danger. She deserved better. Here in the safety of the Brasten Tower, sinking low in a hot bath, Jilssan allowed herself the fantasy of a lover, and hands on her body where and how she wanted them.

As much as Jilssan wished to escape time, the cooling water eventually reminded her of minutes trickling down, turning into hours. She emerged from the bath, dried herself with the softest towels she'd used in years, and headed back into the main bedroom, wine glass and bottle in hand, seeking any clothes beyond her dirty, bloodied Myrian outfit.

A gorgeous dress had been laid out on the bed, its shimmering dark blue pinpricked with golden dots that sparkled in the ambient light. It floated on the fluffy down under it, a piece of the night sky made real. Her heart hammering, Jilssan downed the rest of her glass and glided over to it, brushing her fingers over the velvet. It was so soft, and the entire dress so beautiful. Jilssan pulled on some tights, then slipped into the dress itself, her admiration turned into a concerned frown as it came to rest on her shoulders. The sleeves hung low and the bottom trailed behind her, spilling stars across the floor, which made her steps feel clumsy—Myrian fashion had always been more practical. The worst offender, however, was the front of it, which hung weirdly before her, loose where a woman with bigger breasts would have filled the dress.

She was pondering her options, her glass of wine newly filled, when a maid knocked on the door. A seamstress sent by Lady Brasten, to correct any imperfection in the dress to the extent that she could before the meeting. She was very adamant that the Head of the House wanted Jilssan to look her best, and while it slipped from the aged lady like water bounding down a stream, words upon words without care for their directions, Jilssan heard the melody beneath.

She had not dreamed Lady Brasten's appraising stare or the spark in her voice as they bantered earlier. A shiver danced across her skin even as her body grew hot, the bath-time fantasies turning into a far more concrete image. Jilssan licked her dry lips and held herself still until the seamstress was gone, her dress now pinched and pinned in subtle ways to fit and embellish Jilssan's form. The moment she was alone, however, Jilssan finished another full glass of wine—a questionable decision, but she needed to change her mind. Besides, she'd had a full, glorious meal. Surely she wouldn't be *that* heady!

The time for the meeting unfortunately came all too soon, and as Jilssan followed a steward up the stairs, dress trailing behind her, she had to admit she was, in fact, quite inebriated. Not particularly wise, although she could appreciate how *good* she felt. It would be a simple matter of watching the words out of her mouth and paying closer attention. She was not among enemies, but among potential allies—allies who needed her.

The tight and endless staircase made her long for her magical endurance, but Jilssan eventually reached the top of the tower, where Lady Brasten's office was located. The steward guided her to a cozy circle of seats half bathed by the afternoon light, with a dark wood table with an offering of sweets, tea, and more wine. Sora Sharpe sat at the edge of one seat, nibbling on a yellowed cake, her bloodied outfit replaced by comfortable brown wool and cotton pants. A single tie held her long hair loosely behind her, and one might think her relaxed if not for the stiffness of her posture.

"Why, I think I misread the dress code," Jilssan quipped before selecting a cushioned seat directly in the sun. The wine had been uncorked and set to chill. She had no intention of drinking more, but it might pay to let others think she'd drank more than she truly had—which, admittedly, was already quite a fair amount. "Or is there a fireside party afterwards I'm unaware of?"

"There may be," a third person replied, his voice rough coals burning with distaste, "but you'll forgive me if I don't extend the invitation your way."

Varden approached them, chose a simple wooden chair, and dragged it slightly outside of the circle, closer to the fireplace. He paid no mind to her smile and flipped open a sketchbook, angling it so she wouldn't see inside. It struck her how unusual the sight seemed, even though the art found in his quarters proved he'd drawn a hundred times over at the Enclave. Never where they could see, though, not like now.

Jilssan tore her gaze away, before her discomfort grew enough that she'd feel obligated to acknowledge it. They all hid things. Her, too. Didn't matter what Varden had, or why. It was just how one survived.

"I'm touched you'd even ask for my forgiveness," she said, and the deadpan *as if* stare she received in returned warmed her heart. Some things, at least, had not yet changed.

"There's no fireside, and no party," Sora interjected, as if any of that really needed to be said. The investigator cast a pointed look at Jilssan's glass of wine. "Though you seem quite capable of creating your own."

Jilssan laughed, the soft buzz of alcohol twirled with her voice. "One *must* learn to amuse herself, where I'm from. But you're invited, if you so wish."

She raised her glass. Sora did not appreciate the gesture and rolled her eyes in delightful exasperation.

"The whole city's fate could depend on today—*your* fate, too—and you're soaking up wine like it's all a game."

She did not need to add "have you no shame?", not with that tone. Jilssan allowed her smile to slide into a confident smirk and leaned forward, elbow still on the armrest, her pose as relaxed and confident as she could muster.

"You should try it. It makes the whole ordeal far less stressful."

When everything was a game, the terrifying consequences didn't crush her wits. Wine and wits allowed her to hide the way her stomach tightened at the worst possible futures, like Isra paying for her betrayal the way Nevian had for his master all these years. When she thought of her apprentice—sweet Isra, hiding all these years between so many masks, left at the Enclave at the mercy of Avenazar's whims—the balm of the last hours vanished and the fear threatened to paralyze her mind.

Two quick knocks interrupted them before Sora could retort, and soon Diel Dathirii strode around the corner. A simple braid held part of his hair behind, but the rest caught the sunlight and glowed within it, curtains of gold framing delicate elven traits. Exhaustion had carved new lines around his mouth since their last encounter, but he held himself as straight as ever, chin tipped with defiance. Sora nodded his way.

"Lord Dathirii," she greeted.

Lord, huh? Jilssan couldn't help her snort. "No need for all the 'lord' business. He's just Diel now, and lucky he's even that still."

Sharp green eyes turned to her, staring daggers, but his voice remained smooth and please. "Good afternoon to you too, Master

Jilssan."

"Can't be worse than the last few days," she said. "We may have made a slight miscalculation in our plan. Lord Allastam was very keen on making me pay directly."

"What plan?" By the sharp glare she threw first at Jilssan, then at Diel Dathirii, Sora had already pieced most of it together. She was also looking quite offended, as if any previous teamwork between them amounted to a personal betrayal.

"A question I'd love answered." Lady Brasten swept into the space, and the afternoon light added a soft glow to her golden top. Jilssan's mouth dried as she followed her advance through the room until she stood at the back of a large wing chair with the Brasten crest sewn into the design.

"Oh, it was only a little midnight chat about which lies I planned to tell, and if he could please swallow his pride and not deny it all outright." Judging by the flat line of Diel's mouth, he did not appreciate her formulation. She waved his protests away before he could utter any. "None of it matters. After all, we're planning to move on to the truth, aren't we?"

The regular scratches of Varden's charcoal stopped and he stared long and hard at her, as if he could peel off every layer of half-lies and illusions she kept, layering deception and carefreeness like so many shields. Always better to keep others guessing, to never let them know when she was serious and truthful, and when she played with them. It was lonely, perhaps, but it was safe. She wished Varden's expression would drop that hint of pity, that softness in how his brow pinched something she'd never seen from him.

"Truth," he repeated, as if tasting the word. "If you even know what that is anymore."

It burned. Not in shame or guilt, she'd long discarded those, but in a fierce longing she'd thought buried. Perhaps Varden couldn't see through the layers of misdirection, but could she? Or were they as much her as anything else now? Cursed gods, she really had drunk too much, to let one man's words rattle her so.

"We already know the truth," Lady Brasten said before finally settling into her chair, hands on the armrests as if she presided over this reunion, a queen and her subjects. "This meeting is to determine how we're wielding it."

"Nevertheless, I would like to hear it, if you don't mind."

Diel had tilted his chin up and stared somewhere over Jilssan's shoulder, as if he couldn't bear to look at her.

"You mean here that Lord Allastam and Master Avenazar signed a trade deal involving your delivery, under which Lord Allastam's only requirement was that 'he never hear of you again'? The deal for which Master Avenazar clearly established he wanted to 'make you pay for your insolence'?" The poor elf paled with every new word out of her mouth, his jaw working hard. He was really taking it personally. "Lord Allastam may not have asked for the details of your fate, but he knew exactly what it entailed."

He squeezed his eyes shut, and his chest rose and fell slowly with his calming breaths until he found his words again. "Proof. We'll need proof."

"She is not proof, but we do have Jilssan," Sora Sharpe said. "First-hand witnesses matter in investigations."

That, Jilssan decided, was her cue. She took a very noisy sip of her wine, reclining in her seat, then crossed her legs daintily.

"And right now, I will deny any of this in public and ridicule your accusations until the investigation and everyone's reputation is ashes. I am not your witness until my demands are met."

Sora spun towards with such force that the tea in her small cup overflowed, spilling on her legs. As she cursed and sponged it off, Lady Brasten stepped in, entirely nonplussed.

"Pray tell us, Master Jilssan, what *are* your demands?"

She locked eyes with Lady Brasten. Out of everyone here, she held the power. This was her home, and without her support neither Diel nor Sora would get anywhere. But also, she was quite pleasing to look at. "I want you to extract my apprentice, Isra, from the Myrian Enclave, and to guarantee her safety until these matters are resolved. She and I are to be fed, housed, and allowed free roam of the Brasten Tower until we choose to leave it—at which point we will receive enough funds to either travel wherever we may want, or settle in our own home." She leaned forward, setting her chin on the back of her hand. "I will not say a word until then. The moment I openly defy Master Avenazar, she is in danger, and I wish to spare her Nevian's fate."

Avenazar had been so gleeful about it, eager to tell her all about his apprentice's pathetic shield and the sound of his body hitting a bridge. After that, it had become impossible not to think of Isra in the same situation, and the vision had plagued her, moving her ever deeper into betrayal.

Her words sent a shudder through them, too, everyone shifting in their seat except for Lady Brasten, who tilted her head towards the rest of the group in recognition of their malaise. Jilssan wished she could've seen them better, but she didn't want to look at anywhere but the woman who'd decide.

"Isn't Nevian—" Sora started.

"Indeed," Lady Brasten cut off, her voice carefully neutral. "I think these demands are reasonable."

"We have a deal, then?" Jilssan asked, hope building in her chest and spilling into her voice despite her best efforts. All this time in Allastam's cells, she'd prayed nothing had happened to her apprentice, that she'd kept her head down and avoided Avenazar's ire. No great meals, hot baths or wine could truly relax her until she knew Isra was with her.

Lady Brasten extended a hand, her eyes sparkling, her lips parting into a beautiful smile. Jilssan's gaze trailed on it a tad too long before she caught herself, and shook the offered hand.

"Deal," Lady Brasten said. "You understand, of course, that should you not hold up your end of the bargain once your apprentice is safe, Master Avenazar and Lord Allastam will not be your only worries. I *will* come for you."

"Of course." Jilssan raised her glass and emptied it, setting it on the ground before leaning into her seat, one arm thrown lazily over its back. "I might even have enjoyed the challenge, but in truth, I relish the chance to pay back Lord Allastam for what he did to me."

She kept her tone casual, with the upward lilt of a woman enjoying herself, but she could feel knots of tension undoing themselves within her, one by one. If anyone could save Isra, it was this group. They'd extracted Varden, after all, and Lady Brasten's confidence in their ability to hold up their end of the deal inspired calm in her.

"Then perhaps it's time we discuss the details of this payback," Lady Brasten said. She turned towards Diel, releasing Jilssan from her gaze—and that felt intentional, permission to relax outside of her scrutiny, to wrangle her feelings and compose her persona once more. "Many nobles I've spoken with believe you fled the Dathirii Tower on your own. I danced around any confirmation of events, but now that we have details of this deal between the Myrian Enclave and Lord Allastam, we can dismiss any illusions. We can prove he has worked to see you dead for a profit, and that most of this was conducted at a time you still held a seat at the Golden Table. Isandor's nobles want peers who respect them. You lost their vote when they perceived disdain, and Lord Allastam will lose it when they realize he considers them merchandise at his disposal."

"That's good," Diel said, "but what are our demands? An independent investigation into the full extent of his crimes? Reparations?"

His voice hadn't strained, but when he leaned over to choose a pastry from the tray and as his hand hovered about the cream puffs, Jilssan noted its shake.

"Reparations, yes, but I did not have your home in mind," Lady Brasten said, her tone softening. It didn't stop Diel Dathirii's slight flinch, or the force with which he snatched the puff and shoved it into his mouth. "I think they should come in the form of military help against the very enemy with whom he broke our laws and customs. I fear for your family too, Diel, but the real threat is elsewhere. You were the first to warn us. Don't lose sight of it."

Diel Dathirii swallowed hard, and one could almost blame the pastry if not for the angry pinch of his lips and his whitening knuckles, gripping the armrest tight. The scratch of Varden's charcoal as he drew had stopped, turning the silence almost deafening.

"You are correct, though it pains me to accept it." He looked at Varden, then, for some reason, and Varden smiled at him, soft and sad and ever beautiful. He returned to his art when Diel continued. "Besides, any condemnation of Lord Allastam or loss in prestige is a heavy hit to Hellion's legitimacy and helps us."

"I'd need solid proof to get him condemned," Sora interjected. She had remained quiet for most of the conversation, but now she slid towards the edge of her seat, fire in her eyes. "If it comes down to Jilssan's word against his…"

"Isn't that what your investigation is for?" Jilssan turned to face her and leaned forward, putting her hand on Sora's shoulder as if they were the best of friends. She stiffened. "I promise I'll do my best to spin the tale of an embittered and power-hungry man who didn't hesitate to sell his fellow noble to a painful end over a small disagreement."

"You make the truth sound like a fabricated lie," Diel pointed out.

"And fabricated lies sound like the truth," Jilssan replied with pride. Her words might not cut it this time, not if Sora Sharpe needed something more concrete to make her accusations stick.

Myria loved its bureaucracy, but Master Avenazar had never been one for paperwork and she suspected he'd not have put this particular deal in writing. Not a problem a little creativity wouldn't solve. She turned to Lady Brasten, all smiles, her next lie easy on her tongue. "What Master Avenazar and Lord Allastam negotiated is a trade deal, and those are signed. Usually, at any right."

Sora pushed Jilssan's hand away and crossed her arms. "The Enclave is under Myrian law. I can't demand entrance to gather proof."

"Which is why Allastam soldiers *must* be part of the reparations," Lady Brasten said. "It all ties perfectly together. First, we meet our part of the bargain and reunite Master Jilssan with her apprentice." She raised a finger to count the steps. "Second, we call a Golden Table—quickly, to give House Allastam as little time to prepare as possible—and convince the other nobles to grant us this investigation and the troops for it. Third, we force our way into the Myrian Enclave and get our proof."

"What about Avenazar?" Jilssan asked. "He won't *let* you, and he'll recover from his poisoning soon, if he hasn't already."

"I will take care of Master Avenazar." Flames blazed to life in the fire behind Varden, casting flickering shadows across his face. Some crawled towards him, leaving no room for doubts about his intention. As long as it wasn't her. Still, Jilssan hoped he had a plan. She doubted Keroth's flames alone would suffice.

"This will put us on a tight schedule," Lady Brasten said. "Let's see what groundwork we can lay with Isandor's key actors before the Golden Table convenes. Master Jilssan, I suspect this part will be of little interest to you, if you prefer the comforts of your new quarters…"

Memories of the inviting down bed floated to the forefront of Jilssan's mind, and she returned Lady Brasten's smile with a grin of her own. She didn't mind the dismissal, not when her body so deeply wanted more rest.

"I would indeed prefer to fall asleep in a bed instead of in this lovely seat, bored to tears." She stood up, intending upon a graceful bow and a retreat, but exhaustion and alcohol rushed her head the moment she was on her feet, and she stumbled a step forward, almost losing her balance. So much for her dignity. Jilssan bowed nonetheless. "It was a pleasure, and I eagerly await the return of my apprentice."

Lady Brasten tilted her head in assent. She radiated a confident elegance that set Jilssan's veins on fire. What a gorgeous woman, all deadly edges and brilliant wits.

"Please, Master Jilssan. The pleasure is all ours."

And in the grave warmth of her voice, Jilssan heard another invitation, to make the pleasure all *hers*, specifically. She fully intended to take her up on this specific offer.

AT first, Jilssan thought the two youthful voices were a product of her dreams. She'd collapsed into her bed and fallen asleep as soon as she'd returned to her rooms, the exhaustion of the last few days catching up with her. It had been a fitful sleep, however, full of fleeting nightmares of Avenazar tracking down Isra, of her apprentice calling her name, screaming in pain. But the voice that filtered now was joyful, a first sprout piercing through the snow after a long winter.

"You're the one who cracked it, Nev Nev. You should be the one to show it to her!"

The remnants of sleep still clung to Jilssan's mind, muddling the words even as she pushed herself off, the down sliding off her shoulder. Nev Nev? That couldn't be…

"I should be *working* on it, not flaunting our meagre progress," a sharp voice replied—and that was, without an ounce of doubt, Nevian. How was he even alive? Avenazar had been adamant.

"Well, you're here now."

Jilssan could hear Isra's pout through the door, likely with lips pursed and arms crossed in an ever-familiar expression. She grinned, head light from relief, and flung the down aside as she jumped out of the bed. She was already halfway across the room when Isra's light knocks hit the door.

"Since when do you knock for me, Isra?" she asked, her voice ragged at the edges.

The door flung open and Isra ran in, her mass of hair flying behind. She threw herself into Jilssan's arm with such strength she knocked her off balance and they both fell. Jilssan's head was spinning, the last of her sleep-induced slowness gone.

"Isra! How are you already—?" Jilssan squeezed her, running a hand through her hair. She could not have slept more than a few hours, surely not. Had Lady Brasten already had plans to infiltrate the Myrian Enclave at the ready?

Isra held her tight, fingers clumping Jilssan's nightshirt. When she spoke again, her voice was muffled against her shoulder. "I'm sorry I didn't come sooner! I was with Nevian in the library all day and no one even told me you were here." She sniffed, then pulled back enough to wipe her tears. "I'm glad you're safe."

Slowly, as she brushed away strands of hair from Isra's face, the pieces fell in place. How everyone had shifted around when she'd mentioned Isra and Nevian. Lady Brasten's confidence they could extract her from the Enclave. Sora's interrupted comment about Nevian. They had played her, letting her believe her apprentice was still within Master Avenazar's easy reach even though their end of the bargain was technically already fulfilled.

I think these demands are reasonable, Lady Brasten had said.

Jilssan could only laugh.

It burst out of her, cheerfulness bordering on hysteria, relief washing away any hints of resentment. Jilssan rode the impulse, allowing herself this uncontrolled moment, illusions crumbling for a time. She placed a hand on Isra's shoulder, squeezing it tight, but as her outburst crested and fell, her eyes latched on the teenager still standing in the doorway.

Nevian had changed. His downy blond hair had grown, and he'd filled up to look less lanky, but that wasn't it, really. His shoulders didn't bend inward anymore, and while he was obviously awkward, he didn't slink near the frame. He occupied the space fully, as if he belonged there, instead of diminishing his presence to the best of his ability.

"All alive and grown up, huh?"

"No thanks to you."

Well, that was also new. He wouldn't have dared a retort before, even if every emotion was always etched plainly on his face. That had made him fun to push around. Jilssan grinned at him. "Wouldn't have wanted to fall out of Avenazar's good graces."

Nevian snorted. "That almost sounded like an apology."

He turned away with the obvious intent to leave, but Isra butted in their conversation with unbridled enthusiasm. "You should have seen how fast he solved your notes, Jilssan! You know, about using the rekhemal? One glance at them and he knew what kind of spells we needed against Avez. I'd been reading for hours—all the way through the night, even—and all I got for it was a headache."

A cute pink coloured Nevian's cheeks and when he pressed his lips into a line, Jilssan had the distinct impression he was hiding a smile. "It's not solved," he corrected. "I have to go back to it."

He didn't give any of them time to comment, closing the door on them. Jilssan didn't mind in the slightest. The apprentice she cared for was still with her, beaming and at ease, happier than Jilssan remembered seeing. She brushed her knuckles against Isra's cheek, the sight a balm on her exhaustion.

"I'm sorry, Isra. I've done a terrible job of protecting you." She hadn't planned far enough ahead, hadn't had enough contingencies, and everything had come crumbling down on them. "But you sound like you've got quite the tale, if you've wound up here. Please, tell me everything."

"I-I don't know where to start!" Her hands flew through the air, carried by her excitement. "So much happened. I stabbed Avenazar, and I shapeshifted into water—and I found why I struggled so much with magic before, too!"

Well. For once, there'd been no hyperbole in Isra's words. How had she stabbed Avenazar and lived? How had any of that brought her here?

"Perhaps you should start at the beginning," she suggested. "Or whatever led you to attack Avenazar."

Isra's hands fell back into her lap and she pouted. "The water shapeshifting part is really cool, though. But I guess they're all tied together."

Jilssan couldn't help but grin. Despite all that had happened to Isra, the core parts had remained intact. "We're back together now and we'll have plenty of time for the amazing feats of magic. But I've been cut off too long, and I need your help catching up."

"Right."

Isra hesitated, all her bluster and energy drained away. Jilssan grabbed her hand, gave it a small squeeze, then helped her apprentice up.

"Let's get to the bed," she said, pulling her along. "And whatever happened... what matters is that you did what you needed to survive."

"But I didn't." Isra's voice rose to a higher pitch, and she sat herself down on the bed with dramatic force, making it creak. She avoided looking at Jilssan when didn't look at Jilssan as she sat beside her. "I'd known Nevian was alive for a while. When you told me I should redirect Avenazar's anger if he came for me, I... I thought about him. I know you want me to be more pragmatic, to 'do what needs to be done', but when he attacked me, I couldn't. I did my best to protect everyone else's secrets—yours and Nevian's."

Guilt and worry twisted Isra's voice. Was she afraid to disappoint? Did she fear Jilssan would love her less if she couldn't conform? It seemed impossible from the willful girl, yet she *had* spent years in another skin, doing exactly that—conforming. Slowly, Jilssan slid a finger under Isra's chin and turned it her way.

"Once, in the dead of the night, I met a noble of this city whose idealism and refusal of necessity would eclipse any others. I asked him why he fought a pointless, losing battle, and he told me someone had to. That he was only doing what needed to be done." It had felt like a punch to the stomach, her own pragmatism turned on its head. "I still disagree, but it taught me something: 'what needs to be done' should always be set to your personal goals and ethics, or it'll eat you inside. I'm ruthless because I know what I want and what I'm willing to sacrifice—or makes others sacrifice—to get it. You don't have to be."

Isra's eyes had watered with unspilled tears. "So if I don't want the same things you do… if-if I'm not ambitious or savvy with politics…"

"Then I'll never have you as a rival, and I'll be happier for it." Jilssan pulled her close, wrapping her arm around Isra's shoulders. "I won't be disappointed in you, Isra. I'll teach you what I can, and as long as you don't expect me to be your moral compass, we should get along. If you want to learn how to stand your ground on ethical principles and risk your life for them, Varden is much better mentor. You can ask him."

Isra's brief laugh morphed into sobs as she leaned against Jilssan, tears running down her cheeks. With every new sob, every sniff, Jilssan's throat tightened. She'd never realized how much pressure Isra put upon herself to be like Jilssan, instead of being herself. Perhaps this time apart had provided the space necessary for her apprentice to find the girl hiding under the persona. She was glad Isra still had a sense of who that even was.

Isra sniffed again, lifting her had to croak a few rough words. "Thank you."

"Take a moment. Digest it all," Jilssan said. "After that, though, I really do need to hear what transpired."

They sat in silence as Isra worked through her relief. Once she'd recovered, she slipped out from Jilssan's arm and haltingly started her story, beginning with her painful hours trying to understand Avenazar's spells and Jilssan's intent. She had Jilssan promise she'd look at Nevian's very hard work—which, overly serious company notwithstanding, she *was* curious about—but moved on to more exciting bits quickly. Jilssan let her set the pace, eventually shuffling through the wardrobe available to her while Isra talked. The options remained limited—two long dresses, a practical set of pants with a short skirt, and a handful more undergarments. She'd have to talk about Lady Brasten about her needs, especially if they wanted her to play the part of the dramatic witness.

When Isra explained the poisoned letter opener and her sudden, flowing shapeshift into a pool of water, Jilssan whistled. Isra beamed at her with pride, and promptly explained her father's amulet must have interfered with her magic, and now she'd grown into a much more powerful wizard. She was excited, and Jilssan wondered if she had any idea how many years of training most transmuters needed to achieve nonliving forms. Most rarely even used them without another mage to interfere, as the process could dim your self-awareness unless you no longer wanted to shift back. From the sound of it, fear had driven Isra's form and allowed her to retain her basic subjectivity within it, but still… Jilssan reined in her growing pride and amazement long enough to offer a stern warning about trying again alone. Before long, they were deep into discussions of different types of shapeshifting and their respective dangers, and the tangents carried them late into the night, the idle chatter as restful to Jilssan as the short nap had been.

Chapter Eleven

COME *seek me when you've found your grace again.*

After a sleepless night, the intoxicating power those words had brought Yultes had vanished. Hollow fear replaced it, the certitude his defiance would be met with punishment, the nature of which he could not predict. Would Hellion replace him as a steward? Would he reject Yultes' friendship, casting him out of his circle for good? The possibility lurched into his chest, a heavy ache, yet it had lost its oppressing urgency, this overwhelming sense that his entire life would crumble if he did nothing to fix it. Only phantom pain remained, the ghost of a person he'd outgrown and left behind.

He eventually set about his day, his mind trailing several steps behind his actions, as if barely tethered to his body. In the aftermath of the reception, the Dathirii Tower had gone quiet, its lively stairway meetings turned into whispers behind closed doors, its laughter replaced by the pounding boots of Allastam soldiers. Under the pretense of investigating the previous night's incident, Yultes had met with the staff and reassured them he'd rebuked Hellion's demands. No one looked comforted by the thought. When Yultes passed by Garith's door, he found a guard conveniently stationed there. Any thoughts of a friendly ear he'd had died, and he returned to his quarters.

There was, in truth, another Dathirii he needed to speak with—or write to, at any rate. Amidst the blur of memories from last night, one had remained clearer than any other: Branwen's gaze meeting his, her eyes burning with anger, her lips turning into a grimace as she mouthed 'asshole' at him. Yultes sat at his desk and stared at his blank parchment, the quill spinning under his fingers, the words fleeing his mind before he could arrange them into sentences. What could he say that would convince her he'd never betrayed them? She had no reason to trust him, and he had no proof to offer. Still… His fingers drifted to their previous exchanges; a paper trail he knew he should burn but could not bring himself to. The thought of losing that fleeting kinship paralyzed him more than any fear of Hellion's abandon. He had to try.

~~Branwen.~~

No, that was so dry. He needed to reach her, didn't he?

~~Branwen.~~ *My niece.*

No, no no. She'd hate that, would think him presumptuous—and really, he was. He had not been her uncle for decades, and if ever there was a title one needed to earn, it was that. That, and others like it, others like *Father,* which he had long since thrown so far out of reach that it was absurd to even linger on it.

~~Branwen. My niece.~~ Branwen.

~~I am sorry for.~~ *What happened yesterday was more obscene than any of yours or Garith's pranks. I will make it right.*

He did not know how, yet, did not even know what *right* would mean. For Diel to return, yes, and Jaeger to be safe again. But what was right for him? What was it for Hellion? He didn't know what he wanted to build yet, let alone how. Nevertheless, he could not think of anything else worth writing that Branwen would want to hear—if she even wanted what little he'd offered.

Yultes set aside the letter, put down his quill … picked it right back up, then forced it down with a sigh. He needed to stop, to let go, and distract his mind. He forced himself away from the desk, retrieving the gardening care package he'd moved from his original quarters to these—Jaeger's old ones. Most of his plants still lived several floors down, where they always had. Where they waited for his return. He refused to be entirely without them, however, even in temporary lodgings. Few things calmed his nerves as much as the methodical act of untangling vines, removing dead leaves, and checking the soil, one plant at a time. He was in desperate need of that headspace now.

He set to work on the pothos on the bookshelf near his desk, its vines and leaves spilling all the way to the ground, and then some. Yultes had moved it into a bigger pot shortly before winter had arrived in full force, and the top needed garnishing. He settled on the ground, sitting cross-legged by the trailing vines, gently picking up each of them and sniping cuttings with two beautiful leaves each. The regular, methodical movements soothed him, though it did not last nearly as long as he'd have wished.

What peace he'd achieved shattered with the two sharp knocks at his door.

Yultes startled, swept the cuttings, and dumped them into a small water jug, then promptly rose to his feet. He was about to call for his visitor to enter when they did so themselves.

Lady Viranya Dathirii swept in, a perfect hourglass of broad golden epaulets and fanning skirts, embroidered to look like the branches and roots of a single, beautiful tree. Her eyebrows arched at the sight of him, hands dirty from the plant soil.

"Gardening," she stated, with all the contempt she reserved for servants and their menial tasks.

Yultes' cheeks flushed, guilt twisting his stomach. As if he'd been caught in a crime! He tried to shake off the embarrassment. He loved plants—had loved them long before he had followed Lehran away from their elven Meltara community, always trying to claim gardening tasks first—but it had been a private part of him, one of the few things not even Hellion knew. Lady Viranya was quite low on the list of people he'd wished to share it with.

"Yes. Gardening," he conceded, hoping she would let it rest.

"Never mind that." She sniffed, and added, "We are having a dinner tonight. Hellion's closest allies. His friends."

Which did not, by her own standards, mean him. Had she come all the way to his quarters simply to make it very clear he was excluded from this group? "I arrange *his* reservations, not everyone's."

She laughed, a companionable 'oh Yultes' crossing her lips amidst the chuckles, all edges strangely absent from it. It sounded almost … affectionate? Yultes' heart pounded, the hopes of decades of approval-seeking rising within him. But how often had those been crushed? He had to be careful and guard himself here.

"You're invited, of course," Lady Viranya said. "An hour past sundown, at the usual."

"The usual" would be *The Golden Vault*, one of Isandor's best reputed establishment, reserved only for those with high prestige and the solid coin to back it up. He was surprised they'd even landed a table without titles to their names. How much gold had this group squirrelled away, hidden from Garith's knowledge?

"Right." By the lift of Viranya's eyebrow, he'd failed to infuse the word with sufficient deference.

"Yultes, my dear, we're all very aware that we have not always been fair to you. It is undeniable that you are Hellion's confidant, however, and his speech yesterday gave us much to reflect on. It *is* time to let the dynamics of the past rest and to forge new ones. Wouldn't you agree?"

"I—" Jagged hope tore through his chest, its warmth bloodied from overuse. He smiled despite it all. Perhaps they had seen his worth at last, had gone past his humbler origins now that they were in part forced to share them. "Yes, of course."

"I'm glad to hear it," she said, one hand rising to her breast, as though her agreement personally touched her. "I will leave you to your important gardening, then. May Alluma guide your path."

"And yours," Yultes responded, the usual words spilling from his lips as she left.

YULTES walked into *The Golden Vault* with the distinct impression of marching directly into a trap. After Viranya had left, the glow of her kind words had slowly ebbed, leaving him needled with worries. They had extended friendship to Yultes before, only to spurn him when he'd reached out in return. None of them had been in charge at the time, however, and Hellion had put every drop of his talent into that speech. Maybe, just maybe…

Yet they were as likely to lure him here, under the gilded archways and in a universe of abundance, to tease out his allegiances. If they had the slightest doubt—and after the disaster he'd organized the previous night, Yultes certainly felt like he'd painted a target on his back—this might be a pretext, a game to test him. It might even be the latter without any suspicions, for their amusement. They played those with servants often enough.

He'd nevertheless dug out his best clothes, an outfit he'd had tailored with the Dathirii green, with leaves and vines along the sleeves, some even wrapping into the form of the family's sigil. It matched with one of Hellion's favourites, the same green but with different under undertones. A message for tonight, if ever there had been one. He tried not to think how grating it now felt on his shoulders, a skin he'd once worn proudly but would rather peel away.

He tried not to think about how he still yearned to succeed here, to belong with them, despite all he'd done to help Jaeger and Garith.

Delicate lyre music underscored the low conversations nobles shared with one another, each group seated in a booth surrounded by partial curtains of red and gold. The hushed ambiance had an elegant quality; people with class did not need raise their tone. After a valet retrieved his winter coat, Yultes stepped onto a circular rune which promptly dried his boots, then he was led deeper into the establishment, to their table.

He had expected Viranya to include Enmaris and Iriel, of course—the trio almost always moved as one—but Jayna Dathirii was a welcome addition. As the new liaison with House Allastam, Jayna would hold a key role in the family's future, after all. A nugget of hope formed in his stomach, and he greeted them all as he sat down. A bottle of spicy wine was already open and partway through, and someone filled his glass before he'd even settled in.

No one talked about what had happened yesterday. As a first course of cheese sticks and herbs arrived, the conversation turned to asinine gossip. Iriel mentioned that Lady Shireen Almara had reused the same dress for several soirée already, betraying the House's financial struggles. Not one to let others have the crunchiest gossip, Enmaris mentioned Lord Farron Balthazar had been spied with Lady Adda Carrington, and the two families might be looking to unite one's rising fortunes with the other's lasting prestige. This led to two-course worth of speculation on which of them would divest of their House name in favour of the other. At first, Yultes kept his peace and let others debate, but as the wine flowed, he risked one remark, then another, each earning him effusive praise. Heady from the small victory, he jumped into the conversation more eagerly, his earlier worries melted away by everyone's warmth. Lady Viranya set a hand on his forearm, and her voice seemed silk instead of steel.

"Truly, we have been foolish to forego your insight for so long, my dear."

He beamed back at her and, emboldened by the most pleasant, fulfilling hour he'd had in a long time, he smirked at her. "Your loss."

A brief silence followed his quip—long enough for fear to punch through the pleasant buzz of his mind—then they all laughed. Relief washed through him, and he washed down the rest of the acrid taste of terror with wine.

"If I could then, perhaps, ask for your wisdom?" Jayna said. "As our last illustrious liaison to House Allastam."

"Yes, of course."

"With her lord father arrested, does Lady Mia Allastam have the internal power to carry out the threats she uttered this morning?"

Yultes' brain felt like it had fallen several bridges and splattered on impact. These words didn't make sense, put together. He leaned back and hitched the best smirk he could to his lips, hoping to project the air of someone considering the situation rather than flailing to put together what was happening. Lord Allastam arrested? And *what* threats?

"I'm afraid I'm not privy to the nature of these threats, but Lady Mia Allastam is not one to utter such things on a whim," he said. "What are we looking at?"

"A week."

He arched his eyebrows, a silent invitation for her to go on, but his heart raced and his muscles tensed, his entire body waiting for the blow. Jayna dabbed the corner of her mouth with a tablecloth, then sighed.

"A week before they call every Allastam soldier at our disposal back to their tower and ask to see our books. Hellion was in quite a state when he returned."

In quite a state, and yet he'd not called upon Yultes. The fears that had plagued his night returned in full force, gnawing at his insides, and the rest of Jayna's words were equally alarming. What was Mia's game, here? She had never been in full agreement with her father's actions and she'd connected him with Branwen, so he'd have expected help from her. No matter how he looked at it, however, this seemed like an impeding catastrophe. If anyone competent looked at the Dathirii books, they'd unearth the maneuvers he and Garith had done in an instant. This included Iriel, seated on his left, lips pursed in a smile that was absolutely unreadable. Yultes ought to go. This required his immediate attention.

"Believe her," Yultes said. "I certainly will, and this unfortunately means I have a lot of work ahead of me."

He made to stand, but Lady Viranya wrapped a hand around his arm, stopping him halfway. "So soon, Yultes? We have not even gotten the main meal!" A murmur of assent passed through the others as she smiled at him and tugged down. "These are challenging times, certainly, but we'll deal with them together—tomorrow. Tonight is for pleasure, remember?"

He let himself be pulled down to the chair, let the quiet warmth swirling in his stomach unwind the knots of fear. They'd never asked him to stay like this, as if his departure would create a void. It felt good, and *simple*, and he craved that deeply.

"I suppose," he said.

Jayna motioned at a waiter, and he filled up all their glasses once more. An inch of embarrassment crept into her voice as she spoke. "I apologize. I didn't mean to bring business to the table."

"No worries, my dear," Viranya replied, "but let us move on. I'm certain Yultes would be thrilled to tell you more about House Allastam later."

"With pleasure," Yultes said, and he found that he meant it. Through conversations tonight, Jayna had proven quick of wits and sharp of tongue, with a pleasant laughter and an ability to spin words into the perfect tone. She would manage his old position without trouble.

They left the topic behind, returning to the casual gossip of the city as the main meal arrived. Yultes' pressing concerns slipped away, and as the night went on, it became harder and harder for him to tame his enthusiasm and guard his heart. The wine flowed, he talked and laughed with them—one of them, as he had sought all his life. By the time they waited by the exit for their winter coats, he was humming to himself.

A hand alighted on his shoulder—Enmaris', as he turned to the group for a quip. "I bet Yultes will receive his coat before any of ours, now that he's such good friends with the lower populace."

Yultes laughed; it was expected of him. His heart had stumbled and stopped, however, instincts trying to warn him through the sluggishness of alcohol and the pleasant buzz of the evening. Why would Enmaris bring this up now? Why set him apart when he had been one of theirs all night?

The hostess returned, a colleague helping her carry the coats. She had many freckles, all the way down her neck, a fact he strangely fixated on, distracting himself as the staff helped everyone gracefully back into their winter coats. Everyone but him. She turned to him, then, a rosy colour under the freckles.

"I'm afraid we found everything but Master Yultes' coat."

His companions let out various sounds of surprises, and Yultes' stomach clenched, his vision narrowing to the hostess and her calm and apologetic tone. Perfectly professional. A low buzz grew at the base of his skull and he struggled to articulate. Set apart again.

"O-only mine?"

"I'm very sorry, sir," she said.

The rest of his group stared at him, expectantly, and Yultes absorbed their expression, his mind decomposing each of them with the ease of years of training—Iriel's pinched lips of disapproval, Jayna's horrified o-shaped mouth, the slight smirk of amusement from Enmaris, and Viranya's arched eyebrows, inviting him to do something about it. After all, the *Golden Vault* served high class patrons; it was beneath them to misplace his coat. Yultes tilted his chin up, letting his irritation and dismay flare his temper.

"This is unacceptable," he started. "I trusted you with my coat and—"

"Now now, Yultes," Lady Viranya cut in, her voice a sharpened blade. "You're not going to berate the poor girl for that old thing, are you? It's a wonder you even call that monstrosity a coat."

The air left Yultes' lungs as surely as if he'd been punched, his impetus broken by Viranya's interruption. He stammered on his words, eventually managing a pathetic "It was fine."

"By the lowest of standards, perhaps," she said. "In a way, they did you a favour, losing it. Besides, you did so want to flaunt your perfect little outfit … this is a sterling opportunity, isn't it? Show the whole world your colours."

They all laughed, his supposed friends, and Enmaris's smirk felt far more sinister, in retrospect. Yultes' throat tightened, the acrid bitterness of humiliation splashing in his stomach, turning it. Had they known ahead of time? Arranged this? To what end, except to mock him? Except to remind him that he would *never* be one of them, no matter what Hellion might say or encourage—if he said anything at all. No matter what, or who, he sacrificed.

A hard nugget of anger twisted under his bile—at them, for trapping him like this, but at himself, too, for falling for it. He should've known better, should have listened to his gnawing worries. But he hadn't, and now he was stuck here, high in the Upper City, with no coat to ward the winter chill and no desire to stay with Lady Viranya and the others. He let their laughter carry on to their natural conclusion, a smile forcibly etched on his face.

"Well, it seems I have a long and cold road ahead," he said. "If you'll excuse me."

He left, carrying himself with all the pride he could manage, head high as he pushed the golden doors open and the first freezing gust hit him.

His feet did not carry him to the Dathirii Tower. Yultes didn't feel the cold, not with all the anger boiling within him, and he couldn't bear to lock himself in Jaeger's quarters, the very place a reminder of his situation. Instead, he spiralled downwards, following the Upper City's sweeping bridges and stairs to the lower levels until they lost their railings, growing narrower and more dangerous. More and more towers loomed above him, and while some blocked the wind with their bulk, many clusters created perfect corridor through which it plunged, whistling so loud it covered Yultes' own thoughts.

Good.

He didn't want to think, didn't want to relive every compliment paid to him tonight, every time they'd all hung to his every word, as if he was fascinating, as if they saw value in what he had to say, what he thought of the situation. As if he was truly one of theirs, strategizing with them, gossiping with them. It had all clicked, like he was a puzzle piece finally finding its home, and for one blissful night he had thought he belonged. He had drunk more, and stopped watching his words.

This elation angered him more than their quiet humiliation game. What was he even doing? They had asked him about the household, had inquired about Hellion's schedule and meetings, had teased out which noble houses besides Allastam supported them. They hadn't wanted *him*, they had wanted his knowledge, and he'd almost given his secrets along with it. Had they heard his pauses before he laughed when they mocked the staff? Had they caught a frown when they suggested throwing Jaeger out in the middle of the night? Yultes hoped not, but there had been so much wine…

He should return. Rush to the Dathirii Tower, find Garith, stammer out what he knew of their new deadline, let him know he might have given himself away. But the ground under his feet had turned from smooth bridges to cobbled streets, then from those to uneven, frozen mud. Under the stinging cold, he smelled human refuse, the snow and walls tainted with the stench of local life. The stars above had all but vanished, hidden behind bridges and towers, and the cityscape turned into intermingling shadows with the occasional splash of white, a patch of snow desperately capturing what moonlight filtered through.

In the depths of winter night, Isandor's Lower City felt more like a different realm, a universe of cold and shadow ready to engulf all that stepped in it. Fitting, he thought, even as a shudder wracked his body from head to toes. He was ready to disappear, at least for a little while. Almost ready.

Yultes rounded the last corner—and he knew, as he did, that it'd be the last, that although he had not wanted to admit it to himself, he'd always had a destination. Here, at the bottom of the city, nestled between unforgiving towers, warm light spilled from thick windows and an ill-fitted door. It warded off shadows, promising a refuge against the cold and a warm meal for the empty stomachs—a shelter against the world's cruelty.

Music drifted from it, the upbeat clack of wooden spoons and a rapid-firing violin, their rhythm discordant in a playful, almost competitive way. Every now and then, a burst of laughter or cheering covered it. Yultes sank against the nearby wall, his melancholy turning into a soft smile. The stone was cold against his back and even colder under him, and it slipped through his clothes, seeping into him, numbing the heavy guilt and bitterness within.

Yultes fought to keep his eyes open, to stare at this tiny beacon he'd financed for so long, but as time passed, he grew more comfortable. The drowsiness settled in, and he shushed the little alarm bells at the back of his mind, closing his eyes to listen to the music until it, too, faded away.

Chapter Twelve

V ELLIEN found it strange to return to the Shelter without Nevian, but he had his nose deep in piles of books. Nevian wouldn't miss them. Many here had, to their surprise. When Vellien slipped through the front door, the patrons cheered at them, hurling greetings over the din of the crowd. They returned what they could with a shy handwave, their cheeks burning, their heart hammering as they struggled to control the rising panic at so many eyes on them. Several patrons happily let them know Larryn hadn't left his rooms since his return, and Vellien's worry at that only heightened when an elderly lady grabbed their hands and told them she was glad he had called on them.

Larryn had definitely not called on Vellien, and despite rushing into the Myrian Enclave together to save Nevian, neither of them had really talked, not since he'd kidnapped Vellien. A lot had changed since, yet the memories of a cold blade against their throat remained seared brightly in their mind, and their body clenched in remembered fear as they moved through the common room. They paused at Larryn's door, allowing for a moment to steady themself, then knocked.

A grunt answered from the other side. Probably an invitation, but Vellien didn't dare assume that. "I would like to come in?"

"Vellien?"

There was a crash, then swearing and stumbling. The door opened, Larryn clenching its knob and leaning on it, all of his weight on the wood and a single leg. A deep gash tore through the other, blood pooling in it before trickling down and onto the floor boards. Vellien's gaze bounced from it to the fallen stool in a pool of reddened water, then back to the thick and curved needle in Larryn's bloodied hands.

"What are you doing here?" Larryn asked.

"You're wounded."

They had meant to be more eloquent, but Larryn's tone—flat and exhausted, entirely devoid of its usual flare—had taken them aback. His deepest wounds might not be physical.

"I'll be fine."

Larryn pushed himself off from the door and set his foot down, but never shifted any weight back onto it. He was not fine, no matter his posturing. Whatever had hit his leg had torn through muscles and nerves, possibly damaging the bone, too. It needed medical attention, not a handful of sutures after a quick rinse.

"I will not force treatment on you." Vellien's voice edged into squeal territory within a few words despite their intention to stay firm and calm. "Investigator Sharpe was worried about the state of your leg, and I can see her fears were not unfounded."

"Sora sent you here?"

The lightest red tinted his otherwise pale cheeks. He sounded more embarrassed than angry, too. They had not asked Sora about the nature of their relationship; it had seemed complicated, like most people's with Larryn.

"Not in so many words." She had mentioned a shared acquaintance with a fiery temper whose presence in the Allastam Tower might best be kept secret, and they had deduced the rest accordingly. "If you would please stop deflecting and give me permission? It is a serious wound and could cause lasting damage."

"I've had worse," he muttered, and his hand not holding on to the door for dear life slipped behind him.

Vellien considered leaving. They didn't want to argue with Larryn—the very thought constricted their chest and left them a little dizzy—but it was a very bad wound, and Larryn himself sounded so defeated, like he refused out of habit more than anything. Their heart hammering, Vellien inched closer and leaned down, to force Larryn to meet their gaze.

"You asked me to help the Shelter's people. That includes you."

"Nitpicking my words to get what you want? You've spent too long around Nevian."

If Nevian's pedantic influence granted them the wits and stubbornness to face Larryn, they would not complain. "No one gets special treatment. That was the rule, wasn't it?"

Larryn snorted, but Vellien knew they'd nailed a victory by his brief smile. "All right, golden healer. Come right in."

He hopped backward, into his tiny room, and put the stool back on its feet before slumping into it. Vellien followed, unable to resist a quick peek around—not that Larryn had much to see. A cot with thin furs, dirty pants and shirts, and a plank set against the wall to serve as a desk, with a sewing kit and more torn clothes sprawled over it.

Larryn extended his damaged leg, his arms crossed. "Just the leg. Don't want you snooping around every little thing."

The request surprised them. Did Larryn understand healers could perceive the scars left on the body that were otherwise invisible to the eyes? Cal might have told him. But if so, why was he so self-conscious about his? Vellien would not deny their curiosity was piqued. Not, however, enough to break Larryn's trust and destroy this delicate balance they'd returned to.

"I promise."

Vellien crouched by Larryn's side, closed their eyes, and set to work on the deep cut, careful to keep their focus on the wound. Even so, they couldn't miss the bone-deep exhaustion within Larryn's body, the way it shivered under the blanket of Alluma's gentle energy, craving for more. They resisted the desire to explore the reaction, knitting flesh and nerves back around the bone before sealing the skin. They dulled the pain with a low, steady push of energy, hoping it'd last through Larryn's evening tasks.

When they opened their eyes and straightened back up, they found Larryn with his own eyes closed, his lips twisted in a strange grimace, as if still in pain despite Vellien's help.

"A-are you all right? You look…" *Like you're about to cry.* They knew better than to finish the thought aloud.

Larryn startled, and his stool tipped over. His newly healed leg shot out as he gripped the seat, stabilizing him before he fell. He stared at it in wonder, and silence stretched between them, Vellien's question unanswered. Which was, in and of itself, an answer. Vellien gathered up their courage.

"A-as your healer, I must recommend rest. I know you don't want to hear it from me, but your body is not coping well with recent events. I can't heal that sort of fatigue, only stave it off as I just have."

Larryn neither glared nor snapped at them, and if Vellien had ever needed more proof that something was wrong, this was it. Instead of insults, Larryn offered a weary shrug.

"You're right, but I can't rest. There's an evening meal to—"

"I don't think it's the cooking," Vellien interrupted, only to panic that he'd dared to. "N-not that it isn't tremendous work, I don't want to undermine that, but—"

They stopped at Larryn's raised hand. It had been such a slow, firm movement—so *calm.* "You don't have to justify every word out of your mouth. I promise not to blow up at you if you say something horrendously privileged. I'm… I'm sorry for how I treated you, Vellien. You've done a lot of good here. I can tell you care."

"Oh." They had never expected an apology. A quick flush climbed to their cheeks as they struggled to respond. "I'm—I … it's forgiven."

"I got a feeling you don't hold grudges anyway," Larryn said.

Vellien laughed, and their hiccuppy snorting was buried under Larryn's louder chuckles. It didn't last, this awkward moment of mirth between them, but it soothed Vellien's nerves. Perhaps they *could* truly relax around Larryn.

"Don't worry about me," Larryn said. "It's all this Myrian shit that's keeping me awake, but Nevian said he had a solution, right? I'm gonna hang onto that. Kid's a genius, and we've seen how much power Varden can wield. I… I want to believe they can do this. And then I can sleep."

Vellien noticed the forced optimism at the end, but they let it rest. What good would it do, to press Larryn until he spilled his whole heart? He was probably worried about Hasryan. All of them were, really, even if they didn't know what to do about it yet.

"He is working very hard," Vellien said—every waking hour unless Vellien scolded him.

Larryn snorted. "Of course. Tell him Efua doesn't go a day without mentioning him."

"Neither does he." Vellien could not help their smile. Nevian glowed with pride every time he talked about her, and he mentioned her at every opportunity. It was one of those few times he ever seemed to truly relax.

"Good. Don't want him to forget us."

Larryn threw it out in jest, a vague smirk on his lips, but Vellien only beamed at him. They knew perhaps better than Nevian himself how impossible that would be.

NIGHT had fallen by the time Vellien left the Shelter. Unsurprising, perhaps, with how fast it arrived in winter, but their heart squeezed in fear at the darkened streets. House Dathirii had many enemies, and Vellien had neither titles nor fighting skills to protect themself. They stood by the Shelter's door, the warmth at their back, and hummed the first notes of a prayer.

"Alluma guard my feet, as I walk through the valleys of life." They took a first step, then another. Their voice echoed on the tower walls, soft and trembling, and a pale glow swirled in their right hand's palm, its light glittering on the icy street. It wrapped around Vellien, a reassuring cocoon. "Alluma guide my path, from one cycle to the next, from joy to sorrow, and sorrow to joy. Alluma—"

Their voice turned into a strangled choke as the light fell upon Yultes' familiar figure, propped against the icy-cold wall of a tower, curled in on himself to ward off the cold. Anger flared first within Vellien. He of all people should not be here, at the bottom of the Lower City, on the corner where a small offshoot of a larger street led to a Shelter built by the son he'd abandoned. *I got a feeling you don't hold grudges anyway*, Larryn had said, and Vellien had agreed, but a quiet indignation burned in them now. Perhaps some people deserved the grudges.

And yet, and yet, as they glared daggers at their uncle, they noticed the paleness of his skin and the blue lining his lips. He had nothing but a doublet on—one delicately embroidered with the

Dathirii sigils, as if his very presence here was not insult enough—and no proper winter clothes but his boots. If he could sleep in this cold…

Vellien scrambled to Yultes' side, a needle of fear piercing through their anger. They brushed aside the frozen strands of straw hair to peek at his ears, always a first victim of frostbite for elves—and indeed, the tips had gone a ghastly white. Vellien knelt down and pressed the back of their fingers to Yultes' cheek. Cold. So very cold. Their stomach clenched, and they sank into themselves, seeking that unique peace that marked Alluma's presence.

So, all right, perhaps they *weren't* any good with grudges after all. But the alternative was to walk right past Yultes and leave him out to freeze to death, and Vellien couldn't. No one deserved that.

They placed their palms on Yultes' chest, gathered all the warmth they had, and slowly but surely worked it back into their uncle. Shudders ran through their body as the exchange progressed, bone deep cold and fatigue seeping into them, weighing down their mind. Vellien fought their slipping focus the only way they knew: they sang, a hymn to the sun and warm summers to ward off the cold threatening to overtake them. Their voice was an anchor, every note they pushed tying them into their body, here and now, and keeping them from losing track as they warmed Yultes' core, then his arms and hands and fingers, and finally, delicately, little by little, his pointed ears.

Yultes moaned and curled in on himself, but his breathing had grown steadier. Vellien gave him a surge of energy, dragging him forcefully out of his hypothermic daze.

"Vellien?" Yultes croaked, his eyes fluttering open.

Vellien dropped their song, swallowing back the notes they loved. Those weren't for him, not if they could help it.

"Get up." The fierceness in their own voice surprised Vellien. "You can't stay here."

"Wh-where … oh."

Silence slipped between them, colder than the night. Yultes pushed himself back up into a sitting position and set his head against the wall. He did not get up. Instead, he looked past Vellien, at the Shelter at the end of the alley. His expression softened and darkened all at once, guilt twisted by something else they couldn't identify—nor cared to, they realized. They slid into Yultes' line of sight, blocking the view to the Shelter.

"I know what you did." Anger slipped into their voice, and Yultes' snapped to attention. They straightened, bringing their full height to bear, as if they could ever hope to impose. "You're lucky he made me swear secrecy, because everyone else would, too. How could you?"

A hollow laugh escaped Yultes. "I don't know anymore." He pushed himself up, leaning against the wall for support, and a full-body shiver coursed through him. "I should… go back."

Vellien's anger deflated, as if it couldn't maintain itself if unchallenged—and the husky pain in Yultes' voice *was* an admission of defeat and regret. They huffed and crossed their arms.

"Not alone. I can't let you walk home on your own."

Thinking of their tower as home added sharp edges to their voice. They hadn't been able to go to their quarters since Hellion had taken over. Vellien missed their bed, missed the quiet space they'd built by the large windows, half hidden by curtains, hanging plants, and a shelf, like a secret bubble bathed in sunlight. Their chest ached with it.

Yultes didn't respond. He started off, his strides uncertain, shivers still coursing through his body. Vellien trailed behind, unable to break the awkward silence. They had never spent much time in Yultes' company, and now that he was simultaneously Larryn's awful father, the pivot of their resistance to Hellion's takeover, and a family member who'd almost frozen to death, they didn't know how to deal with him. They bottled it all up, climbing through the city until Yultes' pace slowed again, and his body shuddered with such brutal force he started to stumble.

Shame swirled through Vellien—Yultes obviously needed more help, but they'd been too lost in their own thoughts to properly dispense it. They grabbed his wrist, stopping him, but couldn't think of anything to say, their usual calm reassurances eaten by their indignation. Vellien pushed more heat into their uncle, forcing themself not to be cavalier about it, to heat the core first then direct it towards extremities, slowly, gently. Yultes studied them, his lips pinched into a tight expression that gave nothing away.

"We're not so far," he said. "I can make it the rest of the way. I—" His mask crumpled—only a second, a brief moment of soft anguish he covered almost immediately, smoothing out voice and smile into abject neutrality again. "I think… I think I'd not mind everyone knowing, if he'd let me. It's long overdue, isn't it?"

If he'd let me. They must have talked, then. Vellien tried to absorb that Yultes himself no longer wanted this secret—even if the admission seemed hesitant, like he'd explored this knowledge for himself, too. In their shock, they loosened their grip on Yultes' wrist, and their uncle slipped out.

"Thank you for the warmth," he said, and he walked away, leaving Vellien to stand in the cold, grappling with their knowledge of his past and what to do about it—if they should do anything at all.

Chapter Thirteen

Hasryan spent most of his day sprawled in the hideout's busted couch, his back set against one armrest so that it would dig into his spine just so, dampening the constant throb of pain. It made it easier to think, and as the last string of events sunk in, he found he had a lot to think about.

He tried to focus on the good. He'd survived, somehow! Even stranger: Sora and Larryn had worked together to free him. And the cherry on top? She'd arrested Lord Allastam, effectively shattering her professional life in the long term, all for him. Sora cared, *she cared for him*, and had it not been for Brune, that knowledge would've obsessed him ceaselessly.

But there had been Brune, and their conversation dominated Hasryan's mind. He reviewed every word, every smile, every threat, even, until they merged into an overwhelming and bitter longing.

He missed Brune. He missed her casual earth puns and her

genuine smiles when he brought her salted butterscotch candies. He missed their professional relationship and the confidence with which she entrusted her most difficult tasks to him. He missed the certainty she'd seen something worth saving in his murderous and self-destructive teenager self—the certainty he'd been loved by someone, unconditionally, for the first time in his life.

Hasryan's throat tightened, the thick ball of feelings threatening to choke him. He'd thought her love had been lost—or worse, a lie—when she'd left him to hang, yet after today… Hasryan kept reliving her passing hurt and surprise when he'd refused her apology, or the little cracks in her voice when she'd admitted he'd deserved better. He clung to them, his memory amplifying the hints of love until he was out of breath, his heart erratic, the ache ever growing.

It hurt. It hurt to believe in them, to know somewhere deep in his core that these hints were not lies. She *did* love him, even now, despite using him as a scapegoat. How hard had it been for her, to do that to him? How much did she regret it now? Would she do it again? Brune's love was a spike, and every question hammered it deeper into Hasryan, widening the cracks until his pain leaked out, tears streaming without stop.

Hasryan wiped them away angrily. He had to stop! She had betrayed him. It was over, and he was better off without her, no matter how much she'd given him in the past, and no matter how much she still did.

He hated knowing she'd shielded him from scrying spells, that without her he'd never have escaped his detractors. It made him glad, and angry—and lost, too, because he'd spurned her extended hand and would lose this protection soon. Once that happened, staying in Isandor would become nearly impossible. He would have to give up his home and start over. The prospect haunted him all afternoon, claws of despair gripping his stomach and leaving him tired and empty. As the bright light warming his dusty room vanished, Hasryan ran out of tears and hope. He stayed splayed on the couch, his wounded arm growing stiffer, his chest growing tighter and heavier.

He only wanted a peaceful life with friends, putting his skills to good use, but Isandor would never forgive him.

Steady knocks echoed through the hideout, and his heart lurched into his throat. He wiped his face in a hurry, wincing at the sudden jolt of pain, then rolled out of the couch and to his feet. His whole body throbbed as he waited, tense, to see if he needed to bolt—an eventuality for which he'd failed to prepare. If his only exit route demanded he climb out in winter with a wounded arm…

"It's Sora. May I?"

The familiar voice—hesitant, inquisitive, hopeful—melted his fear away, and the quick beat of his heart took a different turn. She'd not sounded pleased at him, when she'd arrested him in front of Lord Allastam, and now he'd have to reckon with that. Still … he was glad she'd come. Being alone was doing a number on him.

"I'm here," he said, his voice rougher than he'd hoped. He plastered his best smirk on his face, unlatched the door, and cracked it open.

Sora slipped in quickly, forcing him to step back to make room for her. She'd shed off her bloodstained Sapphire Guard outfit and replaced it with casual clothes and a thick winter hood. Snow fell as she pulled it down and tugged her long braid out of it, giving it a small shake. Hasryan's throat went dry, his head hot, and his gaze latched onto the curve of her lips as she smiled at him.

"Good evening."

The soft tremble of her voice burned through him, vaporizing any breath from his lungs and drying his throat. It held no hint of resentment, only fondness and relief, and he struggled to digest it. When she lifted a small basket, he latched on the focus.

"Gifts?" he asked. "And, wait … how did you know to come here?"

"Cryptic note on my door, encased in stone."

Brune, then. Brune had simply told her where she'd sent him. He clamped down on the surge of gratefulness. "An invitation and a threat all in one. How very like her."

Sora grimaced. "I have a feeling she won't be the worst of my concerns in the coming days." She shoved the basket toward him, waiting until he wrapped his healthy arm around it. "It's dinner, and a few changes of clothes."

His stomach rumbled at the mention of food, loud enough for Sora to hear. She laughed, and he let the sound wash over him, pleasant and calming.

"Help yourself."

He would, but he wanted out of his bloodied furs first. As Sora removed her winter coat, he opened the basket and retrieved some very neutral, black and grey clothes. They made him think of his own infiltration outfits, and when he turned to Sora with raised eyebrows, she shrugged.

"Old loose clothes. Haven't worn those in forever. I don't feel the need anymore so I thought you could have them."

She tried to sound casual, but Sora's lying skills hadn't gotten any better, and he caught the weight of history in her voice. He let it go—they all had things in their past best left undiscussed. If anything, this felt like she'd offered a piece of herself, even if they left the story of it untold.

"Thanks," he said.

He slowly pulled the pants on, careful not to pull at his arms or lose his balance. The bottom trailed on the floor, mocking his much shorter height. When he glanced up to confirm just how much taller Sora was—or maybe, just maybe, because he felt like looking at her again—he found her staring at him. She seemed startled to meet his gaze.

"I thought you'd be—what did she want?"

"To apologize." His voice cracked halfway through and he cursed himself.

Sora looked up at his probably-still-puffy-eyes, then frowned. She reached out, frozen fingers landing lightly on his cheek. "Did you…"

Hasryan's world ground to a halt. He could feel his self-control unravel as he simultaneously relived his time with Brune—her love and sincerity and arrogance—and absorbed Sora's concern. He wasn't ready for the surge of feelings, a pressure growing within him until it threatened to burst.

"I told her off. She…" She loved him still, and had protected him, but he could never forget her betrayal. "She doesn't deserve me."

That was it, at its core. He loved Brune. He would never stop being fond of her and the life she had offered him. But he loved himself even more, and what he'd built after Arathiel had freed him … it was a thousand times better. And he deserved better, didn't he?

Sora let her hand fall, slowly, regretfully. "I'm glad you're alive. Whatever comes next, it was worth it."

Hasryan dug deep within his reserves and slapped a smirk on his lips, a familiar anchor against the storm roiling inside. "One can hope, but it won't last. We were right. Brune was the one keeping all those divination spells from finding me."

Sora's expression closed off, softness disappearing as she put up her own barriers. "How long?"

"Until we win." And once all of his friends, old and new, were safe again, he wouldn't be. He'd have to make his exit in the dead of night, House Dathirii's secret help, the one truth too dirty for even them to air out. "Don't worry. It gives us time to figure something else out."

Not that he had any hopes of it, not now. Maybe tomorrow, after a good night's rest, it wouldn't feel as dire. He clung to that thought and shrugged out of his loose fur vest, ready to move on, carried forward by the increasingly tempting scent of a fried dish and tomato wafting out of the basket. Wounded arm close to his side, he picked up Sora's tunic … and struggled to unbutton the front one-handed.

"You're wounded," she said. "Do you—If you need help changing…"

He dared a glance. Sora was biting her lower lip, looking every bit like she wished the words hadn't crossed them. With a breathless chuckle, he shook his head.

"It'll be fine, I'm sure."

It was not, in fact, fine at all.

After fumbling with the buttons, Hasryan reached for the first sleeve and slipped his healthy arm inside. Now he only needed to pull the tunic over his head. He tried to reach the collar with his arm to tug it up, but when he bent backward in the attempt, every muscle in his back screamed in pain. The sudden flare tore a moan out of him, and the world grew blurry, out of focus. He slid a foot backward, desperate to maintain his balance as sweat trickled down his neck. His breath had turned short, erratic. His whole body was calling out his bluff, and all he could do was stare at a knot in the wooden floorboards.

Cool fingers touched his naked shoulder. "It was amusing at first, but I think that's enough of getting hurt in the name of pride. Please, Hasryan. Let me help."

Hasryan closed his eyes and nodded. She clasped his shoulder tighter to steady him, and he belatedly noticed how his skin burned under her hand. He focused on the icy touch as she rolled the last sleeve up, placed it near his wounded wrist, and gently unfurled it, steadying his arm to avoid any jolt, every movement precise but soft. Her touch raised goosebumps on his skin—the fever, he told himself, or the chill in the air.

She gave a tap on his shoulder, motioning for him to bend his knees so she could pull the tunic over his head. Hasryan obeyed but held on tighter to her hips with his good hand, fighting off his dizziness. He could feel the warmth of her body, smell the winter cold still clinging to her. His heart rate accelerated, and he stopped pretending the light-headedness had anything to do with wounds or exhaustion. He wanted to touch her, hold her, kiss her, even, and he had no idea what to do about it.

Experiment, Arathiel's voice suggested in his mind, and never before had Hasryan so badly wanted to snap at a cheeky, imaginary friend in his mind. Experiment? He needed to stop thinking about it, that's what. Where would that even lead? A kiss, a thousand expectations, the necessity to untangle a mess of desires and fear, and before they held anything solid between them—if they even managed—he'd be long gone. No thanks. He let Sora pull the tunic over his head then straightened up, ready to pull the rest of it down over his chest.

Focused on moving on, Hasryan didn't notice how close his face had come to Sora's until her breath caught and her eyes met his. Her hand lingered half on the tunic, half on his chest, the tip of her finger tracing one of his many scars.

Then she leaned in and kissed him.

He froze, shocked—she wasn't supposed to do that! This was *Sora*. Investigator Sora Sharpe, who had tried to hang him, had searched Isandor high and low for him—who had now, quite certainly, found his lips. For one stunned, glorious second, they remained locked together, every inch of Hasryan a slow, vibration of pleasure. Then panic flooded in.

He jerked back and caught Sora's crestfallen look, heavy with the weight of her expectations. She hid it quickly.

"I'm sorry, I—" She scrambled backward and almost causing him to fall as she stopped supporting him. "I shouldn't have. That was— Your dinner's in the basket."

She snatched her wet boots up and pulled the first one on. Even in the dim moonlight, he noticed the depths of her embarrassed flush. She was going to leave him there, feverish and confused, angry that he'd pulled away when he craved her touch still and relieved that it was over all at once. The world seemed to spin under his feet. He couldn't leave them broken like this.

"Sora, wait," he croaked.

She pulled the second boot up, eyes locked onto it. "Just forget it. This never happened."

Her shame hit him deep and hard, clenching every muscle and closing around his heart until it felt like a small, shrivelled thing. It was so familiar, this disgust for him, this will to erase him. Hasryan's throat and eyes burned. He'd been right to pull away.

"Am I that much of a mistake, then?" His voice didn't crack, didn't waver. It was cold, hard, brutal.

Sora snapped up, leaping to her feet, her eyes wide. "No! It's—"

"A secret." The heady rush of *Sora* kissing him had vanished, crashed down so hard and fast he didn't have time to do more than bury the flames devouring him inside and rebuild his usual defences. "Don't worry, I get it. No one can know you kissed the assassin. You're too solid, too incorruptible for that. That's fine. I'm used to being everyone's dirty little secret."

"Hasryan."

He recognized the iron edge in her tone and the way she tilted her chin forward from countless back and forth in the Headquarters. It said: I will get this through your thick skull no matter what. Coat in hand, she strode right back to him, towering over him.

"I shouldn't have kissed you without asking first. When you didn't react, I felt awful for pushing that on you on top of everything else. I am not ashamed of *you*."

"A-A warning would have been nice," he muttered, too scrambled for anything more coherent.

What would he have even done, had she asked? He'd just decided against kissing her, but if Sora had started it…? Now she waited, eyes locked on him, and once again he felt the weight of her expectations in her bright eyes and parted lips, in the way she leaned ever so forward, hoping, perhaps, that he would initiate something. She was waiting for him to kiss her, and the pressure stifled his breath, crushing him. He didn't move.

"I don't think…" He trailed off, not certain what, exactly, he didn't think. Not certain of anything at all, really, and wishing someone would set him back on the simpler path of eliminating targets and infiltrating enclaves.

Sora's shoulders slumped. She reached for his cheek, briefly touched it, then let her hand fall back down. "It's fine, Hasryan. I misjudged." The roughness in her voice said it wasn't fine at all. She must have heard it, because she cleared her throat and forged on. "I don't want this to come between us. You matter to me."

A tightness unwound in him. From the moment she'd backed away, he'd been convinced she was leaving him, another relationship shattered, another person abandoning him. And it'd still felt like his fault, if she left, like existing as himself was fundamentally wrong. Hasryan breathed in deeply, clinging to her reassurance, and forced himself to look up and meet Sora's deep-set eyes. Moonlight fell across her face, highlighting her round cheeks and nose, brightening her dark hair. She was beautiful and so solid, a rock compared to him. She made him want to try to explain.

"I almost kissed you myself, actually," he said, and her strangled surprise drew a sharp chuckle out of him. His nerves would kill him before he got to the end of this. "I, look, the kiss, that's the easy part. But that's not all you're thinking about, isn't it? And romance? All those things attached to it? It just—I never thought about it before, and now that I do, it freezes my insides. I don't know if I'll ever…" He looked at her pleadingly, as if she could complete his sentences. No dice, so he changed tactics. "I asked Cal, once, if he'd one day stop playing matchmaker with others and look for his own love. He laughed it off. Said he had Ren, he had his friends, and nothing could make him happier. That friends part made so much sense to me—it still does—but I don't know."

He'd always figured he was some form of aromantic, like Cal, but that answer left him dissatisfied. He'd just never found anything better, and now he'd spilled all that to Sora, as if it made more sense to her than him. Seconds of awful, long silence stretched on, tiny weights of rocks placing themselves back upon his heart. Hasryan wanted nothing more than to look down, but he kept his head up, even if he was staring a little over Sora's shoulder rather than right at her.

"All right."

She said nothing else at first. *All right.* As if those two words could answer the intense flow Hasryan had dumped on her. It took him everything not to snap at her. She wasn't laughing at him, at least, or preparing to bolt.

"You need time. Maybe even forever." She smiled at him, and while it felt a little strained, it calmed some of Hasryan's nerves. "Right now, you're running a fever, you're wounded, and I don't know when I can next slip unnoticed here. We're dragging Lord Allastam to the Golden Table, to get a full investigation authorized. So this might be our last real time together for a while and I don't want to waste it. I'd brought dinner for two. If you want to hear it, I can talk about the mess Kirio made at home, while I was breaking down doors to save you?"

He laughed, giddy from relief and fever both, and plopped down on the ground, some distance from the pool of melted snow gathering under Sora's boots. This was good. He didn't need to make any decisions tonight, or anytime soon.

"Of course. And I want to know how you even wound up breaking said doors with Larryn at your side."

Sora's face lit with a dangerous grin. "Oh, *he* made even more of a mess, if you can believe it."

Of everything that had happened today, that was by far the easiest to believe.

Chapter Fourteen

SWEET oblivion had overtaken Yultes the moment he'd collapsed in his bed, but only for a brief reprieve. As the alcohol worked his way through and out of his system, he began waking up—hot, then cold, then hot again. His mouth turned into dried paste, his head started pounding, and by dawn the hammering almost covered the insistent knocks at his door. Yultes groaned and shoved one of his many pillows over his head. The banging only intensified, and his headache with it.

"All right, come in!" he called.

Instant regret blazed through him, jolting him upright. What if it was Hellion? Viranya? He was in no state to greet either of them, and— Thick nausea interrupted the line of thought, and he flopped back down before it crawled from his stomach and into his throat. How much *had* he drunk yesterday?

"Yultes?"

Garith's voice arrived muffled, strangely distant. Yultes squeezed his eyes shut. He was in a state, to say the least. It had not felt like it yesterday, drifting through Isandor's bridges and stairs. Then again, he'd been unwise enough to make his way to Larryn's Shelter and let himself freeze against a wall, lost in wistfulness and guilt. A night best forgotten. He called to Garith, mumbling the words past his thick tongue. The coinmaster's footsteps stopped right within the doorway.

"This is a highly disturbing sight," he said. "Did you even change before going to bed?"

Yultes dared a glance down. Great. He indeed still wore his fancy vest. He propped himself up by an inch to peek at his feet and was relieved to note he'd at least removed his boots.

"I daresay cold, drunk stupor prevented me from it."

"And here I thought I was your favourite drinking companion."

With a mock pout, Garith entered the room. He grabbed a chair on the way and flipped it around to sit backwards. Yultes ran a hand over his face and through his hair, untangling some heavy knots. The tugs at his roots sent sharp pain through his skull and he groaned.

"Lady Viranya invited me in person, as a token of … peace, I suppose, and of a brighter future."

Garith's grimace conveyed his full opinion of the matter. How foolish had he been to believe in the ploy? It had been so easy to fall back into these hopes, to give them yet another chance, as if he hadn't made his choice the very night Hellion took over.

"Any idea what they actually wanted?"

To humiliate him? Yet even with the wound still burning bright within, Yultes knew there must have been more. He tried to piece his memory of the evening—all they'd said and asked of him, every subtle smile between them. They hadn't prodded about Jaeger or Garith, and while there had been a few comments about how difficult it must be for him to handle their 'incompetent servants', none had felt like a pointed test of loyalty. Then again, they'd kept his glass well filled, and Yultes feared his control over his mimics might have slipped as the night progressed.

"Either they do not trust me, or they needed to … re-establish a certain hierarchy. Jayna Dathirii was present. This may have been a lesson for her more than me."

Silence met his hypothesis, and Yultes cracked his eyes open to find Garith staring at him in open-mouthed horror. Then his lips closed in a flat, angry line utterly at odds with the coinmaster's usual smiles.

"They're not friends," he said with a force that surprised Yultes. "Has it always been like this, in your little clique?"

Yultes didn't—couldn't—answer. *They're not friends.* He had known the truth of it on some level, in how they inevitably set him aside, loving him only in small bursts, keeping him on his toes. But what else could he have? He had been Hellion's confidant, and those were his people, so they'd needed be his, too. None of this was true anymore, of course. He didn't have anyone.

"You look like shit." Under the playful tone lay a thread of concern. Garith tilted his chair forward, hovering above Yultes, his long hair almost tickling his nose. Whatever he saw on Yultes' face displeased him. "Did you get into a scrape?"

At first the question confused him, but the memory came in a flash—Hellion's hand, backhanding him. The second slap, later on, more predictable. He reached for his cheek, his heart buckling in his chest. Was it that apparent? He'd not dared look at the mirror yesterday. They must have thought it hilarious that he'd arrived so out of sorts.

"Hellion," he admitted, and even that felt like a betrayal, a secret he shouldn't have shared with enemies. Yultes swallowed the bile rising in his throat and swatted at Garith's hair. "We have bigger concerns."

"Do we?" Garith slammed his chair back down, and a spike of pain hit Yultes' temple in response to the snap of the legs. "When we said you needed to be everyone's shield, we didn't mean literally. We need to get you out of there."

"N-no. I don't matter here, we—"

"Yultes." All trace of pleasant humour vanished from his tone. He stared at Yultes, chin tilted up with a solemnity that was strikingly Diel-like. "On my team everyone matters."

Perhaps, but was Yultes truly on his team? Was this not a temporary alliance, with Garith and Jaeger only grudgingly working with him? Part of Yultes wanted to believe that; it made it simpler to think of himself as alone. It felt deserved, the rightful conclusion to his continuous string of mistakes and betrayals. Yet it would also be the easy road, wouldn't it? One where he did not need to change, to fix anything and become worthy of their regard.

"Did Jaeger write to you?"

Garith huffed, not fooled by the obvious deflection, but he answered nonetheless. "Only to tell me he would not accept any criticism of his decision. Curse him, I was halfway through my own letter by then!" He offered Yultes that easy grin of his, all light humour and teasing. "I scribbled a 'you may want to skip this part' around it and sent it up anyway. You are both far too prone to dismissing your personal safety, it seems, and *someone* needs to say so."

Well, that deflection had not lasted long. Yultes propped himself up on his elbow and when his nausea remained tolerable, he sat up fully. His heart lurched at it, but he held tight to glare at Garith. "When did you get so annoying?"

"Countless hours of banter with Branwen." He winked, then stretched with applied laziness. After hours together, Yultes recognized this habit: Garith was making himself comfortable for the bad news. "So, bigger concerns?"

"You might need a drink."

"How bad?"

"Strongest-drink-you-can-find bad."

Garith winced and leaned forward on the chair, pushing it on two legs. "I'm all ears, buddy. Let's hear what our good friend Hellion has in store for us."

Yultes fought his nausea and gathered his strength. "Someone arrested Lord Allastam yesterday. I don't know whom, or on what grounds, but it is sufficiently solid that he was not immediately released."

"Your brain is more scrambled than I thought if you consider this bad news. Or was the drink to celebrate?"

"In response, House Allastam is withdrawing their troops from the Dathirii Tower within a week." Garith tilted his head to the side, his mirth diminishing as he grappled with the potential consequences of this news. Yultes continued, determine to hammer it in. "Once that is done, they will examine House Dathirii's books, as per their agreement with Hellion, and claim their due for the help."

Garith's chair crashed back to the ground and the racket sent a spike of pain through Yultes' skull. He groaned and gripped his head, squeezing his eyes shut as it passed. When he opened them again, Garith was nibbling at the inside of his mouth. "In all fairness, I don't think I have a drink strong enough for this."

"I didn't think so." Yultes brought his legs back to him and set his forehead against them. He felt dirty, the night's sweat still covering his body. "Iriel will want to see the books before House Allastam does so, and we cannot fool him the way we did Hellion. He'll find everything."

"Neither he nor Lord Allastam are getting a single dirty finger on our account books." Garith had recovered all of his usual smoothness, and he rose with fluidity and confidence that Yultes could only envy. "I'm done exposing our soft bellies to all the predators in this city."

"And you intend to do … what, exactly?"

"What I started overnight." A dangerous glint shone in his eyes and something sharp crept into his smile. "Why, I intend to burn all my accounts."

Yultes' bitter laugh escaped him before he could steady himself. "Be serious, Garith." But Garith only grinned wider, and Yultes understood: he *was* serious. He meant every word. "You can't."

"Can't I?" Garith spun on himself, arms spread wide. "Who will stop me? All the books are still in my quarters and my fireplace burns as bright as any others."

"Then what? Get beaten over it? Do you think Hellion will take all of this in stride?" Yultes wanted to rise and glare down at Garith for his carelessness, but he doubted he could stand. "If you don't pay for it, then Jaeger will."

Garith's enthusiasm deflated with a deep huff. "If only he'd left! I would have passed him a core account book with the barebones of our finances recorded for Diel to start over."

It would make their plans easier, perhaps, but Yultes could not fault him. Jaeger had shattered Hellion's hold on the gathered Dathirii nobles by refusing to leave—refusing Hellion's framing of his very presence as a relic of the past. In theory, Hellion's invitation was open; in practice, doing so now would concede the tower to him.

"Jaeger can't leave, not anymore," Yultes said, words halting as an idea formed in his mind, "but you can, while we stay and burn the books."

The more he considered this stray thought, the more Yultes liked it. Garith had not been confined to his quarters yet, or he wouldn't be here. Perhaps, with a sufficient distraction—such as, say, a large fire—they could allow him to escape with this core account book.

"I'm not going anywhere."

"You must." Under the tightness of his skull, Yultes assembled his thoughts into a coherent defence. His heart sped up as pieces fell in place. "You've had to circulate a fair amount during the preparations of Hellion's reception, and it stands to reason your loose ends aren't all tied up. Another trip to the kitchens would not provoke suspicions and they have a door leading outside. You have the means, but more importantly, no one knows the house's finances enough to rebuild them from a skeleton. Only you can do that."

"But I don't want to leave!"

Garith crossed his arms and pouted with such childishness that Yultes was brutally reminded how young he still was, really. He and Branwen weren't teenagers, but compared to Yultes, he had so little experience. His desire to stay stemmed from the same unaware foolishness that had once led Yultes to desert his reclusive elven village and follow his exiled brother on adventures. Garith trusted in the future in the same way Yultes had at the time—in the same way Branwen kept saying her Uncle Diel could work miracles. They hadn't learned better yet.

"People think Isandor's families live and die by their leaders, but they're wrong. We thrive or disintegrate by the grace of our coinmaster." One might blame him for the exaggeration, but truth lay at its core. Good coinmasters could shape the fate of their families, and despite his propensity to keep strange hours and run after every pretty girl in the city, Garith had an eye for numbers. He understood how to analyze the flux of gold in their treasury and draw the appropriate conclusion. Yultes met the younger Dathirii's eyes and held them. "*You* are at the heart of House Dathirii, not Diel. Hellion's ugly act is about to get worse, and we cannot risk your life and knowledge to his whims."

Garith tucked away a strand of his golden hair, as if he could just as easily brush away Yultes' words. Yet he had no witty reply this time, only a muttered "You drank too much."

"Perhaps," Yultes said, "but I am entirely *too* sober this morning, and I mean every word, headaches and nausea be damned."

Garith laughed, but under the exaggerated mirth, he was obviously troubled. He set his hand on his nearby chair and rubbed the back of his neck. "I suppose you might be right. Already started the skeleton accounts either way. You make sure you drink a lot of water while I finish."

"The whole Reonne River if it's what it takes," Yultes promised.

"And Yultes… You don't have to do it alone."

He left *what* Yultes could have company for to the imagination. Long after he was gone, as Yultes painfully went through the motion of preparing for the day, he heard Garith's firm and exceptionally serious tone.

On my team everyone matters.

When Viranya or Hellion affirmed him, their love spiked through him, a brutal surge he desperately clung to. Oh, how he'd scrambled to retain it, only for their affection to crash and him to fall with them. Garith's words instead settled within him, a warm bundle snuggling against his heart. Its weight steadied him, quiet and reliable, and Yultes ached from the softness of it. Garith, who would call him an asshole without hesitation, who had countered every jibe Yultes had ever thrown his way with one of his own, who despite it all had seen something in him, another person, isolated and curtailed, and reached out to it.

This Yultes—this other version of him, lost and buried long ago—was ready to accept the extended hand.

Chapter Fifteen

THE anxious churning of Nevian's stomach settled as he rounded the last corner and found the Shelter's ramshackle structure, squeezed between bigger, sturdier towers. He'd only seen the outside twice—once while leaving for Cal's little bookshop, and a second time leaving for the Brasten Tower—yet the crooked door and discordant symphony had a familiar, homey quality. He tightened his grip on the thin book he'd brought and quickened his pace, eager to be out of the cold and out of sight—not that he held any illusion about whether or not Master Avenazar could find him, here or anywhere else. Knowing nowhere was truly safe had made it easier for him to move about.

Nevian shouldered his way inside, forcing the door to move despite the iced bottom and uneven ground, and heaved a sigh of relief at the blast of warm air that welcomed him. The Shelter's common room smelled of cedar smoke, tomato, and basil, and although he'd eaten already—a lack of foresight on his part—his mouth watered. He glanced around the tables, at the patrons' chipped wooden bowls full of a thick tomato-based veggie mix, and wondered if his stomach had room for more. One of the patrons caught him staring and recognition lit his face.

"Hey, you're that kid from the other day. With the attack."

Panic surged through Nevian and he slid one step back, but the burly man grinned then nudged his table companion, a woman who'd traded quite a few fingers for scars. The scowl she'd harboured vanished as she spotted Nevian, then she slammed her mug down and every discussion around her paused.

"Hey, Larryn!" she called out. "Your saviour's here! Get him a drink, c'mon, we never see his face in here."

"You say that like drinks ain't free already."

Larryn's retort went from muffled to clear as he popped out from behind his counter, at the back of the room. By now most of the common room had tuned in to the exchange and many laughed. As more and more eyes latched onto Nevian, his heart rate sped and his palms turned sweaty. He hadn't meant to be so *noticed*.

"I I-hi," he muttered.

"Nevian?"

Something strange pulled within Nevian at how Larryn said his name, packing it with a world of fond annoyance and a hint of worry. He hadn't thought much of his relationship to the fierce owner of the Shelter, except that he owed him and that they both cared for Efua a great deal. Not until Larryn had shown up at the

Myrian Enclave, wreathed in flames alongside Varden and Vellien, risking his life and all he'd accomplished with it for Nevian.

"Your room's still empty," Larryn said. "Efua might even be in there. She keeps going back to read your cat book thing."

Cat book thing. Nevian twitched at the disrespect. "I brought her another. House Brasten has an extensive library and…"

He trailed off when Larryn gestured him along, pointedly not listening to a single word about House Brasten. As Nevian slipped between the Shelter's tightly packed tables, several patrons slipped a few 'thanks, man' and 'glad you're alive, kid' his way. Nevian's throat tightened. Their gratitude flustered him too much for any words to make it past the lump. He'd caused the problems in the first place—shouldn't they resent him for that? They could have died, any and all of them, at the mercy of Avenazar's whims, all because he'd been amongst them.

Nevian was glad to escape their gaze and thanks when the door clicked behind him, shutting out the common room. He released a slow, shuddering exhale and closed his eyes. Breathe slowly, Vellien had recommended, and feel the ground under your toes or a surface beneath your fingers. Ground yourself in your body. Here in Larryn's Shelter, however, Nevian instead focused on the rich smells of the night's dinner and let the hunger steady him.

"Better?" Larryn asked.

"Much."

"Are the lordlings a problem? I didn't expect you back."

It felt half accusation, half pleased surprise, like Larryn was ready to fight the entire House Brasten on his behalf. He most likely was if his reputation was anything to go by.

"I have had no issue with House Brasten," he said, dissolving any doubts in this regard. "I, however, need to speak with your friend—with Hasryan—if possible."

A myriad of emotions bumped one another from Larryn's face—surprise, confusion, suspicion, even—but he settled on a simple question, his tone miraculously neutral. "Why?"

"I need advice." Nevian retrieved the mirror tucked besides Efua's new book. "Vellien did not know whether you'd have his location, but I thought that if you did not, you would certainly want it. We could scry for him again."

Larryn's eyebrows shot up. "Not gonna charge me for it?"

Nevian stared at him, uncertain whether or not Larryn had meant it in jest. "It is to my own benefit."

He snorted. "Never change, Nevian," he said, and this time his amused tone was a lot easier to identify. "I do know where to find him. Meant to go later tonight, so I can get you there. And I'll do it for free, even!"

Before Nevian could retort, the door to his old room cracked open, and a girl's head peeked through. Efua's hair had been gathered into two beautiful puffs, and her big brown eyes grew ever wider as she spotted him.

"You came back! Is it over?"

The sound of her voice filled a hole within him he hadn't noticed until now, its inquisitiveness like fresh water on dry soil. He wished he had better news for her, that he could stay and sit for hours as they used to, going through the words she most struggled with.

"Not yet," he said. "I'm only—"

"You got time," Larryn interrupted. He set a firm hand on Nevian's back and pushed him towards Efua. "Can't leave so early in the evening. Give it an hour, maybe two."

Then he vanished back into the common room, the roar of conversations briefly crashing through the corridor as the door opened, then closed. Nevian swallowed the tightness in his throat, trying to ignore the way the skin itched where Larryn had touched him, even through his coat and robes.

"I suppose this gives us time for this new book I've brought from House Brasten," he said.

Efua squealed, flung the door wide open, and came rushing at him. His heart leaped in anticipation, but she drew herself short and only stretched to the very tip of her toes, as if she could peer into his bag. Effusive warmth passed through Nevian and he handed her over the slim tome.

"It's the story of a young Brasten girl who wanted to win their flight competitions so badly, she learned to speak with birds and had one fly for her."

"Oooooh." She snatched it out of his hands and flipped through the thick pages. Her eyes scanned the lines—too fast for more than a cursory reading, especially for her, but enough to notice some major differences about this one. "The words are a lot smaller. And I don't have pictures?"

"Very true, and it may be hard at first. We can start together, and if you cannot grasp the meaning of some words, you can always ask Cal."

Vellien had suggested the latter. According to them, Cal would love helping Efua out and was likely to grow lonely now that everyone had deserted his home. Nevian didn't understand how anyone could *miss* having a half-dozen people crammed into their small, private space, but it would not be the first or last thing to boggle his mind about Cal.

"Oh! I will. I will ask him about all the words."

Her resolve melted nuggets of stress within him, dissolving tight balls of nerves lining his stomach and spine, dotting his body with near-invisible pain. Nevian allowed himself this rare moment of relaxation and followed her into his old room. He'd left no belongings in it, yet nothing had changed—it felt as if he'd never left at all.

They settled into the bed, side by side as always, and Nevian set the book between them. Efua brought her finger under the first line right away, leaning forward to squint at the letters, and started off. Her reading speed took Nevian off guard. How had she grown so much faster in a handful of days? These were new words to her, yet she read them steadily, forming each vowel with patience and determination he could only commend. He rarely had to correct or help her every now and then, and inevitably his mind drifted off to the afternoon of research and the unfurling of theories in his mind.

House Brasten often traded in minor magical artefacts, and with time they had gathered a substantial number of tomes related to spellcraft, especially in regards to inscribing supernatural effects permanently within an object. He'd sifted through them, refining his approach to modifying the rekhemal's properties. They had also had a single tome, bound in dark leather, about soul traps of all kinds. At the end of the day, *that* was his plan—a trap for which he set himself up as the bait.

"You're not listening to me anymore," Efua said, pouting. "Not all of you came back."

Nevian doubted he'd ever make it completely back. Parts of him would forever be lost to Avenazar's violence, and even more had been irremediably changed. He grimaced and spared Efua the grim and bitter thoughts.

"I am distracted," he conceded. "We have a plan to take care of the bad man, you see, but it's very complicated and I think of it all the time. It's important for it to be perfect."

Efua pulled the book towards her and her shoulders hunched. "I'm distracting you from fighting the bad man."

That wasn't what he'd meant, but Nevian had no idea how to correct course. She clutched the book hard, her head firmly turned away, and a tight knot of guilt and panic rose within him. He stared, mouth dry and words lost to him, his heart squeezing tighter when she sniffled.

"Do you… Do you think I'll—" Efua stopped, tilted her chin up and turned to him, eyes full of water and resolution. "I want you to teach me magic, too. I want to defend others against bad men and make everyone's life better."

Nevian remembered when he'd first dreamed of magic. He'd been surrounded by arcanists throughout his youth, working at his parents' establishments and selling them the components sometimes needed for their crafts, but it had never occurred to *him* that he could be one. He hadn't had that ambition, not until Master Sauria had noticed him and not until his parents had given him tacit permission. Even then, though, he'd not talked about defending others, or making anyone's life better. He had wanted to be famous, to become a powerful mage known throughout Myria.

Those dreams felt alien now. They belonged to a boy Master Avenazar had erased from existence, and Nevian had clung to what pieces he could, rebuilding himself from them. He still loved magic—the puzzles of runes, the tingling of power at his fingertips, the unravelling of the world's mystery—but he wished Myria would forget him, that he could stay here, in this strange city full of towers and friends, teaching himself the intricacies of magic without any pressure but his own. How impossible it still seemed to have a life without the looming threat of Master Avenazar, and the weight of the dream settled on his lungs, crushing him. Yet when he pushed past it, Nevian saw himself sitting with Efua surrounded by books, showing her same basic runes he'd taught Isra only a few days ago. A fire crackled in the room, and somewhere nearby, Varden sat and sketched it, as he so often had since Nevian had joined him in the Brasten Tower.

He set his hand near Efua's, on top of their shared book. "I would love nothing more, Efua, and I'll make it happen. You'll see."

ARMED with several jugs of thick pea soup and a meat pie, Larryn climbed through the Lower City to the address Sora had given him. She'd sent him a note, not even bothering to show up, and Larryn couldn't decide if he was angry that she'd snubbed him or glad he had some space alone. When Hasryan hadn't come to collect his breakfast, familiar fear and anger had flooded him, motivating him to climb to the Headquarters and rope Sora into a rescue. He'd thrived on the adrenaline, feeding himself on it until Hasryan vanished in a perfect stone egg, taken by his old boss, and Larryn had nothing to fight for anymore—no way to save him.

He barely remembered the rest of his day.

He'd walked home, the armour ditched somewhere. He'd gotten the most makeshift, rotten bandage on his leg. He'd slept, or thought so—he'd jerked up at least once, convinced hands had tightened over his throat, but those nightmares had started trailing him awake, too, so who knew? Until Vellien had shown up to heal him, his day had melted into an indistinct blur of aching body and haunting memories, drifting from one moment to the next, waiting for the world to right itself, too exhausted to *make it*.

Anger had sustained Larryn for so long, he didn't know how to let go and still move through the world. He clung to his love for the Shelter, to what he gave to its patrons. No one had to beg for coins or scavenge frozen food out of dirty streets as long as he fed them, and that should be reason enough, but he'd lost the joy of it. This was what Vellien had meant, with all his talk of rest, and while Larryn couldn't take a real break, he craved a quiet night with his best friend, to maybe sit with him and simply *be*, both of them run ragged by the world.

It'd be easier to do that without Nevian trailing him, out of breath from carrying one of the jugs and climbing so many stairs.

"Think ya need him for long?" Larryn asked.

Nevian bristled, his whole face pinching as if he'd just sucked on a sour fruit or some shit. "I have no intention of lingering there. My time is precious."

Larryn choked down his laugh. "All right, mister high and mighty. I hear ya."

He lengthened his strides, forcing Nevian to pick up the pace. By the time they got to Hasryan's dilapidated hideout, Nevian was panting loudly by his side. Not a peep of complaints, though; the kid had gone through worse, no doubts. Larryn leaned on the door.

"Special meal delivery!"

Complete silence met his call. With every second of it, Larryn's stomach tightened, fear reclaiming its due. Wasn't this the place? Had something happened to Hasryan since? Had this been a trap and not a note from Sora at all? He leaned back and turned on himself slowly, hoping his good ear might pick up a sound he'd otherwise missed. Nothing. No whistles, no footsteps, no voices. Only Nevian's quiet pants.

The door's lock clicked, startling him. He whirled around to find himself face to face with Hasryan's smirk and almost threw one of the jugs at him—half in reflexive fear, half in spite at scaring him like that.

"Welcome to my humble home," Hasryan said, stepping back with a grand gesture. He never fully opened the door, closing it back as soon as they'd slipped in. This 'home' had a rickety wooden chair, and old sofa half broken in, and drawn curtains which had seen better days. Not much, but it did have Hasryan, and that alone washed through Larryn, unwinding him.

"It sucks," he said. "Can't go back to Cal's?"

Hasryan grimaced. "I might. Don't want to show up too soon in case they scope out my friends. No one came to ask you questions?"

Larryn shook his head. It was a little strange; he'd have expected the Sapphire Guard battering down his door again, messing with the place under the pretense of searching for clues. They showed up whenever they had an excuse, and he'd long since concluded Drake had asked them to.

"It's been quiet. Who knows, maybe they don't know how to deal with Sora breaking rank like that."

"Investigator Sora Sharpe and the mysterious Fleece." Amusement bubbled through Hasryan's tone. "You make the poorest guard ever. I never thought I'd see the day!"

Larryn flushed, the memories of changing right in Sora's office still fresh. "Ya got no idea the things I'd do for you, knucklehead. She had a plan—a bad one, but it was more than I did."

"Bold of you to call anyone else's plans bad." A softer undertone threaded Hasryan's teasing, and he gripped Larryn's forearm, squeezing it.

Nevian cleared his throat behind Larryn, before stepping forward and setting the jug of soup down. Before he could place a word, Larryn snorted.

"Ah yes, sorry, kid, forgot your time was so precious."

Nevian huffed. "You're not sufficiently older to be calling me *kid*," he protested, but with that little huff, it kind of lost all its credibility. Larryn's fingers twitched to ruffle his hair, just to make a point and annoy him, but he held back. Nevian would hate it for more than the teasing condescension.

"Am I old enough?" Hasryan asked. "Whatcha came here for, kid?"

Nevian's mouth flattened into a line. "Getting annoyed, apparently," he mumbled.

This time, Larryn couldn't hold his laughter, and Hasryan joined in. Poor kid, he'd only ever seen them fight, hadn't he? He'd had no idea what he was getting into. Nevian waited for them to calm down, although not without giving them the most powerful eyeroll Larryn had seen in a long time.

"I need advice to hire Brune's services."

Hasryan's laugh died instantly, snipped out of existence. Only the smirk remained, but Larryn recognized his friend's habitual mask. "She's a mercenary. You pay her, she'll do it."

"That is false." Nevian crossed his arms. "She told me herself she would not help if it came to Master Avenazar."

"You know her." Hasryan strode back into the room, flinging himself with feigned nonchalance into the sofa. He still kept his wounded arm close, Larryn noted, but he threw the other one over the back of his seat.

Nevian bit his lower lip. "I used to sneak out of the enclave to meet with her. She would teach me magic in exchange for information. I need her guidance again, Lady Brasten has agreed to lend the funds, and she has seemed inclined to help against Lord Allastam, but…"

"You want *personal* advice." He sank deeper in the seat, eyes closed.

Larryn turned a glare on Nevian. Couldn't he see the hurt under Hasryan's smile? The way his fingers had clenched into the sofa's fabric? The tremble in his sigh? Nevian only stared ahead, chin up.

"Yes. We need her help. I cannot build this spell alone."

A soft plea snuck its way under the kid's firm tone, and slowly, Larryn noticed in him the signs he'd so easily spotted on Hasryan—the slight tremble in his voice, the tightness in his jaw, the whiteness of his already pale skin. His anger slumped. Nevian knew what he was asking, but he knew what was at stake, too. Hadn't Larryn said, just the other day, that he trusted him to get Avenazar off everyone's back?

"Give her salted butterscotch candies," Hasryan said. "She'll know what it means."

"Right. Candies." If he had any doubts, they didn't show up in his tone. Instead, Nevian bowed low. "Thank you."

He left them without another word, tightening his coat's hood above his head as he headed back into the winter night. Larryn locked the door behind him.

"You didn't owe him shit," he said, turning to Hasryan. "He's a big kid. Could've figured it out on his own."

A bitter laugh escaped Hasryan. "Maybe? But if she was serious about her apology, she might as well prove it. I don't care either way."

That was the biggest lie in the universe, but Larryn let his friend have it. "Fuck their apologies. It's only good for their conscience." Meat pie, soup, and utensils in hand, he walked across the room and plopped down into the sofa by Hasryan's side. "If you can wrangle something out of her from the guilt, all the better."

He'd certainly gotten Yultes to finance the Shelter's activities over the years. That had stopped with the start of their war with the Myrian Enclave, and he was slowly eating through his reserves. He'd always known he couldn't count on his shit father forever, that a day would come where he'd decide he'd done enough, but the gold he'd squirrelled away wouldn't last, either. Yet another problem he'd tabled, too exhausted to look for solutions.

"We'll see, won't we?"

Larryn didn't miss the spike of anguish in his friend's voice. He pulled the jug's thick stopper off, then shoved it in Hasryan's arms with a spoon. It earned him a chuckle.

"Aah, Larryn's remedy for every wound of the heart." He leaned forward and breathed in the aroma wafting out, before hurriedly shoving a few spoons down his throat. "It never misses."

They shared the meal in near silence, companionship as much a remedy as anything else. Larryn himself scarfed down quite a lot of pie, his appetite returning in full force for the first time since his fight with the Myrians—since he'd sliced a man's throat and stabbed another in the back. Even now, his stomach churned at the thoughts, but Hasryan's very presence calmed his nerves. By the time they'd emptied most of their meals, Larryn felt energized and clear-headed. Almost normal again.

"So … you're friends with Sora now, is that it?"

Friends, huh? That was a good question. He trusted her, and that was more than he'd ever said about anyone with that uniform on—and her willingness to get rid of it had a lot to do with those feelings.

"Well, the law stick up her ass isn't entirely gone, but she's got a solid core."

"That's good. She kissed me yesterday."

"She *what?*" Larryn slammed his spoon back on the jug so hard it flew from his hand and skittered across the ground.

"I'm hurt that you would be so surprised," Hasryan chided, placing a dramatic hand over his heart.

Larryn ribbed him. "It's not you, it's her. Maybe the law stick *is* out of her ass after all." He stood to pick up his spoon, then pointed it at his friend. "So what did *you* do?"

"Panic," Hasryan admitted with a breathless laugh before running a hand through his hair. "Why is this so complicated, Larryn? I never thought about these things until Sora came around, and it's just—it's very different from the excitement of new friends, new people I can trust."

Larryn struggled for an answer. He'd never been great at these conversations, and he'd spent most of his life ignoring his own confusing ups and downs. Self-examination did not agree with him. He had these rare powerful bouts of sexual attraction which he tended to ignore, and he'd set aside any question about that in favour of survival—his, and others'.

"I can send Cal over to help you figure things out?" he

volunteered, returning to his seat. "He's the expert, isn't he? I think he even has a book on it or something. I'm … very bad at this stuff, Hasryan. But I like Sora. She's a good choice."

Hasryan snorted. "At least I pick my existential crisis right." He clapped Larryn's shoulder hard. "Sorry I dumped this on you."

Larryn bit his lower lip, fighting against his rising guilt. Hasryan's trust warmed him, but he had no idea how to help. Did that make him a shit friend? "It's fine, it's just… I'm better at aggressively supporting any decision you make. That's my specialty."

Hasryan arched his eyebrows and leaned forward with a hint of a smirk. "I'm thrilled to know you'd accept an invitation to attend a Dathirii wedding should I be the groom."

A spike of fear ran through Larryn and he opened his mouth to protest. Hasryan's laughter buried his garbled words. The pure mirth out of him washed away his instinctive reaction, and he pushed Hasryan's shoulder. "Stop scaring me like that."

"I'm sorry, it was too tempting. I wish you'd seen your face." Hasryan shoved his hand in said face with a grin, then dodged Larryn's initial attempt to slap it away. When Larryn finally freed himself, he found Hasryan staring with a very serious expression. "Good to see some energy in you. Nothing's more unsettling than flat, exhausted Larryn. I can tell you're barely keeping it together. No sleep?"

Any willpower he had for deflection vanished. "Not a lick."

"It'll come back," Hasryan promised, as if he had it in his power to make it so. "Whatever you gotta do to get there, make sure you hold on long enough to make it to the other side."

"Of course." They'd had these discussions before, sitting together on a tower's balcony where they didn't belong, sharing a drink and their countless stories of survival and crimes. Holding each other up through the worst days. And now, just like then, Larryn recited their mantra. "Out of spite and out of love."

In the past, only the 'out of spite' had truly driven him forward, yet as the words left his mouth, Larryn realized he was more attached to love now. It steadied him when spite and anger ran out. His hand fell to his pocket, where Cal's symbol was ever present—a symbol given to him in friendship, to help him find his way not only to Nevian, but to Cal afterwards, too. More and more, Larryn thought he understood the shape of his path forward.

CHAPTER SIXTEEN

RANWEN pulled her scarf higher over her nose as she surveyed the entrance to *The Golden Vault*, an establishment she had exited no more than twenty minutes ago after the most satisfying stunt of her life.

She shoved her hands in her pockets, where she'd crumpled Yultes' last letter. What was she supposed to make of him? An asshole most of her life, a surprisingly hilarious ally for a brief stint, and now the most likely cause for her failure to extricate Jaeger from the Dathirii Tower—if one discounted Jaeger himself, who in the end had chosen to stay. Then this letter, neither apology nor excuses, as if he'd known she'd hate either from him. She'd thrown it away, only to pick it up a few minutes later. Maybe she could test him? Before the big reception, he'd tipped her about one of Hellion's upcoming all important business meetings—one that happened just a few minutes ago, to disastrous results.

She had disguised herself as a waiter, avoiding any of the actual staff, and passed by his table to 'accidentally' pull the tablecloth. Half the plates and glasses had slid with it, shattering on the ground and spilling the meals. She'd apologized profusely, knocked even more things to the ground in her hurry to pick them up, and listened to the sweet, indignant rant of Hellion's business partner. The chalk-white merchant had turned an angry beet red and declared that if House Dathirii couldn't even guarantee a pleasant evening, he saw no reason to believe they could uphold their end of the deal.

On most days Hellion might have been able to salvage this. He knew how to coat every word with honey and dampen even the most terrible stings, if he so desired, but he'd cracked instead and outright snapped at the merchant. Something about how 'only a fool' would so misplace the responsibility of a ruined evening and take it up with him instead of the restaurant's owner. Branwen didn't stick around to hear the fullness of it. She'd needed time to slip out and hide her disguise under her winter coat and a thick scarf, to wait for her least favourite uncle to slip out.

Hellion wasted no time, stalking out with his coat wide open, golden hair flowing behind him in a perfect image of the indignant noble. Branwen fell into step behind him, humming to herself. She was being petty. She knew she was, that with Lord Allastam's arrest she had bigger priorities than ruining Hellion's day, but she didn't care. Sometimes one needed to nourish their soul first.

Once Hellion's path led him closer to a tower wall, Branwen sped her pace and caught up to him. She grabbed his collar, yanking him down to her height before dragging him alongside the tower, out of view of the busier bridges and into a half-hidden doorway, where she shoved him against the wooden door. Her hands stayed on his chest.

"Hellion, what a happy coincidence!" she exclaimed without any sincerity. He paled at her grin. Good. She wanted him to be afraid. "What are you doing in these parts? Unhappy business dinner, perhaps?"

He released a hiss that sounded suspiciously like her name. Branwen forced herself to laugh—had he, perhaps, finally recognized his clumsy waiter? Or was the sound his unfiltered reaction to her? Whichever, she let her laughter grow unhinged before shutting it down brutally. He recoiled under the glare, all of his countenance from the reception night gone now that they were alone.

"Let's make something clear, you worm," she said. "Your time is coming up. Soon, you'll be the one going down the shitslides, and that day will be the most blessed of my cycle. We got your best ally squeezed now, and what will you have left, once House Allastam leaves you in the dust? Nothing. Nothing but me, watching your every move, eager to make you regret every injury you've inflicted upon my family, physical or otherwise. But—" She lifted her hand from Hellion's chest with a dramatic sigh. "I suppose I ought to extend the same kindness to you as you did us. Leave now. Take whatever is left in our coffers and run, even. Find yourself a fancy city and buy a manor and live in riches far, far away. I don't care if I never have to see your face again."

Hellion sneered, leaning forward. "Do you really think—"

Branwen shoved a hand over his mouth, cutting him off in the most disgraceful manner possible.

"You make your choice, my dear uncle. And if you think a dusty banner collapsing upon you is the most humiliating thing that can happen, it'll be my pleasure to prove just how wrong you are. Bards will write limericks about your fall for centuries to come."

"When I'm done with this House, no cheap lines will erase my legacy. Not even the likes of *you* can ruin that."

"Well, we'll see about that, won't we?" she asked cheerfully. "You have your warning."

She blew him a kiss and strode away, basking in the sweet silence that followed. Maybe the shock of disrespect stole his words—a feat rare enough that Branwen intended to savour it. If anything, his seething anger would keep her motivated as she tried to untangle her network's response to Lord Allastam's arrest, and which key players Lady Brasten and Uncle Diel needed to pressure before the Golden Table arrived.

HELLION flung Yultes' door open with such force it smacked against the wall, and fear shot through Yultes, jerking him to his feet and out of his bedroom without pause. His heart raced wildly, bringing a surge of nausea he struggled to contain as he paused in his quarters' living room, his old friend sweeping in, overflowing glass of wine in hand, bottle in the other.

"How delightful, you still live here after all," Hellion exclaimed, long strides carrying him all the way to Yultes. He flung an arm around his shoulders, squeezing it as one would an old friend.

Which he was, Yultes reminded himself. He was an old friend, and he ought to act like one. Only, he had not left on friendly terms, but on a challenge. Yultes had turned his own words over in his head ceaselessly since, trying to imagine what would follow, what Hellion would do when they next saw one another. He'd created dozens of scenarios, tried to walk himself through any arguments, to prepare himself for the inevitable fight so that he could defuse the situation and hold onto his position a while longer.

All of it flew out the window now, shattered by Hellion's overwhelming presence, the waft of his perfume mixed with the alcohol in his breath, the warmth of an arm on his shoulder, a friend leaning on him, old fears and love rearing their heads. His throat dry, all Yultes managed was a strangled "Hellion."

"I must say, I thought you—my most trusted friend, my closest ally, my one truthteller—had taken the invitation to leave and abandoned me."

"Never," he said, his voice a thin thread. It sounded foreign, as if it didn't belong to him. His whole body didn't, as if Hellion's very presence threatened to swallow him. He scrambled for solid ground to stand on, for something *himself* that was not *Hellion's friend,* but Hellion gave him no time, leaning in closer.

"I'm glad," he said. "I need you, Yultes. I need someone who will stand by my side no matter what. Viranya and the others, they are brilliant minds, but they are opportunists—ready to change House at the first threat. Not you. Never you."

Hellion's fingers dug into his shoulder, plea and threat all at once. Guilt howled through Yultes' mind, a gust as powerful as a windy night atop Isandor's towers, snapping his thoughts in all directions at once. He'd been the first to betray Hellion and turn his back on him. And it was hard, with his friend leaning on him like this, to remember why he'd done so—why Yultes had ever thought it worthwhile to inflict such pain on him. Part of him was terrified that if he opened his mouth, he'd spill all his secrets just to get rid of the nauseating weight against his heart. Thankfully, Hellion had come for an audience, not for advice, and he kept going.

"Branwen threatened me today, did you know that? As if she were some vulgar thug!" His voice tilted up in mockery, but Yultes didn't miss the threads entwined underneath, anger and fear tightly woven together. "She waited for me outside the restaurant—after ruining the dinner, no less! I do not think such behaviour should go unpunished. Do you?"

"A-at the restaurant?" Yultes stammered, avoiding the all too direct question. He'd little doubts that Hellion's punishment involved liberal use of the Allastam guards still within their walls, but this time, he didn't see how he'd stop it. The panic cleared his mind, however, disentangling it from Hellion's dangerous love. "How did she even know to be there?"

Because he had told her, of course. He had shared some of Hellion's key meetings, hoping for exactly this result—except he'd never thought Branwen would speak to Hellion directly.

"What does it matter?" Hellion snapped, his anger flaring as he shoved himself away from Yultes. It'd been a rhetorical question, but Yultes quelled the reflexive fear inside himself and cut in before

Hellion could continue.

"Your schedule is not public knowledge. Unless you've already shared with your new council, no one but you, me, and key Allastam players could have provided this information."

"The merchant—"

"Perhaps, but she'd have to know to track him down."

Yultes clasped his hands behind his back to hide their shaking. He hoped Hellion would mistake his shortening breath for excitement instead of fear. He was walking dangerous grounds, pointing the signs at him, but the outline of a new lie formed before him, one so enormous it might distract Hellion from his vengeful impulses.

"You asked me to investigate what happened the night of your speech." The instant he finished, Hellion's gaze turned ice cold and settled on him. He had neither forgotten Yultes' rebuttal, nor forgiven him. Reminding him of it might have been a mistake, but it was too late now. Despite his quivering stomach, he pushed onward. "We agree there has been foul play. Someone is working against you and set those banners to fall on you. But I do not think it's Diel's people. Not Jaeger, not Branwen, not Garith. No, they're the easy scapegoats."

"You sound quite convinced of this." Hellion's voice had dropped into a dangerous whisper, sweet and intrigued. "One wonders, when you receive visits from Garith as the sun rises and prowl near Jaeger's door a handful of times. You *have* spent quite some time with them after our takeover. Perhaps you have special insight?"

Yultes' insides shrivelled. Hellion had been bound to catch up sooner or later, to piece together all the diversion tactics Yultes had used since the beginning—to notice, after all this time, that his supposed friend was the one link between all of his problems.

"It's best to keep your enemies close." Yultes was forced to pause, his own daring leaving him breathless. Who was the enemy here, if not Hellion? But if he'd managed to guide Hellion where he'd wanted, surely he could at least pretend he could do so with Jaeger and Garith, too? "They would *love* to ruin you, but Jaeger has never left his quarters without my presence and I verify everything Garith has done for us. When would they have had the opportunity? The means?"

Hellion huffed. "And Branwen?"

"We cannot discount her entirely, of course, but Branwen is blunt and childish. She'll spit in your face, not orchestrate a hundred different mishaps during a reception. Look at her behaviour that night and today."

May she forgive him this slight, because it was working as intended. Hellion emitted a pensive hum, his frustrations turning into serious consideration. He swiped the bottle of wine from its precarious position near Yultes' pothos and tipped it over his glass. "So tell me who. I can tell you're leading me somewhere, Yultes. I've taught you these techniques."

The truth in his almost gentle nagging sent fear jolting through Yultes. If Hellion could see through Yultes' build up, what else would he perceive? Was Yultes walking a thin line, or was he hurtling directly into disaster? It didn't matter: he could not back out of it anymore.

"I believe we should consider the possibility that Lord Allastam is behind this."

"That's preposterous." Hellion stopped filling his glass. He'd already nearly reached the upper lip. "Lord Allastam is an ally and a friend. We see eye to eye."

Yultes' thin hold on his veneer of calm almost shattered. A friend? Once, perhaps, he might have been. Yultes could still remember a younger version of him, confident but more open to the world. Bitterness and arrogance had festered within him for years, however, and he'd grown ever more spiteful and ambitious in the recent decades. People had become tools to him, never friends.

"Is he?" Yultes set the quill down as calmly as he could and caught Hellion's gaze. "Why would he want House Dathirii to regain his footing? Lord Allastam leads an upstart house, relatively young in Isandor's history, powerful because of its ruthlessness. House Dathirii instead has centuries of tradition behind its name. Nobles love the oldest Houses. He already betrayed you once, Hellion. And now, right after a disastrous night—one any of his people had plenty of opportunity to orchestrate—his daughter orders all soldiers withdrawn? Demands to see our books and sap your profit? How convenient."

Perhaps that *had* been Mia's game. Yultes might blame the father for it, but removing military power from Hellion's hands while subjugating their finances certainly did no favour to his claim to leadership. House Allastam had motive, means, and opportunity—and Yultes would love a scapegoat for his own schemes. He scrutinized Hellion, desperate for a hint of his old friend's thoughts, but even with decades between them, Hellion remained impossible to read or predict.

Impossible, that is, until he burst out laughing, each chuckle a crystalline spill from his lips, a cutting melody all of their own. "Oh, Yultes. My poor Yultes. You're serious, aren't you?" He lifted his glass. "To your wonderful imagination," he said, before downing half of it in one go. "I forget, sometimes, how unique your mind is and how far it can reach. Irreplaceable, truly."

Mortification dug its way through Yultes, a familiar friend, too. Once, it came with confusion—the shame of failing entwined with the complimentary veneer of Hellion's words and the feeling he should be thankful for them, that they had no right to cut him. Yet he saw it now, how they were designed to slice. He let them—let the insult bleed him inside, an open wound he didn't want to forget, a clear contrast with Garith's gentle concern for his well-being—and he swallowed his most bitter retorts.

"I'm glad you find humour in the situation," he said instead, "but I—"

"I don't want to hear any more of this foolishness, Yultes!" Hellion slammed his glass down, rising to his feet in a sudden movement. Yultes couldn't help but recoil away, his cheek burning as if he'd been slapped again. Hellion's eyes flicked at the movement and the hint of a satisfied smile flitted across his lips. "I asked you to investigate, not to weave a full conspiracy out of thin air to cover your own failure. Lord Allastam is an ally, and he's done more for this House and me than you have."

He emptied his glass over Yultes' pothos, the red wine sliding over its heart-shaped leaves before sinking into the earth below. Then he shoved it to the ground, pushing the clay pot with such force it shattered on impact. Yultes froze, horror and surprise clamping down on him. He'd brought one plant with him, just one, and now—

Hellion's perfume ensnared Yultes as he moved into his space, the warmth of his body so close. Fear tingled through him, but Hellion's anger seemed to have deflated with that single strike. Instead, he slid a finger under Yultes' chin, turning it towards him, and leaned in. His forehead rested against Yultes, and the world around fell away. Nothing else but them, this bubble, this moment, and how it eroded any sense of self Yultes had.

"I need you to be better," Hellion whispered. His voice deftly played the chords inside Yultes, prying a familiar melody of yearning out of him. He squeezed his eyes shut, trying to block it out, but there was no muting the delicate sigh, nor the soul-wrenching "Please."

It reached within him, decades of love and companionship packed into it, and pulled a gasped, frantic pledge out of him. "I promise."

Only with Hellion long gone did Yultes stop believing it, the world righting itself, the cut of his earlier insults returning fresh to his mind. He stood where his friend had left him, his eyes drifting to the broken pot clay and the pothos' roots, still clinging to the earth that nourished it. Mostly intact despite its fall. It would need a new pot, but with a caring hand, it would survive this ordeal, as it had many others before.

CHAPTER SEVENTEEN

N EVIAN hunched his shoulders as he stepped into *The Moonshine* and a blast of noise, stinky alcohol, and smoke hit him in full force. The chaos of conversation and music had an aggressive quality to it, as if to ward outsiders away, and Nevian clutched his knapsack tighter. Everyone knew the small tavern served as a front for the Crescent Moon and hostile or not, he needed to be here. His arrival, however, did not go unnoticed. Conversations died, customers with mean muscles and a plethora of scars turned to glare at him, and one even spat in his direction. A complete reversal from the Shelter's welcome. His mind screamed at him to run, but instead he pushed deeper inside, towards the counter. His heart pounded and with every table he passed, he expected hands to reach out and grab him.

"You're late."

Brune's voice carried over the din, rooting him to the spot, and he found her leaning in a doorway, impassive. Late? How could he be late? They didn't have a meeting planned this time and hadn't talked since deciding the last one would be on—oh. He was late for the winter solstice meeting. Weeks late, now. How long ago that felt… Nevian gave her a curt nod.

"I'm sorry. I couldn't make it."

"I don't appreciate my time being wasted." She crossed her arms, and a month ago Nevian would have been terrified she would stop teaching him, that this one chance he had at becoming a stronger wizard would vanish. Now he pressed his lips together and did his best to conceal his own irritation. "Congratulations on surviving."

"Thank you." He loosened his grip on his knapsack and breathed in. He'd gone past surviving. It was time to fight back. "I'd like to talk in private."

Several of the tavern's patrons snickered at his demand. Nevian's head grew hot, his chest tightened, and the edges of his vision blackened. He'd hated the attention in the Shelter, where it had been friendly, but now it pressed on him, stealing his breath. Through the ringing in his ears, he heard someone joke that Brune had no time for a whiny kid's ass. Nevian gritted his teeth. He was neither whiny nor a child, and she knew as much.

"Consider me intrigued, Nevian." Brune stepped back from the door and gestured for him to follow. Dismayed silence spread through the room as Nevian scrambled across its floor, a thin smile on his lips. At least the first, scariest step was over.

Much like Larryn's Shelter, *The Moonshine* occupied a large area at the bottom of a tower and Brune had acquired the rest of the floor for her business. She led him through a corridor lit by stone globes giving off a warm brown hue and inscribed with familiar runes. He recognized the patterns for Creation and Body, intertwined into other scripts he couldn't identify. Some of the runes ran from one globe to the other, and he noticed several he'd often come across while deciphering protection spells.

She pushed a door on her right and stepped into a small office with a perfectly clean desk and two small chairs. Nothing personal decorated the desk—in fact, nothing occupied it except an inkwell and a black quill. It reminded Nevian of the stale rooms one could rent in Myrian schools in order to study.

Brune settled in the chair behind the desk, and he forced himself to sit down in front, pulling his sack on his lap. She gestured for him to go on, so he gathered his courage and plunged in with words he'd practised a dozen times in front of Vellien.

"I need help with a spell from someone who works both divine and arcane magic."

Brune's eyebrows shot up. "I am no priest, Nevian."

He frowned at the blatant lie. Why would she waste their time with such an answer? "You are. Not a clergy priest, perhaps, but you can channel Gresh. And you're an expert with runes. You're the person I need."

She tilted her head to the side, perhaps wondering how he knew about her ties to Gresh. Many believed Brune's lieutenant was the source of the Earth magic in the Crescent Moon, but he'd noticed how magic current shimmered around Brune's palms whenever she touched a stone surface, shivering in anticipation. Her affinity needed no runes.

"You have always been a bright mind," she said, and the hint of regret in her voice startled Nevian. He stiffened, too aware that fake regrets always preceded violence with Avenazar. "So I'm the person you need, fair enough. Now you must convince me I should waste my time on your spell. You can't afford my services."

"House Brasten can," Nevian countered before fishing through his sack for his letter from Lady Brasten, sealed and signed by her hand. She had asked him, handing over the scroll, if he was confident in his choice, and he'd replied with fervent bluster. He tried to summon that energy again now. "Besides, allowing Master Avenazar to rampage through this city unchecked is counterproductive for you."

"Is it now?" she asked.

Nevian tilted his chin up and held her gaze in the silence. It stretched on, the weight of her thoughts pressing down on him, trying to crush his certainty. When they had been working on his arcane runes, those long pauses had instilled a constant sense of inadequacy in him, as though no matter how well drawn, she'd find his runes lacking and inevitably decide he wasn't worth what information he could provide. Today she was judging him by a different metric.

"You have been helping Lord Dathirii. Against House Allastam, one might say, but you have been an established presence in this city for years—longer than the Enclave—and I do not believe you feel threatened by local nobles. You did, however, tell me you'd not confront Master Avenazar for my sake, which implies you consider him sufficiently dangerous."

"And yet here you are." She leaned back into her chair and a flat, coin-sized rock appeared between her fingers, dancing between them mindlessly.

"I am not asking you to confront him directly."

"I'm no fool, Nevian. He'd read my help in your mind."

Nevian's stomach tightened. He could not deny this. If Avenazar discovered who had designed the magical trap, he would add the Crescent Moon and Brune to his list without the slightest hesitation.

"Indeed, if he gets the chance. You are a master of your craft and a professional, however. You would not accept my gold then let me face him with a shoddy rune, knowing your own peace is on the line."

She laughed. They both knew a perfect rune alone wouldn't save Nevian, but she seemed to appreciate the cheek of his response. Before her mirth vanished entirely, Nevian retrieved a small brown box with a golden bow from his knapsack and slid it across the table.

"I have these, also," he said.

Brune caught her coin and leaned forward. "Are those…" Her voice trailed off and a rare smile curved her lips, soft and genuine. She pulled the box closer, fingers sliding within the bow's loops. "Did it come with a message?"

"It comes with me and my request."

When Hasryan had promised she'd know what the salted caramel candies meant, Nevian had not expected her to recognize the very box they came in. He hoped it would help.

"That's typical," Brune said. "First he refuses my apology, and now he's asking for a favour and sanding off the edges with sugar."

"I'm not asking for a favour," Nevian said, gritting his teeth. She wasn't talking about him, but he refused to let the conversation stray. "I'm asking to hire you."

Brune leaned back into her chair with a long, amused exhalation. She toyed with the golden bow, and her expression had something so intense and undecipherable Nevian felt like he was intruding on a private moment. He focused his attention on his knapsack, closing it back again. Brune tapped the top of the box. "Very well, I'll help. I never could refuse my pupils."

Nevian dug his fingers into the leather of his knapsack, his chest swelling at the word 'pupil'. Did she really think of him that way? They hadn't often collaborated, restricted by his ability to escape the enclave.

"If you had a message, I could pass it on. As an apology for my lateness."

Brune wrapped both of her hands around the caramel box with an unsettling tenderness. It didn't transfer to her voice when she responded. "No need. He's heard all I had to say and made his choice. One day, I suppose I will have to allow others than you through the scrying protections I've built around him."

Allow others than you. Nevian remembered how he'd struggled with his spell, bent over a mirror with Larryn. It'd felt like he'd slammed into a wall at first, as if another force meddled with his vision. That must have been Brune, then. After that night, Nevian had reviewed his runes over and over, convinced he'd find a mistake in them to explain the experience. It was a relief to learn there had been none to find.

"Very well," he said, rising to his feet. His voice trembled, trepidation at what he'd just accomplished overtaking his professionalism. Nevian cleared his throat to steady it. He'd *hired* Brune to help them, and he ought to act like it. "We'll be awaiting you tomorrow morning at the Brasten Tower. If you have any resources on the marriage of divine and arcane magic, I recommend you bring them."

Brune flicked a knowing smile at him. "Always eager to lay your hands on new tomes, aren't you? Very well. Don't stand me up again."

The edge in her voice at the end sent a quiver through Nevian. He struggled to keep his outward calm and nodded before leaving the office. Excitement lengthened his strides as he found his way back into the common room. He looked forward to working with a such an experienced magic user—he would learn *so much*! Trying to devise a runic structure on his own had already offered him great insight into the relationship different runes could have with one another. How different types paired gave you access to new magic, or widen or narrow the scope of a spell, for example, and he'd found indications on how to integrate body, mind, and spirit all together in a single series of rune. The endless possibilities sent his mind in a gleeful frenzy, and between Varden and Brune, he was about to innovate and open a whole new range of possibilities. This was why he'd always wanted to become a wizard, and for once in his life, Avenazar would not ruin it.

NEVIAN presented the key elements of his plan to trap Master Avenazar in House Brasten's great library, his hands flitting with anxious energy as he worked his way through it. Brune sat across the table, awash in light from the high windows. None of it felt real—not his voice fluttering through the halls, not her attentiveness to his ideas, not the burgeoning of confidence in the pit of his stomach. He had seen students in lecture halls present theories to Myrian Academy Masters, their own mentor off to the side in support, and here he was, exposing big magic ideas to Brune, citing sources. When the enormity of them grew too much, his gaze flicked to his right, where Varden sat in silence, as he had through almost every hour of research on this spell.

His heart hammering, his palms sweaty, Nevian finished his presentation of his imagined trap—a way to invert the rekhemal's property from an extension of the body to a containment of spirit and mind. A soul trap he could spring from the confines of his own mind and which would rely on the rekhemal's divine nature, inaccessible to Master Avenazar.

Brune tilted her head to the side, eyebrows raised. Every nerve in him vibrated as he awaited her opinion.

"Ambitious," she said with obvious approval.

Thrilled elation ballooned in Nevian's chest until he thought he'd burst from it. Then she battered him with questions on the specifics—what runes did he want to use, how did the rekhemal work, how would he trigger the trap, had he ever cast anything remotely like this—ripping away any pretense that he had more than a surface understanding of what he was attempting. As he stammered his way through an answer, she cut him off with a dramatic sigh.

"I guess that's why you hired me," she said. "You understand, of course, that you'll live or die by this spell."

Nevian nodded. A heavy weight had replaced the lightness in his chest.

"Good. You've always learned well under pressure. If any beginner can do it, it's you."

Had he ever learned *not* under pressure? Nevian had never had any choice—and he didn't today, either, not if he wanted a future. "Let's get to work, then."

Brune laughed, motioned for him to sit down, and turned towards Varden. "I understand you have this rekhemal with you?"

His eyes flicked up from his sketchbook to settle on Brune. She met his stare, and a tingling run across Nevian's skin—a building of power, like an invisible pressure in the library. He held his breath as the silent exchange raged. Then Varden offered a polite smile and nod, retrieved the artefact, and the pressure dispelled.

He spread the long band of dark fabric on the table with reverence, his fingers trailing on the soft surface a moment before he let go. It looked so ordinary, just a black piece of cloth with orange flame-like triangles near the eyes, but Nevian had experienced its power. He'd never forget the enhanced mental acuity; how awake and alive it'd made him feel.

Brune hovered her palm above, without touching it, and let out an appreciative hum. "Interesting. I would not want to meddle with this without the active collaboration of Keroth's flock. I'm glad we have Their benediction."

"It's a blasphemy I take upon myself."

The strain in Varden's voice alarmed Nevian. Would this have dire consequences for him? Was he hiding something from Nevian? He bit back the tangle of fears and questions rising. They'd decided to shoulder the risks together. Varden hadn't tried to dissuade him from this plan once he'd known it might trap Nevian alongside Master Avenazar if done wrong. Nevian had to trust he could choose his own risks and sacrifices.

"As long as it's not on me," Brune said. "We can use its inherent power to hide the trap's signature."

"We'll use it," Varden reiterated.

"Then we'll need to understand it first, won't we?"

She set her palm against the table's wooden surface, her fingers spread out. Two lines of stone coursed from it with a joyful crackle, circling the rekhemal several time before spiralling to each end of the bandana, encasing it. The stone rose into a spike with a quick succession of layers, lifting the rekhemal from the table and above the circle formed by Brune's magic. The latter glowed a soft brown then spread inward, tracing brand new lines and arcs. Nevian leaned forward, drawn to the familiar patterns—this was a rune! He recognized the sharp triangle used for enhancements and the thick arc connecting the Body and Mind components of it, but the rest of its meaning was lost to him.

"Please pick up ink and reproduce it, Nevian. The spell isn't forever."

"Hold it."

Varden flipped his sketchbook to a new page and retrieved a thin stick of charcoal from their wooden box. His hands sped over the paper as he drew, every line quick and self-assured. In less than a minute, he turned the image of the rune towards Brune and Nevian. Not a single detail was missing.

"A man of many talents," Brune said, and she dropped the spell.

Unravelling the exact meaning of the rune proved harder than obtaining it, however—in part because Brune had him work for every inch of it. Nevian spent hours drawing separate runes and researching for elements in a handful of tomes either from the Brasten library or Brune's personal belongings. She'd send him off with a clue, and while he scrambled to piece together the next element, she shifted through his collated notes on divine magic, protections from mental assault, and soul traps. He struggled to focus on his tasks, always on edge for a grunt of disapproval or a mocking sort, but the most sounds Brune ever produced was a pensive hum.

By the end of the day, Nevian's head throbbed from the research and his fingers cramped from all the runes he'd drawn, but when he stared at the one translating the rekhemal's power, he grasped its parts. He could tell the repetition of the enhancement triangles signalled a powerful increase in ability, and their repetition on the outer edges of the Body and Mind forms meant a casting outward of them. It was growing late, his eyes burned, and he wistfully wondered if Vellien would be in their quarters, but Brune had him run through the explanation one last time before they concluded.

When he finished, Varden—whose main participation today had been to force food and water on Nevian—retrieved the rekhemal and brushed his fingers against it.

"So this rune … is the arcane equivalent of the rekhemal?" he asked.

Nevian grinned at him, ready to confirm, but Brune cut him off.

"No. It's an interpretation of it."

"A portrait." Varden tapped his sketchbook.

"Indeed. That is a very grounded imagery. What we have built today is a reference that Nevian can use. Tomorrow, we will need to use it and create a different piece—one you and I will collaborate to reintegrate into the rekhemal itself." She turned to Nevian. "I recommend you rest early. These runes are how you access the world and change it. The best wizards can evoke them with a few key movements without even drawing them. Use a tool often enough and it becomes second nature."

She snapped her fingers and glinting rocks grew over her nails. Nevian frowned. For a brief instant, brown threads had shimmered to life around her hands, entirely unfamiliar to any arcane magic he'd manipulated before, but so much closer to the sharp energy Varden's fire emanated.

"But you cheat," he protested. "That was divine magic."

Brune's eyebrows shot up, and she rose. "Was it now? I suppose you'd know better than I would."

She bowed her head, and her whole body turned into friable

earth then dust, collapsing on the ground before sinking into the wooden floor. Nevian gaped, his initial rush of fear quickly turning into wonder.

"Now I understand why you risked everything to meet her."

"She's a good mentor."

"She is both straightforward and needlessly dramatic," Varden countered with a smirk. "Let's get some rest."

They had long since gone their separate ways by the time Nevian understood Varden had implied he, too, was straightforward and needlessly dramatic. Too late for a retort, but that did not stop Nevian from mulling over one all the way to his door. The strange sight awaiting him there turned the tides of his thoughts, however.

A pile of beautiful leather-bound books had been left for him, tied with a bow. Nevian counted five, each of them an enviable thickness and devoid of title, all with a different shade of leather. A silvery silken rope held them together, and on top of it rested five ink bottles of matching colours, set in a wooden holder. This one had a gigantic pink bow on top, and a scroll had been tied to it. Nevian approached, intrigued. Someone had put a lot of time into this, and while everything pointed towards a gift, he had a hard time believing it. No one made him gifts like that.

The scroll didn't lie, however. The wax sealing it held the Enezi seal—one Nevian had most often seen as an embossed header to important magical treaties on transmutations than he had in wax, especially addressed to him. This wasn't from Master Enezi but from his obnoxious daughter, who had insisted on hanging around him for two years and only learned not to annoy him over the last few days. Books, though... She was learning fast. Nevian broke the seal and unfurled the message.

Practised with Jilssan today. We changed simple properties in objects, so I made this for you! A powerful wizard needs spellbooks to write in, and the coolest ink to go with them.

She hadn't even signed it properly. Typical. Instead of irritation, however, a wave of fondness crested at the thought. Nevian crouched by the books, set the inks aside, and undid the knot in the silk rope. He ran his hands over the dark green leather of the top book before cracking it open and inhaling the delightful scent of old books. He stared at the empty pages, waiting for him to fill them with notes and runes and hypotheses. A future for him to write, if he survived—one Isra did not seem to doubt for a second.

CHAPTER EIGHTEEN

TEP. Step. Swing. Step. Swing again—left, then right. Arathiel's sword connected with the training dummy, again and again, the sharp *thwack* marking the cadence of his training. He kept his eyes locked on the target and his focus on his body, tuning his senses towards every hint that made it through the numbness—the strain of muscles, the slight pressure under his bare feet, the tilt in his body as balance shifted. It was different than *before*, he knew it on an instinctive level, years of practice as House Brasten's swordmaster drilled into his muscle memory. But the Well had stolen that before, and he could no longer count on it. He needed to keep his skill sharp and understand himself *now*, so he'd established regular practice session within the Brasten training hall.

A century had changed the room, its old wooden panelling walls gone, giving way to a maize-coloured stone engraved with pale blue designs, yet something in the room's energy had remained through the decades. It sank in him, familiar and motivating, calming the nerves he'd come here to evacuate. Every day spent in the Brasten Tower ratcheted his tension, prompting him to pace long circles in his room or on the roof above. It helped, for a time, but the stress returned, nodes lining up against his spine as events unfurled, bringing them ever closer to a serious confrontation.

He would be ready when his turn came. One step at a time. One swing at a time. Arathiel pushed himself through another routine, speeding his footwork despite the limited feedback, spinning and—

His sword whacked against the wooden shaft of a spear, startling him, and he jumped back. Amake Brasten faced him, her elaborate dresses traded for simple cotton clothes hanging freely around her body and a sturdy pair of boots scuffed several times over. His eyebrows shot up, half-surprise and half a question. She grinned at him, spun the spear, and brought it back in a ready position—an invitation of her own.

"With pleasure," he said, and he leaped into the match.

Arathiel started slow, taking the measure of his adversary. Amake had already proved formidable in verbal sparring, and he refused to underestimate her. He tested her defence, chaining a handful of strikes and feints, and she matched him with ease, parrying every attempt. Every time he plunged closer, she slid back, her footwork quick and secure. Inevitably, Arathiel studied her technique—how she used her weight to absorb his more powerful blows with ease, the weight transfer as she shifted to the offensive, the grip on her shaft and the areas of his body she aimed for with her jabs. She was fluid, well trained, and determined—and after the initial trading of blows, his critical swordmaster eye faded and he let himself enjoy the sparring match.

He'd not had a partner since before leaving for the Well, and the melody of blades felt both old and new—familiar in its rhythm, yet both muted and more urgent than ever. Arathiel's movements had lost a lot of his ancient subtlety—a talent for grace and minuscule shifts that had earned him his reputation as a battle prodigy—but some instincts never vanished. Amake held her own, sweat beading on her brow and running down her neck, and when their gazes met across weapons, she grinned at him, fire in her eyes. She launched herself at him, her spear bending and curving and stabbing with slender power as she strained his defences. He laughed, breathless, as he barely knocked her latest strike aside.

"You're good," he said, "but are you good enough? Surely you've read my history."

"I have." She followed the matter-of-fact statement with a jab directly at his head, forcing him to dodge aside. "According to it, you used to spar with Kellian Dathirii."

"Few others could keep me on my toes."

A hint of smugness slipped into his voice, surprising even himself. It was a memory of who he'd been, confident to the point of bluster, so convinced his skill with a sword could get him anywhere and anything—including a cure for his sister's illness. Back then, he had welcomed all challengers, but only the older, more experienced Dathirii guard had managed to knock him down a peg. And for all of his youthful arrogance, Arathiel had recognized the opportunity to learn.

"I think it's time you started again,"

Amake timed her words with a new series of offensive jabs, forcing Arathiel to dodge and spin, straining the limits of his balance. His entire focus went into the dance, the timing of his feet on the ground, the shifts in his weight he struggled to perceive. More than once, he saw a chance to reverse the flow—an opening he could slip into, flip from defensive to offensive, force *her* to parry his strikes—but this was better exercise than he'd ever come up on his own. Arathiel had no interested in a win if it deprived him of practice that might save his life later on.

Amake focused on the fight for a time, leaning into the exercise with obvious enthusiasm. He hoped she wasn't pushing her body too far but withheld any comment. She was more than capable of handling her own limits. For all that she enjoyed the sparring, however, she'd obviously come to talk and broke off after a particularly vicious exchange.

"We need to know the extent of his newfound powers, and he needs practice with them. I daresay you'll find yourself on your toes once again."

"Oh, I don't need convincing," Arathiel said, "but isn't he under arrest?"

"Aren't *you*, after a fashion?" she countered with a smirk. "We'll arrange supervision, but as long as this happens within my walls…"

Her dismissive gesture said it all. Arathiel suspected it'd best happen away from Sora's gaze, if only for plausible deniability, but he'd let her handle the politics.

"So you want us to train…"

"And if he happens to open up about his time in Brune's captivity or the nature of their arrangements, all the better."

Arathiel laughed. There it was. "Sure. I'll spy for you if you free him up." He didn't expect Kellian to share anything he'd not want repeated. They had never been that close.

Amake's mouth quirked into a smile quickly growing familiar to him, self-satisfied, shameless, and amused all at once. Her victory smile. She brought her spear at the ready again with a defiant sweep. "Shall we go again, then?"

They continued sparring for another hour, a comfortable back and forth with the occasional pauses to catch their breath. Arathiel began to exploit Amake's repeated mistakes halfway through—a technique she spotted immediately, only to demand he show her what she was doing wrong. They fell into an easy rhythm of matches and exercises, and Arathiel forgot about the world for a time.

Amake, however, clearly never did. Not even in the middle of a sparring match, weapons clashing as they pushed at each other's defences. He should have known, perhaps, that her best weapon would always be her words.

"I trust you've received news from Hasryan?" she asked, right after he'd dodged a nasty blow.

His heart slammed against his rib and panic flooded through him—how did she know? Sora had told him, of course, but— Before he could finish his thought, her spear swept his feet, stealing his already precarious balance. He fell hard on his back, the wind knocked from his lungs. Arathiel rolled to the side, bringing his sword to bear as he rose, the hilt catching her next strike. He held steady, one knee on the ground, halfway up, and met her eyes.

"That almost worked."

"It did." She stepped back and set the butt of her spear on the ground. "You wrongly assume my main objective was touching you."

The knots of fear returned to his stomach. She'd always known he valued Hasryan, so why bring him up now? Arathiel waited, his breath heavy. If Amake wanted something from him, she wouldn't waste his time. Amake lowered her spear back into ready position again. Her own chest heaved with slow, deep breaths.

"Have you told Diel yet?"

Arathiel eyebrows shot up. At a loss for an answer, he dashed forward and pressed a series of attack, focusing on her lower right, where she'd struggled to parry before—and indeed, she grimaced as he forced her to step back and spin away, unable to keep her grounds. He wondered what her underlying goal was. Did she want confirmation Diel had involved himself with Hasryan, or did she already know and wanted to test what Arathiel would readily reveal?

"Diel Dathirii has always known where my allegiances lie and was the first to disregard them."

Amake found her footing, then caught his downward swing with the shaft of her spear, leaning forward. Her voice dropped as she got close.

"Disregard or employ?"

Arathiel pressed his lips together. He trusted her, but this was not his secret to share. He held the position steady for a few seconds, then pushed her back and disengaged. "If you need Hasryan for something…"

"I might." She set the butt of the spear on the ground, signalling an end to their sparring match. "Thank you for the exercise, Arathiel. It was quite refreshing."

Their conversation stayed with him long past the end of his training. He didn't mind Amake putting one and one together when it came to Hasryan's involvement in their group, but he could not help but worry about who else would start to see the threads connecting them all, a quiet network of friends and allies building around Hasryan, keeping him safe.

Sooner or later, the one asking questions would come with ill intent. They needed to be ready.

Chapter Nineteen

"THERE'S something fishy about this Sora, sister, and I will find it."

Drake slipped one arm through his winter's coat sleeve, grimacing through the pain. In other circumstances, Mia would have been more sympathetic to his pain, but her ever-headstrong brother had hopped out of bed against every healer's orders. Not even their magic could erase all the damage of a crushed ribcage.

"It can wait," she said as he buttoned up. "You need more rest."

Ugly splotches of red rose to his cheeks. He snatched his rapier from where it lay in a pile of bag, clothes, and other miscellany the staff no longer bothered to clean, and he tied the belt with angry, jerking movements. Hiding his shame under bluster, as usual. He certainly would not meet her eyes, no matter how hard she tried.

"I'm not *waiting*. Father is in prison and the House is in complete disarray. I have to do something."

Mia resisted the urge to roll her eyes. Father was under house arrest, at best, and she had no doubts Lady Brasten treated him a thousand times better than he had those who'd just escaped from their own cells. Plus, every aunt and uncle had swarmed in as soon as the news had spread, splitting the leadership between themselves—and bickering about it—leaving nothing for Mia. She hadn't been able to protest. The exhaustion from that first day had wiped her out, and she'd needed to recover. Pushing herself *then* would have ensured she'd struggle to keep the pace for far longer.

Not that she felt particularly useful here, trying to convince Drake not to rush headlong into another ill-conceived decision.

"And that 'something' should be planned, Drake. We need to think carefully about our next move."

He snorted, and finally dared to meet her eyes, chin tilted up. "I have a plan. You'd have me sit until every detail is hammered out and our chance to act would be long gone. I'm not like you, Mia. I don't like idling."

Anger devoured her next words, every inch of her energy redirected into maintaining her façade and swallowing her hurt. Of course he thought of rest as idling and a waste—and associated both with her. That he also considered her a thorough planner only showed how little he knew and would have been funny on most days, but she had no patience for it now.

She left his quarters, frustrated and at a loss about the next step, only to spot Yultes coming down the stairs to the audience hall—a frazzled Yultes, in crumpled clothes and with deep creases under his eyes. It seemed the last few days in the Dathirii Tower had not been kinder to him than her own here. Mia tightened her grip on her cane and sped up.

"Master Yultes!" she called out, and he stopped at her voice, leaning closer to the stairs' railing to look down at her. Even with the open space separating them, his smile was unmistakable and genuine. She replied in kind. "I had not expected to see you within our halls."

He bowed and started down the steps. "I've made proper introductions between our new liaison, Master Jayna Dathirii, and your aunt. I believe they are going over the matter of guards and accounting?"

By the lilt in his voice, he'd love to do the same. Mia motioned in the general direction of her own quarters. "A tedious subject, I'm sure, but if you have time for some tea, I may provide more entertaining conversation."

"I have a limited amount, but I'll gladly accept this invitation."

If her eyes did not deceive her, he had an extra spring in his steps as he descended the rest of the way. In all honesty, she found herself looking forward to it, too, her prior frustration washed away by the prospect of an agreeable time with an old friend and a key player in these events. It had been difficult to track the results of putting him in contact with Branwen, but judging by the rumours of Hellion's disastrous reception, she hadn't misjudged her target. She signalled to a servant to prepare them tea, but otherwise waited for them both to reach her quarters and be truly alone.

"You look troubled," she said.

A sharp laugh escaped him and he rubbed his face. "That obvious, is it?"

"I'm an acute observer." She motioned for the seats but did not wait for him to move before settling into her own. Her leg muscles had been building a low scream of pain over the last hour, and the instant relief drew a groan out of her. Mia closed her eyes and leaned back. A dull throb still reverberated through her body, from deep within her bones, but this was already better. "Apologies if I am not the best company today. The offer for great conversation may have been a lure."

"Then you must have had something in mind to bait me so."

He sat across from her in a rustle of clothes, but she didn't open her eyes to meet his gaze. She could feel it on her nonetheless. "Nothing so specific, I'm afraid." Or it had slipped her mind, drowned by the thud at the base of her skull. "I suppose I wanted to clear the air. Play cards on the table, as they say."

Silence stretched between them—either Yultes glaring at her, or considering her words. Perhaps she *should* look at him, to get a better sense of his mood, to be careful, but she did not think it necessary. Strange as it was, she had always felt safe enough around him to drop her guard.

"I would like that very much," he said softly.

The problem, of course, was that one of them needed to take the plunge in order to clear the air, and Mia was no good at it. She had learned to keep her heart close early on in life, concealing her joy and anger as often as she concealed her pain. She may not need to actively hide herself to the same extent around Yultes, but to bring forward more vulnerable parts felt like another matter entirely. Yultes did not provide any words of his own, perhaps equally at a loss of where to start. She opened her eyes to study him again despite the harsh light threatening her with a headache.

"Every day I live under my Father's rule, I chafe at the expectations of meekness set upon me. My ideas and dreams rarely align with his, and my voice is disregarded at every turn. But I have built my own life out of their sight, and they will not stop me forever."

No surprise touched Yultes' expression. He was looking away from her, ostensibly towards the windows, but Mia suspected his attention was turned inwards. His lips pressed into a tight line.

"What if they try?"

"They will."

All her family would, if she made a move for leadership. She'd yet to form a plan for the specifics of it. The Allastam soldiers were far more dedicated to her father and Drake than her, and most of her relatives would have her hauled up to her quarters 'for her own good'. Mia Allastam had no plans yet, but she had allies, within the staff and outside, and one day she would see her opportunity. Until then, however, she meant to nudge what she could in the right direction.

Yultes perked at the certainty in her voice and finally fixed his pale eyes on her, a small girl sitting straight despite the pain in her back and the fatigue in her bones. Frail, despite her best wishes, despite her resolve not to let it stop her.

"I can only admire how well you know yourself."

His voice wavered before he finished the sentence, snagging on the ocean of feelings she heard roiling inside. Did he imagine himself lost at sea, then, while she had her feet on firm land?

"I think you know yourself better than you give yourself credit for."

It dragged a laugh from him. "Do I? I have been—Well. You connected me with Branwen, so I must assume you are well aware that I've been …" He trailed off, as if he could not bring himself to voice his allegiances aloud. "Yet it brings me no joy, to do this, and no sense of rightfulness. Every new betrayal leaves me more wretched. He trusts me—loves me."

"Love."

Mia repeated the word, bitterness on her tongue. It had been wielded as a weapon against her too often, the source of endless justifications. *I do this because I love you, Mia, to protect you.* Always, always, they set her aside out of love—trapped her, ignored her, diminished her—all out of love.

"Love is not pure in and of itself, as many tales would have us believe. People can love you wrong. They can love their idea of you—and if that is who they are enamoured with, are you really betraying anything?" She waved at the air as if chasing a stink. "Have you told Hellion you disapproved of his path? Of his ideals? How did *that* go?"

Yultes flinched as if she'd struck him, and that was all the answer she needed. He squeezed his eyes shut, shoulders hunched, as if he needed a moment to process his own reaction. It was strange, to watch the guilt ebb away from his grimace, drop by drop, until a grim determination remained.

"Thank you, Mia." He unfurled from his chair with renewed energy. "I must go. Our new coinmaster, Iriel Dathirii, insists on seeing the books before your people arrive. Unfortunately, someone left us with very limited time to plan our counter move."

His mouth quirked into a smirk, and she replied in kind. "Never renege an opportunity to improvise."

Polite society would have her stand to wish him a good day, but she could not care less. If anything, Mia sank deeper into her chair as he headed for the door. Yultes stopped with his hand on the handle.

"You should call on me tomorrow night. For tea, of course. And perhaps, one day, I will be in a position to return the favour."

Mia saw no favour to return, but she caught the amused lilt in Yultes' tone as he mentioned tea. He had something else in mind than quiet conversation, and she was eager to find out what.

CHAPTER TWENTY

HASRYAN regretted knocking on Sora's door the moment his knuckles rapped against the wood. He had no business coming here, at the risk of ruining everything she'd accomplished, but inside this flat lived the one person he was desperate to talk to. With Sora busy getting Lord Allastam's ass nailed for his crimes, he had his chance.

Warmth slid from the slight crack in the door and Hasryan huddled closer, flashing a smile at Camilla's gentle surprise. "May I?"

"Of course," she said, throwing the door wide open and stepping aside. "Sora's not home."

Hasryan slipped inside and shut the door behind him, cutting off the cold breeze. His hand flew to his chest and hovered above his heart. "I'm wounded you think I came for her."

Camilla's smile was honey through his veins, sweet and warm and reassuring. It soothed more aches than he was willing to admit, even though he'd come exactly for that. She brought wrinkled fingers over her own heart, mimicking his gesture.

"I implied no such things, dear. Quite the contrary."

Even with her clue, Hasryan needed a moment to understand she meant he could talk freely, without worry of what anyone but her might say or think. Did she already know what had happened? Before he could bring the question up, a grey blur zoomed at the edge of his vision, a sleek feline body slipping between chair legs as it rushed towards him with an interrogative *hrm?* Kirio didn't leap *on* him, however, instead pouncing on a long pole wrapped in rope long frayed by the assault of his claws. He climbed with equal speed, stopping as abruptly as he'd come once level with Hasryan's head. Feline eyes met his, black pupils wide, then Kirio leaned towards him, stretching the whole of his body and posing there, expectant.

"Kiss his nose," Camilla said. "It's the only proper greeting."

Hasryan's gaze flicked between her and the tiny grey snout awaiting his blessing, and he laughed. It was such an absurd thing, yet he couldn't help but image Sora walking home day after day, to be greeted by the speedy trample of her grey fur ball across the little flat and the incessant demand for love. Warmth unfurled in his chest like a thousand tiny sprouts and he bent forward to land a peck on Kirio's nose. The cat rewarded him with another happy rumble before climbing all the way up, and ... vanishing into the ceiling? No, not quite. Now that Hasryan paid attention to it, Sora's 'ceiling' was not full at all. It was, in fact, a mix of glass platforms, long walkways, baskets and other beds, as well as long square planks with the occasional in them. One to two feet of space separated the arrangement from the actual ceiling—ample space for Kirio.

"And she's surprised he's such a sneak," Hasryan commented.

"You'd get along," Camilla said. "He loves to watch when I'm in the kitchen. Look."

She pointed at a glass layer lower than the others, then traced a path from it to the shelves forming a staircase to the counter. Kirio had made his way to the glass, exposing pale toe beans to the world as he watched them.

"Should I expect cat hair in the next cookie batch?"

"He's never come that close. I think the ceiling satisfies him."

A feeling Hasryan easily understood. He had spent large chunks of his life keeping a wall at his back or seeking perches where he'd have a good view of the room. Always on the lookout for aggression. Always ready to bolt. The Shelter and the Crescent Moon hideout had been rare locations where he hadn't felt the need for such caution. With time, that had also become true of Camilla's quarters.

"I'll get a proper welcome too, won't I?" Camilla asked.

"A peck on the nose?"

Her melodious laugh filled the room. "If that is what you're willing to give, I will accept, but this old lady was daydreaming about a last hug, while she still could."

Hasryan had begun pulling off his thin gloves and boots, but he froze at her last words. "While you still can?"

The question came out more strangled than he'd intended. Of course she knew that his time in Isandor was fading, grains of salt slipping through an hourglass, but to hear her acknowledgement of it reopened the wound anew.

"I'll be moving into the Brasten Tower later today," she said, thwarting his expectations. Even with his eyes firmly on his boots and the puddle forming under them, Hasryan heard the sad smile in her voice. "We've not made a secret of my presence here, but with the Golden Table approaching, we think it's best if I leave Sora's immediate vicinity. It is hard to convince anyone she is unbiased while housing a Dathirii."

No way he could visit over there. He hated it, pragmatic though it was. This sort necessary secrecy was exactly why he refused to stay in Isandor. He couldn't live forever as everyone's secret, always hiding and sneaking, one misstep away from a scandal. With a heavy sigh, Hasryan removed the rest of his boots and set them to the side. When he straightened up, Camilla was waiting for him with open arms and raised eyebrows.

All Hasryan had to do was take that one step forward. Just a step, a sliding of his body, a shift in his weight. Yet his throat closed, and he found he did not know how to move in this way yet, how to be *casual* about it. Camilla's expression softened, the teasing smile turning into a sad recognition, and she closed the gap herself, putting a hand on his shoulder, her longer fingers applying pressure on his back. He let it guide him, leaning towards her, closing his eyes as she enveloped him in tender, lavender-scented warmth.

After that, they fell into comforting patterns: Camilla shared bits of her life while preparing a batch of tea and providing another plate of cookies for them to consume. She had visited some of her regulars again, helping to clean their houses or bring groceries over—a task that grew more essential as days with high winds and frozen bridges multiplied. Esmera had quite a range of complaints about the weather, but she'd also asked after Hasryan. It seemed she'd been thrilled for him to 'throw the whole city into chaos again', as she'd put it. And he had a reward: a pair of mittens of the same deep red as the scarf he'd left at Cal's. His throat tightened as he ran fingers over them and he garbled some rough thanks.

Camilla indulged his messy feelings by not poking at them, giving him the space to digest the new kindness. She led the topic elsewhere, narrating with great enthusiasm her walk with a grumpy old man—one she'd been with when she'd first met Arathiel, it seemed—and Hasryan let the quiet rhythm of her words wash over him, lulling him into a false sense of security. Then Camilla cut her story short.

"Oh, but listen to me rambling." Camilla set her teacup down and met Hasryan's gaze. Something sharp glinted in her eyes—his only warning sign. "I'm sure you had something in mind when you came here. You've had such a difficult few days."

The opening shouldn't have felt like such an attack, but Hasryan's chest tightened, his breath suddenly short. He squeezed his teacup as his defensive smirk returned in full force. "First you imply I come for Sora, and now that I have secret motives?"

"It's not a secret motive to seek advice or comfort from trusted family."

The word 'family' dropped right as he was pushing off the ground to get on the chair's hind leg. He shoved with far too much force, swung overboard, and flew out of the chair, hitting the ground on his back. Amidst the clattering, he caught Camilla's stunned "Oh!" then her stifled laugh. His back hurt where the wooden chair had dug into it and new pain lanced through his arm, but he managed to a chuckle alongside her.

"Words are a weapon," he said.

"And my best one," Camilla agreed. She sipped her tea, never getting up to help him. "But in this case, I mean only to defeat the demons in your head, if there are any. It's an offer, Hasryan. An open door."

He knew that, but struggled to accept it in a more visceral way. Hasryan picked himself up, scooped up the thankfully unbroken teacup, set the chair right once again, and settled into it. An open door. He ran a hand through his hair and a breathless chuckle escaped him.

"You've lived a long time. Bet you captured your fair share of hearts through the decades."

Her melodious laugh filled the room, frank and sudden. Camilla needed a minute to get it under control, but she eventually managed, fingers over her lips.

"You flatter an old lady," she said, her eyes twinkling. "But you're quite right. Are those the stories you wish to hear? Because I assure you, there are many—two brilliant trickster girls, a mild-mannered butter maker who had the most incredible talent in bed, a sailor who dropped by every other month, Garith's grandfather… I've loved and dated across the whole spectrum of gender and lived some fantastic experiences, in and out of bed. I wouldn't say I did it all, but I certainly covered some ground."

Heat burned Hasryan's cheeks. He hadn't expected Camilla to bluntly mention her sex life like this! Yet it helped, that she'd disclosed so much all at once without the slightest hint of shame or regret. Those couldn't have all been perfect experiences.

"Th-that's good, I suppose. It's just that I…" Did he even want to bring Sora up, in her own house, while she wasn't there? It felt like a betrayal. But Camilla was right. He'd come because he had too much roiling in his mind and while she couldn't fix all his problems, she might ease this one. "I don't know what to do with myself anymore. I think I messed it up with Sora."

Camilla filled his cup again and leaned forward. Listening, silent, and open. Hasryan cleared his throat and took the plunge. He explained, as best as he could, what had happened with Sora, his sentences strings of broken and confused fragments, his words escaping him more often than not. He didn't know how to describe the mix of thrill and confusion and fear storming inside of him, how even now, he wished he'd kissed her longer, or at least responded, but the thought of everything else around—a romantic relationship? Love with the big L?—paralyzed him. Those fears he kept close to his heart, however, brushing it all under a generous 'I panicked' immediately followed by 'everything's ruined now' even though he truly didn't know whether that was a good or bad thing.

Camilla let him unwind everything bouncing in his head, interrupting only to advise he set down the teacup as he grew more agitated, and once he ran out, deflated, she leaned forward and put her pale wrinkled hand over his darker skin.

"You set a healthy boundary. Sora accepted it. It sounds to me like the two of you are working out what you can and cannot be, according to your respective situations and needs." She squeezed his hand. "Feelings are spiky, hurtful things. It sounds to me like you're handling yours with care to avoid further injury. No sense in adding scars, after all."

They both knew his heart was riddled with them. Hasryan hunched his shoulders, mulling over her words and the rest of his night with Sora. It had been peaceful and simple. They'd both acted like nothing was amiss. Maybe *everything* wasn't ruined.

"Do you think I'll ever be ready? Would I even know?"

"I'm afraid that is for you to discover, Hasryan." She released his hand after one last squeeze and leaned back. "Chances are you'll make mistakes, no matter how careful, but they don't need to be the end of the world. You're in charge of what you risk and when."

He smirked, then, because that was her way of hinting that he might have been a little overdramatic. And maybe he'd been; it *had* felt like the world ending, even if the rest of his night with Sora had disproved that. These particular demons felt calmer—dormant, most likely, until he poked them next. Hasryan leaned back into his chair, kicking it off its hind legs.

"Good talk, good talk." His exaggerated casualness wouldn't fool anyone, but Camilla allowed him to bring the topic to a close. "Need any help with dinner? Something to slice into tiny pieces? I have a lot of energy to burn."

She set him up with thick cut of beef—from the chuck, or so she'd said—to cut down into small cubes, promising carrots and potatoes could come next, if he wanted. He set to work, happy to have something to busy his hands and mind, and Camilla started her stories where she'd left them earlier. They fell into a familiar rhythm, a calming reminder of his days hiding in her quarters. Kirio perched on the nearby shelves, sometimes stretching his neck to sniff at the air. He never snatched at any pieces, though. How different from all the street cats Hasryan had frequented in his youth, as desperate for a meal as he'd been. Hasryan sliced a thin piece off and leaned towards him conspiratorially.

"I'll give it to you if you don't tell your mom," he whispered.

Kirio's ears perked up and Hasryan's grin widened—until the cat's head snapped towards the door and he fled up the shelves and to his roof with an interrogative rumble. Alarm shot through Hasryan and his grip tightened on the bloodied knife.

Someone hammered on the door. The sort of loud knocks Hasryan associated with guards, more a warning that they'd destroy the door than an ask to be let in. Camilla paled as she stood up, her fingers trailing on the table. Every smash of fists worsened the lump of panic in Hasryan's throat, but his muscles moved of their own, years of practice kicking in. He followed Kirio up, grabbing thin shelves to lift himself up to the ceiling and squeezing himself in the tight space. The platforms creaked as he crawled towards one of the many glass panels.

They smashed the door in as he reached it.

Drake Allastam strode in, flanked by two goons in his house's colours. Snow gusted inside after them, but they didn't bother closing the door, surveying the area as if they owned it. Hasryan gripped his knife so hard his knuckles ached. Everything had started with this jerk harassing Larryn, with a single headbutt, and it was all Hasryan could do not to drop on him now.

"What are *you* doing here?" Drake asked, a finger pointed towards Camilla. A self-satisfied chuckle escaped him. "Always knew this Sora Sharpe was full of lies."

The two Allastam guards stepped forward, responding to the obvious aggression in their lord's voice. Camilla's figure drew up, her chin lifting in defiance. Hasryan couldn't see her expression from above, but the pride of her posture warmed his heart.

"Lord Drake Allastam." She greeted him with a brief curtsy, but every word held a steel edge. Hasryan braced himself for impact. "I must say, I am surprised to see you barge into someone's home like a vulgar thug. It's quite unbecoming."

As she stepped forward, a quiet war waged inside Hasryan between his desire to listen to her cut Drake into ribbons one sentence at a time and a visceral fear for her safety. From further up in the ceiling, Kirio let out a worried rumble. Camilla either did not share their fear or hid it perfectly under her poise.

"You have no right to be here," she said, "and if you think I'll let you rifle through Investigator Sora Sharpe's home because you brought beefcakes along, you're sorely mistaken."

An angry red stained Drake's cheeks. He closed in, a step away from Camilla, his two brutes on each side. "Stop me with what? Titles you don't hold anymore? Your big muscles?" He snorted. "I don't care what you or anyone in your piss family wants, hag—"

The sharp crack of Camilla's slap silenced the room, and Hasryan's world slowed down to crystallize the moment: Drake's stunned expression as he jerked back, Camilla's huff, Kirio darting away in a scramble of claws. The two guards' protest—a cry and a grunt—as they moved in unison, one pushing Drake protectively back while the other shoved Camilla.

Time snapped back to regular speed as she crashed into the table. Its legs scraped against the floor, the grind ringing in Hasryan's ears and covering startled cry as she tried to catch herself. She hit the ground instead and the guard snatched her extended wrist. Hasryan's stomach clenched, panic flooding in every muscle.

"She *slapped* me!"

Incredulity coloured his voice, but Hasryan heard something far more dangerous under it: wounded pride, and a promise the insult would not go unanswered. Anger contorted Drake's face. His chest heaved, a hitch in his breathing, and his fingers rested where Kellian's stone had pierced him. This slap, it occurred to Hasryan, was the second humiliation he suffered at the hands of a Dathirii recently, all in front of Allastam guards.

They yanked Camilla up and she huffed again as she landed on her feet, her hair escaping in wild strands to form a silver crown.

"How uncouth," she said, centuries of dignity filling her voice with such power the two guards shrunk away, barely holding on to her.

The warm pride within Hasryan tightened into an unbearable ache. He loved her. Loved her kindness and wisdom, loved her strength of character and clarity of purpose, loved how she dominated the room with her presence—and he could not stay hidden and watch Drake hurt her.

Hasryan pushed to the side, squeezing himself between his lower platform and the second layer of cat maze, then off the ceiling entirely. He twisted midair as if he was just another feline, getting his feet under him and the knife at the ready as he dropped right by Drake. Terror flashed through the young man's eyes as Hasryan unfurled, slapping a hand over his mouth to stop any scream, then spun around the noble to get behind. He brought his knife about as he did, placing the blade against his victim's throat. The two guards had barely started turning by the time he got into position. Hasryan winked at them.

"If you don't mind, I'll be taking this one with me."

He hurried back, dragging Drake along with him and out into Isandor's freezing winter. Cold gusts hit him in full force as he stepped onto the icy bridges and snow seeped into his socks. Guards came rushing out after them, and Hasryan prayed they wouldn't notice how underdressed he was, wouldn't realize he'd been relaxing in Sora's home by the boots in the entrance and his coat on the hanger. How foolish. He should never have let his guard down like that, never allowed himself such a sense of security. But now his best chance was to keep them too occupied.

"Tell them to stay back," he told Drake, releasing his mouth but placing his hand next to his newly healed wound.

"I'll kill you," Drake said instead.

"They might," Hasryan agreed, "but *you* will be long gone, throat slit and body falling down a couple bridges."

Hasryan kept backing away, one step at a time, Drake held firmly in his arms. He wondered how that looked, with the beef's blood already on the blade. It would be so easy, to add Drake's to it. A flick of the wrist, a movement practised dozens—hundreds, perhaps—of times, as natural to him as breathing. What was one more death to his name?

But this would be personal, a death *in* his name, and there had only ever been two of those—his first at his mother's betrayal, and the second when he chose Brune over her partner and his boss, Enmaris. Two people he had loved, in their own way. Drake did not deserve to be with them—even Lord Allastam hadn't, but there had been necessity then, the fear rippling in Larryn's voice carrying him forward as he'd climbed the Allastam Tower.

Hasryan set a first step on a set of stairs, pulling Drake up with him. The young noble fought back with invectives and fists, but Hasryan pressed his fingers into his wound, shutting him up. He didn't need that noise right now. The cold had infiltrated his very bones, his toes freezing more with every second. He didn't know how long he could keep his body from violent shudders or his grip from slipping. Every gust of wind snapped at his clothes, slipping icy air within. He needed to make a break for it and hope they'd follow.

When he'd put a dozen steps between him and the two Allastam guards, he pushed Drake down at them, hitting the back of his head with the knife's hilt on the way. He sprinted up the rest of the way as Drake fell, the sudden burst of action pushing some warmth into his toes as he dashed away. The alarmed exclamations and crash behind him were the only signs his plan had worked, but he couldn't afford to relish that victory.

He sprinted across slippery bridges, turned around a tower to cut line of sight, then latched to its wall and climbed down, wet socks sliding on the stone, his frozen fingers almost relinquishing his grip more than once. He shimmied closer to the next bridge, two levels down, and managed to set foot on it as the angry boots of his pursuer passed above. Hasryan released a shaky breath, allowing himself a few precious seconds to recover. He hoped they'd look for him long enough for Camilla to get to safety. Nothing else mattered—not his body shaking with the crash of adrenaline or the cold snaking into every inch of it, not the inevitable consequences of his actions. Whatever happened now, he'd have no regrets as long as she was safe.

Chapter Twenty-One

NEARLY half of Nevian's life had consisted of a difficult grind to master new magical knowledge in unfavourable conditions, and still he struggled with the gruelling process of building a rune to integrate into the rekhemal's. Brune had him run through different drafts, adding one layer after another, forcing him to justify every line he placed down. At first, he hesitated at every step, memories of similar exercises Master Avenazar had used to humiliate him still fresh in his mind. Varden encouraged him, a gentle reminder that he'd escaped those times and wasn't alone, not anymore. And as he got over that first hurdle, Nevian gained in confidence with every new attempt—even if most were wrong. Brune corrected him, direct but never unkind, leading his way through several iterations and solidifying the knowledge he'd cobbled together.

Despite the hardships, constructing the rekhemal's reversal rune was the easiest part of the day. Nevian thrived on mental challenges. The difficulties had only brought satisfaction, and he'd felt as if he was constructing a puzzle from scratch, one piece at a time. He loved the result, a perfect circle embedded with an 'x', along which lines new patterns grew according to their desires. This beautiful rune was his future.

"Take a break," Brune had said. "Eat something, too. You'll need every ounce of energy this afternoon."

When he'd returned, she was waiting for him with several runes already drawn, most of them simpler versions of their final sigil.

"Theory's only good if you can put it into action."

Nevian grimaced. He'd always struggled more with the actual *casting* part of spellcraft. Still, he set to work without complaint, activating each rune provided by Brune one after the other, using appropriate words and gestures. She corrected Nevian's motions and pronunciations over and over until he began to wonder if it wouldn't be simpler to cast with smells and tastes. Any sense could be used in theory—some were just more reproducible than others. Brune must have judged his reproduction inadequate, though, because despite the dark blue shine of the runes every time he cast, she had him do it again, and again, and again.

Magic tingled through his body, stronger with every new attempt, a growing buzz that left him feeling both hyperaware and numb to the world around. He touched power with every activation, pushing it into the rune's lines—his tools—and bending the magic of the world with it. He created a shimmering cage of pure force, filled the library with a sharp tang scent, snuffed all candles then relit them. On and on he went, repeating the maneuvers, power coursing through him, but still it wasn't enough for Brune. She pushed him until his skin grew so sensitive the clothes burned it and the light streaming through windows threatened him with a migraine.

"You feel it now, don't you?" Her words hammered against his skull. He held himself tight, every inch of his body brimming with power and hurting from the effort to contain it. "How long has it been since you last cast a spell, Nevian?"

"The scrying." The two words ripped at his throat. He didn't look at Brune.

"And before?"

"Defending … against Avenazar. Winter solstice."

She sighed and placed a different rune in front of him. A perfect, empty circle.

"Activate this one."

The sink. He'd seen it drawn in theory books. Circular runes could absorb magic and a perfect circle often served as a way to contain overflow. Nevian placed his hand above and released his power. It slid out of him brutally, a flow of magic pouring out of his muscles and head and mind in an indistinct blue wave and sinking into the drawn circle. Black stains crept across Nevian's vision. He tried to catch the table but couldn't feel it under his palms, couldn't feel anything, really.

A chair of stone formed around him, soft sand cushioning his fall. Why was he sitting? Nevian shook his head, trying to clear the disorientation. He must have fainted. Brune watched him in silence.

The magic, right. Nevian exhaled slowly and waited, curled on himself, for her to scold him on his weakness.

"This is why regular practice matters." Her tone surprised him. She sounded … concerned? "Complex spells require you to hold onto enormous amount of power. You need to train your body to do so. Take an hour to rest. Go drink some water. I'll test out the rune we devised yesterday."

Nevian didn't dare stand, so he stayed to watch. Brune drew several variants of their sigil across the table using stone she conjured and spent several minutes staring at them in silence. The air around them shifted, growing thicker, and the stone chair under him warmed. He leaned forward, eager to catch glimpses of a master at work. Brune crooked two fingers on her left hand, then chopped through the air with a low, throaty rumble. Dust flew from the nearby bookshelves, sucked in towards her, then settled on the rune, perfectly lining its form.

"Was that supposed to happen?" he asked.

"Of course." She set that particular rune aside. "This one holds the elements we used to create a pulling effect. I modified it to affect the environment instead of the mind, so I could easily test the pull. All of these are variants are meant to test one specific property, out of its overall context. When you build complex spells, you ought to be systematic … unless you want them to blow in your face."

He definitely did not. Nevian studied each variant rune after she'd finished with them, trying to decipher what property it tested. Varden joined them during this time, and when he caught sight of Nevian's peculiar seat, he asked if everything was all right. Only once reassured did he settle in a chair and open his sketchbook. Nevian's heart jumped as he caught a glimpse of himself on the page, deep into one read or another. It made sense, as Varden had had very little else to draw over the last days, yet Nevian couldn't help his embarrassment.

Brune continued for a while, and once Nevian had mostly recovered from his near-faint, she set him to work again, asking him to reactivate the very first rune. He obeyed, his movement less sharp, his fingers not quite right, and he still pulled storms of dust to himself twice. Every time, power coursed through him, turning his muscles tense and his head light, leaving his skin burning and his breath short. He didn't understand how Brune managed to trigger her magic without breaking a sweat. How many hours had she practiced?

"Now do it without moving," she asked.

"What?" That's not how it worked! Without the movements—

"You heard, Nevian. Avenazar will be rampaging in your mind when you'll trigger this. Do you believe you can both stay clear of him and make those gestures? Because if you fail to keep your mind safe, the spell will trap you, too."

Nevian had always suspected this could be a consequence of failure, but the reminder set a dull panic winding around his stomach, constricting it. Was he throwing himself into a fate even more terrible than his previous life? But he couldn't think of it this way. Doing nothing would lead to an awful conclusion, too. He had to keep going forward.

"Then I'll do it." His voice was steady, unlike the rest of his shaking body. "With or without the movements, I will spring that trap."

"Excellent." Brune swiped away the first set of drawn sigils she'd greeted him with and set them in a neat pile next to him. "Keep practicing, Nevian."

And she vanished again, dust in the library. Nevian gripped the paper tighter, his resolve crystalizing as he watched the cloud that was Brune settle on the ground. He turned to Varden.

"You're staying, right? I might need a boost."

"How far we've come, that you ask for my healing instead of having me foist it on you."

A deep fondness laced Varden's gentle ribbing, flustering Nevian. He tried to cover it with a snort. "I said a *boost*. I liked it when you infused energy in me."

Varden's eyebrows shot up. "Well, I'm here for both, as always."

THAT night, Nevian sought Vellien out.

He'd buried his head in books and theories ever since arriving, seeing little of them despite sharing the same tower. It was necessary, he'd told himself. Isra's poison would only grant them so much time to build a riposte. He didn't have *time* to spend with Vellien, or to figure out how he felt about them. But also … he was nervous about that and how his feelings had shifted again, the anxious butterflies gone and giving him his focus back. Was that supposed to mean he wasn't attracted anymore? Because he still cared—cared so much that his throat tightened as he knocked, knotting itself until he struggled to breathe only to loosen as Vellien opened and beamed at him.

"Hello," Nevian squeaked.

Vellien laughed their perfect snort-laugh, and all the butterflies lurched back into Nevian's chest, so intoxicating they ripped a chuckle out of him. Vellien motioned for him to come inside, eager to close the door behind Nevian.

They'd been granted a small room, made even smaller by the soft curtains hastily hung from the ceiling, delimiting a cozy corner with a single chair and a few candles. The rest of the space was dominated by a very large bed, so long it went from one wall to the next. They settled on it, each on one end, their feet stretched towards the center, never quite touching.

"I need your help with my plan."

As Nevian explained his soul trap idea, Vellien turned progressively paler, but they didn't protest. They must have known there was no point.

"You said you needed my help?"

Nevian met their eyes, hesitant. They would not like this. "I need you to chase me through my mind. A mental game of cat and mouse. You…" Heat rose to his cheeks and he cast his eyes down to his hands, fingers wringing together. "You know its paths almost as well as I do. If I can escape you, then perhaps I can face Master Avenazar."

"He will not care to keep it intact as I will."

Nevian squeezed his eyes shut. "So neither should you."

A strangled sound escaped Vellien. "Nevian, I can't do that. And forgive me, but I think you are wrong about this approach." The determined note in their tone made Nevian look at them. Arms crossed, a fierce stare, their cheeks so flushed all of their freckles shone. "What we have rebuilt together is fragile. If I destroy it, I weaken your defenses. I can chase you through it, but only so we can find where we still have work to do—memories still escaping you, knowledge fragmented, that sort of thing—and make it better. You will be stronger for it, and healthier. More pain is not always the way to train."

That had never been Nevian's experience. Myrian training philosophy involved gruelling exercises and the overhanging threat of humiliation upon failure—unless, of course, your parents were important mages themselves. Nevian had had neither the political importance to shield himself nor the wealth to afford private tutors, so he'd learned the cost of mistakes the hard way—and learned not to make them. All until he'd earned his rank as acolyte and Master Sauria, who had sponsored him to begin with, took him as an apprentice. A brief lull of peace in his life, one Master Avenazar had torn to pieces.

Brune's training today had been brutal, too, but it hadn't felt malicious. Their time was limited. If he wanted to succeed, he needed to learn to hold the world's magic within himself, and fast. His timeframe to train his mind was equally short, but he'd started early, as he pieced his memories back together with Vellien. Perhaps he could afford a gentler approach and conserve his strength for the rune activation.

"If you think it's best…" Nevian said.

Vellien crawled on the bed to get closer then extended a hand. "Let me show you."

Nevian braced himself for the touch, knowing he'd lose track of it as Vellien brought them both within his mind, then laced his fingers within theirs. The world faded, leaving behind his sense of self and Vellien's tranquil presence by his side.

When they had done this before, memories would shape their surroundings—his parents' shop, the streets of the Myrian capital, the Enclave's darkened courtyard as he snuck out at night. The landscape would reflect what Vellien worked to repair, allowing Nevian to guide them or push memories away if he wished to avoid them for now. The same push and pull had let him stall Master Avenazar and escape him, creating a path of his own choosing.

This time, only shades of memories unfurled, following the path of his thoughts but never materializing. Nevian's confusion rippled out of him in visible ripples in the grey void, and Vellien's amusement touched him in response.

Give it time. Let yourself feel safe.

At first, Nevian didn't understand. They were in his mind, in himself. Why wouldn't he feel safe? But the very thought brought in an anxiety so brutal it materialized as black cracks in their surroundings, a hundred holes in which to hide. Master Avenazar's cackle echoed all around, coming from everywhere at once, and Nevian plunged into the cracks, slamming them close behind himself. A gentle warmth welcomed him there. Vellien, reminding him that they'd come together, that he was safe.

Safe.

Now it made sense. He had never so consciously inhabited his mindscape before Vellien had guided him through healing it, but he had been here, repeatedly, always in great pain. This situation—his body faded, his emotions and memories easy to access—had never heralded anything good for him. Even through the healing, he'd had to relive horrible memories, had to endure a process that remained exhausting at its best.

Nevian tried to relax. Master Avenazar wasn't here. If he wanted to remain in control while confronting him, he'd best start by keeping his cool while he wasn't even around. Slowly, the blackness around faded away, the conjured cracks giving way to grey once again. He felt exposed, but every time a new crack tried to form— every time he tried to give himself an escape—he forced it away. He was safe, here. He was safe.

At the corner of his eyes, the grey coalesced into a simple table surrounded by two chairs. They reminded him of the Brasten library, although these had a darker wood, more to his taste. On the table rested a pile of three books, with a fourth invitingly opened. Nevian hovered closer, his curiosity growing, and as he did, towering piles of books emerged all around him, forming walls throughout the space, reaching ever upward. Many floated midair with a faint rustle of paper, literary butterflies populating the sky. The peculiar scent of old pages filled his nostrils and soothed his nerves.

May I? Vellien asked, the words brimming with amusement.

Nevian needed no words to transmit agreement, and they

materialized from grey fog into one of the chairs, lips curled into a soft smile.

"A fortress of books," they commented.

"I suppose I have always felt the safest with them."

It felt strange to hear his own voice here. He didn't need to speak for Vellien to understand, but they both felt almost physical in these surroundings.

"Play with it," Vellien suggested. "Change its shape and nature. Let it shift to your whims or match memories. Master Avenazar can destroy your memories, but this place is a reflection of your state of mind. It can be rebuilt, but that will be difficult in the heat of the moment. I–I don't know if it's even useful to you. I just thought you'd like to see it."

"I do."

He'd never thought he had such beauty inside of him. Hundreds and thousands of books all around, flitting or resting, the stacks curling protectively over his head and never falling. An inner paradise uniquely him and entirely his.

"Thank you, Vellien."

They didn't chase each other that night. Nevian played with his sanctum, transforming piles of tomes into proper shelves, creating whirlwind of pages that burst in all directions at once, crumbling the stacks and reshaping them into corridors. He created new areas, his inspiration surfing on any thread that passed his mind. The table received crayons, a higher chair, and a children's book. A section of the stacks receded into a proper wall with a fireplace, large seats, and a pile of hand-sized charcoal. Hints of music drifted in, spoons and violins and homemade percussions sometimes covered by a burst of laughter. Vellien sat at the center of it all, a silent witness of Nevian's experiments, their quiet affection rooting itself within him, growing ever stronger. Vellien belonged here, in his sanctum, a part of what made Nevian safe and happy—a part of the future he'd fight for.

CHAPTER TWENTY-TWO

GARITH was unrecognizable.

He and Yultes stared at his reflection in the tall mirror, looking for flaws in the disguise, but even knowing who stood besides him, Yultes had trouble identifying him. He had raided Branwen's gigantic walk-in of disguises and brought scuffed brown pants and a rough, loose linen shirt to replace their coinmaster's usual fancy and ornate doublets.

More striking than the change of fashion, however, was the new haircut. Yultes had shorn Garith's hair down to an inch, leaving only a golden tuft on top. The elf had looked ready to cry when the long locks drifted to the ground, but the signature Dathirii golden curtains would have been a dead giveaway. Once it was gone, they'd rubbed charcoal in it to darken the colour, dulling the hue. Unless Garith brought attention to himself, he should go unnoticed even among his peers.

"I look… modest," Garith said. He laughed and scuffed his foot through the golden hair littering the ground. "Pretty sure those were my biggest draw."

"Think of it as a new challenge," Yultes replied.

Garith grinned at his reflection—and just like that, he looked more like himself, easygoing and confident. Then he pulled the cap over his ears. "You always know just what to say, don't you, Yultes?"

Yultes ran a shaky hand through his own hair, uncertain how to respond. He caught his smile in the mirror's reflection, though, and the slight blush on his cheeks. Caught, too, the twinkle of amusement in Garith's eyes. Yultes grabbed the sack with the transcribed account books and shoved it at him.

"You should go."

All mirth vanished from Garith's expression. He slung the bag over his shoulder, readjusted his disguise again, and sighed. "I hate this."

"I know."

Garith had made it known every step of the way that he hated leaving them behind to burn the books. Jaeger would hear none of it—he'd been too glad for a concrete plan that placed Garith out of harm's way, even if it meant bearing the brunt of it. Especially so, perhaps. Yultes had only risked one visit to his quarters, pretending the need to rescue more of his plants, and the steward had been restless, vibrating with the same defiant energy he'd unleashed the night of the reception.

"You think Branwen got our message?" Garith asked, his voice tight.

He was delaying now, even though every minute in Yultes' quarters could turn into a disaster. "If it'd been intercepted, we would all have heard of it in very unpleasant ways."

"Right, right. And you'll watch over Jaeger, won't you?"

"With my life, if I must."

Instead of reassuring Garith, it deepened his frown. "No. I want you both alive when all is said and done. Even if you're right and I'm the heart of this House—whatever *that* means, really—I'm useless without the body around. I told you: everyone on my team matters."

Yultes let the words wash over him. Everyone, even him, no matter how hard he'd worked against them before, how he'd contributed to the rot surrounding Hellion for decades, eroding their family's cohesion. Garith clasped his shoulder, drawing him out of his darker thoughts. "May Meltara watch over the course of your life, and Alluma bless this cycle."

The blessing caught him off guard. When had he mentioned Meltara in front of Garith? The Water Dancer felt like such a distant part of him, buried with everything of his past upon joining House Dathirii. Wherever Garith had heard, he'd remembered, and that alone was more than Hellion and his entourage had ever done— than Yultes himself had, really.

Sharp knocks at his door startled them, and panic sparked as Enmaris' gravely voice passed through it.

"Yultes, your presence is requested."

"A moment," he shot back.

He met Garith's eyes, mouthed a quick *Alluma guide your path*, then let himself fall into a persona he'd worn for decades, the second skin so familiar he'd mistaken it for his. His voice changed, sharpened into a cruel point.

"This *isn't* what I asked of you. Is it so hard to put two thoughts together in that head of yours?" He grabbed Garith's shoulder and dragged him towards the door, his rant spilling with every step. "You best come back with the correct tomes, or it'll be the last time you show your face in this Tower. We have no room for crass incompetence."

He grabbed his doorknob, flung the door open, and pushed Garith out—past Enmaris, waiting with his eyebrows raised, and the three Allastam guards right behind him. Yultes' heart shot to his throat at their sight, and he forced his gaze away from Garith's exaggerated stumble, as if done with the servant now that he'd been properly chastised and dismissed. Enmaris' gaze flicked over Yultes' shoulder and his mouth twisted in a grimace. Yultes' stomach plummeted, one hard rock of horror.

"You need to get this house in order," Enmaris said. "Servants have been worse than ever. Worthless, the lot of them."

Relief almost choked him, and it was all Yultes could do not to grin. "I've noticed." He let his gaze slide pointedly to the three guards accompanying Enmaris. Garith might be out of immediate trouble, but these didn't bode well for Yultes. "You said my presence was requested?"

"Indeed." He squared his shoulders and affected an official air. "Garith may think he can keep the Dathirii books from Lord Iriel, but we have no time for his games. We'll search his quarters and take them. As you've spent quite a considerable amount of time in them, we thought your input could be of use."

"Fair, though I doubt Garith revealed any secrets to me." Yultes pulled his door closed behind him, shutting off the glimpse into his quarters—where, with the right angle, any of them might still catch sight of the golden locks on the ground. "Lead the way. I'll try to think of any areas he's systematically avoided during our forced collaboration."

Enmaris grunted in agreement, and they set off, the three guards fanning around Yultes as though escorting him. The thump of their boots scraped against his ears, discordant echoes of his flight with Jaeger, when Hellion had first taken over the Dathirii Tower. They'd heralded violence that night and might do so again tonight.

At Enmaris's command, the guards kicked down the door as soon as they arrived, snapping it off its hinges. Yultes stared as they rushed in, hands on their pommel, his mind drifting to better times, when interrupting Garith without warning meant risking the presence of a very naked partner. There'd be no one today, not even Garith himself.

"Come," Enmaris said, and they walked into the quarters, past the guard at Garith's door.

The guards ransacked through every room, pulling out drawers and flipping their content onto the ground, throwing entire rows of books out for Yultes to examine. He directed them at times, leading them to Garith's stash of alcohol, of which only the Flirt remained. The guards laughed about the rewards of the job before moving on.

They pulled the mattress off from the bed, tore through the pillows, and tipped over furniture with visible glee. Yultes tried to steer clear as best as he could, navigating the chaos towards the bedroom and the one window that mattered. There, hanging outside, a darker shape in a dark night, was the lower half of the basket with everything they wanted. Garith had packed everything he could there, tying it to the one rope that had served as communication between Jaeger and him … but Jaeger had yet to pull it up.

Yultes tore his gaze away, his heart pounding. If anyone noticed—if anyone thought to check the windows—they were done for. Should he try to pull the curtains close, or would that draw attention to it? What was the best course of action here? No, he needed to distract them, perhaps bring the search to an early end. Yultes gathered his courage, smoothed his expression, and stalked back to Enmaris.

"He must have hidden them. I've seen him pull out information from the archives." He gestured at the empty shelves where the tomes and scrolls had once been, neatly packed. One could still see the dust outlining their shapes. "He's not here, and neither are the books."

"Your meaning?" Enmaris snapped.

Yultes had no trouble icing his voice as he retorted. "Garith's current location is not my responsibility."

It was a dangerous game, to send them after Garith. If they caught him before he left the Dathirii Tower, it wouldn't matter whether or not they spotted the accounts still hanging by the window. But if they saw them before they could be burned…

Yultes resisted the urge to glance at the basket again, instead meeting Enmaris' glare with a questioning eyebrow.

"Well?" he said. "Ask your man."

It wasn't *his* man—Enmaris had yet to recruit new soldiers into the Dathirii guard—and the reminder stung.

"You're growing quite the sharp tongue," Enmaris said, his voice dropping into a low growl. "Might want to watch that."

No one could mistake the threat there and it rooted Yultes where he stood, decades of learned fear mixing with his current gamble.

Enmaris left him, demanding answers from the guard at the door—a young man who was quick to babble that his orders did *not* include keeping Garith inside, and, of course, he'd asked where he was going, he was going to the kitchens, and yes, he'd had a bag with him but—

He never got farther. Enmaris snapped at him, stomped inside, and told his trio of guards to follow him. As he passed Yultes once again, he slowed and sneered at him.

"Dismissed," he said, as if Yultes himself was one of the servants. "You've outlived your usefulness."

No pretend love for him tonight—not that Enmaris had ever been very good at it. Still, the brazen hostility shocked him. Weren't they supposed to be a team, each essential to Hellion's leadership? Was this normal enmity, or had Enmaris sensed something? How thin was the ice he walked on? He only needed to keep it long enough to destroy the historical accounts and deal this one serious blow to Hellion—after that, there'd be no avoiding the fall into freezing waters, and Yultes could only hope Meltara would see him through.

When Yultes turned around once again, the basket was gone. Jaeger must have pulled it up, alerted by the sounds from below. Or so he hoped. Freed from Enmaris' surveillance, he slipped out of Garith's quarters and hurried up the closest stairs. If he could reach Jaeger, if they could burn all this key information under Hellion's nose…

He turned the last corner, steeling his nerves as he approached the pair of guards at Jaeger's door. Yultes turned his nose up and strode directly to the door, ignoring them entirely. He was Hellion's right hand, his closest ally and most trusted friend, and he didn't need to explain himself to them. Except they slid in his way, hands on their sword and professional scowl well in place. Yultes bristled even as his insides squeezed, and he glared at each in turn—one of which he recognized as the strong-nosed man he'd once interrupted as he dragged Jaeger up towards Hellion's quarters.

"What is the meaning of this?"

Pure arrogance added a dangerous edge to his voice, but neither guard flinched. "No one's to come in, sir. We have orders."

He scoffed. "From whom? There is only one person who outranks me in this House."

"Indeed."

The honeyed voice extinguished all of Yultes' hopes. Hellion, his oldest friend, who had built him piece by piece, taught him everything about Isandor, shaped him into a different person—into the only acceptable version of Yultes, grinding away everything he deemed unworthy, anything that made Yultes unique, that afforded him a sense of self outside of Hellion himself. Hellion, who loved an image of Yultes that existed only in his head and to which he could never measure.

Hellion, who advanced on him clutching a clump of beautiful golden hair, the undeniable proof of this other Yultes he'd refused to see, and of his best friend's betrayal.

CHAPTER TWENTY-THREE

A S SOON as Branwen Dathirii had laid eyes on Garith's message and read his cheeky *see you tonight, dear cousin,* she'd known he was about to do something foolish. Even in cursive, she heard the forced bravery of the declaration, the way he tried to manifest it by putting the words on the page. If he had been certain, he would have surprised her with it.

She didn't know what to make of the rest. He still trusted Yultes, that much was obvious, and while she couldn't shake all of her doubts away, she found herself hoping he was right. Regardless, there was one thing she did know: she couldn't stand waiting to see what happened. It felt like all she'd done recently. Waiting for information, untangling the lies, passing what she learned along to Uncle Diel and Lady Brasten, then back to waiting. Bullying Hellion had helped her mood a great deal, but she was growing restless again, and if Garith had a plan in mind, she wanted to be ready.

So she'd asked herself what they might need, alone in the Dathirii Tower, surrounded by Allastam soldiers and at the mercy of Hellion's whims. The answer? Reinforcements. She didn't have a lot of time, but Cordelia might help her build a small team of the Dathirii guards that had moved on. Branwen had thought first to talk with Kellian about it, but the moment she'd laid out her idea, he'd swept it aside.

"They're in too small numbers compared to the Allastam soldiers. I'll do it."

"Because you alone isn't too small?" she'd retorted, irritated at his dismissal. "Besides, you forget one important detail: you're under arrest."

Kellian had rolled his shoulders as if warming up for exercise. "I am not the same I was. Stone walls can't contain me." He'd stepped closer to said wall, then pressed his palm against it. His hand had slowly turned into stone itself and sank in. "Get me a sword, and I'll be there. They can decide what punishment I get for it after everyone is safe."

Branwen had wanted to protest, but she'd feel much better with Kellian by her side. She'd missed him, with all his gruff bluntness. Maybe this was a mistake, but she found that much like him, she didn't care to think that through now.

"Strike team, then," she'd said with a smile.

And so they'd found themselves at the foot of the Dathirii Tower when a lone figure slipped out of it, underdressed for the freezing weather, a small bag slung over their shoulder. One might think him a messenger boy too poor for proper winter clothes, but Branwen Dathirii was as adept at seeing through disguises as she was at constructing them. Especially those from *her* wardrobe. More importantly, she and Garith had grown together from tiny children into who they were today, never leaving each other's sides for long, and she would know him out of thousands.

He'd exited the Tower two levels below, from the kitchens' doors, but she bent over the bridges' railing and cupped her hands around her mouth.

"Oi, message boy!" she called.

He startled and looked up, the familiar grin on his lips. "Milady!"

Kellian gripped her forearm. "Branwen, what are you—"

"It's Garith." She relished the stunned shock on his face and chirped. "Won't you make him a fancy bridge, Uncle?"

Kellian crouched down with a grumble. "How you two manage to play tricks on me, even now..." He shoved his hand through the thin layer of snow, set his fingers against the stone bridge, and slowly stretched it out into thin curling stairs. When they touched near Garith's feet, the stone from *that* bridge began crawling up, thickening the pathway and providing a railing. Garith climbed right up, bare hands gripping the cold stone as he joined them.

Now that he was so close, her eyes caught on the cap covering his head. She'd assumed he'd tucked all his golden hair within, but it flattened in the wind, empty, and his hairline had this darker colour to it...

"Wait, did you ...?"

Garith bowed, sweeping his cap off in a grand gesture, and

nothing spilled out. They'd cut it all off, leaving a tiny soft inch on, and it was so bizarre she burst out laughing. He placed a hand over his heart.

"I'm wounded."

She should stop, but she couldn't. The frank laugh turned into a series of giggles, her head light from relief at seeing him again, at him being safely out of the tower after all, even if it had cost him his beautiful golden hair. She flung herself at him, bringing him into a hug as an apology, and Garith squeezed back, holding her tight.

Kellian, bless his heart, ruined their moment. "Do we have time?"

Garith sighed and withdrew, a new heaviness weighing down his shoulders. "No, you're right. I have to get these to safety." He patted the sack by his side. "I worry about Jaeger and Yultes, though. They'll be burning every important archive of our accounts soon, and that won't go over well, especially with the Allastam audit coming in a few days."

"Where?" Kellian asked.

"Yultes' old quarters, right above mine. Wait—"

Kellian had dashed off, sword sliding out of its scabbard with an eager whisper. The stone steps he'd created flew to him, moulding themselves into plates around his body as he rushed for the door. Garith gaped, and Branwen couldn't help her laugh at his pure shock.

"What—"

"It almost makes him cool, doesn't it?"

He laughed. "Uncle Kellian? Never."

The quick back-and-forth filled Branwen with a sense of rightness she hadn't experienced in weeks. Being separated from Garith was like having half of her torn away, and she'd been bleeding from that hole non-stop since the reception. She drank in the moment, knowing it couldn't last, then pulled off her mittens and shoved them against his chest.

"Here. Freezing your hands off doesn't make you look sexier or whatever got into your head. You'll need them more than me."

He rolled his eyes at her but slipped them on without protesting. "Be careful, Branwen. Hellion must know he has his back against a wall, and you know what they say about cornered animals."

"Yeah, yeah."

She had a hard time being afraid of Hellion after the restaurant. He was all talk, and with his tiny little empire crumbling around him, he was as likely to collapse as he was to strike. Garith caught her forearm, digging his fingers in even through the newly put mitts.

"I'm serious," he said, his mouth a grim line. "He's hit Yultes a few times. The tantrum might be pathetic, but it'll be ugly, too."

Under his fear, she caught a whiff of guilt. Branwen looked at him again, more carefully this time, and she absorbed the deep creases under his eyes, the way his smile didn't touch his eyes, which kept flicking back towards their home, where he'd left his companions behind. He didn't want to leave and would only abandon the others if he'd thought it absolutely necessary. Garith had lived within the Tower; he'd know better than her how dangerous Hellion could be.

"Gotcha," she said, meeting his eyes. "Take care of the books.

We'll get Jaeger and Yultes out."

He pulled her in for a last, heartfelt hug, over almost as soon as it'd started, and then he was gone without another word to deliver his precious cargo to the Brasten Tower. Branwen turned back towards their home, the great tree shape dark against the sky, and headed in. She hoped Kellian hadn't left her too far behind.

"I TRUSTED you."

Hellion flung the accusation at him as one would a dagger, and the words punched through his stomach, their strangled betrayal a better weapon than any blade. Yultes flinched and stepped back, desperate to catch his breath, to fight the searing guilt rising through him, carrying with it endless apologies. The guards' iron grip clamped around his arms, their fingers digging into his skin. Panic deployed frantic wings within his chest.

"Hellion, listen—"

The slap came hard and fast, snapping Yultes' head to the side. Pain rang through his ears, almost covering Hellion's retort.

"No. I am done listening to your poisonous words."

His thoughts jostled, dislodged by the slap, scattered between the remnants of his past self, now demanding that he beg for mercy, the need to keep his head clear, and an ever-growing anger. It had started so small, a kernel of rage at the decades he'd lost, more directed at himself for getting roped into Hellion's aura than at Hellion for the endless manipulation, the back and forth between praise and mockery, the slow isolation from everyone else. But here and now, as Hellion accused *him* of poisonous words, that anger blazed to life, devouring everything else.

"*I* am poisonous? You've spent years dripping venom into my ears. One word at a time until I thought nothing but your praise mattered." He drew himself to his full height, forcing his wobbly legs steady. "Was I ever going to be good enough, Hellion?"

Yultes regretted the question as soon as it left his lips. He didn't want the answer, and every fibre of him braced for impact as Hellion's furious snarl morphed into an incredulous chuckle. He laughed, a cold waterfall that had nothing to do with his usual warm chuckles and froze Yultes to the bones. Hellion's hand flashed, gripping his chin as he pulled him close. The familiar perfume wrapped around Yultes, and even now, held by two guards, the taste of blood on his tongue from a slap, Yultes could not help mellowing inside, tilting forward as he waited for Hellion's words. His old friend brought his lips to his ear.

"You were *dirt*," he whispered. "A speck on our boots who aspired to be more—and I gave that to you. I made you better, elevated you, and this—" His grip tightened, nails digging into Yultes' cheeks, and he forced him to look at the scattering of Garith's hair on the ground. "—This is how you thank me? The one person who was there when they all abandoned you? I saw you when no one did."

"Hellion…"

The name escaped him, more a plea than Yultes had ever intended to give. He felt dizzy, almost feverish. Somewhere deep within, on a visceral level he didn't understand, Yultes didn't want their friendship to end. Even though he could see how Hellion had played him, plucking on his loneliness and frustration, even though he saw the lies and knew he could become so much more than what Hellion wanted for him, he had to try.

"I'm sorry, Hellion. I'm sorry I betrayed your trust. But if you ever loved me—for your sake, you have to stop this. You know Diel—"

The second slap knocked his head against the guard's armour and split his cheek. Yultes squeezed his eyes shut, fighting his nausea. It was over. This was what he had chosen. Why did it sicken him so?

"I see now what Viranya meant," Hellion said, and that thread of hurt had been schooled out of his voice. "It doesn't matter how many pretty paints one applies; it's impossible to hide the ugliness underneath forever. I was foolish. You were dirt and will always remain so. But that's all right." Hellion leaned in again, voice dropping to a whisper. "Here's your last lesson, my friend. I don't adorn myself in ugly things."

Yultes caught a glint of metal, then a sharp pain shot through his stomach. He gasped, his legs giving in from the shock, and only the guards' iron grip held him up. Had Hellion just … stabbed him? The blade slid back out, blood spilling from the wound in a deadly confirmation.

Hellion stepped back with a disgusted sound, withdrew a handkerchief, and began cleaning the blood from his fingers—Yultes' blood. He dropped the handkerchief on top of Garith's shorn hair and a predatory smile curled his lips.

"Best hope you live to learn from it. Now if you'll excuse me, there is another gangrene someone must cut from this House."

Hellion turned away from him, towards Jaeger's door. Shock and pain narrowed Yultes' vision to his immediate surroundings—the searing in his stomach, the red drip of his blood sliding along Garith's hair or soaking the handkerchief, the hands holding him, keeping him from even staunching his wound. He might bleed out, held between them, and still a part of him refused to believe it had happened.

Distantly, he heard Hellion's angry exclamation as he opened Jaeger's room, then noticed the smoke billowing out the open door. That was good, at least. Yultes managed a smile. You could always count on Jaeger to get the job done. He, on the other hand, didn't have the strength to escape two trained soldiers, to protect Jaeger as he'd promised Garith. He wondered how long a stomach wound took to kill you and whether the guards would still hold him up after he'd lost consciousness, like a trophy for Hellion.

They dropped him while the question crossed his mind. He smacked onto the ground hard, his head ringing from the impact. Garith's hair stuck to his tongue as the two soldiers rushed past him, sprinting across the wooden floor and—was that stone, bounding down the corridor like a living animal? It crackled with the movement, every leap a confusing melody of cracks and pops, then flattened itself along the ground as it reached the pair of guards, slipping between their legs to resume its run. Its run to him, Yultes realized.

The bounding stone slammed into him, wrapping itself all around Yultes, encasing legs and arms and hips then lifting him back to his feet in a sharp and painful movement. He stumbled as it released him, sloughing off in chunks—all but a thick layer that settled over his wound like a bandage, and a sharp fragment in his hand.

The clang of swords meeting snapped him out of his shocked reverie, and his gaze found Kellian, now engaged with both guards, a layer of stone plaques forming an esoteric armour around him. Their gazes met briefly over the melee.

"Get in there," Kellian snapped, head jerking towards the smoking door.

Yultes' grip tightened on his stone fragment and he dashed off. Pain shot through him with every step, Kellian's strange stones grinding against his bones, but he gritted his teeth and rushed into the room.

Smoke greeted him first, prickling his eyes and grating the back of his throat. A thicker layer swirled around the ceiling, curling over his trailing tradescantia's purple leaves and along the string of hearts he'd kept dutifully full and lush over the last decade. It twisted something deep inside to see them caught up in his mess, but he tore his gaze away, focusing on the two elves facing each other.

There had been a scuffle—a full cabinet of plants had crashed to the ground, littering glass and soil, and many of its inhabitants now fell prey to the flames licking out of the basket of accounting books. A thin burning log stuck out of it, right next to a broken bottle of wine—Jaeger's weapons, his last statement before Hellion had come crashing in. Now Hellion held Jaeger against the wall, and in the flickering light, his old friend looked like a leaf trembling in the wind, fragile and pathetic.

"It's all smoke now," Jaeger was saying, rock-steady despite everything. Confident in himself in a way Yultes could never be.

"Every debt, every transaction, every deal. Gone. And you are no phoenix, to rise from its ashes."

"I don't care!" Hellion snapped. "The House is mine. You-you think you're so clever, so pure, but look where it gets you. I'll give Diel a loss he'll never recover from."

Jaeger laughed in his face. He did not look at Hellion's small blade, glinting red from Yultes' blood. He laughed and closed his eyes, exuding defiant confidence.

"Go on, then. Get your petty revenge in. We'll see if your Allastam allies protect you from the consequences, or if you're as wrong about their loyalty as you were about your best friend's."

The retort stung Yultes as badly as it did Hellion, but decades of watching for the slightest sign of anger in his old friend told Yultes the exact moment he snapped. He sprinted forward at the first twitch of Hellion's jaw, lengthened his strides as tightness ran up his old friend's spine, and barrelled into him as Hellion sliced at Jaeger. Yultes caught Hellion's wrist and they crashed into the spilled glass.

The impact jostled the stone shard plugging his wound shut, slamming it deeper in Yultes' gut. Pain thundered through him, knocking out any sense of self and surroundings. He thought he heard Jaeger call his name through the roaring in his ears, felt Hellion's body nearby. His consciousness was slipping, blood pouring out of his wound again. But he still had something solid in his hand, still clung to Kellian's stone-shaped dagger and the one promise he intended to keep.

He would keep Jaeger safe.

He dug his fingers into Hellion, not caring which part of him he held, and stabbed. Hellion jerked under his grip, his scream of pain and shock tearing through the room. Nausea surged through Yultes, but he crawled farther up Hellion and stabbed again, and again, and again, putting every ounce of diminishing energy he had into it. He tried not to think of the way Hellion jerked under every strike, of the stench filling his nostrils, of decades of twisted friendship ending in a pool of shared blood. Tried to ignore the tears pouring out of him as every strike opened a different wound inside of him, shattering the version he'd spent decades trying to be. Yultes pumped his arm again, ready for another go, but cool fingers caught it.

"Yultes," Jaeger's voice cut through his daze with startling clarity. "You can let go now. It's over."

He pried Yultes' fingers from the stone shard, gently unfolding them one by one, then pulled him away. Yultes' breath had turned into sharp, heaving gasps and blotches of darkness crept along the edge of his vision. Red blood and mangled flesh filled everything else, so he squeezed them shut, blocking out the world—all but the burning pain in his stomach and Jaeger's cool touch, brushing away the strands of his hair stuck to his forehead. He could feel himself sinking into unconsciousness.

"Garith…" he croaked. "Enmaris might—"

"Don't worry," Jaeger said. "Garith will be fine, and we'll find you a healer. I have this under control."

It made no sense, of course. Jaeger had been isolated, with no way to come on top of this, but he when had he not been a solid rock to steady you in a storm? You could always count on Jaeger, and as the last of his consciousness slipped away, Yultes found himself believing in their future.

Chapter Twenty-four

ANY illusions Mia Allastam entertained that Yultes' invitation to enjoy tea in his new quarters had not been a plea for her aid at a crucial moment vanished when she noticed the smoke billowing out a window carved into the great Dathirii tree tower. She gripped her cane tighter, pausing on their doorstep for strength. She'd almost excused herself, the needling pain threading through her muscles and bones enough to knock her down, but he'd sounded like he needed her. She was the one who'd put new pressure on Hellion Dathirii and hastened whatever schemes Yultes had been running. As an ally and a friend, she owed him her best, even if the current version of 'best' had her mind mired and her thoughts scattered.

One step at a time, she reminded herself. Do not let others see your pain, and never miss an opportunity to improvise. With the medicine she'd drank before leaving, she'd have one to two hours of this low, constant ache before the pain returned in full force. She could hold that long.

First sign of chaos: no Allastam soldiers were guarding the front entrance. The two large doors led into a great hall out of which several staircases grew, and not a single soul was there to greet her. Mia stopped after a few steps, listening for any unusual sounds. Distant conversations echoed down into the hall, words distorted by distance and twisting corridors, but their urgency was unmistakable.

"Milady?"

A voice startled Mia. Three of the Dathirii staff had emerged from a side door, buckets of sand between them. She smiled, hoping to ease the obvious fear between them.

"I was invited for tea. Seems a bad time now, doesn't it?"

"It is," a young man answered, his voice melodic and firm. "There's fighting in the upper floors. You might want to head home, milady."

"No." She hardened her voice so that no one would challenge her decision. It wasn't their place, but sometimes people saw the cane and decided they had all the rights. "Which way to the commotion?"

They exchanged glances and at length, the young man pointed at one of the four staircases. It ran along the side she'd spotted smoke from. The steps were large and low, but they nonetheless made her wistful of House Brasten's elevator. One day, she'd have one built within House Allastam, too.

"Thank you for your information," she said and headed up, her hand wrapping around the branch-like rail as she climbed.

Two floors later, she found the first of her soldiers—four of them in a huddle, in the middle of a heated strategy debate. She cleared her throat loudly and all conversations died. They saluted, forming a quick line—but their obedience stopped there.

"We have a situation, milady, Go home."

"I will not."

Mia drew herself up and glared at the older woman who'd dared to speak to her so. Allastam soldiers had always disregarded her more easily than her peers and she'd learned to avoid them and rely on the rest of the household instead, but tonight they *would* recognize her authority. She let diamonds slip into her voice, bringing forth the full force of her heritage.

"I am Lord Allastam's first daughter and until his name is cleared and he is returned to us, you will heed my command. I expect you all to fall in line and escort me as I resolve this situation. Is that clear?" A pause. Their uneasiness angered her, but she kept her deadly cool and headed for the next step, as if there could be no doubts that they'd do as told. The soldiers scrambled to catch up and form around her, providing protection on all sides. Good. "Now, tell me what we know."

The older woman laid it out quickly as they continued upwards. At Enmaris Dathirii's orders, several soldiers had followed the newly anointed Dathirii Guard Captain as he'd attempted to track down Garith Dathirii and important documents. This had left their troops in disorder—or, Mia suspected, served as an excuse for the chaos that followed—and Kellian Dathirii had caught them off guard, bringing forth the full force of his Earth powers against them once more.

He'd left a trail of guards trapped against walls and floors on his way to the quarters where Jaeger was being held. The guard's information after that became more disjointed. They'd received no news regarding the two soldiers at Jaeger's door, but rumours said Hellion had been present there, along with both Yultes and, of course, Jaeger himself. This was where the fire was coming from.

"Seems to me Kellian Dathirii was dispatched here because they knew an incident would happen," the old woman concluded.

"Indeed." Mia, who had arranged for the channel of communication between the people in the Dathirii Tower and family safely within House Brasten's walls, was not surprised. "Am I to understand that Kellian Dathirii alone is preventing you from putting an end to this?"

The woman stammered. "Well, milady, he wields power unheard of. Even here, with limited access to stone, he is formidable. That's to say—"

"Please stop," she interrupted. She didn't need their excuses. She understood perfectly the difference between their soldiers, used to dominate through numbers but with limited real experience, and Kellian Dathirii, who had centuries of experience and a new boon. "Stop talking, and stop fighting him."

"But, milady…"

"When you cannot defeat an enemy with brute force, do you throw yourself at him until everyone lies dead? No, of course not. We have better weapons." She made her cane snap on the ground as she pulled herself up the last step, punctuating her words with the sharp strength of it. "Fan out behind while I negotiate."

They had reached the right landing: the remainder of her troops had gathered on it, blades drawn. Three of her soldiers littered the corridor, squirming within rock cases, arms strapped against the walls or the floor. Two more were unconscious, if not dead. Eleven guards, counting her escorts, and all had been stalled by the single elf at the end of the corridor.

Kellian Dathirii waited with his weapon drawn, the tip in their direction. He'd armoured himself in stone, though the plates had been chipped and removed in parts, and her men had left a few wounds on him. Smoke poured from a door behind him, and a few steps away, Jaeger and Branwen crouched near a very pale and distinctly unconscious Yultes, pressing bloodied clothes to his stomach. Her stomach tightened. She hoped she wasn't too late to save him, or those he held dear.

"If I may have a word?"

She cast her voice out and walked through the crowd of soldiers. They split on either side of her, forming a beautiful inverted V behind her as she passed. Mia let the clacking of her cane fill the silence as she strode down the corridor, past the three stuck soldiers, and stopped near the two fallen ones, halfway to Kellian. All eyes had turned to her now. She tilted her chin up and held herself still and proud, resisting the weight of their stares and the constant pull of her pain.

Kellian Dathirii lowered his sword and bowed. He'd barely straightened when Branwen materialized at his side.

"You here to call your goons off? We need a healer."

Mia raised her eyebrows, her calm a striking contrast to

Branwen's agitation. As much as she wanted to expedite a healer, she could not afford to look weak and compliant in front of all her soldiers.

"I'm here to re-establish order," she corrected. "If you need a healer, then we can negotiate."

Branwen scoffed. "Hellion's dead. Every trace of our accounts has been burned. There's nothing left for you here." She gestured at the tower, and it felt to Mia as if Branwen was growing in stature with every firm word crossing her lips. "Leave our home. You're not welcome here."

Mia's gaze flicked to Yultes, still partly held by Jaeger. He needed urgent care, but how could she navigate this and still save face? "I'm afraid it is not so simple," she said. "We had warned Hellion of our intentions to withdraw from this Tower, and while I am not unwilling to hasten that process, it was meant to come with an audit. House Dathirii owes us a debt."

"If you think you'll see a single piece of gold—"

"Don't be foolish." Mia sliced through the retort, leaving Branwen no time to mount an assault. "One does not trifle with debts in Isandor and your House's reputation has suffered enough without denying this one, regardless of how it came to be. But neither you nor I are leaders of our House, Branwen Dathirii, and I understand a Golden Table has been called for tomorrow. Perhaps such things can be settled there, in fairness and by the agreement of Isandor's governing body, and we can focus on preventing unnecessary deaths here and now."

"So our healer—"

"*Our* healer will take care of Yultes Dathirii, and I will personally see to it that no harm comes to him while within our walls."

This time, it was Kellian Dathirii who bristled. "I'm not letting a single member of my family go with your men. They held him while he bled out."

Mia's stomach clenched at the thought, but she kept her disgust from her face. Instead, she turned slowly from Branwen to the older Dathirii, whose words were more than empty threats. She hoped her posture conveyed presence and power. It could be difficult to tell what others perceived when she could never forget the pain.

"Correct me if I'm wrong, sir, but you should be under house arrest within the Brasten Tower, alongside my father. Do not mistake my willingness to talk here with forgiveness. I have not forgotten what you did to my brother, nor how you allowed my mother's killer to escape." She let her words carry, sharp as Kellian's blade, but he did not flinch. Unsurprisingly hard to impress. "In fact, my second condition to a full removal of our Allastam guards within these walls is as follows: I want you in the Sapphire Guard Headquarters, under shackles that will keep your newfound abilities contained, until the Golden Table has convened and discussed your fate."

"That all?" Branwen asked, her voice dripping with sarcasm.

"For tonight."

She imbued her tone with a light smugness she'd often heard from her father, and Branwen grimaced as if she was asking the world from them. She'd fallen into the steps of Mia's dance, performing for their audience, but they both knew that in the circumstances, Mia's demands were quite reasonable. She could keep Yultes safe, and Kellian should always have been in a neutral prison.

"Branwen." Jaeger's voice rose from the back. "I'm going with Yultes."

She spun about. "I haven't agreed to anything!"

"But you will," he countered, and Mia wondered if he'd caught up to their improvised scene. He might even have known ahead of time she'd been invited tonight, or that she'd helped put Yultes and Branwen in touch to begin with. "These are fair terms. Diel will handle the rest tomorrow, and Yultes can't wait an hour while you argue over this."

"You're not under any obligations to come," Mia said. "If you'd prefer to be somewhere else…"

A hollow laugh escaped him. "Of course I would, a thousand times over. It can wait, however. Yultes saved my life and he deserves a friendly face to wake up to."

Mia Allastam might have argued that she was a friendly face, but she doubted she'd be awake by the time the healers finished their work. Her time was limited by her waning energy and the pain in her bones hitching ever upward. It'd be a relief to have someone else by Yultes' side, even if Jaeger had no real power within House Allastam. Sometimes, an observer was enough to keep everyone on their best behaviour.

"All agreed, then?" she asked, turning her gaze to Kellian.

He pressed his lips into a flat line, then slid his sword back into its scabbard. "All agreed."

"LET me get this clear."

Diel stared at the family gathered around him, late into this Golden Table eve, determined to spend this one night with everyone who could make. Camilla had arrived earlier in the day, her belongings packed in a hurry—although not so quickly that she'd forgotten a jar of fresh cookies—and urgent news of Hasryan on her lips. Her grandson had followed much later, several hours after sunset, his golden hair cut to an inch and his mind still in the home he'd left behind. Diel had listened to Vellien's anecdotes with a distracted ear, unable to relax until Branwen's return. For the second time, Diel had watched his niece walk in without Jaeger by her side, forcing him to swallow bitter disappointment. They'd all sat together, traded stories and worries, and as the astounding tales of the day compiled, Diel's mind inevitably turned to his confrontation on the morrow.

"In the last twenty-four hours, Kellian escaped his house-arrest quarters to lead an assault on Allastam soldiers—" He raised a first finger. "—Hasryan mysteriously appeared in Aunt Camilla's defense—" A second finger joined the first. "—and Hellion is dead, presumably killed by his trusted right hand." The third finger followed, and he sighed. "But I'm supposed to convince everyone Lord Allastam is the one who needs investigating, and not I?"

Branwen snickered and raised the cup of wine before her. She and Garith had unearthed a stash from Alluma-knew-where and had shared a bottle of it. "Sorry, Uncle. We didn't want it to be too easy?"

"Clearly not," he replied with a breathless laugh. "I hope I haven't grown too rusty."

"You will do fine," Camilla assured him. "He sold you out to the worst of fates while we've been fighting back. Those do not measure on the same scale, and as long as you don't let anyone lose perspective, you can lead the Golden Table where you want."

Diel wished he shared Camilla's certainty. He'd failed once before and it had led to their downfall. Would he truly fare any better tomorrow? But he'd fought alone the first time, on the defensive from the start and with no concrete plan. Now he'd be seconding Lady Brasten, who navigated these events with a deftness he lacked, and they'd carefully built their case over the last few days. It would be different. It had to be.

"I say we forget all that," Garith declared. "Let's tell stories and drink and laugh or something. It's been too long since I heard all of your beautiful voices."

"And us yours, Garith," Diel said softly, "but you sound like you have something in mind."

Garith flashed him his easy grin, and the very sight was a balm on Diel's weary heart. He wished Jaeger was with them, quietly sitting in a corner, speaking only for one clever remark here and then—or even better, sitting behind Diel, slowly braiding his hair as they both listened to the endless banter between Garith and Branwen. As soothing as this family reunion felt, having so many once again together only highlighted those missing.

"I just thought … you and Aunt Camilla, you must have stories of when Yultes arrived, right? How he was back then, before he turned into a constant jerk?"

He ended with a quip, as if to apologize for even bringing it up. And it was true that they never talked about Yultes before—why sour the mood, after all? A lot had changed since Hellion had taken over the Dathirii Tower, however, Yultes perhaps most of all. Diel smiled at Garith.

"I do. He was quiet and eager, anxious where his brother Lehran was daring—the protector of a trouble-making sibling. He hadn't wanted to settle with us at all, at the time, and I'd catch him arguing with his brother that it wouldn't work out, that sooner or later, Lehran would want to leave again. I suppose he was right in that regard."

It had taken a few decades, but eventually Yultes' brother had left again—called by the rivers, or so he said. Tatiel had gone with him, leaving Branwen in her two uncles' care. Neither Diel nor Yultes had really measured up and even now, as she listened to tales of her parents, he could see the quiet pain in the pinch of her lips, the way her smile didn't quite stretch fully.

"We didn't get along so well at the time either. I liked to be very wrong, very loudly, and he avoided confrontations as best as he could. But there was that one time I'll never forget, when I convinced him to go rafting down the Reonne's affluents. Yultes had turned into a different person once over the water, energetic and commanding, alert and knowledgeable. He kept us from turning over quite a few times."

Diel launched into the story proper, and it wasn't long before

Garith, Branwen, and Vellien all leaned forward, ears perked. Eager, perhaps, for a tale they hadn't heard a dozen times before. Diel focused on the telling, adding the appropriate dramatic flourish here and there, slowing to ratchet up the tension whenever appropriate. He wove words into an entrancing tapestry, jumping from their exciting ride down rapids to a quieter moment, the two of them side by side on a flat rock and staring at the canopy above, trading childhood stories from two very different worlds. That was the first time Yultes had mentioned Meltara to Diel, and the only he could recall.

He finished to a round of applause, and Camilla passed them tea she'd steeped while he'd entertained them all. Diel accepted his cup graciously then sat back down on the ground, in their small circle. He sipped in silence while Aunt Camilla shared her own stories of Yultes and how he'd come to her for care tips about the near-dead plants he'd found in the quarters assigned to him.

As the night progressed, Diel became calmer and drowsier, and he suspected his aunt had chosen herbs with the intent to knock him out. A wise choice. As much as he loved this time with his family and energized himself with their laughter, he had a long day ahead tomorrow and they were all counting on him. He turned to her as sleep gained on him, only to find her winking at him. He could only smile when she waved him goodnight. Aunt Camilla had always known exactly what he needed.

CHAPTER TWENTY-FIVE

JILSSAN stared at the door to Lady Brasten's private quarters, uncharacteristically nervous.

The last few days had been a string of long naps longer nights, plagued by memories of Lord Allastam's cold cell and the reimagined pain of a spiked mace through her back. Even during the day, as she chatted with Isra or deepened her training in shapeshifting magic, she could not entirely keep her mind clear.

She'd dropped in on Nevian to see what he'd built from her notes, but Varden's unceasing stare had made it clear she wasn't welcome to stay. She'd left them once her curiosity had been satisfied, and returned to this peculiar cycle of interrupted rest and limited energy, until the worst had passed and her body slowed its tantrum of forced rest.

Today had been a lot better. While her back and the long scar across it itched ceaselessly, she'd felt invigorated through most of it.

So tonight she'd slipped back into the gorgeous dress left for her the first day, pointedly ignored the bruises still showing across her arms and back, and climbed her way to the promise of a delightful night. She hoped her absence wouldn't be mistaken for disinterest instead of sheer exhaustion.

When Lady Brasten called for her to enter, Jilssan's heart stammered with anticipation. It'd been so long since she'd experienced such flutters, let alone allowed herself to pursue them. But this? Lady Amake Brasten was a brilliant negotiator who'd outplayed Jilssan with outstanding ease. The seamless lie around Isra's safety had trapped Jilssan, but instead of causing bitterness it had only increased her admiration for House Brasten's leader. Not to mention that she was gorgeous, and when Jilssan stopped dreaming of the Allastam cells at night, she imagined her pale fingers running across those full curves and conjured the taste of her lips. She was confident the real Amake Brasten would be a hundred times better than the fantasies of her mind.

"Good evening," Lady Brasten greeted.

She was lounging in a long chair near the hearth, a book in hand, one of her legs stretched out towards the heat and the other folded closer. A slit in the skirt of her light, black dress let its fabric conveniently slide down, revealing the thick curves of her thighs. Golden beads along her body caught the firelight, reflecting it like waves of shining stars on her fat rolls. Jilssan's mouth dried at the sight. The bold, enticing position felt intentional. Grinning, she closed the door behind her and leaned against it, hands still on the knob.

"I thought I'd return the gorgeous dress you had set aside for me," Jilssan said. She was relieved by the smoothness of her voice.

Amake Brasten lowered her book and looked Jilssan up and down with raised eyebrows. "You appear to be wearing it."

"Am I?" Jilssan faked surprise and looked down at herself. "That might be something of a problem."

Lady Brasten's quick and sudden laugh sent warmth coursing through Jilssan. "You don't deal in subtleties, do you?"

"You wound me." Jilssan pushed off the door and strode across the room, to sit at the end of Lady Brasten's long chair. The fire's warmth prickled her skin so close to it. "I picked up your very subtle clues and responded accordingly."

"Clues?"

Jilssan loved the little quirk in her smile, the unspoken challenge. She wanted a demonstration.

"At first I thought Sharpe had chosen to wear simple pants rather than a dress, but she wouldn't have dared refuse if you'd offered only that option. Not to mention her bath wasn't scented, unlike mine, and she asked me how I'd managed to pick up wine so fast, which means she had no bottle in her room. Now, I suspect that last part was to get me inebriated before the meeting, to better your chances at a *very bold* lie, but still… A nice touch."

Lady Brasten stared at her, her smile widening with every point Jilssan made. She sat up, facing her. Her eyes glinted in the shifting light, captivating pools of confidence and desire. There was something intense there, a constant evaluation, like she couldn't stop assessing, calculating, predicting. "What took you so long, then?"

Jilssan's laugh cracked despite her best effort at levity, and she turned away from Amake, towards the fire. "I needed rest. I don't think milady would have enjoyed my catatonic self."

Warm fingers brushed the nape of Jilssan's neck, sending a shiver down her spine. "I hadn't expected an honest answer."

"I don't make a habit of it. Surprise is too powerful a weapon."

"A wise decision." Lady Brasten's body shuffled nearer, and the delicate smell of jasmine filled Jilssan's nostrils. She'd expected Lady Brasten to choose a stronger perfume, something spicy and unforgettable, but this pleased her. It was soft and reassuring, and she relaxed as Lady Brasten pushed the dress off Jilssan's shoulders in a slow, delicious movement. It clung to her body partway down, held by the seamstress adjustments before it could slide to her hips.

"Do you need another night of rest?" Lady Brasten asked.

"If you want to call it rest." Jilssan didn't care to wait. Her entire body had tensed under the light fingers running across the top of her back, bumping her scar. She needed this—the intimacy, the space away from her recent pain, the permission to be weak, shattered, and in need of another. "One night won't make me forget the spike slicing my back, the subsequent violence, the stone floor, and numbness in my toes. I'd need a dozen massages and several weeks of rest to overcome the bone-deep weariness of magic overuse. I need to know I'm safe again, or something close to it, and now that I've said all this, it occurs to me I've needed someone to speak with for a really long time and should have, perhaps, taken more care in choosing with whom."

Lady Brasten's hand stilled, and Jilssan regretted saying so much. Opening up always scared others away. She should've gone down the playful path, made a straight line for what they both wanted here, and kept her problems to herself. She waited, breathless, unable to find a quip that'd break the heavy silence and at the mercy of Amake's response.

Solid hands wrapped around her hips and pulled her until she rested against Lady Brasten. Jilssan's breath caught as the other woman pressed herself close and whispered. "I can provide for some of those needs."

Her right hand slid forward, its thumb describing a large arc to caress the upper part of her ass. Jilssan's thoughts scattered as the hand moved farther down, wrapping around her thigh with a firm grip. Amake's hand stopped as it reached the edge of the dress, then slid under and started its slow way back up. That simple movement left her mouth dry and her body aching. She'd come for this, but she hadn't realized how shaken and needful the last few days had left her. Jilssan leaned back into Amake, a little breathless.

"I hope you define massage the same way you define rest."

"At times," Amake replied mildly, with an unmistakable playful undertone.

Part of Jilssan wanted to turn around and bask in Lady Brasten's beautiful smile, in her self-confidence and its unsaid promises, but that would interrupt the slow movements of her hand and break the warm embrace. She hadn't felt this safe in years and was mellowing more with every circle of Amake's thumb. It was easier to let her talk, and allow the soft voice to envelop her too.

"It sounds like you, Master Jilssan, need not only a lover, but a friend." Her left hand left Jilssan's hip to trace the scar on her back, all the way to her neck, as if she could see it through the fabric. "You're not what I expected. Softer. More vulnerable."

Jilssan's instincts flared, warning her to close up before she left herself open for attacks. She stiffened and covered her panic as quickly as she could. "No wonder, if your only source is Varden. Did he employ words such as 'morally corrupt' and 'power hungry'? I suggested them to him once, and he seemed to agree."

"He said you had a heart under all that ambition, but that you made sure to keep it buried most of the time."

Jilssan laughed at the description. She couldn't deny its accuracy, and it was amusing to imagine the disgust in Varden's tone as he explained. "So you found the heart and immediately exploited it to bend me to your will."

"Of course."

"I'm not sure Varden would approve of such ruthlessness. 'What needs to be done' is a difficult concept for him, I'm afraid."

"You underestimate him." Lady Brasten kissed her nape then wrapped her hands around the bunched-up dress, slowly pulling it all the way down. Jilssan struggled to focus on the conversation as Amake's fingers and velvet fabric brushed against her back. "He's perceptive and unburdened by doubts. Your perception is skewed because his goals don't align with your understanding of ambition and ruthlessness."

"Perhaps." Under different circumstances, Jilssan would've argued, but Lady Brasten had bared most of her back now. Her hands ran from Jilssan's shoulders to the lower back, careful never to do more than brush the still-painful scar, and the shivering pleasure of her touch scattered her thoughts. "Admittedly, the minutiae of Varden's personality and goals are not currently a major concern for me." She turned her torso to face Lady Brasten. "We should stop talking about men."

Lady Brasten grinned and pushed down the remainder of her dress. She looked at Jilssan with satisfaction—it was lovely, how she managed to feel calm, inviting, and victorious all at once. She made Jilssan feel in control despite her inner voice whispering that she'd slipped and lost it, that intimacy would lead her to her ruin. Lady Brasten pulled her into a kiss, slow at first, but more heated and demanding with every passing second, and the night grew more intense—clothes strewn to the ground, skin held firm under pressing hands. Jilssan's concerns melted away, and she let her illusions of control go with them. Lady Brasten led their dance, always a step ahead, picking her up to move to the bed, taking surprising initiatives, and Jilssan was more than happy to let go. She plunged into the sex, hot and shivering, her hands running along Lady Brasten's delicious body, all curves and rolling belly and thick thighs, her mind occupied by nothing but their movements and the pleasure that came from it. She forgot the atrocious pain, the freezing cell, and the dangerous politics of the coming days, burying it all under the powerful jolts of pleasure until they collapsed side by side, out of breath, sweaty, and satisfied.

Jilssan stared at the ceiling, relaxed. *Content.* Part of it was the afterglow, of course, but beyond that… Lady Brasten made her as if she could let go of the posturing, the word games and manipulations, the constant alertness to schemes and dangers. As much as she loved those, they had taken a toll and she welcomed the pause. She turned and nestled her nose in the nook Lady Brasten's neck with a happy sigh.

Her partner's whole body stiffened. Jilssan would have missed it, had she not been snug against it. She leaned back.

"Is there an issue?"

"Some clarifications are in order, I believe." Amake stared at the ceiling above. "You need a friend and a lover and I am comfortable with that, but there is a world of difference between a lover and a romantic partner."

"You're afraid I'll fall in love with you?"

Amake laughed and turned around, tugging half the blankets in the process. She stared at Jilssan, that beautiful confident smile dancing on her lips. "I think you're already smitten, dear, and I worry about the desires such feelings bring."

It took a moment for Amake's seriousness to pierce Jilssan's pleasant afterglow. She meant this—the playful self-confidence masked very real concerns. About Jilssan expecting… what, exactly? A full-blown romance? What an absurd idea. "Myria has long since taught me to handle these."

She'd lost her first love to airheaded romance and carelessness, and she'd never risked it again. Isandor was far safer, of course, but she didn't intend to stay … right? Jilssan closed her eyes, willing away any thoughts of her current situation and uncertain future. Those could wait. She wanted to enjoy Lady Brasten's company.

Amake's fingers ran the length of Jilssan's arm. "Good. Romantic gestures leave me uneasy, to say the least. I find having those feelings foisted on me unsettling. If you ever make me feel like I *should* reciprocate, I will show you the door."

"I shall consider myself warned, then." Jilssan brought herself closer and landed a slow kiss on Amake's lips before grinning. "Maybe I'm a little smitten, but what we have now suits me. Tonight is perfect. Watching you trap Lord Allastam like you trapped me will be perfect. Beyond that…"

She trailed off. Jilssan had no idea what happened beyond that, and she'd rather not dwell on it. Personal ambition had driven most of her life. She'd climbed through the Jaheera Coast's Academy ranks, making her mark with innovative use of power runes to enhance physical performances. Few Myrians had played with one-word runes and powerful spells, since it was much easier to achieve complex ones through several runes, and Jilssan had spent a few years between boring piles of books to stretch the potential of power words. As dreadful as academia had turned out, it drew many powerful figures, and she'd managed to catch the attention of Master Enezi, Isra's father. With both the backing of a reputable transmuter and her own personal achievements, Jilssan had only needed to establish herself as a competent leader for more political missions. Thus, a position as second-in-command here in Isandor.

That … had not turned out so well, and now she found herself adrift, uncertain about her next goal, once she and Isra were safe. Perhaps the last few exhausted days were a signal to slow down, to take a deep breath and realign her path. After all, '*what needed to be done*' only worked as long as she had a clear idea of where she wanted to end up.

Chapter Twenty-Six

DIEL Dathirii swept into the Golden Table's building with his head high, a dusting of snow shining in his golden hair and a glorious green cloak trailing behind. Lady Brasten accompanied him on his right, her eyes painted gold to match her dress, while Arathiel, Sora, and Jilssan followed a few steps behind. An unexpected team for this final play, one devoid of any other Dathirii. His family had stayed at the Brasten Tower, their hopes and future all in his hands. The warmth of their well wishes nestled against his heart, soothing his nerves.

To his surprise, Lady Mia Allastam waited for him in the lobby, a picture of the delicate lady, her hair held back by a plaited braid through which she had woven the artificial flowers she was known to handcraft, her sky-blue dress pooling around her, her smile steady and soft. The blush on her cheeks and carefully applied makeup couldn't hide her exhaustion and he caught the crispness of her posture, betraying the pain needling at her. He was all the more grateful for her presence, if it cost her to have come.

"Lord Dathirii," she greeted, and the use of his lost title startled him into a full stop.

"Lady Mia Allastam," Lady Brasten replied, filling his awkward silence. "It is always a pleasure to see you. Have you, perhaps, had the chance to read my last correspondence?"

"Indeed. Your cousin's tips have saved a few of my days since. Please let them know I'm grateful for the wisdom. And it so happens that that correspondence is why I've come. I thought it best delivered in person." Mia offered a slight bow, then she retrieved a parchment from her sleeve and extended it towards Diel. "From yours."

What wits Diel had managed to gather in their brief conversation almost scattered at the mention of 'his'. He snatched the message from her hand and unfurled it with shaking fingers. Branwen had been confident they could trust Mia Allastam to hold her end of the bargain, but less so that Yultes would even make it to the Allastam Tower alive. The message held only a few lines, all in Jaeger's flowing handwriting, and for a time Diel could only stare at it, the beautiful letters so familiar to him, so loved. Then he forced himself to read.

I'm sorry, Diel. It seems I am no good with construction, only destruction. I've done my best to keep your architect safe for when you return.

Y.

And then, under the two lines:

See you soon, my love.

It needed no signature, and Diel traced the letters with his fingers, inhaling deeply in an attempt to keep his composure. He turned his gaze back to Mia Allastam, who had waited patiently for his attention before she spoke again.

"Yultes is recovering well and first awakened near dawn," she said. "You should know he has confirmed that in the course of yesterday's events, he repeatedly stabbed Hellion Dathirii. We questioned him before he could speak alone with Jaeger, and their versions match."

In other words, they did not have time to build a lie to cover for each other. Diel suspected this was not information Lord Allastam would have wanted shared, but nothing in Mia's posture betrayed nervousness or guilt. She had helped them a great deal since he'd lost his house, at significant personal risk. He tilted his head in a grateful nod.

"House Dathirii will not forget your consideration in this matter." He couldn't keep the roughness out of his voice and bowed to her. "I hope one day we can repay you for it."

Mia Allastam returned his bow. "So do I, milord."

She wrapped her winter overcoat over her shoulders then left them. As he watched her disappear in the curtain of snow still falling, Diel Dathirii had the distinct impression she knew when and how, perhaps, he could pay his debt. He filed that information away for later; for now, they had more immediate matters to attend to.

"Master Jilssan," Lady Brasten said, "be ready for your grand entrance. We'll call for you."

"As long as you set the stage properly, I'll wow even the crusty curmudgeons."

Lady Brasten laughed, but behind her, Sora Sharpe was rolling her eyes, as annoyed as Diel. A lot of lives depended on their success today—a lot of people relied on him saying the right words at the right time and, perhaps more importantly, keeping quiet when the wrong ones threatened to burst.

Diel slid his thumb over Jaeger's words one last time, then slipped the paper in his vest, so that it could rest close to his heart.

THE decorum usually in full force during gatherings of the Golden Table had vanished. Instead of standing by the Table with solemn expressions, the noble representatives of Isandor's great houses had gathered in clumps, whispering to one another in covert tones, restless and ill at ease. Most had been kept in the dark about the details of Lord Allastam's arrest, but all knew it had happened—and all had seen him arrive earlier, flanked by five soldiers in House Brasten's livery. Lady Brasten and Diel hoped the shock and spontaneous outrage at today's revelations would carry them through, and it seemed the dramatic arrival had stoked everyone's emotions.

Their own entrance brought quite a few stares and a renewal in the hurried conversations. Diel caught snatches here and there, split between their surprise at Arathiel's presence—and the lack of any armed escort for him beyond Sora, who kept a hand on his elbow— and speculation about what Lord Allastam had done. House Allastam kept to their own, aligned around their places, Lord Allastam and his son in a quick, heated discussion. In another corner, Lord Balthazar leaned on the wall and listened to Lord Lorn with a disaffected air that felt forced. Their families, the two biggest players besides House Allastam, had been the only two Lady Brasten had met with directly, hoping to convince them this was a good opportunity to stall their rival's constant growth.

Eventually everyone reached their seats around the table, and as Lady Brasten and Arathiel claimed the family's two spots—one of which they had inherited from House Dathirii's fall—Diel was forced to step back. The relegation left a bitter aftertaste on his tongue. He was a guest here, permitted to speak only by the Table's grace and at their command, and in no way their equal, not anymore. It grated him more than he cared to admit.

As the last conversations dwindled, Lord William cleared his throat, calling everyone's attention, and opened the meeting by intoning the traditional "We are the Golden Table, the heart of Isandor, the creators of its future."

Sora Sharpe choked at the words and brought a hand to her mouth to quickly camouflage her disdain as a cough. Lord William moved into the beginning's procedural, and although no one protested Diel's or Sora's presence, many snorted and scoffed. He endured, gaze straight ahead, and graciously thanked the Golden

Table for the honour of his presence as if each word didn't burn his tongue.

"Now," Lord William continued, "it is customary for new members sitting around the table to be introduced. Lady Brasten?" His eyes rested on Arathiel and he smiled, a strange, self-satisfied expression that sent a wave of unease through Diel. "Would you do us the honour?"

"With pleasure, milord, though I'm sure Lord Arathiel Brasten needs no introduction." She set her hands on the table, perfectly at ease despite the incredulous whispers and Lord Allastam's deadly glare. "As I've stated during our last meeting, we have confirmed beyond reasonable doubts that Lord Arathiel is exactly who he claims to be. Considering his involvement in the matters we have to discuss today, I judged it appropriate for him to occupy our new seat."

"If I may, Lady Brasten?" Lady Carrington was poised by the table, about halfway between House Brasten and House Allastam, who today faced each other. Despite leading the smallest house around the Table—one who rightly should no longer have a seat— she was often awarded the spot directly across Lord William's as deference to House Carrington's status as a founding family. "Has he not been arrested for freeing Hasryan Fel'ethier?"

"Indeed." Lady Brasten smiled, a discreet expression Diel had come to identify as the personal pleasure of leading a conversation exactly where and how she wanted it. "He is willing to step aside and act as a guest, but if the reasoning for it is that nobles under investigation for criminal acts should not participate freely, then I'm afraid Lord Allastam should also step aside."

"That's preposterous!" Lord Allastam exclaimed.

Before he could edge another word in, Lady Brasten clapped her hands and grinned at him.

"Then we agree, and he stays. After all, we're all equals here around the Golden Table."

Lord Allastam's mouth clamped shut. He could either ask for special permission and imply he deserved better, or endure Arathiel's presence. It was a power play—their plan didn't rely on Arathiel at all, but they'd all agreed that giving him the second Brasten seat would put Lord Allastam off balance and prove to smaller houses that they didn't need to bend to his threats. Diel exhaled slowly in the heavy silence that followed. No one had any objections. Fuming, Lord Allastam introduced the holder of the seat he had inherited from House Dathirii's fall, and they could finally move to the hardest and most important item on the agenda.

"Lady Brasten," Lord William called again, "if you would please explain to the Golden Table the reason for this second special meeting? I'm certain we're all eager to hear the details."

"I will speak plainly: the Golden Table is more than a council of law makers. For better or worse, we, as a collective, stand above any court of justice. We have the power to begin and stop any investigations, and indeed, many of us here have done so on an individual basis." She set her hands down on the table, her tone calm and solid. Convincing. "Have we not all, at one point or another, asked investigators to look into a matter for us? Or slipped a few coins in an open palm, distracting unwanted eyes? Bribery and intercession are so common we don't even think of them as crimes."

Sora Sharpe emitted a low hiss by his side. She stared ahead, stiff, trying to disguise her scowl under a professional mask. The supremacy of the Golden Table was an open secret, one she had herself railed against in the past, but he doubted she'd ever witnessed thirty nobles acknowledge it with shameless nods.

"If I have brought so many guests with me today, milords, it is because I believe the Golden Table is the best suited to examine the gravity of Investigator Sharpe's accusations against Lord Allastam, listen to the central witness in her investigation, and decide whether or not we want her to pursue this course. Lord Allastam will forgive me his brief but comfortable stay in my tower, I'm sure. His decisiveness regarding matters concerning his family might not have given us time to convene properly."

What a cutting way to imply he was harsh, deadly, and cared little about the Golden Table unless it served his schemes. Diel couldn't quite hold back his smile, and judging by the snickers around the table, several other nobles agreed with Lady Brasten's assessment. Their mirth relaxed the tense atmosphere, and the scowls vanished from most expressions.

Lord Balthazar pulled at his thick beard. His fast-rising family would have much to gain from House Allastam taking a hit, and already a glimmer of interest shone in his eyes. He was one of the few gathered who'd known the nature of today's discussions ahead of time, and he obviously approved of Lady Brasten's handling of it so far. "We've already cleared our schedules to be here today. I supposed we might as well hear it. I do believe, however, that Lord

William should be entrusted with our guests' right to speak, as he does when our own discussions become too heated."

Several murmurs of agreement followed his suggestion. Lord William accepted the role, as gracious and a tad dramatic as always. Diel had expected more waves about it after he'd voted in Diel's favour at the last Golden Table, but that was the strength of Lord William's reputation as a mediator. Even when he took a side, he was trusted to be fair.

"Let us begin, then," Lord William said. "Investigator Sharpe, please present the crimes and accusations you would be investigating."

Sora steadied herself with a deep breath and stepped forth, to stand beside Lady Brasten at the table. Drake Allastam slapped a palm on the table, but before he could edge a word in, his father's hand landed on his shoulder, heavy with meaning. The young man bit back his outburst, but no one could mistake the hatred in the glare he directed at Sora. She raised her eyebrows at him.

"I will not bore you with every crime I'm investigating. Most are not worth the Table's attention."

Sora had never been a good liar and couldn't disguise the hint of annoyance in her voice. No doubt she thought none of these crimes should be their business and they shouldn't interfere. But she played the game nonetheless, and as long as appearances of deference were maintained, the Table wouldn't hold it against her.

"The Sapphire Guard allows great latitude to the noble houses of Isandor in matters of justice, asking only to be kept informed of potential prisoners in their cells or judgments being meted out." Her disgust increased, but she pushed on with her speech, hands behind her back in apparent calm. Diel wished he could see her expression, but he had to stay one step behind, like a ghost over the table. "Without this information, we cannot sanction one's actions. It's in this context that I first entered the Allastam Tower, to arrest his lordship for detaining Master Jilssan of the Myrian Enclave and Hasryan Fel'ethier, as—"

The Golden Table erupted in exclamations as she named Hasryan, burying her voice entirely. For a moment the conversation was nothing but a chaotic mess of questions and answers, sometimes confused, sometimes angry, then Lord William's voice rose above the din, as smooth as ever. "Everyone, please."

They calmed, and Sora finally finished. "As well as torturing him."

Lord Allastam snorted. "He tried to kill me. Do you want to see the scar he left me, ten years after he killed my wife?"

Sora glanced his way and as Lord Allastam reached for his shirt, she raised a hand. "I assure you; this won't be necessary. No one questioned whether he deserved it." She said every word like they had been ripped out of her forcefully. Diel's stomach twisted, and it was all he could do not to step forward and question it himself, ruining their chances. He had to admire Sora's self-control—he wasn't certain he'd have managed to say that, or to smoothly continue. "I am only stating that by law, you were obligated to alert us, and you did not. These are minor crimes, but they matter. They are indicative of your disregard for laws and customs that apply to you."

Silence returned to the Golden Table. The gathered nobles leaned forward, their gaze alternating between Lord Allastam and Sora. Lord Balthazar had yet to let go of his beard and was stroking it eagerly, his interest clear. Lord Lorn kept his thoughts closer to himself, but Diel had worked with him long enough to recognize the spark in his dark eyes. Everyone was curious and tense, and the Table's early hostility had mostly vanished. It could return quickly, however. When you attacked a force like House Allastam, you pushed against the noble institution as a whole.

"An impressive appetizer, Investigator Sharpe," Lord William said, "but I believe it is time to move to the main course."

Sora squared her shoulders and spread her palms across the table, taking charge of the space around her. When she spoke, she threw the accusation out with force, putting years of confidence behind her steady voice. "The crime worthy of the Golden Table is as follows: Lord Allastam actively conspired to assassinate Lord Diel Dathirii, at a time when his lordship still held his title and led his House."

The nobles of Isandor's Golden Table stiffened, as if withholding a collective gasp. Their expressions varied between surprise, indignation, and calm masks. Sora held her chin high under their scrutiny, and many turned to Lord Allastam, awaiting his response. He sneered and waved a hand, dismissing Sora.

"I understand Diel is eager to shift the blame for his failure, but I cannot be made responsible for the in-fighting in House Dathirii. All I did was have his titles removed and his family put back where it belonged."

A burst of anger blossomed in Diel's chest, rushing up and spinning his head. Hellion had been nothing but an easily manipulated puppet for Lord Allastam, a gateway to sink the house and drain it of its resources—and now he was dead, eaten from inside by his arrogance and ambition, set up to fail from the beginning. Diel stepped forward, bristling. "You were—"

"Mister Dathirii, please wait for your turn," Lord William interrupted. "There will be ample time for your side of the story."

It took everything Diel had to swallow his words, nod, and step back. His face had flushed and he didn't bother hiding his anger. He hated the ready dismissal, the reminder of his new station, of how he could no longer speak whenever and however he wanted. Lord Allastam was smirking at him, enjoying every moment of humiliation. Diel turned away from him and found Arathiel looking back, silently asking if he'd be fine. Diel allowed himself a long, slow breath to calm the furious pounding of his heart, then he smiled back. He needed to trust his allies to speak for him when it was needed.

"I believe we should call our main witness, Master Jilssan of the Myrian Enclave," Lady Brasten said. "Her story is at the heart of this matter, and rather at odds with Lord Allastam's."

A page was sent to collect Jilssan from the lobby. In the tense silence of the wait, Lord Allastam bent over to whisper something to his son. Drake snickered, patted his father's arm, then they straightened back. Lord William stared at them both, unamused. Diel wished he'd tell them both off at the same speed he had interrupted him—whatever mockery Lord Allastam had just said didn't have its place here.

Then Jilssan stepped in, and Lord Allastam's antics were immediately forgotten. She'd shed the large winter coat she'd worn to get here and strode in adorned in a well-adjusted wine-red dress, cut open to reveal black pants embroidered with intricate patterns reminiscent of Myria's official garments. The dress flared behind like a cape, and its low cut revealed much of Jilssan's pale shoulders. She looked ready to conquer the room, an impression reinforced by her clacking heeled boots as she strode to the table. Jilssan didn't walk to Lady Brasten and Sora, instead heading for the closest end of the table. Lady Carrington and Lord Serringer reflexively made room for her.

"Greetings, everyone," Jilssan intoned in a solemn voice, the lilt of her Myrian accent out in full force, before setting her gaze upon Lord Allastam and smiling. "Long time no see, milord."

Lord Allastam's grip on his cane whitened, but he replied with surprising warmth. "I see your tongue never suffered from our hospitality. How fares your back?"

Jilssan's smile crispened. "As well as can be expected." She turned to the room as a whole and spread her arms. "So, how do these things go around here? Do I tell you everything I know, or do you ask pointed questions until you hear what you want?"

"We're gathered here to judge whether or not the accusation that Lord Allastam conspired to have Diel Dathirii killed is worth investigating further." Lord William spoke with renewed enthusiasm, and Diel suspected Jilssan's entrance had appealed to his personal dramatic flair. "So why don't you start with that?"

Jilssan's eyebrows shot up, and she threw the table a contemptuous look. "I'm surprised there needs to be thirty of you to do this," she muttered. "But as you wish. Here is what I know: shortly after Diel Dathirii requested Arathiel's temporary freedom, Lord Allastam travelled undercover to the Myrian Enclave to meet with Master Avenazar."

Arathiel's shoulders stiffened. Diel wished he could reach out and let him know it wasn't his fault, that the decision to free him had been Diel's alone and that he had no regrets. Someone had needed to save Varden, and the way those two got along now only made Diel even gladder he'd chosen Arathiel.

He turned his attention back to Jilssan, who had already given the Table a few more details about the first meeting. "The proposition was quite the pleasant surprise for the Myrian Enclave. We had been under the impression that House Dathirii and House Allastam were tacit allies and would at least make sure not to get in each other's way. Yet here was Lord Allastam, eager to seal a trade deal and an alliance with us by offering Lord Dathirii up on a silver platter."

In front of her, Allastam fumed quietly. His upper body may have projected calm, but his eyes promised death and he tapped his foot, a discreet sound Diel suspected few ears but his elven ones could pick up.

"This doesn't hold water for two seconds. An alliance? You tried to have my son killed!"

With a small cough, Jilssan corrected him. "Master Avenazar tried to have your son killed. I had nothing to do with it.

Furthermore, this would all make a lot more sense if you let me tell the story in order, and I'm sure your colleagues would appreciate it."

Diel had to admire her audacity. She'd come up with the very idea of setting Lord Allastam against Master Avenazar and no one else could have fed Avenazar the correct information to make him give that order.

"Indeed." Lord William almost purred the word, and his smile seemed more sincere than usual. "Please go on, Master Jilssan."

"I'll be quick, since some people here seem to lack patience, and hearing two men plan the demise of another gets tedious after a while." Jilssan made a dismissive hand gesture that clashed completely with the building horror inside Diel. Boring. They had been preparing his death, and while he didn't care to hear the details, the thought they could *bore* anyone made him sick. He closed his eyes, trying to let her words wash over him. "They met a total of three times that I know of. The negotiations bored Master Avenazar to no end, but I reminded him we needed to get something out of this to satisfy our superiors in Myria. I don't think assuaging his petty grudge would have been enough."

Jilssan looked at her bright red nails for a moment, then caught Lord Allastam's gaze and held it. Her smile had vanished. "I asked Lord Allastam later if he realized how Master Avenazar treated prisoners—if he knew he'd sold someone to torture and death. He answered some men needed to be taught a lesson and that he was glad the enclave worked under Myrian laws despite opposing it two years ago."

Lord Allastam's cane slammed against the ground, shattering the heavy silence of his fellow nobles. "Now this is just outrageous!"

"Now?" Sora repeated. "Why now, milord? Was the rest more in line with your memories?"

"Of course not."

"Ah," Jilssan said. "Are you going to deny also stating you'd give that lesson yourself if the Golden Table wasn't so restrictive about assaulting other nobles?"

"Obviously." He snorted, reclaiming some of his calm. "All of this is a fabrication."

Blood pounded in Diel's ears at the brutal denial. He tried to remind himself that they'd expected this, even counted on it, but it didn't make it easier to tolerate. The memories burned too brightly in his mind—finding Hellion on his desk, his goodbyes to Jaeger, chains on his wrists and a hard carriage bench under him. He swallowed hard, desperate to stay composed for the entire Table, but already a thin film of sweat covered his forehead. When Arathiel's steady voice rose, he was grateful for his calmer friend.

"If all of it is a fabrication, then I have to wonder how Diel Dathirii came to be in the Myrian Enclave, in shackles, the very night his house was taken over by Allastam soldiers. Are you suggesting he walked there?"

"I'm suggesting he never went. You've all had ample time to come up with this lie and slander me."

Members of the Golden Table had started whispering to one another, their tones a mix of concern and anger. Diel wondered who they believed and if they realized how accurate Jilssan's portrayal of Lord Allastam was. He couldn't even tell if she'd embellished anything; it was too easy to imagine the man casually uttering every horrible word she'd attributed to him.

"I'll admit, we had also originally concluded that Diel Dathirii had never come to the Myrian Enclave." Jilssan raised her voice to cover the growing din. "We thought we had been tricked, that the carriage only contained an elite infiltration team meant to rescue a prisoner and hinder us." At this, she nodded in Arathiel's direction. "This is what provoked Master Avenazar into sending assassins after Drake Allastam. He had been grievously wounded and sought revenge." Jilssan heaved a dramatic sigh, then fixed her gaze back on Lord Allastam. "Even the best of us are wrong sometimes. You vehemently denied this when I sought an audience with you. You told me you had delivered, and it was my problem if we'd lost our prize. That's when you threw me in your jail."

Diel wondered if they gave badges for professional lying in Myria. Jilssan was obscuring huge elements of the story, mixing in solid truths with her countless fabrications—enough that he wasn't quite certain where one began and the other ended. He'd need to be careful around her. Lady Brasten might think they had her pinned, but watching her spin an effortless tale now, he wasn't so sure.

"You can see why I thought Sora Sharpe's accusations were worth taking seriously," Lady Brasten said. "She must be allowed to proceed."

Lord Allastam clapped slowly, and rocks stumbled to the bottom of Diel's stomach. He was smiling, a dangerous glint in his eyes.

"A wonderful tale. It's quite admirable how Lady Brasten's little crew dances around the matter of Sora Sharpe's less than stellar records when it comes to my family. You might be led to think she's a neutral party, doing her best to do her job, and yet her path has crossed ours on a few interesting occasions. She was present when the Myrians first assaulted my son, seconds away from attacking him, even! Then, on the fateful day she arrested *me*, she also watched as Kellian Dathirii crushed Drake's ribcage under magical stone and even let the good captain send Hasryan Fel'ethier back to his boss! Twice, now, the assassin has escaped her—and one might think it unlucky, if not that we'd then found him hiding in her very home."

The rising murmur of whispers around the table crested into open exclamations and protests. Sora Sharpe had frozen by his side, eyes wide with shock but guilt thankfully kept off her expression.

"He attacked me," Drake put in, voice pitched high with fear. "This demon, he jumped me with a bloodied knife and took me hostage. Dragged me into the cold and even tried to throw me off the bridges! If our guards had not caught me…"

He placed a dramatic hand over his mouth, and the overacting might have been amusing, if not for the sickening anger rising within Diel. Drake had been about to assault an old lady, and *he* was the victim in this story?

"You broke down my door," Sora retorted between gritted teeth.

"You consort with filthy criminals that trawl the shit-stained bottom of the city. I knew you weren't neutral—I'd seen you with that wretch. Someone needed to prove it—and I was right! You're in cahoots with my mom's killer!"

The trap became clear, then. Lord Allastam had waited until their case was inextricably tied to Sora Sharpe's actions: they intended to ruin her reputation and discredit any investigation before it even began.

Alarm prickled every inch of Diel's skin. Lord Balthazar let go of his beard while visible discontent and faint disgust marred Lord Lorn's expression. Several of the other nobles hovered between indignation and shock, and with every second that passed, Diel could feel the collective sympathies of the Golden Table slip away.

They couldn't afford Sora and Hasryan to be linked like that. So Diel did the one thing he was best at: he stepped forward, and said the wrong thing at the wrong time.

"Your accusations are misdirected. Hasryan Fel'ethier is under my employ, and if you have concerns about his actions, *I* will answer for them."

Chapter Twenty-Seven

HE roar across the Golden Table was only equal to the one pounding in Diel Dathirii's ears. Every ounce of good grace he'd had as a victim of Lord Allastam's machinations had evaporated. Nobles turned towards him, some demanding explanations, others an immediate arrest. In the chaos, Arathiel slid closer to him, to stand by his shoulder, but Lady Brasten had stepped back, uttering his name with a perfect mix of betrayal and shock. She had told him once, in no uncertain terms, that they couldn't afford an association with Hasryan—and this was her reiterating that she wouldn't follow him there. He didn't need her to. He didn't *want* her to.

Diel steeled himself and stepped into the space she'd vacated and placed his hands on the Golden Table as if it belonged to him. He'd caught even Lord Allastam off guard, but he wouldn't have long before his enemy recovered.

"Do not expect me to beg forgiveness, as I have neither regrets nor remorse. I needed his help to make a move on the Myrian Enclave, so I hired him—and it saved my life. Were it not for Hasryan Fel'ethier, I would never have escaped Master Avenazar's clutches. Who do you think formed the elite infiltration team mentioned by Jilssan? The one who intercepted the carriage carrying me to a brutal and bloody fate? I count him as a friend, and he has done more to protect this city in the last few weeks than anyone else here."

"All under your orders," Lord Allastam repeated. "Orders for which you claim full responsibility."

Diel knew where this one was heading. He'd looped the noose around his neck himself. He met Lord Allastam's gleeful gaze and offered an apologetic smile and a shrug. "His orders for you were non-lethal, milord."

When a new uproar followed, Diel took consolation in Sora Sharpe's strangled noises behind him, adding credibility that she'd had no idea any of this was going on right under her nose.

"They didn't feel non-lethal," Allastam retorted.

"And yet you're alive, and … remind me, Miss Sharpe, how many charges of murder you've put to Hasryan's name?"

She stammered for a second before asserting some self-control. "M-more than a dozen, milord."

"More than a dozen," Diel repeated. He could not keep the smugness from his voice.

Lord Allastam's face had grown a deep, blotchy red, his rage so intense that Diel thought he felt the heat all the way across the table.

He should be afraid, really—Lord Allastam was no easy prey and would retaliate—but all fear had left Diel. He floated, light-headed and empty, soaked in the brief rush of adrenaline after a dangerous leap of faith.

"Look at him," Lord Allastam said. "He truly *is* proud of it. Since you're so eager to claim this wretch's crimes as your own, perhaps you should hang for them."

And there it was, the point when falling no longer felt like flying, the ground rushing up at him. Diel braced himself. He wasn't done fighting.

"If that is the price I pay, then I must wonder what the Golden Table would consider just punishment for your crimes, Lord Allastam."

"My crimes?" Lord Allastam spread his arms wide, as if embracing the Golden Table. "Unlike you, I've admitted to nothing. You built a nice, provocative lie to be sure, but without proof, is it really worth anything?"

"Witnesses are part of the proof," Sora pointed out, not bothering to disguise her irritation.

"What is one outsider's word against Lord Allastam's, however?" Lady Carrington asked. "Your accusations are grievous. We need more to substantiate them."

An unmistakable murmur of agreement ran through the crowd, and Diel's stomach sank. What would it take for these nobles to believe them?

"Do we really?" Lord Lorn asked, the scorn plain in his voice. "Lord Allastam is eager to focus our attention on Hasryan Fel'ethier, but I remember when he still blamed House Freitz. We've all witnessed their downfall. Let's not pretend we're not aware of how far he can go."

"Are you implying I killed any of them?" Allastam countered, lifting his chin. Several voices rose at once to reply, talking over one another.

Any sense of conversation was temporarily lost as the leading nobles of Isandor yelled their thoughts into the melee, hotly debating Lord Allastam's potential involvement in the suspicious deaths of two members of the Freitz family, almost ten years ago. Accidents happened fast on a boat and the Reonne was an unforgiving river, but no one had ever had more than rumours. They had never been discussed so publicly, and with Hasryan's arrest, everyone had been ready to bury the story forever.

Lord William allowed the chaos to continue until Lady Brasten caught his attention, and he raised his hands to interrupt. "Everyone, please." He never needed to raise his voice to calm the Table. "Let us return to the matters at hand. Lady Brasten has something to say?"

"Indeed. Something escapes me." She reached for her necklace, playing with the beads as if she searched for her words. Diel doubted she hadn't prepared every single one of them before asking Lord William to speak, and he was glad to leave her the limelight for a moment. "We ask the Golden Table to grant Sora Sharpe unhindered investigative power to dig into this matter. Is it not normal, then, that we have no concrete proof to substantiate our claim? This would be precisely her work. Any paper trail is likely located either in the Allastam Tower or the Myrian Enclave, neither of which could be searched without the Table's permission."

"We'll have a contract," Jilssan provided. "Trade deals involving human beings are nothing out of the ordinary in Myria. There's no reason for us not to seal it with signatures."

Diel stared at Lord Allastam's face, trying to judge by his reaction whether or not he'd truly signed anything of the sort. The lord tilted his head to the side and smiled right back at him, oozing complete confidence. Either he was bluffing, or Avenazar had never bothered with paperwork.

"The solution is simple," Lady Brasten continued, unshaken by her opponent's confidence. "We allow Sora Sharpe to investigate this matter and provide the necessary resources to retrieve this proof."

"You mean to assault the Myrian Enclave?" Lord Lorn asked. After House Allastam, they had the largest number of soldiers and would have to contribute significantly to such an assault.

"Why shouldn't we?" Lord Balthazar replied. "Between their assault on Branwen Dathirii and Lord Drake Allastam, they have proven they are dangerous foes willing to resort to violence against the nobles of this city. We need to get rid of them."

The five Allastam members at the table tightened around Drake at the mention of the attack. He'd grown paler and turned towards his father, who nodded.

"On this, we agree. They have to pay for this ignominy. But as we've established, they're not the only ones who tried to have my son killed recently." He turned fully towards Diel, then, and his cane snapped against the ground, killing the few whispered conversations still ongoing. "Tell us, where is Hasryan right now?"

Diel pressed his lips together, but his silence weighed heavily in everybody's eyes. They wanted him to surrender Hasryan, to cut ties now that he had been exposed and cut his losses at the same time.

"As I've said, I count Hasryan as a friend."

"Sir, I *will* have to place you under arrest," Sora Sharpe said, and although her voice was strained, he was glad she'd caught up to the part she was expected to play.

Lord Allastam snorted and discarded the idea of an arrest with a wave of his hand. Clearly, he was not done.

"Lord Dathirii, you are a menace."

Lord Dathirii. How interesting, that Lord Allastam would recognize him as a peer now that he believed Diel could be equally ruthless. But whatever respect might lay under the title's return, it clearly wouldn't spare him the full onslaught. Diel waited, bracing himself. They were so close now, had everyone's agreement that the Myrian Enclave needed to go… But there would be a price to pay for that success.

"You provoked this war with the Myrians. You hired a known assassin and now protect him from our laws. Your familial infighting led to Lord Hellion's murder. Wherever you go, you create chaos, pain, and death. What is next, pray tell me? Enter a bloody struggle to weed out the Crescent Moon on behalf of your betrayed assassin friend? Give power to the Lower City and watch them tear down all that we stand for?"

Diel opened his mouth to deny these suggestions, but he couldn't bring himself to. Lord Allastam had phrased those ideas in the most alarming way possible, but they were fundamentally excellent ones.

Faced with his silence, Lord Allastam only laughed. "You're as much a threat as the Myrians. I'll gladly help the city get rid of these outsiders if I'm promised the more pernicious, inside problem will also go away."

"Say what you mean," Diel snapped. He could feel Lord Allastam circling him, a predator closing in on prey, and he was tired of the wait. He wanted Allastam to pounce, even as his entire body tensed, his insides recoiling from the inevitable consequence of boldly claiming responsibility for Hasryan.

"Isandor would know peace again if you were gone. Everyone else is only following your lead." Lord Allastam rested his hands on his cane, one on top of the other, his entire posture relaxed. "Renounce any claim to the leadership of House Dathirii. Exile yourself. Leave the city, never to return, and I will lend my troops to an assault on the Myrian Enclave. I will even submit myself to this disgraceful investigation and, the Golden Table willing, would consider extending pardon to some of your underlings. *You* are the problem."

Diel's head rung. Exile, then. Quit and leave his entire family behind. He spread his hands on the table, nauseous, half-convinced he would faint. He had fought so hard for this city, over so many decades. He couldn't give up now, not after he'd stood up to Master Avenazar and triggered this war, not after he'd shattered his family's reputation to rescue Varden or risked Jaeger's safety to deny Hellion the very title Lord Allastam wanted him to abandon. His entire life was in Isandor—past, present, and future.

Yet if he let the last one go, if he gave up his future here, the investigation would proceed. They had a chance to run the Myrians out. And this pardon… What if Arathiel could go free? If Yultes could be spared any accusations for saving Jaeger's life? And none of his family could be indicted for helping Hasryan; that was all on him now. It was exactly what they'd fought for from the very first day. Everyone won if *he* chose to lose everything.

Diel lifted his gaze and took in Lord Allastam's smug smile, his utter confidence, and he understood a fundamental truth about him. He didn't believe Diel could accept. This was an attempt to ridicule him because he couldn't comprehend that anyone would sacrifice their position. To him, every battle was one of revenge or power, a slow climb up a ladder which left enemies in the dust. But funnier, perhaps, was the idea that exiling Diel would end House Dathirii and their pesky demands for a better society, that they were all obliging him. Something warm and light ballooned in Diel's chest, untying the knots in it and expanding. The sensation spread to his head until the buzzing receded, leaving him giddy and grinning and on the verge of tears. It was laughable, really, to believe he was the only troublemaker in this city.

"My good lord Allastam," he said, a light edge of hysteria to his voice, "when your soldiers dragged me to the Myrian Enclave, I made my peace with dying to see this through. Do you really think I can't accept exile?"

Lord Allastam's palpable shock reverberated through the Golden Table, and flat silence filled the room. Diel swept everyone into a wide stare. They'd all thought that. Dark fingers alighted on his shoulders, and he turned towards Arathiel, who mouthed 'are you sure?'. Diel nodded, even though his insides felt like they were slowly disintegrating, like a huge part of him was slipping away—he was no longer the Head of the House Dathirii, the uncle who worked miracles, who salvaged everything from wreckage, who always found a way. There was no way, not for him, not if they wanted to finish this. Lord Allastam had given him an opening to make his choice count and he would take it.

He returned his attention to his nemesis, his heart pounding. When he spoke again, his voice had regained countenance and power. "You want me gone, and I want the Myrians ousted and the truth about you revealed. It sounds like the premise of a deal, doesn't it? So let's negotiate, and let the Golden Table serve as mediator and witness."

THEY fought over every detail in a bitter and exhausting back and forth, bringing every grievance to the table. Diel had lost count of how often he'd repeated 'You want me gone, don't you?', wielding it as a weapon, forcing Lord Allastam to relent. Lord Allastam tried to claim the debt owned by Hellion, but Diel countered with a list of the damage done by his soldiers within the Dathirii Tower, to the rooms and people both—and in particular to Yultes, who'd been held by his men as he was bleeding out.

Over the course of the debate, he clarified the details of Lord Allastam's offer to stop him from worming out of it. All Allastam soldiers available would be participating in the assault on the Myrian Enclave. Provided they found proof of this deal in the Myrian Enclave, Sora Sharpe would be granted one year to further investigate. During that time, Lord Allastam would remain under constant surveillance by a rotation of guards from other Houses sitting on the Golden Table, limiting his ability to tamper with the evidence.

Then came the time to negotiate the pardons, and Diel equipped himself with Lord Allastam's own accusations, shouldering the blame for anything Branwen, Kellian, Arathiel, Aunt Camilla, or anyone in his family had done. Everyone was only following his lead, weren't they? Yultes and Jaeger were not only included in the immunity, but they'd be allowed to return home at their earliest convenience. He covered for everyone from Jilssan to Cal, getting their names written down—everyone except Hasryan. The name had barely crossed his lips that Lord Allastam jumped his throat.

"His crimes predate your little alliance. We are *not* pardoning him for killing my wife."

Diel gritted his teeth. He'd not had much hope, but he'd had to try. "But those under my orders?"

Lord Allastam hand waved them away. "If it amuses you."

It had nothing to do with what amused him, but he smirked at his opponent nonetheless. "Interesting, how his past crimes are his responsibility and not his boss'. He was hired in both cases."

It earned him a scowl, but before he could push this angle, Lord

William interrupted, asking him to stay focused on matters related to current events. The Golden Table would not hear more of pardoning Hasryan.

In the end, he also bought himself another month in Isandor as well as a review of House Dathirii's accounts in two years' time. He would have time to return home and put his things in order, at least, before he left it forever.

When Diel Dathirii finally stepped out of the stuffy, windowless room of the Golden Table, he felt stunned and hollow. He knew he'd accomplished a lot—that with a single decision, he had set Isandor firmly behind their fight against Avenazar and greatly diminished the lasting consequences for all of his allies, but he could not conjure any sense of joy. He ignored Jilssan and Sora, who'd been asked to stay outside during the negotiations and now eagerly awaited news, and strode directly to the large window overseeing the city. Isandor spread above and below him, golden lights filtering from the Higher City through a myriad of bridges and cold-resistant vines. In the growing darkness of dusk, he couldn't see the bottom at all.

He had never in his life considered what he'd do outside of Isandor. There wasn't supposed to be an after, and while he'd travelled in his youth, he had no idea where to start or what to do. It didn't even feel real. But he had a whole month to figure it out, and in truth there was only one place he wanted to be right now: by Jaeger's side.

Diel motioned for a page to bring him his coat then strode out without another word.

Chapter Twenty-Eight

Relief flooded through Diel as his gaze latched onto Jaeger's sleeping form. Despite Lady Mia Allastam's assurance that he had been safe, it hadn't felt real until he could watch a strand of hair rise and fall with each breath, or trace the line of his jaw with his eyes, or simply sweep the whole of his beautiful self, half-sitting on the faint couch by Yultes' bed. The bruises on Jaeger's cheeks had faded since last time, but their sight still constricted his heart. They'd heal, in time, just as the cracks in Diel's heart would.

He had Yultes to thank for that blessing.

Yultes, who might have been like a brother, had their cycles joined more closely. Yultes, who for so long had been a thorn in his side, a family member to placate or chastise, a cause he'd given up on—and why wouldn't he, the way he'd sneered at Jaeger and mocked him? When Hellion had taken over, however, Yultes had lost that arrogant veneer. His panicked promises that he'd had no parts in it had reminded Diel of the anxious newcomer from all those decades ago. So he'd chosen to believe in him, to challenge him with that faith, even if he'd doubted he could outweigh Hellion's influence. He was glad to have been wrong.

Yultes lay in an actual bed, so pale and clammy his skin looked almost translucent. Asleep, too, his breathing even if shallow. Diel had no idea how to thank him, or if he'd even be wanted. He had no idea what kind of relationship to expect from him now, and with only a brief month left in Isandor, he suspected they'd never have time to find their way to it.

Diel's gaze inevitably returned to Jaeger's form; Yultes wasn't why he'd rushed all the way to the Allastam Tower. He wanted to curl up next his love, to wrap a hand around his chest and let himself nap—simply pause their lives and sleep besides him again, nose in his hair, Jaeger's scent and warmth his entire world. Soon, he promised himself, but not here. Besides, he longed for Jaeger's voice as much as he did his warmth. Slowly, he sat next to him, set a hand on his shoulder, and squeezed.

"Good evening, love."

Jaeger startled at his whispered greeting, sitting up with such speed he almost slid off the seat. Diel steadied him before he fell, smiling as the fear in Jaeger's expression morphed into a soft, disbelieving smile. Jaeger reached out and cupped Diel's cheek. His fingers brushed against skin and hair in a gentle movement, then he pulled Diel into a kiss—as if he needed to confirm what his eyes and fingers were telling him.

Diel melted into it, his hand sliding along Jaeger's arm until he clung to his elbow, tugging him closer. Jaeger's hand slid into his hair and they stayed locked together, time skidding away from their consciousness, leaving only the taste of each other's lips and the overwhelming joy of being together again. Diel never wanted it to end—would never have stopped, if Jaeger had not pulled back, leaving him lightheaded and breathless. His love leaned his forehead against Diel, eyes closed. They breathed in the silence for a last, precious moment.

"You attended an important meeting today," Jaeger said.

Diel pouted. He wished he could leave the city's politics behind the door to the infirmary and forget it all, but Jaeger hated being left in the dark. If he asked, then he wished to have at least a quick rundown of what had happened—and he deserved to know, even though Diel couldn't bring himself to break the news yet.

"We … succeeded. The investigation into Lord Allastam's actions will go forward. The Dathirii Tower is ours to return to, free of soldiers. You're safe, now."

Shadows passed over Jaeger's expression. "You'd asked me to stay alive through this—to be safe, for everyone's sake. I apologize, but I could not. It is my family and home, too, and when asked to defend it, I stepped forward without regards for my safety, or my promise to you."

Diel's lips tugged in an amused smirk. "You apologize, but you're not sorry."

The solemn expression on Jaeger cracked into a smile, and he released a breathless chuckle. "I am not, and I would repeat every act without the slightest hesitation."

"I know." Diel slid his hand in Jaeger's smooth hair and leaned forward, to whisper in his ears. "This is why I love you."

Jaeger closed his eyes and leaned into the touch. Diel let Jaeger's proximity fill the void that had thrown him out of sorts over the last weeks. Every second in his company breathed new calm into him, anchoring him into the present. Slowly, Diel settled into Jaeger's arms, shifting until they were both comfortable—he against his love, and Jaeger against the seat. He still had to tell Jaeger the cost of their victory.

"Tell me everything I missed," he said instead. "Branwen only had bits and pieces of the story, but what I heard from Garith was quite startling."

"I suppose I can allow you to further delay whatever news you're keeping from me."

A startled laugh escaped Diel. "That obvious?"

"To me? Always." Jaeger pulled Diel closer, squeezing him. No need for Diel to turn around to image the loving smirk on his lips. "You'll owe me as many details as I give."

"As if my memory is good enough for that," Diel countered.

Jaeger agreed with a hum then picked up his story. Diel listened to every word, savouring the sound of Jaeger's voice as much as the story and his commentary. More than once, Jaeger lost him with the details of their accounting acrobatics, but he loved hearing of their early days, before the reception, when he'd been allowed to work alongside Garith and Yultes. By comparison, the isolation that had followed sounded awful—and the steady calm of Jaeger's voice roughened through the telling. By the time they arrived at Jaeger's pulling up Garith's heavy basket of accounting books, it had morphed into an angry and stubborn staccato so unlike Jaeger that

Diel found himself gripping his hand, squeezing it in reassurance. Not every of Jaeger's bruises could be seen on his cheeks, and these, too, would need a long time to heal.

Eventually it was his turn, and Diel—delaying still, perhaps—started as far back as his rescue by Branwen's team, before he reached the Myrian Enclave. He hid nothing, sharing every detail he could remember with Jaeger, as he always had. Sometimes Jaeger stopped him to ask pointed questions, and before long he was guessing half of Diel's story before it happened. Diel tried not to think about how much better things could have gone if Jaeger had been by his side, putting things in perspective. He had never been the miracle maker, not on his own. Jaeger was essential to those.

As they drew nearer to the end, however, Jaeger grew increasingly silent. He no longer asked questions or commented, allowing the retelling to come to its crashing conclusion: Lord Allastam's demand for Diel's exile.

"You accepted, didn't you?"

The softness in Jaeger's voice only deepened Diel's anguish. Talking about their time apart had created a hundred tiny hooks of love for his people into Diel, each fastening into his flesh and heart, desperate to hold him down. He thought of Branwen holding the fort as he'd drifted, leading negotiations and establishing contact with their family stuck inside the Tower, of Arathiel's nostalgia transforming into renewed familial tied as he spent time in the Brasten Tower, of Varden's fiery rebuttals at his inaction and his own willingness to jump into any danger for Nevian's sake. Of Kellian, sullen since Brune had taken him, a new darkness underneath his love for the family that Diel hadn't had time to crack. So many people to love and befriend and care for, and so much to do to keep making the city a better place for all. But he would never, now. He had made his choice. It was the right one—the only one—but he hated it nonetheless.

"I did," he answered, his voice cracking. He turned around, to catch Jaeger's dark eyes, desperate to convey how much it hurt. "I'm sorry, Jaeger. Everyone's hard work to corner Lord Allastam hinged on my answer, and I could clear everyone's name except Hasryan's, and get—"

Jaeger placed two fingers on his lips, interruption him. "Stop, Diel. You apologize, but you're not sorry."

Diel's throat dried. Could anything surpass the little amused crinkles at the corner of his eyes, the knowing smile, the tenderness with which he held Diel's gaze as he teased him? Could Jaeger be more perfect? Diel was every bit as smitten as on the day they met—the day Alluma had irrevocably blessed his life. He grinned. "I'm not, and I'd do it again in a heartbeat."

Jaeger leaned forward, mischief shining in his eyes. He placed a short kiss on Diel's lips. "I know. This is why I love you."

Diel's breathy laugh didn't last—he dove in for another kiss, lightheaded and hot, his blood boiling with soft desire. Jaeger allowed him the moment, but it wasn't long before he broke this kiss, too. His frown doused Diel's elation.

"I—" Jaeger broke off, his voice tight with worry. "I've had … a lot of time to think about you while you were gone—about us, and what mattered to me. I have an important question to ask of you, Diel."

Cold, tight claws clamped down around Diel's stomach. Jaeger's attitude reminded him of their early years together, when he'd so often felt inadequate to the task—a commoner among nobles, and more often the source of problems for Diel than the provider of solutions. Although he'd held his head high in public, it'd taken time for Jaeger to trust his value and let snide remarks from Hellion and his crew slide off him. Diel picked up Jaeger's chin, lifting it so he'd look at him rather than the ground.

"Go ahead. I'm listening."

Jaeger shifted, bringing his knees under him. His eyes shining, he picked up Diel's hand and laced their fingers together. "I know this has been a hundred thirty-seven years in the making, and I was never quite comfortable with the idea before—with the title, it never seemed proper—but I ramble now…"

He steadied himself with a deep breath. Diel waited, his heart pounding. Under pressure, Jaeger either used a few, exact words or shut down completely. He needed time, and Diel gave him all the space he could, resisting even the urge to squeeze his hand encouragingly. He should have used the time to brace himself for the words to come.

"Will you… marry me?"

Intense dizziness rushed to Diel's head. He crushed Jaeger's fingers in response, not quite believing he'd heard right, his heart expanding until it threatened to burst. How often had they discussed this before? Jaeger had always been reluctant to go through with it, for reasons that had varied with time but which, ultimately, hadn't mattered. Diel had refused to pressure him into it and had resolved to let his partner ask, if and when he was ready. And Jaeger *had*. Just now, he had!

"If I want… I mean—yes! Yes, a dozen times over. Of course!" He grabbed Jaeger and kissed him, hanging tight to him, close once more, at last. He wanted to laugh, but instead tears spilled down his cheeks. How many human weddings had he witnessed, daydreaming of his own? By the time he let go, he was out of breath. Most elven cultures celebrated cycles together without marking their romantic unions with weddings, but House Dathirii had lived in Isandor for centuries and adopted the tradition, often for political reasons. "I love you. You know I love you."

"I do." Jaeger wiped the tears away with his thumb, smiling. "A month is a short time to prepare a proper ceremony, but we'll follow it with the longest honeymoon of all. After all, we're elves. We have all the time in the world and can turn one moon cycle into hundreds, if we want."

Diel stifled a sound halfway between sob and laughter. This sounded better than 'exile'. All smoke, perhaps, but Diel welcomed the reframing in his mind. Out of words, he kissed Jaeger again— just kissed him until he could finally form a coherent thought.

"You're perfect, did I ever tell you that?"

"I do believe you have, and your inherent bias leads me to question the truth of your declaration. But thank you, good sir."

It occurred to Diel, laughing now with Jaeger, that he had always known Jaeger would follow him into exile—and that if the roles had been reversed, Diel would have abandoned everything for him, too. They were meant together, hands linked as the cycles turned, and soon they would seal that fact before gods and family alike.

Chapter Twenty-Nine

HOSTILE silence greeted Sora when she stepped into the Shelter and she questioned her impulse to come here. Lady Brasten intended to host a celebratory dinner at her tower—one that, according to many, should see the return of Lord Dathirii's beloved—but she'd not been in the mood for their laughter and cheers. She'd needed to sort through her bittersweet thoughts with someone who'd understand, and her feet had led her downward, away from nobles and their infuriating control over any semblance of justice in Isandor, to the angry cook who'd first helped her save Hasryan and set her on this path. Larryn would understand her frustration more than anyone else in this city.

The Shelter's reaction to her entrance confused her—until she realized she'd arrived straight from the Golden Table, clad in her cleanest and most decorated Sapphire Guard outfit. No amount of mud at the bottom of her light blue cape could erase the signal this sent to them. With an awkward cough, she unclasped the cloak, rolled it, then removed any decorations she could easily unclip. It triggered a few snickers and renewed glares, but she steeled herself to them and searched the room for Larryn.

He was weaving his way between the tables, hands and arms full of bowls and plates, halfway in a conversation with one of his patrons. They leaned forward and pointed towards the door, and he turned. His spontaneous grin was a breath of fresh air when she'd felt stiffened.

"Sora!" At the warmth of his tone, most of the Shelter returned to their conversations. "Why would you wear something so ugly? And in here?" He snorted and waved away any reply that might cross her lips. "Give me a moment, I'm coming."

He continued his run through the tables, greeting people as he set down bowls and plates. The former contained a thick brown broth with chunks of carrots and meat—beef, most likely—while a mix of beans, tomato sauce, and various vegetables filled the latter. Everyone had one of the two meals, and Sora was surprised Larryn had had time to make two. He seemed more relaxed than she'd seen him before, and when he looped back towards her, his hands now full of empty plates, he was smiling.

"You look like someone had you working the shitslides for three days straight," he commented. "Wasn't today your big day? We've been hearing lots of strange rumours from above."

Sora stared at him, taken aback by the simultaneous rudeness and friendliness. "It was," she said. "You have time?"

Larryn stared pointedly at his empty plates, then at the packed room around, and finally back at Sora, eyebrows raised. "Do I look like I do? Where's that infamous acute sense of observation? It's dinner hour."

Sora ran a hand over her face, only to immediately regret the coldness of her fingers, not yet warmed from the winter trek down. "Right. I can… I can go."

"No, no! Just pull yourself a seat." He spun on his heels and strode through the room, towards one of the rare unoccupied tables. Patrons stared at Sora as she followed, visibly still uneasy. "Here," Larryn said, pointing with his chin. "Sit down and relax. It always dies down."

Larryn said nothing of how long that might take, and Sora soon regretted not asking. He'd brought her the thick stew and a tall mug of ale before returning to his work. After one sniff of her meal—a delightful puff of garlic, rosemary, bay leaves, and several other things she couldn't place—a gaping pit of hunger opened in Sora's stomach. She dug in, savouring each salty and flavourful bite, every spoon a comforting weight healing her weary soul. Compared to the heavy taste, the beer went down light and quick, and it was a while before Sora's attention left her meal again, to observe her surroundings.

She'd never watched the Shelter at its peak of activity, when Larryn scrambled from one table to another to keep everyone fed, the tables clean, and the mugs filled. Sometimes he paused to chat for a moment, and over the din of other conversations, she heard him ask for news from someone's family, promise an old lady that young Vellien would return, and rant with a young man about his abusive landlord. Although he'd worked up quite a sweat and must have been exhausted, he made the service look easy—agreeable, even. Some patrons stayed past their meal, but most came only to eat, squeezing around a table with perfect strangers, then returned to their homes.

After an hour, musicians in the crowd grabbed makeshift instruments—wooden spoons, a cracked crate, even a violin with two snapped strings—and settled on a pile of debris from broken chairs and tables, vestiges of the too-recent attack. The melody was unlike anything she'd ever heard—lively, unfettered by rules and conventions, moving with the moods of the players and their spontaneity. Sora lost herself in it, eyes closed, its rhythm as unpredictable as they were entertaining. Between the music's charm and the exquisite food, she readily understood why everyone was so attached to the Shelter.

By the time Larryn returned to her, patrons had begun clearing part of the tables and lining them against the walls, creating space to sit on the floor or dance—and, in time, sleep. Larryn let them to the work and plopped in the seat across from hers, mug in hand. "So what's the bad news?"

"Bad news?"

"Yeah. You came in here with a long face, so I'm thinking your stunt didn't go as planned." Larryn drank long and deep, and if he was remotely anxious, it didn't show.

"It worked, actually. After a fashion. The Golden Table is requesting every House to contribute to an assault on the Myrian Enclave, to oust them from our neighbourhood, at the end of which

I will be permitted a search of Master Avenazar's papers for proof of a deal with Lord Allastam. Provided it exists—and Jilssan thinks it does—I will have the full blessing of the Golden Table to investigate Lord Allastam for a year. Should have plenty of time to dig out even more and build a case to be remembered by."

"Shouldn't you ... be happy or something? It all sounds like bullshit and fancy proceedings to me, but that what's you're in it for, no? You want it official."

Heavy stones settled at the bottom of Sora's stomach as she considered Larryn's words. It should have felt like a victory. She'd worked hard for this, and now she'd be able to put all of her skills towards cornering one of Isandor's real criminals. But doing so because others like him had decided this was a good opportunity to eliminate a competitor didn't sit well with her. Worse, still, was the price paid to keep her reputation intact.

"I feel dirty, Larryn." She wrapped her hands around her mug, her gaze firmly on the pale liquid sloshing within. Part of her regretted saying even so much, knowing the explanation would infuriate Larryn—and that he might rightly direct that anger at her. "They went for my reputation. House Allastam put two and two together, with Hasryan and me. He was at my house yesterday, too, with Lady Camilla, and—"

She had felt the floor open beneath her feet as Lord Allastam had accused her of cozying up to Isandor's most famous assassin. Her cheeks had burned so hard she'd been convinced they could all see the truth on her face and guess at the awkward kiss they had shared, or the quieter laughter that had followed. Words had lumped in her throat, refusing to leave it. She still struggled to find them now and put a finger on what bothered her most.

"I didn't defend him," she said at last. "It didn't even occur to me until Lord Dathirii did."

Larryn choked on his drink and spat it out. "Who did *what?*"

His surprise was an amusing balm on her weary heart. "He… He told the whole Golden Table that Hasryan was under his employ and none of it could be associated with me. Told them he was a friend, even. And I stood there and held my mouth shut, because I knew he was salvaging my reputation to give me this investigation, but it felt so *wrong*. I hated it. I still do."

"So do I," Larryn said, his voice still distant from shock. He wiped his mouth and huffed. "You sure about all this?"

"I *just* lived it, Larryn." She reached over the table and pushed his forehead with two fingers. "Best get it in your head that sometimes even *nobles* know to do the right thing. Got himself exiled for it, too."

Larryn batted her hand away. "Technically, he's not a noble anymore, as Vellien has pointedly reminded me a few times."

She rolled her eyes at him, so he smirked, and within seconds their respective façade crumbled and they were laughing. Sora let the absurdity of Larryn's defence wash some of her melancholy away, then drowned the rest in her ale. When she lowered her mug, Larryn was staring at her, back to this strange serious calm she'd never seen on him.

"For what it's worth, you *should* feel like shit for letting it all slide. Maybe it's the only way, and that means you gotta sit with the bitter lie for a year or more, but if you'd been fine with sinking him for your reputation, I'd have kicked you right out. This just proves you got a soul for the system to try and suck it out of you."

Sora grimaced. Once, she might have argued the latter point with him, even if she'd already been disenchanted with the rampant corruption within their ranks. Now even thinking about the parody that Isandor called justice left a deep exhaustion in her bones.

"Well, it's got one year to get that done, because after that I'm gone. Not waiting for House Allastam—or any other big names scared I'll come for them next—to seal me out. I'm putting this asshole behind bars and quitting."

"Now *that*—" Larryn raised his mug. "—is worth celebrating."

Sora snorted, but she clanked her tankard against his nonetheless. Larryn's cheer couldn't quite pierce her melancholy, but it helped to have him so enthusiastic about her career's eventual end and the bang that'd go before it.

To her surprise, Larryn didn't leave her once his curiosity about the day had been satisfied. He hung back, and she asked him about the Shelter—how many he fed, if the musicians were regular, how he'd managed to build the place. Everything except where he found the gold. Larryn explained the various routines, from the musicians he tipped when he could to how most patrons who spent the night had learned to clear the tables and retrieve the blankets to set the beds on their own. He told her of the secondary rooms, for the locals with sensory issues or trauma that required quieter environment. Every now and then, he stopped to bring ale to another patron or to serve a late comer, but he always returned with new stories and explanations, as if the brief pause had only fed his hunger to talk.

When she'd drank the last of her ale, she declined a refill. As relaxing as this had been, Kirio would be pacing the house waiting for her and she'd had an exhausting day. Besides, she didn't miss the increasingly frequent glances Larryn threw at his Shelter and the door to the back area, where his kitchens waited.

"You've still got quite a lot of work ahead of you, don't you?" she asked. "I'm sorry I took up so much of your time."

"You didn't take anything. I *gave* that time to you, and you should cherish it. I know I will."

He turned away from her, then, as if to hide the shy smile creeping up his lips. The softer expression made him look younger, and for the first time tonight she noticed the lines of exhaustion through his face and the way his shoulders drooped. He'd talked with such enthusiasm that she hadn't picked up all the small signs of fatigue until now.

Sora reached across the table and squeezed his wrist. He turned to her, startled and confused, and she let go right away, scrambling for her small purse and enough coins to cover her meal and then some. He grinned at her.

"Always one to respect the rules," he said, scooping up the coins and vanishing them with a flick of his wrist—the sort of sleight of hand tricks she doubted he'd acquired by practising legal flourishes. "Ya take care, hear me? I'll be counting the days until you get rid of that uniform."

It didn't feel like a reproach, but like an encouragement—a

promise he'd be there through the coming year, and perhaps long after that. The hardest part of her job had not even started, and Sora already knew she'd rely on the Shelter's warmth and this strange, newfound friendship with Larryn to carry her through.

⌘

ONCE Cal had finished setting down his bags, Hasryan could hardly see his friend behind the towering stacks. How the small halfling had managed to carry all of it through the windy, icy bridges would forever remain a mystery.

"What even *is* all this?" Hasryan asked, gesturing at the dozen bags.

"Stuff!"

Cal set his hands on his hips, proud and confident, as if he'd explained anything at all. Hasryan raised a single eyebrow at him, however, and his friend's composure crackled immediately, giving way to a healthy fit of giggles.

"It's not much, really. This one's the clothes you'd left at my place. Figured you might want a change or two—and I can take back dirty ones to clean, if you wanna." He pushed a smaller bag towards Hasryan. "The rest's really stuff, though! I figured if you stayed here instead of sneaking back to my place, you must think it'd be dangerous for me, yes? So if this is your new hideout, we ought to make it a little more homey while you're here."

Two competing surges of feelings reared within Hasryan: the warmth of Cal's simple friendship and his implicit invitation to return to his house, if he preferred, and the terrified pinch in his stomach as he recalled what Cal thought of as 'homey' according to the colourful decor of his own home. Hasryan's gaze snapped to the biggest bags, which had seemed exceedingly light.

"Cal," he said, and he imbued in that one syllable all the love, fear, and amusement whirling within him. "How many pillows did you bring over?"

"Just a few! And they're all red, I promise!" He extended a protective arm between Hasryan and his pillow bag, as if Hasryan had been about to chuck them out. "I got blankets, too, and I even found a curtain to match! It's all totally your colour palette. Except without the fancy black and white. I don't do those, you know that."

Hasryan could not contain his laughter. "All right, all right. I can accept all red. So you came to decorate?"

Cal grinned. "Sort of. I brought cards, two wooden puzzles, and a few of those skill games with sticks *you* always win. Oh, and this bag there is all cheese. The healthiest of diets!"

He had, in short, planned a whole day with Hasryan. No urgent news, no mention of the recent events, nothing but a ridiculous number of decorations in the hopes he'd feel less like a fugitive and a variety of games to keep themselves occupied. Pretexts to do something as simple as spending time together, same as they always had.

"You're making a face," Cal pointed out. "I can pretend I didn't see, or we can talk about it?"

"Pretend you didn't see." No hesitation there from Hasryan. "Just happy for a day with my friend, and if we say more, it'll ruin the effect."

Cal kept his words, but he did give Hasryan's forearm a quick squeeze before he turned to the largest bag, untied its top, and spilled the bright red pillows all over the floor. Hasryan felt lighter and lighter as the pile grew, as if every new addition shaved off the worries weighing him down. He'd had a shit time since escaping Drake and his cronies, nursing both a sore throat from the time outside without proper winter clothes and a circling anxiety about Camilla's safety and the ramifications of his presence in Sora's house. He couldn't do anything about it except worry, so he'd done almost nothing but since, and this would be a welcome distraction.

They chatted as they redecorated the empty wooden interior of Brune's hideout, scattering pillows on couches and hanging curtains that burned a bright red in the sunlight. Cal talked about Branwen's occasional visits, since he had been designated as the safe house for her messages with allies within the Dathirii Tower. It seemed she stayed with him whenever she came, sharing the whispers her network had brought with Cal, unloading some of her worries concerning Lord Dathirii's state of mind or the increasing dangers she perceived within Yultes' messages—letters that, Cal admitted, he had taken to reading.

"Was I supposed to resist secret correspondence between none other than Larryn's father and the Dathirii spymaster? It's too juicy, Hasryan, and I am weak of will."

"So … what's in them?" Hasryan raised his eyebrows. They had been passing hooks through the curtains' holes, readying them to be hung, and he stopped entirely. "My friend, you can't admit to this and keep the best parts for yourself!"

Cal laughed. "You won't even pretend to scold me!"

Hasryan brushed those thoughts away. "If Branwen didn't want them read, she shouldn't have chosen a gossip as her message host. *You* want to share. You're practically vibrating with the need!"

A gentle pink rose through his cheeks. "Maayybe." Two whole seconds of silence followed—the most Cal managed before it all burst out of him. "It's just so strange, you know? In my mind, I know this is the same elf who dumped Larryn's mom on the streets. I expected an asshole. But reading his words, he sounds … anxious and gentle, almost."

Hasryan acknowledged the strangeness with a pensive *hm*, but he could not say it surprised him. People could have all the kindness in the world for those they considered equals, only to turn around and treat others deemed below like dirt. He'd never given much thought to the kind of man Larryn's father might be. Hasryan was quite comfortable disliking him on principle and in solidarity with his friend.

"By the end, they were teasing one another." Cal's tone had dropped, more subdued. "I found myself laughing alongside them, and then I just—I got very angry! This could have been Larryn's family!"

He huffed and passed one of the hooks in with a furious movement, then let the curtain fall on his legs. Hasryan set his own hook down.

"It's not."

"I know, I know."

He *said* that, but the yearning lilt in Cal's tone and the way he wrung his hands betrayed him. Hasryan stared at him in silence, hoping to convey the weight of his disapproval without words. Cal meant well, but he was a nosy little bugger who loved it when everyone got along and had one thousand friends.

"Cal," he said, a warning in his voice.

It earned him a laugh. "All right, all right! Can't swear on Ren's illustrious figure while Larryn holds my coin, but here." Cal raised a hand, palm out, then dropped his voice into the most solemn of tones. "I hereby promise not to push Larryn to mend his relationships with anyone in House Dathirii. Good enough?"

"Good enough." Hasryan grinned back at him. "He's still got your coin, huh?"

"Yes." Cal's hands clenched as though the absence pained him. "I told him he'd know when to give it back, and I've done my best to leave him alone since. It feels like I haven't stepped into the Shelter in forever."

His voice tightened towards the end. Cal used to spend entire days in there, arriving early and staying throughout to lend a hand, heal minor bruises in the patrons, and catch up with everybody's lives. Now that everyone he'd housed at his own place had moved somewhere else, he must feel the Shelter's absence—and what it said about his relationship to Larryn—stronger than ever before.

"He'll come around," Hasryan said. "Give him time to unscramble his brain from everything that's been happening, and he'll find his footing and return that coin."

Cal nodded, but the movement had little of his usual enthusiasm. Hasryan sidled closer, threw an arm around his shoulders, and pulled him close. It drew a wet laugh out of Cal, who returned the hug in full force, squeezing him tight. Hasryan closed his eyes, basking in the familiar softness of Cal's embrace, of his hugs given so freely and with so much love. He had missed it—would miss it again, once forced to leave Isandor behind. It was always *simple* with Cal.

"Thank you for coming," he said.

"Would've come sooner, but everyone's been so busy, they neglected to tell me where to find you. Arathiel said he'd be on his way later, too, if the Golden Table allowed."

It did allow, although not until very late into the day, long after Cal himself had returned home. They had stayed together until late—long after every curtain had been hung, every blanket placed, every pillow relocated multiple times, and after half a dozen different games and more cheese than anyone should eat in a day. As the hours trickled by, each with its lot of laughter and quiet joy, Hasryan's nervous energy dwindled, soothed into a low and manageable thrum. He had been ready to crawl into his hard bed with a new cozy blanket when Arathiel's soft knock brought the outside world back to his mind.

Arathiel whistled as he stepped in, taking in the sheer amount of red scattered around the place. Hasryan smirked and twirled.

"You think Brune will approve of the new decor?"

"Who wouldn't?"

By the slight slur of his voice and the very emphatic grin he offered Hasryan, Arathiel had had a fair number of drinks tonight … and was in a good mood? Hasryan's heart fluttered.

"You've been celebrating?"

Arathiel confirmed with a sing-song *hm* and lifted a half-empty bottle. "Brought you the rest. It's a little tactless, I suppose, but I knew you'd appreciate it nonetheless. And it's red wine, so I'm in line with the theme!"

They found their way to the couch, Hasryan's legs half entangled with Arathiel's, the bottle passed between them. Reassured by Arathiel's general happiness, Hasryan avoided the subject at first, prodding Arathiel for anything new about Varden—and being rewarded with uncharacteristic shyness and tales of pleasant evenings and respite by the fire. They were taking it slowly, nourishing their flame in small moments, each of them otherwise busy. Varden spent most of his days with Nevian—and often, it seemed, fretted over him in the evening, too—while Arathiel had intensified his training and slowly started helping others, too.

"Kellian should be allowed to join me, too," he said. "I wonder if I can still give him a challenge, or if I've lost too much through the decades."

"His fancy earth tricks won't make it easy."

Arathiel laughed and gestured for the bottle. "I dare hope he'll accept a more straightforward duel."

"So he's free now?" Hasryan asked.

"So am I." Despite his words, Arathiel's mirth dampened. He passed the wine back to Hasryan. "I suppose it's time I caught you up."

His reluctance washed away any of Hasryan's calm. He downed the wine, understanding its return was as much advice as kindness, and braced himself for the inevitable bad news Arathiel had delayed. The tightness in his stomach became a vice-like grip as Arathiel went over Lord Allastam's attempt to use him to discredit Sora—not that he was entirely *wrong* about it—only for shock to disperse it as Arathiel described Lord Dathirii stepping in.

Whatever else Arathiel said, Hasryan missed it. A low throb had overtaken his skull, white noise blocking out the world as he tried to wrap his mind around the very public, very firm endorsement he'd just received.

All of his life, he had been everyone's secret, loved behind closed doors, disavowed when consequences came calling. Even Brune had dropped him after more than a decade of tight collaboration. Those who loved him unconditionally and openly could be counted on a single hand. Yet here was this lord, with all his lofty ideals and a profound dislike for violence, so close to losing the life he'd spent decades—centuries, even—building, putting that life on the line, calling Hasryan a *friend* in front of Isandor's highest political body.

And it had, without a doubt, led to Diel's exile.

"He's really something else, isn't he?" Hasryan said, his voice quiet.

Arathiel laughed and gestured for the wine to be returned to him. "I used to be completely smitten with him, and he's grown into an even finer man. For a moment there at the Golden Table, I truly thought he'd convince everyone to pardon you, too."

Hasryan snorted. As floored as he was that Diel Dathirii had even tried, he'd never expected any forgiveness from the city. They might forget in time, but it seemed best to make himself scarce until then. At least House Allastam would have to deal with the upcoming investigation and might not be hard on his tail. Perhaps he didn't need to vanish the moment the assault on the Myrian Enclave was over. After all, if Diel Dathirii could afford one last month to say proper goodbyes, why couldn't he?

CHAPTER THIRTY

WHEN Yultes' mind emerged from the morasses of unconsciousness to humming, he first thought young Vellien was by his side. He let that knowledge sink in, reassured, and drifted back into feverish darkness. He had done all he needed, even if he could barely piece together what that might have been. He could rest, now, and his entire body demanded that he did.

But the humming was out of tune. Horribly so, even. It could not be Vellien, and if not them, then who? The mystery nagged him, keeping him aloft and on the verge of consciousness until his mind untangled words out of the notes.

"And down the column goes the hundred gold, down into our receivables, oh beautiful benefits oh *ooh*."

Garith.

Yultes choked at the realization, and the movement sent pain wracking through his belly. His eyes flew open and he curled up, as if it could make the sudden jab in his midriff vanish. Garith's song died, an ink pen clattered down, and soon a pair of hands held him through the surge of pain. It dampened as quickly as it had come, leaving Yultes panting and all-too awake. Sweat covered his body, and he felt almost as if he was floating on the bed, not quite there.

"That was awful," he croaked.

"Sure looked like it." Garith squeezed his forearm. "Want me to get Vellien?"

Yultes snorted and offered his best smirk. "Not even Vellien can fix your singing, Garith."

Garith laughed, a sound far more melodious than anything else he'd produced so far today. Yultes' pain had fallen to a low throb, and he risked a few deeper breaths as he looked around.

He had been surrounded by greenery of all sorts—but not just any of it. These were all his plants, from the tiniest spider plant to the majestic monstera and the entire collection of prayer plants he'd bought from a southern merchant. He recognized the pots and the plants even though a few showed new growth he'd missed. The mint and other edible plants had been suspiciously gathered on the desk, where Garith must have been working moments ago. Yultes would swear they'd had more leaves when he'd last seen them— when several had been splayed on the ground. The chrysanthemum he'd seen near the flames then wasn't anywhere around. It stung, and he felt childish about it, but he clung to the loss and tried not to think of what else he'd done that night.

Yultes focused back on Garith, on the immediate here and now.

No amount of greenery could transform these quarters—Jaeger's rooms, where he'd spent his time as Hellion's right hand—into his. He should not be sleeping here still.

"This isn't my bed," he said.

Garith shrugged. "It is for now. We brought you home from House Allastam as soon as we could, but your own corner of this tower stinks of smoke and blood. I thought you'd rather wake here, with all this." He gestured at the array of plants around them.

"Where's Jaeger?"

Yultes had clung to him as the last of his consciousness slipped away, but what if something had happened? Had Allastam guards reached them first? Horror scenarios spilled through his mind, a dozen different ways Jaeger could have died after he'd lost track— but no. No. He had awakened once, burning with fevers, in a room of white curtains and deep blue walls. Jaeger had been by his side, eyes creased from sleeplessness. They had written a message for Diel. Jaeger was safe, he had to be.

"By Uncle Diel's side, wherever that is." Garith stretched out his chair and threw his feet over Yultes' bed, making himself comfortable. "You're stuck with me, I'm afraid."

"A tragedy."

His retort had no bite to it. Garith's presence had anchored him through the worst of the last weeks, a refuge when Hellion's love had turned into a battering storm. Now the storm was gone, but Yultes felt no relief, only emptiness. He clenched and unclenched his hands, half-expecting to still feel the stone dagger in his palm or the sudden jerk of Hellion's body as he plunged it in. Yultes closed his eyes, but it only made his memories more vivid, so he forced himself to look at Garith instead. Worry creased his face.

"Jaeger told me…"

Garith trailed off. Yultes only offered a noncommittal grunt in response. Words couldn't cover all that had happened and all it had broken in him, so why try?

"What of Viranya?" Yultes asked instead. "Enmaris? Iriel?"

Garith grimaced, as if their very name brought him pain. "If you think my singing is awful, you should hear them since they changed their tune. Iriel dared to scold me for having the accounts burned. Took it as a personal offence—which, honestly, he should. Better ashes than in his hands, if you ask me."

So they would escape consequences, for the most part. Yultes dreaded his next encounter with them in the tower's corridors. No amount of scolding would stop the remarks about him after what he'd done, and he didn't know if he could bear to hear aloud the whispers of betrayal already growing at the back of his head.

"S'all right, Yultes," Garith said, his slow drawl not quite hiding a quiet fierceness. "Let them think they're safe because Diel's gotta leave. They don't know I've got a long memory, and Branwen's longer still."

Any thoughts of Viranya and her crew scattered away at Garith's words. "Leave?"

Garith huffed and curled up on his seat, bringing back his long legs. He'd never looked so young as now, his hair cut short and his chin resting on his knees. "The self-sacrificial fool somehow negotiated his way into absorbing all the blame for everyone, and got himself exiled from Isandor for it. All this work to get him back home, and he'll be gone in a month."

Roughness twisted the last of Garith's words, and a sniffle followed. Garith laughed, his voice broken, and wiped away his eyes.

"I'm sorry. You just woke up from some tremendously traumatic shit and I'm crying 'cause my Uncle's gotta wait out some jerk's anger somewhere far away. I just—" Garith broke off and cried harder, the tears streaming faster than he could wipe them, hiccups wracking his body. He apologized again and again, but no amount of deep breaths and held in sobs could stop the floodgates.

Yultes sat himself up, gritting his teeth against the lancing pain in his midriff, and set his hand on Garith's shoulder. He had no idea what to say, or even what to feel. Vague shock had spread through him at the news, but he didn't feel sad or frustrated … or anything, really. That overwhelming emptiness remained. Maybe Garith could cry for the both of them.

Minutes passed them by, stretching the moment into a short eternity. Garith's tears dried out, and he patted Yultes' hand before stretching his legs back out. The red-rimmed and puffy eyes didn't help how young he still looked.

"Thanks, Uncle," he mumbled.

Warmth thundered through Yultes at the family epitaph, the first thing to nudge his numbness. He clung to the sensation, the steadying love he'd come to associate with Garith, quiet and reliable in a way Hellion's had never been. Part of Yultes wanted to melt away and slip into the cracks of the floor to handle the emotion alone, but Garith had just cried a long, long time. He forced himself to meet the younger elf's gaze.

"You don't have to always smile around me," he said. "I don't care."

"Yeah, I—I figured. Like I knew you'd stripped away enough of your own bullshit not to mind if I dropped some of my layers for a time." Garith said. "But don't tell the others! I have a reputation to maintain, and I *like* my pep."

Yultes did not understand when he'd become someone their flirtatious young accountant would unburden himself on, but he welcomed the change. After everything Garith had done for him, sitting there in silence while the other cried was the least he could do.

"Your secret is safe," he said. "Until, of course, Branwen and you find another scheme to have me read erotic retellings out loud— then it will be my revenge."

Garith laughed, and it had all of its usual sprightly mirth. "I'll keep that in mind," he replied, and it didn't sound at all like he'd reconsider such a prank, and more like he'd make sure the punishment would be worth it.

They fell back into an easier silence, and from there Yultes slipped in and out of sleep again. The first few times he'd woke up, Garith had returned the desk and worked, his off-key song back in full force. Once, he was also joined by Jaeger, who was going around the plants, rearranging them so they'd be in the best light conditions. Yultes kept silent, eyes closed, uncertain what to even say and too exhausted to search for words. The next time he came to was to sharp jagged pain and a stronger fever than he'd had all day. He was dimly aware of a rush around him, and then two lithe hands on his belly and a song so ethereally beautiful it could only belong to Vellien. It carried Yultes back into a darkness more restful than he'd known all day, and the light had vanished from his quarters when he re-emerged.

No one was left but Diel, dozing in a thick seat, near-extinct candles on the table besides him. Yultes was tempted to ignore him, but there could only be one reason he'd wait there, sprawled in an uncomfortable seat, instead of spooning somewhere with Jaeger. He wanted to talk.

"I'm awake," he said.

Diel's eyes flew open as if he had been waiting for this all along. They caught the flickering candle flame, somehow greener in this limited light than in the full breadth of the sun.

"Yultes."

The intense softness wrapped around his name as it emerged from Diel's lips wrapped in left him speechless. He had known Diel for over a century, and never had he heard his own name like *that*. From young Diel it had come as a call for attention or a challenge, the golden extrovert pulling all eyes to him. The longer Yultes had spent with Hellion—the more he'd demeaned Jaeger—and the more his name had been uttered in irritation, disgust, or as a warning. When he had come to see Jaeger one last time, the day Hellion took over, it'd held a frayed hope under the numbness. Never this fondness, however, and Yultes had no words for it.

Thankfully, Diel was never one to run out of words.

"I've come a few times, but you were always asleep. Everyone kept telling me I'd just missed you, so I made sure I wouldn't." He straightened up, stretching to work out a few kinks in his back. "Not the best seat, but I'm glad I stayed."

Another pause. Diel no doubt expected an answer, but Yultes had no idea what to even tell him. That he had used Diel's words about his role as a guiding light when his conflicting loyalties threatened to break him? That he hated how he'd failed to *build* anything, only staving the worst of Hellion's violence and eroding both Hellion's influence and his own sense of self? He admired Diel's daring, but trying to light a similar flame in himself had only burned him inside-out, leaving him hollow.

"I, huh… I wanted to thank you, mostly," Diel said. "Very few cared for Hellion the way you did. I understand how difficult this is, and I'm sorry for your loss."

Yultes squeezed his eyes shut. The worst was perhaps that he sounded sincere—that Yultes knew he was, because this was Diel, who could despise someone with every fibre of his being and still care for those enmeshed with them and left to deal with the tear where they'd been ripped away. Yultes didn't want to have this conversation—not with Diel, and perhaps not with anyone.

"You're leaving," he said instead.

"I am." Diel leaned forward, hands clasped together. "To refuse this exile and the opportunity it presented would have betrayed all I stood for. I can't say that I feel my work here was complete, but someone else will have to carry that battle."

Yultes had the distinct feeling that 'someone else' included him, and that, too, was not a conversation he wanted to have. He didn't know how he fit in the vestiges of House Dathirii. All he imagined when he gave it any thought was Garith's laugh. The rest was lost to an undefinable, overwhelming ache.

"Any idea where you'll go?"

"Me? None at all." Diel grinned, a child eager for a surprise. But there was something else to the light in his gaze and the way he radiated joy, a deep and all-consuming love that seemed to breathe its own unique life within him. "Jaeger has an itinerary and travel schedule already drafted, I'm sure. Though I suppose I do have two ideas, but they are less about where than who."

"You should warn him."

Diel laughed. "He'll know it's coming, but yes, I should, of course." His mirth settled into something quieter, though to Yultes it still felt as if Diel vibrated with it, the emotion as intense as ever, even if contained. "Since I'll travel… I thought I might look for them, actually."

Them. Diel didn't need to specify who, not when two ghosts had existed for decades between them, missing pieces of their lives never entirely forgotten. A missing brother. A missing sister. The ultimate romantic couple, off to great adventures while their siblings remained behind in an awkward conflict. There had been a time, after Lehran had left, where Yultes had regretted not staying with his younger brother. He would spend entire days at a cliffside park, watching the Reonne's tumultuous waters, wondering if he should have followed its flow, too. Hellion had been the one to convince him he'd made the right choice, that his place was in Isandor, in this illustrious elven family, by his side. Perhaps it had been wrong after all.

"You'll want to go to the ocean," Yultes said, and the words *bring me with you* danced on his tongue. It seemed easier than to stay here and pick up the shards of himself. He couldn't bring himself to say it, though. Even that felt like too much of a decision. "It always called to him, as if he was but one of many affluents destined to join with it."

"It sounds … grand," Diel commented, "but then again, I suppose that everything always was, with Lehran."

Yultes squeezed his eyes shut, overwhelmed by the surge of love and brotherly irritation. Everything truly *was* always grand. No half measures, no small destinies, not for Lehran.

"If you do find them … tell him I miss him, and Meltara can wait while he pays a visit."

"I will. That, and so much more."

It sounded more like a threat than a promise—perhaps, Yultes thought, for Branwen's sake. Would she even want to meet her parents at this point? They had left her decades ago, putting her in the care of two uncles who'd either drifted away or grown busy. But who was he to judge? He'd not only failed Branwen, but thrown his own child to starve in the streets. In the competition for bad parenthood, Yultes would always remain far ahead of everyone—and unlike the many relationships he'd slowly been mending, this one would remain broken forever.

CHAPTER THIRTY-ONE

WARM currents swirled all around Varden as he sat in the heart of House Brasten's main brazier. This was the first room Arathiel had shown him, all the way to the ground floor and adjacent to the kitchens, and it remained Varden's favourite. The fireplace sat in the middle of a circular space, at a place of honour. From the chimney above stretched four elegant swirls of white marble, reaching down in a delicate cage that remained pristine and free of soot despite the constant flames within. Two of these had been engraved in the same style of geometric patterns common around the Brasten Tower, but the others featured common phrases of gratefulness to Keroth for keeping Their fire alive and warming their halls. It wasn't a formal temple, but Keroth lived within every flame, and Varden had returned to pray every day, as he once had in the Myrian Enclave. He had missed the fire baths, flames all around him, the world burned away until nothing but he and the Fire Dancer remained.

"Always so easy to find."

Jilssan's voice shattered his peace of mind, and Varden sighed. He might be easy to find, but one would think that his sitting in the middle of a fiery blaze would properly signal he wished to be left alone. He raised a hand and parted the fire before him, letting it flow backwards as he raised a questioning eyebrow.

"You think you stand a chance against him?" she asked.

That was a more honest question than he'd expected of her. He'd not seen much of Jilssan over the last few days, but she'd never let a hint of doubt show when he'd been around. Then again, they had never been alone together, and few in the Brasten Tower truly understood the threat they were up against.

"That is impossible to know. We have a plan of impeccable theoretical underpinnings with a hundred moving parts and as many ways it could go wrong."

"Reassuring."

Varden waved her comment away, and the fire snapped around him in response to the gesture. "It's the best we'll have, and every day Nevian is a little more ready and a little more determined."

It had been a quiet pleasure to watch him train under Brune, flourishing in his understanding and use of magic. As wary as he'd been of the mercenary leader, she taught Nevian with efficiency, if a harder pace than Varden would be comfortable with under other circumstances. They paid her for it, of course, but he'd come to suspect she wanted Master Avenazar gone from the city's politics and they'd provided her an opportunity to get rid of him without major risks to herself.

"So you think he's got it in him? The kid?"

Varden dropped the fire into low, slithering flames, and let them spin around him slowly, like an animal stalking protectively. "He always did."

Jilssan strode closer to the fire, unaffected by the unspoken threat of his flames. She tapped the pristine swirls encasing the fire with her finger, and once satisfied it wouldn't burn her, she leaned on them, one arm above her head as she met his gaze.

"No need to get all riled up. I'm just worried. That's all our lives he's got riding on a plan I'd barely sketched out in the margins." Her usual smile tightened and she reached within the flames. Varden let them sting without burning her, and she grimaced. "All this stuff about Lord Allastam is theatre. A pretext to get this assault going, so the two of you can have Avez alone."

"This contract you dangled in front of everyone ... does it even exist?"

Jilssan's smile stretched wide, and her eyes shone bright in the dancing flames. "Does it matter?"

"Avenazar has always hated paperwork. He had you write most of the formal deals and messages we sent over the last years."

"Indeed. He even had me sign them for him." She wrapped her hand around the swirl and met his gaze. "So the contract exists, yes."

He did not trust the note of self-satisfaction in her tone. It *existed*, that much Varden was willing to believe, but something about it must be off, or wrong. Even if he pressed Jilssan for more information, however, he doubted she'd be forthcoming with it. He had no interest in whatever game she was playing and he trusted Amake Brasten to beat her to it, should it prove dangerous for her family.

"You know, I've been wondering something." Jilssan turned her back to him, leaning against the swirl and staring towards the majestic doors leading into the brazier's room. "Why didn't you run? You were free, nothing held you in Isandor, and you could have escaped and lived your life wherever you wanted. Avenazar's vindictive, but he's lazy, too."

What a strange question. Even had Isandor not housed friends—first Nevian and Branwen, and then Arathiel and all others—did Jilssan truly not know him better than that? Too often, Varden had had to let evil run amuck to keep himself out of trouble. In Myria, doing anything else would have meant death. But here? "I can't fix Myria on my own," he said, "but I can scorch one infection out of this city, at least."

She made a pensive sound in response. Varden released the flames and left their protective warmth, slipping under the lowest swirl and stepping out of the brazier. He kept only a small flame with him, letting it dance across his fingers as he turned towards Jilssan.

"But why *I* didn't run isn't the question you're asking," he said. "I am not the pragmatic one, unattached and unscrupulous, who should flee in the face of an unpredictable and devastating threat. So why don't *you* flee, Isra in tow? It would be safer."

Jilssan snorted, but the dismissive sound couldn't cover for the way her back had gone rigid. "This city's 'army' is a bunch of overhyped guards. Most of them haven't seen a real battle in their life, let alone an assault on a magically fortified location. Someone knowledgeable needs to take down the Enclave's wall, or they'll never stand a chance."

Varden lifted a single eyebrow. "And you care because?"

"Maybe I don't." She shrugged. "Maybe it just sounds like fun."

Varden didn't ask again. He doubted Jilssan even had an answer, and he had no desire to dig through her mind until they unravelled what was going on. As wary as he'd been of her help, she knew more than anyone in Isandor about the Enclave's defences and what to expect from this battle, and her presence on the frontlines would help keep the Myrian forces busy. They could only hope that when Varden and Nevian showed up within the Enclave, Avenazar would take the bait—and then, of course, that they would be able to spring the trap at all.

THE following day, Varden returned to the brazier to finish that very trap: the final step in their preparations.

Nevian had insisted on coming, but after another day of gruelling training, they'd convinced him that rest would be more beneficial to the challenges awaiting on the morrow. That they'd succeeded at all proved how exhausted he must have been to begin with. For the first time since hiring her, Varden was alone with the Crescent Moon leader.

She did not seem like much, truly. Average height, with a square jaw and thick nose, outfits always in shades of deep brown or ochre, and nearly no jewelry to speak of. Brune was unremarkable— purposefully so, he'd wager—unless one had an affinity for magical energy. Even when she made no use of it, it pooled around her like metal dust to a magnet. Varden had first felt it as a pressure in the air, something heavier than usual, but when he'd let his consciousness slip into the candles strewn around the library and, with his senses merged with the fire's, the trail of magic had flared to life. Any doubts he'd retained about her power vanished; only the most skilled could gather as naturally as they breathed.

"A decent sized fire," she said. "I've heard quite a lot about your strength with it."

"You would have."

He wondered what, exactly, she'd heard. That the Myrian Enclave's High Priest had a reputation for pyromania and would gladly burn down houses and people alike? Or had her sources been more neutral, more inclined to detail his control than the destruction he could bring? Had his reputation changed since he'd escaped the enclave and joined Diel Dathirii's crusade? He liked to imagine it'd be more in line with reality or, even better, that his existence had stopped being subject to gossip of any sort.

"It had been quite intriguing, how the story diverged according to the source. I suppose now I can make my own mind."

Varden could only think of one source that'd give her a different story than others: Nevian. He'd so often wondered what the young man was up to when he sneaked out of the Enclave in the depths of the night, to make his way to Isandor. A new, better master made perfect sense. What felt less obvious is why Brune had accepted the bargain—and after what she'd done to Hasryan, Varden had a few latent qualms about it.

"Why help Nevian?"

She raised an eyebrow. "You hired me."

Varden turned towards her, tilting his head in a clear *'I know your relationship predates this contract'*. After a few seconds of silent stares, a light smile curved her lips.

"He had information. I had magical knowledge. Why deny us both a useful exchange?"

One might believe that, if not that Hasryan had clearly established few could rival Brune when it came to magical spying. "Somehow, I doubt one of your scrying talents struggles to acquire the information she needs."

By the widening of her smile, she enjoyed having her responses challenged. Varden wished he didn't have to play these games with her—or anyone, for that matter—but on this particular subject, he was willing to put the time and energy to corner her into the truth hidden behind layers of vague non-lies.

"Correct," she said, "although I cannot scry on everything and everyone at once. Besides, people are more interesting. What they choose to reveal and why is its own information, and often more interesting than the information itself."

Once again, none of what she offered him was *false*, but none of it applied to Nevian directly. "I do not think that is all," he said. "You like Nevian."

She laughed—a sharp bark that echoed against the room's wall. "Not as much as you do."

Again, he tilted his head and waited for her to say more.

"He could have made a good recruit," she said.

Now *that* made more sense to him. She hadn't approached Nevian only as an informant: she'd tried to build him into a future member of her crew. Nevian was diligent, resourceful, and loyal to those who'd treated him well. If Brune had extracted him from Avenazar's domination, he would have grown into a fierce ally. Instead, he had been caught on the night of the winter solstice, wound up at the same Shelter that had first welcomed Arathiel back, and became close to both Vellien Dathirii and one of Hasryan's friends. By her use of the past tense, Brune understood he might be out of her reach now. It was a relief, considering how she'd treated Hasryan in the end.

"Not good enough to risk Avenazar's retribution for," Varden pointed out. Her only response was a shrug, and he doubted he'd get more out of her. That she had deigned tell him anything at all was a surprise. "Let's finish this, shall we?"

"Very well." Brune strode to the marble swirls around the fire and ran her hand over them. "These will do nicely. You've been used as a conduit for magic before, if I'm not mistaken?"

Ice spread through Varden, freezing the air out of his lungs. Not 'you've acted as', not even 'you have been', but *used*, as if she knew exactly what Avenazar had done to him, that night in the temple. Remembered cold clung to him, stronger where the golden link had sunk into his chest, eating away his free will. His fingers clenched and the brazier's flames snapped as if blown by a hot wind.

"I have, yes," he confirmed.

"What I need is very similar." She spread her fingers and the marble seemed to melt under it, the liquid floating in a sphere under her palm, growing as more and more of the swirls gathered there. "Most objects I've imbued were ordinary tools before I touched them, but the rekhemal has a strength and a relationship of its own—one *you* can access and understand better than any other. Fire is..." She waved a hand at the ever-shifting flames, her nose scrunching in distaste. "It is flimsy and unstable, without substance despite its strength, and we do not agree well with one another."

Varden couldn't help his smile. He had always loved the flames' endless dance, how it could burn so hot yet not have a physical presence when he reached for it. As a child, that more than anything had felt like proof of its divine essence. To learn that these very things unsettled someone like Brune … well, sometimes life offered small pleasures.

"So I am less of a conduit, and more of a guide to this particular dynamic."

"I suppose that is another way to describe it."

Varden fully intended to think of it this way. A conduit had no willpower, no choice in what went through it, and he had no intention of relinquishing that to Brune. As a guide, however, *she* depended on him. He didn't think the distinction was purely theoretical, either. Varden might not understand the arcane rune Nevian had built with her, but he could attune himself to the flow of divine magic. He hoped he'd understand it today, and that perhaps by guiding Brune through some of the operations now, he'd be of more help to Nevian when they faced Avenazar together.

With the marble all gathered in her hands, Brune gestured for him to step into the fire. Varden obliged, closing his eyes as the flames snapped at his robes and licked his curls. He let the raging heat surround him and sink into his bones, filling up every part of his body and melting away the rest of his unease at Brune's all-too-specific description of Avenazar's magic. When his mind was at ease again, he sat on the incandescent logs and retrieved the rekhemal's long box. Slowly, reverently, he lifted the bandana from its cushion and set it on his crossed legs. Then he let his own senses fade away, giving himself fully to the fire.

Shadows and ember glow replaced human sight, tracing everything touched by the flames in his mind, painting the great room in expressive, ever-changing light. Always, Varden wished he could capture the delicateness of their movement, the ethereal beauty of divine fire and the joy it inspired within him, filling his lungs with warmth and hope. He had yet to sketch a single fire that captured this, but if he could do this—if they could trap Avenazar tomorrow—he would have his entire life to keep trying.

A stream of power prickled the edge of his awareness. Brune stood by the fire, a deep shadow more solid than any other, unaffected by the wavering light of the flames, sharp as jagged rocks emerging from the ocean. Her hands and the marble she'd bundled were infused with a golden-brown glow—Gresh's power, flowing through her and into the world. She flicked her fingers up, and the marble extended into thin swirl again, tracing long lines against the ceiling. In but a few gestures, Brune replicated the rune of inversion she'd devised with Nevian above their heads. She kept her arm up, palm extended towards it, and power build between it and her hand, a pressure his flames skirted around. With her other hand, she signalled for the rekhemal.

He sank deeper into the flames. They built in a whirlwind

around the artefact, Keroth's power growing with every spin, rivalling the pressure Brune had created between herself and the ceiling. Varden twirled the flame, creating a controlled air current, lifting the rekhemal with his tiny fire tornado and inching it ever close to the pressure. A vibration built within the artefact as it approached, subtle at first but increasing at an alarming speed. The energy within fought back, the ripples in the fabric threatening to tear its brilliant light as it snapped about—flimsy, unstable, and strong, as Brune had described. Varden reached for it as he did any other flame, and the rekhemal responded.

It expanded his awareness, as it always did, but this time the pressure of Brune's magic transferred into his mind, heavy and intractable, a mountain threatening to crush him—crush them. Varden gritted his teeth, struggling for control under the sudden assault. He could see now why Brune needed him: her strength and Gresh's could not have been more hostile to the nature of Keroth's power.

But that was all right. Varden had faced brutal adversity before, and he had also reached for divine energy of a different source than his. Certainly, Ren's luck charm manifested in a light and airy glitter he'd found easier to scatter about, and Vellien had ceded Alluma's grace to him, helping in its control, but this was only a different challenge, and Brune herself was not trying to stop him. She simply had no idea how to shift her willpower and strength to better suit the rekhemal.

Varden gathered the brazier's power about him, concentrating all of its warmth close to the rekhemal, shaping it into a singular point of unbearable heat. He floated it upward, scorching the surface of this earth pressure, scoring black marks against it. The power cracked, shards falling into the heat below, and they melded together, fusing into a slow-moving liquid. Varden pushed on, eating his way through the overwhelming sphere of Brune's power. His muscles trembled with the effort, and lancing pain settled at the base of his skull as he pushed more and more of his strength into the mix, fusing it with Brune's.

The rekhemal's vibration subdued as the pressure lessened, but Varden didn't know how long he could hold. Already, his own link to the flames weakened, his sight sliding back to normal. Sweat ran down Brune's face and neck, and dirt seem to cling to her skin where it trickled. He had no idea where it'd come from. She met his gaze and offered a tight smile.

"Reproduce the rune."

He heard the words as much as he felt them vibrating through their shared magic, the magma power crawling upward, directed by Brune's will. He joined with her push, guiding the shifting mass towards the ceiling, following the marble guides she had established. They worked in concert, each aware of the other's consciousness, and the effort lessened with every moment in harmony. Varden allowed himself to relax, falling into the rhythm of the work until they'd finished another replica of the rune.

Brune didn't need to explain the next step. He understood it instinctively, guided by her consciousness and the way their gathered power thrummed above their heads, desperate for an anchor. He swept the rekhemal upward with a single hot current and sank it in the middle of the sizzling divine magic. The impact spread through the rune like a shockwave, but he held on to the artefact as Brune fused the rune's power within it. Varden felt the change of its nature within himself, his acute sense of his surroundings fading as the rekhemal's magic inverted. The world closed in on him, his body growing more and more distant—inaccessible, even—with every second.

Panic slid within him. They'd built a trap, a way to cut the physical body from the rest, and he stood within it, linked to it. Varden scrambled to untie himself, but he could barely feel the heat around him, or any trace of Keroth's power. He reached within, for a strength that was his own, for the sense of self that had survived so much. It was still there, still his, body included, and if he could just…

The world rushed back in, heat and bright colours and the sting of smoke. Even dizzy with a hundred sensations, Varden's instincts kicked in and he shielded himself from the scorching flames. Brune was on one knee by the side of the fire, her skin covered with plaques of stone, her breath short. The rekhemal lay halfway between them, caressed by the fire and cradled in a bowl of stone, unharmed and seemingly unchanged. Brune flew the bowl to him with a flick of her wrist.

"Your one chance at freedom, good sir," she said. "I'll await my last payment."

She left him with the changed rekhemal and the distinct impression the best pay would not come in gold coins, but in an unexpected success.

Chapter Thirty-Two

THE Myrian Enclave's wall did not seem as impressive in broad daylight as they had on Arathiel's first visit, looming over them in the dark, the slow-moving torchlight above their best guide of its height. Armoured figures lined them, however, each in identical gear, perfect statues staring out at the eclectic gathering at their door.

Lord William stood at the head of the small Isandor force, clad in a regal armour meant more for ceremony than war. Lord Allastam rode at his right, the head of his own soldiers, dressed for an actual battle, with plate, chainmail, and a helmet in hand. Diel rode on the opposite side, and he'd instead retrieved an ornate doublet emblazoned with the Dathirii tree and woven his hair into a complex braid worthy of the fanciest balls. Jaeger probably had a great deal to do with the latter; the two elves had been inseparable since their reunion. Arathiel waited a step behind, along with

Amake, Jilssan, and Sora—all of them equipped to fight, too. They had come to demand entry into the Myrian Enclave, in the name of Isandor's Golden Table. If refused, they would force it.

Everyone knew they would be refused.

They'd failed all attempts to scry into the Myrian Enclave ahead of time and gauge Avenazar's health and the state of chaos left by Isra's assassination attempt, so they'd relied on Jilssan's best guess. Unfortunately, with no one to *keep* poisoning Master Avenazar, he was likely on his feet at the moment. Any battle plans needed to account for him.

Which, of course, was where Varden and Nevian entered the picture. Once the battle joined, they would firestride from House Brasten and into the Enclave, baiting Master Avenazar to them. The very thought nauseated Arathiel. They should not have to face him alone, the two he'd hurt the most, but when Arathiel asked Varden to bring him, he'd received a kiss on the forehead and a reminder of the fast and painful way fire spread through him.

"They need you on the frontlines," Varden had said, squeezing his hands hard. "We're ready, Nevian and I. This is a risk we chose, not one forced upon us, and we will have one another."

So Arathiel had stayed with the army, where a significant number of soldiers—especially Lord Allastam's—gaped and glared at him. He kept close to Kellian, with whom he had trained intensively since the Golden Table and who elicited a similar response. With all his close friends out of reach—Cal had joined Vellien at the healer's tents and Hasryan had to remain hidden— Arathiel was glad for at least one person to have his back as the battle unfolded.

Lord William finally rode forward, trailed by Diel and Lord Allastam. Of the three, only Lord William seemed at ease on a horse, and Arathiel had to suppress a smile as Diel struggled to remain seated upright in a dignified manner. Horses never climbed Isandor's higher bridges, and nobles favoured riding rapids over beasts, or skinny-dipping in the Reonne's affluents. Since few left the city on long travels, horse riding remained an obscure interest to most. Lord William must have found time and passion for it, considering the grace with which he handled his black stallion. He raised an arm high, clearly enjoying himself, and cast his voice out.

"In Isandor's name, we of the Golden Table demand the Myrian Enclave's surrender. Submit now and you will be treated fairly."

Arathiel's heart picked up pace. 'Entry' and 'surrender' were two very different concepts, though everyone was of the mind demanding either led to the same conclusion. Still, Lord William's use of the much more dramatic one heightened his nerves. Anticipation built within the army around, soldiers shifting in hushed silence, the clinks of their metal armour carried across the snowy plain. Near him, Jilssan placed a hand on her hip and snorted lightly.

"Myrians aren't in the habit of submitting to anything, let alone threats of force," she said.

And indeed, a woman with short-cropped curls stepped up at the wall, spreading her hands across the battlements. Her pale skin seemed to glow in the sunlight bouncing off the snow, and even at this distance, Arathiel would've sworn her eyes crackled with golden energy.

"Surrender?" Her airy voice carried down to them easily, as if gliding on her condescension. "Pray tell, oh lords of Isandor, who will make us? Your piss poor soldiers, who have never seen a real battle in their lives? Your pretty nobles, who dress for banquets instead of war? Or should I fear your wizards, who dabble in the arts with no sense of direction, more interested in making flowers glow in the dark than harnessing the power of the world?"

Arathiel gritted his teeth. Her assessment of Isandor's forces was correct. The city resolved most of its conflicts through trades, deals, and sabotage. Most soldiers present today had seen more fights in tavern brawls than proper assaults, and gathering them had been a show of force more than anything else. Faced with the Myrian Empire's war-trained units, they'd struggle to hold their grounds.

Yet Jilssan—who should understand this more than anyone else—laughed. She stepped forward, her smile wide and her posture relaxed, and touched her throat as she stopped by Lord William's horse. When she spoke again, her voice boomed across the battlefield.

"Master Hann, please, we both know your guards have never seen war either. They don't send veterans on a diplomatic mission to a backwater city." Whispers of hope ran through Isandor's troops at her counter. "Or did you forget that *diplomacy* was our original goal here? One we have thoroughly failed at? Stand down. I have Myria's backing in the removal of Master Avenazar."

Silence met her bluff—surely, Arathiel thought, that was the only way to qualify her claim to Myria's backing. This kind of bald-faced lie seemed perfectly in line with everything else he'd seen from her pull lately, and it hadn't been part of any tactical decision until now.

"Tell me, Hann," she continued, obviously amused by the lack of answers from her Myrian counterpart. "Is your refusal to surrender a personal belief in your troops' strength, or are you too scared of Avez to do the sensible thing?"

Another silence, flat and angry. Arathiel had to admire the ease with which Jilssan had rattled the other mage and boosted their own morale. The troops whispered behind them, encouraged by her words. She stretched, then lazily turned towards Lord William.

"Milords, I think you have your answer," she said, her voice as loud as ever.

"Indeed," Lord William said.

He turned his horse around and swept the small Isandor force behind him, meeting the gaze of each Head of the House present, collecting their assent. Their horns blew one by one, filling the plains to the brim with the sound of war, each new call reverberating through Arathiel's chest and tightening his throat. The soldiers marched forward.

Arathiel turned back towards the Myrian Enclave and found Kellian Dathirii and Jilssan waiting for him, weapons at the ready. Jilssan grinned at them.

"My two bodyguards," she declared, before bowing to them. "Let's redefine 'chaos of battle' for them, shall we?"

ISRA flapped her tiny chickadee wings as she circled above the Myrian Enclave, surveying the soldiers lined below, bows drawn, their armour shining in the sunlight. Wizards waited a step behind, chain shirts concealed by long robes, energy crackling in their hands and ready to be unleashed on the opposing troupes gathered below. Isandor had managed to piece together more of an army than Isra had expected, but what good would it do them if they didn't have the magic or discipline of Myrian forces? She didn't envy Jilssan and those with her on this assault—though she doubted any of them would envy her, either.

When Jilssan had outlined the strategy she'd devised with Lady Brasten, it had become clear Isra's role would be to stay home and stay safe. Indignation had flared through her like one of Varden's sudden flames.

"I want to help," she'd declared, and fear had tightened in her stomach, a hundred tiny knots pinching in alarm. But she would not be safe in the Brasten Tower, not if everyone else failed on the battlefield.

Jilssan had stared at her, a hundred logical counters at the tip of her lips. Instead, a laugh emerged, breezy and incredulous.

"Ah, you want to do the foolish, righteous thing," she'd said. "Very well. We have need of an infiltrator, and between your shapeshifting skills and your knowledge of the Enclave, I do believe you're better suited than the one we had in mind. Less of a political risk, to be sure."

She had given Isra a single scroll, the wax holding it shut imprinted with the sigil of the Myrian Empire, the great boar tusks swooping on each side of its snout.

"Is that ..."

"One more piece of paperwork Master Avenazar had me do. Complete, of course, with the magical imprint on official Myrian documents." Jilssan waved at it dismissively. "It ought to be stored in the last drawer of the cabinet behind his desk."

Lord Allastam's signature had been obtained from several examples Lady Brasten had kept from deals over the years. Isra had marvelled at the lady's willingness to rely on a forgery, then returned to her training with renewed intensity. Without her father's amulet, her magic flowed without interference and her years of struggling suddenly paid off. The currents of magic responded to her will, sinking into her as she'd transformed from girl to hawk to mouse and back to girl without a hitch—skills she would need now to go unnoticed.

The first horn warned her of the approaching battle, and Isra dove down, towards the great tree Nevian had once used to escape from the Enclave. The ongoing chaos at the walls would be her best opportunity to go unnoticed and she would not waste it. Her wings folded and fused in her body, feathers turning to fur and her tail extending into a fluffy duster as she turned into a squirrel and scrambled down the trunk, towards the building in which Avenazar's office waited. Snow chilled her small paws as she hopped across the open space, then ducked behind a haphazard pile of half-rotten crates and shifted again, into a mouse small enough to squirm her way inside. With every new shift, the world around grew bigger and more terrifying, every instinct on high alert, but she kept her wits about and proceeded around the walls.

Everyone depended on her success, and she would not let them down.

As Arathiel soared through the air, piggybacking on Jilssan while Isandor's mages deflected a volley of arrows with summoned wind, he revised his expectations of her battle prowess. She'd leaped the entire fortification with a single jump and now landed with impeccable balance at the top of the wall. Kellian had already cleared the area—Jilssan had flung him first, magical strength pumping through her arms—and he was holding off two terrified Myrians, his sword flashing as it caught the sun. Arathiel drew his own weapon as Jilssan crouched down and slammed her palms to the ground, pulling a staff out of it.

"I need access to the base of the wall," she said. "Clear a path down the stairs while I knock some wizards out."

"On it."

He dashed towards Kellian and surveyed the troops around them. Myrian bows sang as they rained arrows down on Isandor's soldiers, and a small squad of more heavily armoured soldiers waited in the courtyard below for the first enemies to make it inside. They'd be trouble if Jilssan needed extended time by the wall, but perhaps Kellian could trap some of them with stone.

"Coming up behind you!" he called as he arrived.

Kellian stepped aside with perfect timing, giving Arathiel full room to maneuver. His adversary had followed the turn, not expecting another fighter to step in, and Arathiel slid his longsword between the joints of his armour. He didn't feel the sword enter, and the little jerk when it hit a bone caught him off guard, tilting his balance. Arathiel slammed his foot down and pulled his weapon out, eager to find his footing as more enemies arrived. Blood splashed from the open wound, and for once he was thankful of the dampened colour of his sight.

New soldiers came running, and he didn't have time left to think of lost lives, blood, or anything but the quick flow of parries and attacks. The hours spent with Kellian in House Brasten's training room paid off, the two of them dancing around one another with wordless ease. Kellian's sudden stone pillars and walls kept the Myrian troops from staying in formation, disrupting their practised tactics and creating openings for Arathiel to dive in. More than once, the floor's rough stones shifted under his feet, but they'd clamped thin stone bracelets around Arathiel's ankles, which Kellian modified as warnings. It allowed Arathiel to adjust posture, never lose his precarious balance, and sometimes even somersault off the growing pillars and behind their enemies. Whatever training these troops had received didn't help against the whirlwind of blade and stone they formed, and soon they began toppling soldiers off the wall instead of outright killing them, with Arathiel shoving them as Kellian pulled the ground up to trip them.

They'd carved their way to the top of the stairs leading down and inside the enclave when Jilssan caught up with them. She'd strewn her own set of bodies of the ground, many in robes, and

Isandor's soldiers had now managed to get a handful of ladders up against the parapet.

"You boys look like you're having fun!"

Arathiel couldn't entirely deny the thrill of the fight and the natural flow of his partnership with Kellian, who never forgot to warn him of incoming magic, never placed himself where Arathiel would bump into him, unable to hear him through dulled senses and the chaotic din of battle.

Kellian ignored her comment. "You said any inside part of the lower wall." He gestured at the section below them, partly obscured by the steps. "How long do you need?"

"Hard to tell. I never had to undo Hann's work before, and it can be quite complex. I'm hoping it's easier from this side, where it needs not be as strong."

Soldiers came rushing up the stairs before they could ask anything else. Jilssan sprinted right at them, spinning her staff, and with each rotation the weapon elongated until she wielded an enormous pole of rock—something only her enhanced strength would allow her to carry. She promptly smashed it into the legs of several rows of soldiers and they toppled over one another, falling down the stairs in a clanking pile of armour. Jilssan brought the pole back, grinning, and used it to vault over them. It bent with surprising flexibility. Either that pole had never been all stone, or she changed its composition as she fought. Either way, Arathiel was impressed.

"I think she's trying to outdo us," he remarked.

Kellian snorted. "Fancy moves get you killed in a fight."

The reprimand would have been more believable if he hadn't then sprinted down the stairs two-by-two and, as he approached the fallen soldiers, leaped on the helmet of a Myrian slowly getting up and used it as a springboard to somersault. If Arathiel tried anything like that, he'd land on his ankle wrong and twist it again. He shook his head and hurried after Kellian before the soldiers found their feet and cut him off.

JILSSAN had forgotten how much she enjoyed the thrill of an uneven battle. All those poor Myrian soldiers had no idea how to deal with her magic, and while she was no expert in staff wielding, she combined her skills with her enhanced strength to devastating effects. With Arathiel and Kellian ensuring no one flanked her, she had an easy time pushing for the wall.

Then there were no soldiers at all blocking them and they could run straight to it. Kellian raised the earth under the untouched snow banks, scooping it all up in a gigantic shovel and pushing it aside. The battle raged on the rampart above their head. Flashes of heat marked every flame conjured by Myrian mages, most of which had mastered destructive magic above all else. Jilssan blocked out the screams of pain. They weren't her problem.

"Some projectile protection would be welcome," she told Kellian as she pulled off her winter gloves. "Don't let me down, boys."

She set her palm flat against the freezing stone, enduring the biting cold for the sake of direct contact. She'd need every leverage she could get against this wall, and touching materials always helped transmute them.

As Kellian erected a thin layer of rock above her head, Jilssan sank into the spell. The stones turned into grains before her eyes, with lines of power running through them, akin to a super-concentrated cloud of material coursing across the structure. These occurred naturally in most materials, but here they existed in a set pattern, a man-made net meant to bolster the wall's solidity, to convince it to treat every stone as part of a whole and stand in solidarity with itself.

This was Hann's work, her specialty. She imbued objects with partial consciousness, giving them an awareness of their most essential components and, more importantly, of their ultimate goal. She had convinced the enclave's wall to hold steady and keep outsiders out, and it'd defy her attempts to transmute sections of it into sand or mud, refusing to abandon a single part of itself to her magic. When they'd first arrived, she'd tried to understand the nature of the magic, which had roots in both transmutation and abjuration, but the details of it escaped her. She'd never cared to discuss them in depth with Hann and regretted it now. One thing was certain, however: she needed to dismantle this enchantment if she wanted to pull the wall apart.

Jilssan pushed her consciousness against the most concentrated areas of magic lines, feeling their power, tugging at one with her own to see how it'd react. It shimmered brighter in her mind, hardening the stone. Jilssan moved away from the lines of power, to the parts in between, but the moment she touched those the lines spread out, forming a wide web that pushed back at her. She pushed harder, and Hann's magic responded by concentrating around her point of impact. Jilssan groaned and pulled completely away.

Around her, several Myrians lay dead, and her two bodyguards had engaged a coming group of four. The din of battle from above had dimmed, leaving behind the hurried stomps of soldiers running and a return to the bow's songs. What troops Isandor had managed to get up there must have been pushed back. She didn't have long before reinforcements overwhelmed Kellian and Arathiel.

She set back to work, multiplying the technical attempts: assaulting several points at once, trying to overlay her own will on the consciousness—a technique Avenazar might've mastered enough to use, but not her—until she had only one idea left: transmuting the consciousness itself.

Jilssan picked up snow from the ground and used it to smear a basic transmutation rune for Spirit on the wall, hoping to guide herself better. No doubt Hann's spell was more complex, but she didn't need the original rune itself, only access to the consciousness. She set her hand against the stone and activated the rune, sending her magic searching for a sense of self that was unusual in stone. She wished she had more experience with the material, but her own expertise rested in transmuting and enhancing bodies, not inanimate objects. Still, life had its signature and even the faintest form of sentience had a unique presence, the instinct of another's will brushing against yours. The hardest was to block out the chaos of swords clashing and soldiers screaming, to ignore the damp cold slowly freezing her toes, to bypass the hammering in her heart at the distinct possibility a blade could pierce her at any moment. She kept her focus strictly on herself and the wall, isolating her mind until she finally caught a flicker of Hann's magical conscience.

Jilssan snatched it, bringing the sensation to the forefront of her mind until it felt clear, easily distinguishable. Then she started manipulating, pushing and pulling at it in directionless attempts to change its nature and desires. The magic pushed back, but the consciousness had been designed to resist attempts to change its body, not its spirit, and it couldn't counter her with the same efficiency. Slowly, she guided the consciousness into a calmer, more pliant state of being, amorphous and soft. Instead of the defensive presence she'd first sensed, the wall now felt lazy, agreeable. Satisfied, curious about her limits, Jilssan pushed her spell even farther and tried to create a new desire within the consciousness— one of fluidity, of becoming sand.

It hated it.

An intense vibration passed through the wall, a concentration of energy as the consciousness fought the impulse. That energy met Jilssan's spell, and before she'd understood the scope of the wall's reaction, the vibration turned into a rumble. The wall cracked, bright yellow light escaping through the fissures, its power overwhelming Jilssan's mind, searing pain blazing through her skull. She bucked forward and collapsed with a cry. The last thing she heard as the wall exploded was Arathiel calling her name.

Chapter Thirty-Three

I SANDOR'S battle horns echoed across the plain, all the way to the top of the Brasten Tower, where Varden and Nevian waited for their signal.

"It's time, isn't it?" Nevian said.

It was the first they'd spoken today. After days of preparation and training, words had seemed superfluous. They knew the consequences of failure all too well. Yet despite the fear tightening his voice, Nevian stared towards the enclave with intense determination.

"May Keroth's flame shine bright within us and set our hearts ablaze."

They left the Tower's barren roof and the cold winter to descend in the brazier room Varden had become so familiar with. Its flames flitted about with renewed enthusiasm as he arrived, responding to his presence as if they'd met an old friend, and

Varden pulled them to him, wrapping himself in their warmth for a few, calming seconds. When he turned his attention back to Nevian, the young man nodded, pale but ready.

Varden pulled at the fire, winding the flames around their ankles and torso, and plunged them into the firescape. He kept Nevian's spirit close by as he navigated the distorted space of the plane, willing them towards the many fires dotting the enclave. Varden approached a room at the edge of the mages' wing, close to the largest courtyard. He wanted space for his flames—space to fight however he needed to. Nevian's fear heightened as they neared, so palpable it almost overwhelmed Varden. He wished he had any reassurance, but he refused to make empty promises. The only certainty Varden held about today was that Keroth would stand by him until the end.

A powerful sense of wrongness jerked him as he crossed the threshold, and agonizing lines lit across his back—his burn scars coming to life, as if peeling themselves open. Pain and panic slammed into Varden as his knees hit the wooden floor of the enclave's room. The world spun around him, a blur he struggled to parse. What had happened? The fire …?

Whips of energy burst from the flames behind him, pulsing red-green-gold, and clamped down around his shoulders and torso and arms. Their icy touch froze his breath and seared the skin they touched. But worse was the recognition, how his entire body bucked at the knowledge of what would follow, of ice sinking into him, forming an easy path for Avenazar to walk. His ears buzzed and his vision dimmed, his mind slipping away as fast as it could.

"Truly, Varden, I'm surprised you fell for this."

Avenazar's smooth, mocking voice echoed his recent nightmares. Varden choked on a sob, struggling to keep his self-control from crumbling entirely. He had been so worried about how Nevian would fare when faced with his persecutor, he'd never stopped to consider whether or not *he* was ready. "How often did you think you could carelessly stride into our fires before I made them more … welcoming? And you even brought a gift."

Avenazar gestured towards Nevian, cowering by the desk, pale and in obvious shock. The sight struck a spark in Varden, a tiny flame of defiance. He couldn't fall apart, not now. They'd had a plan—this *was* the plan. And no matter how many magical ropes Avenazar wrapped around him, forcibly holding him down, the fire remained. Keroth had not abandoned him. His palms firm against the floor, Varden pulled on the heat, drawing upon the remembered serenity of countless fire baths and the exhilaration of flames coursing through him, responding to his every whim, and he gathered it all within himself.

When Avenazar crouched down and grabbed his chin, bony fingers digging into his cheeks as he forced him to look up, Varden met his gaze and smiled.

"Here's another gift."

He released all the gathered power through his palms.

A great burst of flames erupted, climbing all the way to the ceiling and tugging at Varden's loose clothes. The heat rose in a glorious whirlwind, every inch of his world turning bright and white and scorching. Varden lost himself within it, the world blurring into one surge of power until he could no longer feel the green ropes holding him, nor Avenazar's hand on his chin.

Then the cold intensified, a whip of pain as ropes tightened around his torso and dug into his back. The flames' wild air currents all siphoned forward, into Avenazar, stealing his breath until the fire within him died out, snuffed. He struggled for air, struggled to keep his momentum as the cold crept into his mind, chipping away his control. When he lost the last of it and his flames died, he realized with sinking despair that Avenazar hadn't even let him go.

"Predictability will get you killed. Or worse."

Varden's slippery consciousness muffled the voice. Avenazar's ropes had coalesced into the thick red and gold conduit that had dug into his chest in Keroth's temple. It should feel awful, but that, too, was fading.

"Now, now… If your little tantrum is over, I—"

Nevian's pale, lanky body smashed into Avenazar, sending both of them skidding across the floor. The pressure in Varden's lungs released as the ropes loosened, and the fresh air rekindled him. His mind cleared, and he fought for a better grasp on himself as Nevian rolled on top of Avenazar and smashed an ink bottle on his head.

MASTER Avenazar's brutal trap had shattered Nevian's fragile courage. It shouldn't have—they'd have to face him no matter what—but as it had sprung around Varden, his entire body and mind had clamped down, and his head turned so light he'd expected to faint. He'd scrambled away from the fire until he'd hit the desk's corner, then the wall behind. The office swam before him, yet the rekhemal—still in its inactivated, normal state—tied to his arm let him experience everything in overwhelming detail—rough walls under his fingertips, burnt wood filling his nose, and ringing in his ears. Master Avenazar's gleeful cackle and his confident threats, a promise of retribution tearing through him as visceral fear. He would pay for his defiance.

They would pay, Nevian corrected himself. Varden first, even. Master Avenazar held him tight, laughing as great flames burst all around them, leaving the wizard unscathed and amused. But at least Varden had fought back, even as that ugly red line dug into his chest—even now, as his body slumped, he still had small flames flickering upward, a desperate attempt to counter the grip Avenazar had on him. And he relied on Nevian to try, too, and help if he could.

If he could.

Avenazar clearly thought he couldn't. After his initial cruel jab at his presence, he'd completely forgotten about Nevian, his attention all on the bigger threat. After all, why waste energy keeping an eye on his pathetic apprentice, a toy he'd broken over and over, when a far glossier one stood before him? But Nevian wasn't a toy anymore, and if Avenazar couldn't see that, then he would make it his downfall.

Nevian cast a panicked look around until his gaze latched onto the ink bottle on the desk. Heavy looking, probably breakable. He scrambled for it. His throat shut as he clasped his hands around, ready to fling it—to immediately bring attention to himself. He froze with his arm pulled back, the throw interrupted. Avenazar still wasn't looking. This might not be enough, not when the goal was to get him to attack Nevian and come into *his* mind. He needed something bigger, something more inescapable. Something physical.

Nevian squeezed his eyes shut, fighting the bout of nausea at the idea of Master Avenazar's hand clamping down on his forearm. His stomach rebelled and he almost dropped the inkwell. This had always been implied in the plan—how else would Avenazar follow him into his mindscape?—but rushing towards it contradicted every survival instinct he'd developed. One last time, he promised himself. They had a plan. He had the rekhemal. He could do this.

Nevian gathered the shattered pieces of his courage then dashed for Avenazar's stocky body, inkwell tight in his hand.

They hit the ground in a confused pile of limbs. Nevian's skin crawled, every inch of him screaming to let go and run. Tears welled in his eyes, but he focused on the sharp tightness of the rekhemal around his arm, like a shield where Avenazar always grabbed him—a promise of freedom, if he could follow the plan. He smashed the inkwell hard on Avenazar's face, felt the vibrations of shock go through the glass under his palm as it shattered, then sharp pain from a shard slicing through his skin. Ink fumes filled Nevian's nostrils and turned his throat raw, leaving him dizzied, confused.

Avenazar splayed blackened fingers across his face and all Nevian knew was the overwhelming presence crashing into his mind. Nevian sank with it, allowing the bloated force to drag him without a fight.

In the grey of his mindscape, Avenazar materialized as a vast distortion, twisting everything towards itself. Deep black cracks formed in the walls opposite of him—Nevian's refuge, where he had weathered so many of these attacks. All but the last, when he'd lured Avenazar through a maze of memories of his own choosing, desperate to safeguard those most precious. All but this one, where he was in control.

He had chosen to be here, chosen to let Avenazar into his mind, chosen to risk the destruction of his memories as he baited him. But now that he stood here, a small terrified speck at the mercy of Avenazar's immensity, he could barely keep himself together. How had he ever thought this possible?

Possible or not, he'd had to try. He still did.

The grey shifted around Nevian, a splash of colour replicating one of Isandor's arching bridge between Avenazar and himself—the start of the chase through his mind. The meagre dirt road distended, immediately crushed by the advancing bloated presence, shape and colour and texture pulverized.

Is this a new game, Nevian? Avenazar's voice rattled through him.

Nevian ignored him. When he'd practised with Vellien, he'd built walls and landscapes from memories, focusing on the anecdotal to conceal the meaningful. He reached for those now, and found them crystal clear to his mind, an array of vivid sensations. The rekhemal, providing acuteness to his mind, enhancing his own self-awareness to new heights.

Nevian latched onto the gagging stench of the Lower City, filling his entire mindscape with a single overpowering smell, hiding his own presence within it. It didn't stop Avenazar, only confused and slowed him, but as the wizard's distorting void shredded that memory into a distant echo, Nevian flung another at him, then another—Isandor's biting winter winds, the dust of Myrian streets after a drought, the familiar halo of light from late-night candles in the enclave's library. A lifetime split into shards, as detached from his core as he could, forming a twisting trail as he strung Avenazar along.

Avenazar destroyed everything Nevian offered, tearing them into flimsy pieces, and every loss left him dazed, his focus briefly shattered from the brutal assault. He struggled to keep going, building and rebuilding, one memory after another, dragging him ever deeper.

You can't run forever.

The curious amusement had eroded from Avenazar's voice. His power expanded tenfold, surging outward in a mental shockwave that slammed Nevian against the edges of his own mind. His control slipped, his latest memory—the spicy-sweet taste of Larryn's soup—crumbling to dust as Avenazar yanked other pieces to the surface. Varden's steady and tranquil presence as he sketched by Nevian's side. The echoes of music from the Shelter. Vellien's unique laughter and the sparks of joy it lit in his brain. Efua's bright smile as she ran to him, book in hand. Precious memories, each a fundamental part of him, exposed and vulnerable.

Each a core he had vowed to protect.

He couldn't hide them again, but he let them distract Avenazar, let him gleefully turn the lively jaunt of violins into an ear-bleeding screech, let him shred his memory of Varden's company as if it was paper itself.

And as he did that, Nevian yanked control of his mindscape again, focusing every inch of willpower and energy he had left on the rekhemal's new rune. The pattern bloomed around them, repeated over and over as he brought to mind every line with perfect clarity, imprinting it into the walls around him.

Avenazar's carnage stopped. *What is this, Nevian?*

Nevian ignored the taunting tone or the pounding in his mind, torn and scratched and bloodied from offering up so much as bait. He envisioned himself activating the rune, sharp movements and commanding tone, as he had so often while training with Brune. All of his will into this one wish: invert the rekhemal.

Avenazar cackled, the nightmarish sounded rebounding into every crack of his soul.

Trying to cast a spell? Oh, but you've lost track of something, haven't you? Let me help.

Brutal, physical pain shot through Nevian's wrist as Avenazar released his mind—just for a moment. Long enough to find himself pinned under the smaller wizard. Long enough to register the long shard of glass in his wrist, the blood welling from the jagged wound, and the sudden rush of nausea. His fingers twitched as he tried to replicate the gesture he'd envisioned with such clarity, and a long whine escaped him.

"Now, where were we?"

The world faded again as Avenazar's overwhelming presence pressed against his mind, ready to pluck him and all his carefully hidden memories, now defenceless.

Chapter Thirty-Four

STONE debris and sand hit Arathiel in full force, the brutal thump of a massive rock smashing into his body as he rushed towards Jilssan. It sent him flying into a snowdrift and a cloud of white puffed around him as he sank in. Arathiel lay there, stunned, nauseated by the intense, rippling magic in the air, leftovers from the explosion. Snow fell around in a slow powder and dust obscured his sight. Shadows moved through it, soldiers locked in battle or rushing about, but his ears buzzed and he couldn't understand any of the words said. Everything was impossibly distant, even the spinning ground under him, the strange sensation of a slow, eternal fall.

Then the aftershock of magic receded, and so did the disconnect between body and mind. The hum in his skull vanished, leaving a dazed emptiness behind. Arathiel tried to shake it off, to focus on the ice against his back, solid beneath the snow. To perceive words amidst the clearer battle cries and cling to the present. He was still *here*, not a ghost, never a ghost, and he was still in danger.

Arathiel tried to brace himself with his right hand on the ground, hoping to push himself up, and immediately toppled, out of balance. A wave of nauseating alarm rose through him. He'd never felt *any* pressure on his palm, not even the distant and delayed sensation that had become his sense of touch. His stomach churning, Arathiel brought his arm in front of him.

He squeezed his eyes shut the moment he registered the bones protruding from his wrist, his hand attached at a horrific angle, his fingers bent all out of shape. And blood, so much blood, in spurts out of his arm, on the snow around. His mind spun and spun, as if it wanted to escape but couldn't choose how or where. This should hurt—blazing agony, enough to knock him unconscious—yet it didn't. He didn't feel a thing beyond a distant throbbing across his skin, and a pinch near the bone.

Which didn't mean the wound wouldn't kill him. He needed a healer. He needed to get up and find his way to the tents at the back, to Vellien and Cal, needed to calm his rising panic and shocked queasiness and move. And he couldn't. A sob caught in his throat as he stayed paralyzed, too overwhelmed for even a stunned crawl back.

Booted feet stopped next to him. Not Myrians. An Allastam soldier. Words spoken—something about a chance at a promotion. Arathiel struggled to comprehend, to process the world around at all. A sword flashed, poised to kill. *That* was easy to understand, and it unlocked something in Arathiel, a surge of bitter anger he'd rarely experienced. It splashed, acid in his stomach, as the sob in his throat turned into a growl and he brandished his maimed hand.

"You think your sword can kill me? That it's that easy?"

The soldier flinched, disgust and horror written all over his face. In the second of hesitation, a familiar blade pierced him through from behind. Kellian's sword. The elven captain slid it back out, pushing the body to the side without sparing it a glance. He crouched next to Arathiel.

"Let's get you a healer." His gruff voice grounded Arathiel. "Can you walk?"

Walk? He was dying. Dying fast, blood rushing out of his bizarre body. "I can't feel it. Any of it. I'm—"

"That's fine," Kellian said with placating calm. "I'll find a way. You just hang in there. It's nothing Vellien can't fix."

Arathiel didn't contradict him, even though he knew the unique strain of healing his wounds. Even someone of Vellien's skill might not work fast enough to avoid the numbing cold. But they'd want to try and Arathiel did not want to die. He had found his life in Isandor again, and if it was on borrowed time, then he refused to give it back just yet. He brought his mangled hand close, pressing on the open wound as best as he could while Kellian surveyed the battlefield, seeking a path through the chaos.

"I'll carry him."

Jilssan's voice came from his other side. Her light armour and the red clothes beneath had been torn and sliced through, and a thick layer of dust covered her entire body. A cut ran along her forehead, oozing blood down her cheek, and up to her elbow, her right arm now seemed made of stone. She waved it at them.

"I'm in need of some fixing too, you see." She set her stone hand back on her hip, unbothered by the new state of her body. "I got enough energy to sprint all the way there, and I'd say speed is of the essence, don't you think? Besides…" She pushed the dead Allastam soldier with the tip of her toe. "One of them came for me, too. I think they have orders to use the battle's chaos as cover for some very timely death. Which makes me think Investigator Sora Sharpe is in urgent need of a diligent bodyguard."

All hesitation melted from Kellian's expression. "Hurry, then. I'll find Sora." He dashed for the main cluster of Myrian buildings.

And so Arathiel found himself carried by Jilssan again, in her arms rather than on her back—extracted from the battle instead of being brought into it. They passed through the large hole she'd created in the wall, the result of the deadly explosion he still struggled to comprehend, and as the clash of swords and screams of soldiers receded, Arathiel finally fainted.

SORA Sharpe had started her assault of the Myrian Enclave alongside Lady Brasten, the only sword-and-shield in a tight group of six spear wielders. They had hung back from the initial fight, silent as troops assaulted the walls, trying to get a foothold on the parapet. Sora's chest tightened as the battle unfolded, the itch to join in growing stronger by the minute. She didn't like staying behind, regardless of what the strategy devised with Jilssan said.

Not a moment passed without a fiery explosion, or boulders crashing into Isandor's ranks after a brutal telekinetic flight. Every time, their line of soldiers scattered, the fighters untrained in this sort of warfare panicked then emerged from the magical assault only to find Myrian foot soldiers bearing down on them. The city had brought its own mages, of course, but the skill set prized within the spires involved deception and embellishment, mobility and ruse. Their role would come later, same as Sora's. All they needed was one key event, their signal to go.

Then a bright yellow fissure ran across the Myrian wall, and it exploded with a resounding crack, showering the surrounding battlefield with dust and stones.

Lady Brasten raised her spear, her lips flattened into a thin, determined line. "It's our turn."

They rushed in, long strides carrying them past clusters of soldiers rearranging their formation, and they plunged into the cloud of dust and snow as one. Pale blue livery became shadows against the backdrop, spears flashing when a sunray pierced the cloud of dust. They moved in pairs, circling one another, a practised dance in which Sora had no role. She'd no time to find one, either; Myrian soldiers bore down on her.

The ensuing battled consumed every inch of her. Sora's sword met her enemies', her shield blocked slashes meant to kill, her feet moved every forward as dust clung to her throat and stung her eyes. Her ears rung from the clash of metal and scream of soldiers, yet she strained for any hint of someone behind her, of a warning cry she'd need to heed. Discipline gave way to instincts, training merging with reflexes, strikes and parry melting into one long string.

She barely registered when she emerged from the cloud of dust, her heart hammering, her muscles strained from the effort. She set her back against the wall and tried to get a sense of the tide of battle.

Myrian mages had inflicted heavy losses on them, but with the wall breached, Isandor's troops had gained a solid footing in the inside courtyard—and now, their own mages could do their work. Isandor nobles and the Sapphire Guard Commander had selected some twenty soldiers across their troops, all best known for their precision and agility, and formed strike teams out of them. Endowed with slow flight and camouflage, they moved about the battlefield, weaving through pockets of battle or shooting from above, targeting key points of Myrian operations. No sooner had a mage made their presence known that death rained on them. Myrian discipline devolved into chaos at the loss of their leaders. Jilssan had been right about that, too.

Even so, Sora didn't want to bet her investigation on a victory. She needed to get to Master Avenazar's office as soon as possible, in case Isandor needed to beat a hasty retreat. Unfortunately, she ran afoul of Master Hann almost as soon as she made for the correct buildings, dodging pockets of battle.

"Investigator Sharpe," Hann said, cold steel in her voice. "I hear we owe this deadly masquerade to you. Good people are dying for your little game, and I find you weaving your way through the battle, ignoring most of it?"

Sora ground her teeth. Even if it wasn't her game that'd brought them here, she'd taken part in it, pushing for this investigation, and it made her all too aware of every death. Still. They had come with a purpose. She readied her blade, still slick with dark blood from the last Myrian to stand in her way.

"I've been cutting my way through, you mean."

"Well, I'm afraid your path ends here."

Hann extended a hand, fingers crooked. The snow drifts swirled to life, the quick whirlwind of white powder gluing together ice shards and rocks into two small humanoid constructs—snowmen with jagged ice for arms, and white glowing pinpricks where eyes should be. At a flick of Hann's wrist, they surged forward.

Sora fell back in a hurry, giving herself just enough distance to sidestep the first swoop, her body moving on instinct—instincts that betrayed her an instant later, as the second construct rushed her and she tried to block the attack by slicing through the arm. Her sword ran through the snow, slicing the powder and catching on the side of a rock to no effect. The blow struck her square in the chest, sending her reeling from the weight of impact.

Her back hit the second construct.

She sank in—or rather, it absorbed her in parts, snow wrapping around her shield arm and pinning it down while one shard sliced between two ribs. Her vision blurred and her knees buckled, but she didn't fall, held tight by Hann's creation. Sora elbowed into it, only for her blow to hit solid rock and shoot pain through her whole arm.

"I have to admit, I expected you to put up more of a fight," Hann said.

Anger flared within Sora, but as her head snapped up to reply, one of the constructs slammed its fist over it, forcing snow fingers down her throat. She choked, her throat freezing up, her nose buried by the creature. The battle had been over before she'd even had a chance to think of a good tactic against these creatures. Now she was drowning in snow, the door leading to Avenazar's office building a dozen feet away, her hopes to reach it dwindling as her lungs burned harder and harder, the edges of her vision darkening, her hold on consciousness slipping.

The constructs brutally released her. Sora crumpled to the ground as air rushed back into her lungs, pure and cold and invigorating. She gasped and coughed, then fresh snow slammed into her and she rolled over, half-expecting another blow. When she found her feet again, one knee still on the ground, she found the source of her sudden freedom: a stone formation rose from the ground, curved like a giant shovel, and scooped one of the two creatures, flinging it away. Kellian hopped onto it as it finished its throw, sliding down its curve as he sprinted to Hann. She conjured a new golem in his path before he could reach her, so he slammed a heel in the ground and brought a few slices of stone floating up, hovering about like so many shields. Sora scrambled for her fallen weapon, eager to join the battle again despite her aching lungs and muscles.

"You have to keep going, Sora," he said as he caught her movement. She scowled at him, but before she could argue, he flicked his hand up and a sheet of rock rose from the ground, walling him off. "Don't lose track of the goal, and watch out for—"

A hard *thump* cut off his words, and even through the stone wall, she heard him roll on the ground. Sora cursed. She hated leaving him behind like this. He better be alive when she returned.

She turned heels and plunged within the office building. Darkness surrounded her as her eyes adjusted to the sudden absence of blinding sunlight on white snow, and she slowed her pace, ears perked and sword raised. The burning pain in her back and recent brush with death scrambled her brain, and she struggled to recall the layout of this place. Avenazar's office was down the corridor, but was it the second door on the right or left?

Hurried footsteps interrupted her scrambled sifting through her brains and she spun about, weapon at the ready. Two soldiers sprinted down the hall at her, neither in the red Myrian uniform, and one with a hand raised in peace.

"Investigator Sharpe!" His gravelly voice had something appeasing, like a balm on her frazzled nerves. He and his companion stopped closer. "We caught sight of you slipping in. It's dangerous to stay alone, so we hurried in."

"Right. Thanks."

They weren't wrong. What would she have done, if she'd ran into Myrian troops, wounded and out of sorts as she was? Her mind split in a dozen directions at once, scattered to the point of uselessness. If she could get to Avenazar's office, she might manage to focus again—to close the door and push away the deadly battle raging outside while she searched for the proof she needed.

Which was on the *left*. Slowly but surely, the maelstrom of her thoughts was starting to settle.

"We're almost there," she said.

The two of them stopped—then she caught it, the exchange of glances, the slight nod—and her whole body tensed. Too late, she realized they might not be Myrian-red, but they were certainly Allastam-blue. Too late, she understood the real danger of being caught *alone*.

She turned on them as a first blade slid under her armour, plunging near where Hann's ice construct had wounded her, and a large hand quickly muffled her scream. The close quarters offered no room to maneuver her longsword in position, and the two Allastam soldiers worked in perfect unison, slamming her against the wall and holding her as pain shot through her veins, locking her muscles. Poison. She couldn't even fight back, couldn't move as they turned the knife in and pulled it out, spraying her blood against the wall.

With Kellian occupied by Master Hann, she had no one to save her this deep within enemy lines.

Chapter Thirty-Five

VARDEN stared at his pale brown hands, flat on the ground. *His* hands, he reminded himself. It felt important. He coughed, and pain shot through his lungs as if a great cold weight pressed against them. Avenazar's rope, still embedded deep in his chest. Its shifting glow cast mesmerizing patterns against the floor, a beautiful dance of colour he could lose himself into. And he had. Seconds trickled by, each stretching into a fuzzy eternity, his mind numbed by the cold.

He remembered Nevian's scream. A shard in his wrist. A last attempt to reach into the blaze and the brutal ice clamping down on his mind. It had taken so little, and already he felt himself slipping away.

"Varden."

That was his name. Varden. He tried to focus on the voice, to tear himself from the inertia.

"Varden!"

Delicate hands gripped his shoulders, shaking him. He curled up his fingers and watched them fold excruciatingly slowly. They were still *his*. His fingers, on his hands. Every inch moved felt distant, as if through molasses—as if he'd been almost split from his own body, sequestered away from bones and muscles.

"The rope," he rasped.

He managed to tilt his head up, ever so slowly, and found Isra staring back, eyes wide with panic.

"I-I know. It's like the first one."

The first one, by Keroth's great brazier. When he had almost killed Branwen, unable to resist control. The link connected him to Avenazar still, casually wrapped to the wizard's hand as he wrestled Nevian under him. A plaintive whimper escaped the young man. Forced to deal alone with Avenazar, because Varden was here, unmoving, strung up and powerless. He needed to free himself, but he could not even feel the flames behind him. The world felt distant, inaccessible.

"Isra …"

He didn't understand why she was here, instead of safely in the Brasten Tower, but it didn't matter. They needed her to help. She turned to him, and a terrified smile flitted across her lips.

"I-I learned something special recently. Did you know powerful magic can interfere with other spells? A-anyway." Something between a laugh and a sob crawled out of her throat, and a slight glow spread across her body. The texture of her hair began to shift into soft brown feathers. "You might need to apologize to Jilssan on my behalf. Sorry."

She completed the transformation she'd been holding back, her entire body retracting into the hawk form they'd all grown familiar with. She hopped back once, then flew straight at the large, pulsing link connecting him to Avenazar. Her claws dug into the magical thread and it wobbled under her weight before it merged with her, the golden-red light sinking into her talons and crawling up to her body. Her form stretched and snapped back, imbued with a light brown glow that swirled in and out, pushing at the very shape of her until she was less hawk or girl, and more an amorphous, ever-shifting ball of energy. Sometimes Varden discerned feathers or fingers, but the shapelessness always snapped back into place—and every time it did, it sucked in the gold and red hues of his link to Avenazar. The rope tightened around him, pulling him closer as it grew shorter. Varden gripped the nearby fireplace, and a wave of relief washed through him as he realized how fluid his movements had become, and how clearer his mind.

It was short-lived.

A distressed whine escaped the ball of light, distinctively Isra. It filled the entire room, a ripple of energy as much as sound, and Varden's insides squeezed, his body recognizing the danger before it hit. The shining ball of energy Isra had turned into exploded with a dissonant pop, evicting her body from it.

No ropes held him back as the blast hit him, sending him tumbling into the desk. Varden fought to clear the blotch of white in his vision and the ringing in his ears, struggling to his knees. Isra had flown across the room and smashed into a wall, but the force of the explosion hadn't even budged Avenazar and Nevian. They remained locked, one on top of the other, Nevian's eyes glazed over and his face contorted in pain.

Varden's heart stuttered with hesitation. He wanted to help Nevian, felt that impulse in every inch of him, but if Isra had cracked her skull... He darted to her first, one hand extended behind him as he pulled the dwindling flames closer and stoked life into them. Calm washed over him as the warmth flowed through him then into Isra. His head pounded for an instant, an echo of her internal damage, then it was gone. Enough to save her; enough to lift any guilt as he left her there and turned towards Nevian and Avenazar.

The pool of blood had widened under Nevian's wrist, but he didn't seem aware of it or anything else in his surroundings anymore. Neither did Avenazar, for that matter, and Varden's flames flared as he considered incinerating him then and there. Would have, if he hadn't watched his divine fire dance harmlessly around Avenazar but a few minutes ago. Varden anchored himself in Keroth's proximity, breathed in, and exhaled. His breath turned into a brazier, the fire around him springing to life and rising to the ceiling.

In Myria, divine and arcane magic had always been divided by clear lines. Wizards practised the latter, and with it came more prestige and thus more power. Faith was a secondary means of accessing power, lesser by its very nature, and no one with proper arcane might would waste time with it. Until he had stood in Keroth's brazier, melting his way through the mountain of power

Brune wielded in order to carve a brand-new arcane rune within the rekhemal, Varden would never have thought to blur those lines.

If arcane runes were but a tool—a way to shape the power roiling within him—he could use them, too.

Flames coursed over his sleeves as he raised his arms, commanding the ever-growing blaze in the room. He painted walls and ceilings with them, sinking ever deeper within their dancing forms until he saw through them, the world a landscape of flickering light and shadows, bathed in Keroth's swirling power. A small fireball nestled in his palm, a blinding pinprick even amidst the other ever-shifting light. He aimed it at Nevian's arm, where the rekhemal hid under his clothes, and the flames enveloped Nevian's limp limb, coursing up and down, staunching the incessant bleeding.

The artefact lit up in his mind, a beacon of power. Exactly as it always had been, a blessing of Keroth, allowing one to stand vigil through the Long Night and perceive the world. Its trap unsprung. And Nevian was in his mind, alone with Avenazar, his body bleeding, perhaps in no state to trigger the inversion. Varden had promised to stand by his side—to shoulder the burden with him. He would not break his word.

"Keroth, bless me with your eyes." The words spilled as a chant, an echo to the Long Night Watch's prayer—as much a tool to shape Keroth's power as any rune. "Let me see his bright flame, surrounded as it may be by unrelenting darkness. Let me be his candle, to ward off any shadows."

The world shifted, flames blurring together as a flurry of new sensations crashed through him—fear and exhaustion and pain, resolve collapsing bit by bit, eaten away by despair. An inescapable pressure that became razor-edged in sudden, agonizing bursts. With every one of them, something tried to shift in Nevian, to mould itself around the pressure in a weak attempt to soften the brunt of the assault. It wasn't working. Varden could feel it in his bones and blood, Nevian's horror adding to his own. Nevian fought with reflexive stubbornness, the path for his defiance long lost to Avenazar's darkness.

Varden let his presence light it back up.

The fire spread across the ceiling swirled, reshaping itself into a large circle. Varden swept his arm, as if sketching with fire, and formed the lines of the rekhemal's inversion rune. With each new movement—each strike of fire above—power rose within him. This was his last offering to Keroth, one more drawing to feed the fire, one more prayer for help—and as the rune neared completion, a quiet serenity washed over him, an otherworldly sense of rightness that Varden willed to burn bright and high, a beacon for Nevian to see.

Brimming with hope, he traced the last line and finished the rune.

SHREDDED pages floated around Nevian as he crawled away, the battered remains of his mind desperate to escape Avenazar. The mage's pressure had only grown, a hungry void lashing out at everything around—every wall of emotion, every memory, every imagined furniture Nevian conjured to keep him occupied. Avenazar walked through the shattered remains, more physical than ever before, examining his handiwork like a casual stroller through a garden. Every now and then, he'd pluck a memory forward only to tear it apart, until Nevian's past and present blurred away, lost to a sea of pain and the never-ending cackles. Every expendable memory was long gone, and Nevian clung to his new friends and loves, all too aware it was only a matter of time before Avenazar reached those, too. He no longer had any strength to defend them with.

They had failed, predictably so, and Nevian could no longer remember why he'd thought they had a chance, or that the price would be worth the attempt.

Warmth spread through his arm, a gentle touch filled with hope, a brief relief against the pain. A tiny flame danced on it, almost shy. A friend, Nevian thought, before his mind scraped the truth from his scattered debris. *Varden.* Varden, in the room with him, every step of the last few days and today, too. Quietly present, sketching, always there when Nevian found himself looking for him. Always there when Nevian had needed it, whether Nevian had seen or wanted it.

The flames spread from his palm, coursing around the ground as if following trails of oil, each line building a familiar pattern. A rune, *his* rune. Nevian's whole being tightened as he recognized it, Varden's tender hope latching within him and hardening. The fire wrapped around him, breathing new strength into him until he stood again, steady in his own mind.

This again? Avenazar mocked. *You've never learned any humility.*

Magic swirled around Nevian, a power not entirely his own, filled with Varden's soothing confidence. Pieces of the decor rebuilt around him—the tall bookshelves, the table to study, the fireplace behind, all of it wreathed in flames. And in the walls and ceiling around, repeated over and over, shining white with heat, the pattern of the inversion rune.

You don't want humility, he shot back. *You'll never accept anything but complete submission or annihilation. But I'm not a toy, to use or break as you see fit.*

Every inch of him trembled as he replied. Nevian drew on Varden's presence and the power growing all around, on those who had helped and loved him, on all his hopes for the future, and he grew himself, enlarging his presence to match Avenazar's vast power. His old master rushed him in response, eager to teach him a lesson.

Nevian had nothing to learn from him. Here, in his mind where he could be anything, *do* anything, he envisioned himself performing the gestures to activate the rune, put all of his will into that one final act, channelling the power that had swirled around him into the large inversion rune hovering above his head.

Hot wind snapped to life, sucked upward and towards the rune, pulling and pulling relentlessly. Panic coursed through Nevian as it all rushed past him, threatening to drag him along with it. Then it all died out, as suddenly as it had started, the crackling of power gone. Had it failed? Avenazar cackled, his entire self oozing with mockery, and he bore down on Nevian to laugh. He never got a word out.

Magic exploded from above, casting a wide net of burning lines. It landed over Avenazar's bloated presence then stretched out, expanding all around it with leaping flames until it had somehow encompassed the vastness of him. Anger and confusion passed through the wizard and he flung his power against the spell's hold, ramming the brunt of his strength on it. Each hit rumbled through Nevian, a shock he felt to his core, an attack against him—against his magic.

Not just his, though. He might be weaker than Master Avenazar, but the rekhemal held its own strength, a conduit for Keroth's power. And at the edge of his mind, his faith in Nevian its own divine blessing, Varden continued to nourish the flame of their spell. Nevian clung to his presence as the inverted magic tried to pull at him, too, to extend its trap to his mind as it had Avenazar's. Power tingled across his skin, a first hint of his body as they kept the magic directed entirely towards the Myrian wizard, filling in the net's hole more and more, covering it. The sphere distended as Avenazar pushed against it, stretching its surface to the extreme. Nevian strained against the onslaught, control slipping from his fingers, threatening to unravel entirely. He clung to it, scraping every second of containment through a lifetime of stubbornness. Power left him raw and hurting, and still he refused to let go.

The immense ball of fire encapsulating Avenazar vanished, snuffed out with a gust of wind. One moment it had encompassed every inch of Nevian's mind and willpower; the next it was gone.

The spell ended as suddenly as it had triggered, leaving a stunned Nevian behind.

Avenazar's physical body crumpled on his, crushing his breath. Nevian scrambled from under it with a strangled cry, then collapsed as soon as he no longer touched him. His entire body itched, raw from magic and touch alike, and his mind felt like a shattered piece of pottery. Tears blurred his vision, his throat tightened, and a long whine slipped past his lips. They had done it. He knew they had done it, but he couldn't understand it—couldn't understand what it *meant*. He didn't even feel himself, wasn't sure what himself meant now.

"Nevian." A soft voice, warm and full of worry. A shadow fell over Nevian. "I'm here, Nevian. You did it. It's over."

Nevian wiped his tears, but he couldn't bring himself to look at Varden, couldn't do much but cry harder. Varden crouched down, his hands hovering near Nevian but never touching him. Never without his permission. Nevian choked back another sob and wrestled control of his voice.

"T-take it off," he said.

"And your wrist? I staunched the bleeding but…"

A full-body shudder wracked him as he realized the glass shard must still be there. He curled on himself but managed a small nod. Varden needed no more. Warmth spread through Nevian's entire arm, numbing all other sensations. He squeezed his eyes shut as a steady hand gently held his elbow down, then the pinch of pressure in his forearm warned him of the glass shard had slid out. No pain at all, only the eerie feeling of not having truly returned to his body yet.

"I'm almost done," Varden promised.

He tore Nevian's sleeve farther up until he could reach the rekhemal and untie it. The soft fabric slid off in a last caress—Avenazar's final touch. Nevian flinched, yet in its absence he felt as if he could breathe again. It was gone. Avenazar was gone. Not even his vessel touched him now. Nevian was free—to study, to heal, to build a life from the scattered remains of his memory without ever looking over his shoulder.

It should excite him, but Nevian only had emptiness within, his emotions as grey as his mindscape. Joy required energy, of which he had none. It would come, in time, but for now, Nevian was content to close his eyes and let the tears flow as body, mind, and soul accepted what had come to pass.

VARDEN sat cross-legged in front of Avenazar's body, the rekhemal in his upturned palm. Once upon a time—not so long ago, really—he had retrieved it from its delicate box and foregone the clergy's rules on their holy relic to lend it to an exhausted, distrustful Nevian. He had teased him about his wariness, promising that once one wore the rekhemal, their very soul would belong to the Fire Lord.

He'd never thought they would carve the jest into reality.

The rekhemal had changed, the energy within chafing at his fingers, no longer steady and warming, but angry and foreboding.

Nothing in it felt like Keroth anymore, and the power brimming from it would love to escape. Brune had had no input on whether it was at all possible, but Varden had no intention of risking it.

He closed his eyes and let his surroundings guide him once more, expanding his senses to cover the flames still licking at the ceiling and all around him. His head pounded, sharp repeated lancing of pain through his skull—a clear warning he was fast approaching his limits. He'd channelled everything he had into his tenuous link with Nevian, hoping to transfer the fire's strength into his young friend as he activated the rune. It would be good to return to the camp after this and rest, but Varden would not leave this task unfinished, no matter how unpleasant.

He pulled fire down to him, letting the heat swirl around his arm and into his palm, then shot it at Avenazar's body. The stench of charred flesh quickly filled the room, adding nausea to his pain. Just the rekhemal left now, then they could wake Isra and leave. Varden didn't want to linger.

"Is this it?" Nevian asked, his voice hollow. He hadn't moved from the spot where he had collapsed, but he'd turned his head in Varden's general direction, his mouth twisted in a grimace.

"Yes."

He nodded. "Do it."

He watched as Varden stirred up a warm air current, lifting the rekhemal closer to the ceiling and the large version of the inversion rune now charred into its wood, as he had in the Brasten's brazier. The flames reached for it, snapping at the fabric, and Varden encouraged them to, slowly building their hunger. The rekhemal fought back, resisting the flame with ferocity. He could almost *hear* Avenazar mocking his predictability still. It did not matter. Nothing could withstand Keroth's flames forever. Varden gritted his teeth, dug even deeper within himself, soaking every drop of heat within the room, and intensified his assault. Slowly, as an excruciating pain built under his skull, the rekhemal's fabric coiled on itself. Blinding white light gathered around its edges then ran across the entire bandana as its magic unravelled and the artefact turned to dust.

Varden released all the magic, snuffing out the flames with one wide sweep of his arms before crumpling into a sitting position. His head pounded, an echo of the previous pain, and he half-expected to faint from exhaustion here and now. He closed his eyes, forced his breathing to slow, and let the enormity of what they'd accomplish sink into him, and to examine the churn of emotion swirling within. He had not expected to feel so *satisfied.*

"May Keroth show no mercy and reduce his soul to a charred, useless crisp," he said.

A strange squeak halfway between laugh and sob escaped Nevian, then silence curled around them both, a quiet understanding neither needed to spell out. Varden knew they should be moving, that despite the weariness spreading through him, they were far from safe. He'd never manage to firestride in his current state, however, and in the quiet of the room, the echoes of the unfolding battle oozed through the walls, muffled. Could they even get through unscathed? Perhaps if they exited the building, he could signal for an ally to escort them.

After either an age or a second of silent recovery, Varden broke their restful bubble, dragged himself to his feet, and made his way to Isra. He had so little warmth left within himself, but he wrenched what he could to the surface and transferred it to her, further tending to the wounds he'd patched hastily. Her eyes fluttered open, then widened as she saw him.

"Did we—?"

A strangled scream and the sudden metallic screech of armour on stone interrupted her question. Varden's heart rate spiked; it had been right outside the office door. Isra found her feet right away, a hand on the wall for support. Varden motioned for her to stay and padded his way to the exit, the light glow of flames running along his fingers guiding him.

Two soldiers held a woman against the wall, blood dripping from the knife in one's hand. Varden registered the Allastam colours, and just as he relaxed, the torch ensconced in a nearby wall flared to life, shedding light on Sora Sharpe's face—a warning from Keroth, a nudge to act. He let the fire at his palm climb along his arm, growing stronger. His ears rung at even that small trick of magic; he was in no state to take them both on.

"Piss off," one soldier said.

The other dropped Sora. She crumpled to the ground, a rag doll, her life quickly spilling out around her. If he left, she'd die. Even staying … did he even have it in him to heal her, if he had to fight first?

"I don't think so."

He pulled the torch's flame to himself, hoping to fuel his own fire with it. Sharp pain coursed through his body at the simple act, as if he'd burned himself. Another sort of warning, that, but Varden clung to the flame nonetheless. The guards laughed and readied their sword. One still had the bleeding knife.

"Don't blame me cause you weren't wise enough to save your life."

Varden slid back one step as they advanced. There had to be a way. After all they'd accomplished today, two soldiers couldn't be their undoing. Should he keep them talking? Hope Nevian had one last surprise spell in him? He was rifling through possibilities, holding tight to the small flame still within him, desperate to find the one way to use it that'd solve this predicament, when a gust of wind tousled his airs. Wings beat at his ears then smacked his cheek as a bird flew over his left shoulder. It stretched midair, talons turning into paws and claws, wings folding back into a long feline body, beak opening into a mouth full of teeth. Orange stripes lit like bright flames in the changing light as a tiger landed on one of the guards, claws digging around the armour plates and jaws clamping down on its throat.

Isra— who else could it be, shifting shape to suit her needs? It was all Varden had time to think before the great cat tore the first Allastam guard's throat out, spraying blood across the corridor. A terrified scream tore itself out of the second soldier, and they scrambled away, turned heels, and ran. Varden couldn't blame them. Horror and relief churned within as Isra sat atop the body and calmly began to clean herself, one lick at a time, evidently self-satisfied. He forced himself not to think of it and edged towards Sora, one hand on the wall as support. Isra's eyes tracked him every step of the way, and he found himself viscerally afraid.

"Everyone all right?"

Nevian's question jarred him out of the instinctive fear, but it seemed to hit Isra even more strongly, and her form retracted, fur turning to skin as she regained her human body. She hurried off the body, her still-bloodied lips parted in horror, then spun over and was sick against the wall. Nevian turned to Varden, vibrating with awkward confusion, clearly at a loss what to do.

"She saved my life," he said, hoping that perhaps the reminder would help ground Isra. He had no time to go to her, not when another life hung in the balance. "And Sora's too, perhaps."

He plunged in, and his muscles locked tight as the echoes of her paralytic poison in her veins reached his body. Varden ignored it, first closing the deadly wound at her back—then felt a tear in his own. He gasped, pain flaring along his spine, thought he heard his name called. He struggled to focus and keep his body and Sora's separate, to heal without taking the pains onto himself. Too little energy left. Varden shot an emergency burst of magic through her, hoping it'd suffice, and pulled out in a hurry.

Nevian crouched over him, long fingers digging into Varden's shoulders, lips moving. It took a moment for the sounds to resolve into words.

"—can't just collapse like—oh! You're awake." Nevian jerked back, bringing his hand back as if it'd burned him, before offering a watery smile. "I wasn't panicked."

"I'm sure." The words stayed thick on his tongue. He pushed himself in a sitting position, and the stone under him tilted sideways. Nevian grabbed him again, steady hands on his shoulders, and this time he didn't let go.

"Can you walk?" Nevian asked.

"In a moment." The memories of Sora's paralysis and pain were ebbing, leaving him with only his own exhaustion and the distant throb in his back. His garb had turned wet near the open wound, but he'd closed it at the same time as he had Sora's. It had been a long time since his healing had been so sloppy. "I can't carry her, though."

Sora had not regained consciousness. She lay by his side, still pale, but the grimace of pain and anger previously locking her face had smoothed out. She ought to make it, if they could extract themselves from here.

"Kellian can," Nevian said. "He came upon us while you were healing her. He's in there now, searching for the proof with Isra. You … spent a lot of time with her. Not moving. And then bleeding—and then you fell over."

"But you weren't panicked," Varden reiterated, a smile creeping to his lips as he met Nevian's eyes, so blue and open now, an invitation to see his world through them he'd never extended before.

Nevian's smile bloomed on his face, freed from years of anxiety and fear, beautiful and open and eager. When laughter spilled after it, a flighty joy bouncing within it, Varden knew every moment of pain and recovery would have been worth it.

CHAPTER THIRTY-SIX

VELLIEN'S stomach churned at the sight of Arathiel's mangled hand. The day had already dragged a plethora of open gashes, bloodied limbs, and magical burns through the flap of the healers' tent—more so than they had cared to see in their lifetime—but the bone sticking out of Arathiel's wrist, a streak of white in the bloody red of crushed muscles, was more than they could handle. Nausea rose within, an implacable wave that rolled over all their defences until Vellien rushed out of the tent and surrendered their dinner to the once-white snow. They stayed there, heaving, struggling to recover from the shock and humiliation.

"I set him down on a cot," Jilssan said, a step behind them. "Will you manage? No one wanted to try. He's got something of a reputation, seems like."

Vellien wiped their mouth, squared their shoulders, and turned around. Her entire arm had turned to stone and she had a minor cut on her forehead, but unlike Arathiel, she didn't seem in immediate danger. Others could care for Jilssan.

"I–I will, yes. I just didn't expect…"

"It's not pretty, I'll give you that."

Her shrug let Vellien know she'd seen worse dozens of times over. They forced a mask of professionalism upon their face, then slipped back into the heated tent that had been their refuge for the day. Jilssan grabbed their arm before they could enter.

"One of the healers in there—someone from the Sapphire Guard, I think—said Arathiel was cursed. Dangerous. Something about Ezven's magic coursing through him or some similar nonsense. He sounded serious, and I'm a good judge for deception."

"You would be, I suppose."

The retort had escaped Vellien before they could think better of it, brought forth by the memories of Jilssan that Nevian had shared while Vellien helped him recover. So many cruel games had casual lies, for no other purposes than her own enjoyment. Enough to anger Vellien for months, if not years. She laughed, nonplussed, and Vellien turned an embarrassed shade of red at her lack of guilt. They hurried inside.

A nurse had summarily bandaged Arathiel's hand, but blood soaked the fabric already. How much had Arathiel lost on the way? Vellien pushed down their latent nausea and unwrapped the hand, careful not to look too closely. They couldn't afford to be sick again, and they didn't need close visual inspection when Alluma guided them. Vellien began a low, wordless chant, a string of notes they left to mindless inspiration. It didn't matter what they sang, only that no prayer quite appeased them like a song, their voice a soothing echo through their own mind, growing until Vellien's palms glowed with a soft light. Vellien steeled themself for the rush of pain and dizziness to come and plunged their magic into the wound.

There was no agony.

Arathiel's body was a spiral of cold force tugging at Vellien, grasping at their magic and pulling hard and fast. The current swept them off their feet, plunging them deep within it and barring Vellien from their surroundings. Ezven magic, Jilssan had said, and Vellien understood the warning. They felt the thread of His presence, Death and Rebirth entwined within the cold force surrounding them, reaching for Vellien. They pushed back, gathering Alluma's power to them like a protective cocoon, their voice rising until it covered the rush of Arathiel's magic in their ears, the only outside sound they still perceived. Breathless, Vellien expanded their focus on the wound slowly, steadying themself as the pull grew stronger.

In most bodies, Vellien easily perceived muscles, nerves, and blood flow, but Arathiel's anatomy was buried under a storm of magic. It existed, threaded through the current of Ezven's strength, accessible if one managed to repel the intense numbing effect of the force.

Vellien reached for Arathiel's wrist and wrapped soft, healing magic around it. It felt like plunging into a pool of viscous and freezing sludge, and Vellien's song faltered as the sensation pressed in on them, enveloping them. The world faded further away and they let it go, to focus on their task. They could still perceive fractured bones and burst blood vessels through the haze, distant and coated in Ezven's power, so they reached for it. The cold magic reached back, leeching at Vellien's strength with alarming hunger, soaking it up. Vellien scrambled to push past it, slamming what they could into the bone before rebuilding the arm around it, yet even that became difficult, the sludge slipping between them and their patient, cocooning them thoroughly. Only their song remained, gentle notes drifting into the void, a reassuring melody Vellien latched onto. It was comfortable here, and if the magic sustaining Arathiel needed Alluma's power to work, perhaps the best they could do now was let it do its thing and sing onward.

"Vellien."

Their name. It sounded so distant, worlds and ages away. Whoever called them, it could wait. They were working and needed to give Arathiel all they could.

"Vellien!"

A hand grabbed their shoulder and shook them hard, the rough movement piercing through the soft void of their healing. They felt tired, all of a sudden—utterly hollowed out, their song so weak they couldn't hear their own notes anymore. Someone shook him again, sloughing off more of the daze, and Vellien's sight returned, the darkened edges crawling away. Arathiel stared at them, propped up on their healthy arm, searching their face. A strange pinch lined Vellien's wrist, a sucking sensation they belatedly realized was their magic flowing into Arathiel. It was all they could feel of their entire arm.

They snatched their hand away and were relieved to see it move at all. The jerking movement set their body off balance, and they tipped backward. They couldn't feel their feet either, or the freezing ground under their too-thin boots, or anything much. Panic flooded Vellien as the world tilted, but Arathiel caught them before they fell and held them by the bed.

When their eyes met again, understanding passed between them. Vellien had heard of Arathiel's capacity to ignore pain—receiving open wounds without a flinch or running on a broken ankle—but they'd not realized what it had meant, how Arathiel moved through the world. They wrapped their fingers around the wooden beam of the bed, staring at them to make sure they were firmly latched because they couldn't feel them, and glanced at their feet. Firmly spread and flat. Good for balance. Hopefully they wouldn't fall again.

"I'm sorry, Vellien," Arathiel said.

"Don't be. Healing always involves taking part a person's wounds upon yourself. I failed to anticipate what that might mean, in your case."

"You're very kind, but I am well aware my *arm* was wounded."

Vellien considered that very carefully. They had barely felt the pain of the arm as they healed it, cocooned as they were in the strange numbing sludge of Arathiel's body. Had they inadvertently tried to cure that instead? It explained the current state of their body, though less how they'd so completely lost track of themself in the process, or how their magic had seemed sucked towards Arathiel on its own, by the end.

"Regardless, I will gladly lend my help again when needed. Show me the arm?"

Arathiel turned it around, exposing the reddened gash along his forearm. Vellien carefully placed their palm over it and nudged it with magic, but they only sensed the cold swirl of Ezven's magic within. No telling if they'd properly healed the bone and muscles under the skin.

"We'll have to assume nothing is amiss, I suppose," they said.

"It cannot be worse than it was."

Vellien agreed with a pensive *hmm*, even though they disliked leaving things in their current state. They wanted to verify their own work and have a better idea of Arathiel's current state, and to be blocked out unnerved them. The healing had taken its toll, and even their current numbness notwithstanding, it would have been risky to push it. They conceded with a sigh.

"Don't use the arm for now. I advise a lot of rest until I can do more."

"Would you perhaps consent to passing your healer's duties to someone else?"

High Priest Varden's voice drifted from the tent's flap, weighed by exhaustion. Yet there was something joyous in his tone, and Vellien was not surprised to find a smile curving his lips as they turned around.

"Not in your current state," they said, noting the distinct sway of exhaustion in Varden, "but in time, certainly. If Arathiel does."

Arathiel's soft laugh and the warmth with which he pronounced

Varden's name left little doubt about his opinion on the matter. Vellien wanted to ask if his counterpart had any experience healing Arathiel, but when Varden swept forward, he left behind a dazed Nevian, eyes puffy and lined with red. Worry shot through Vellien and they rushed towards him, only to stumble the moment they'd released Arathiel's bed. They fell forward with a surprised yelp, then their knees hit the ground—they felt that shock, at least.

Nevian rushed to them, kneeling in front, hands hovering about. He'd started crying again, but a wobbly smile made it through the tears, and that alone told Vellien all they needed to know about their mission.

"He's gone," Nevian whispered. He wiped away his tears. "Why did you fall?"

"I misplaced some of my sense of touch. But I'm all right, don't worry." Their hands flitted around again, eager to hold Nevian but knowing he'd hate it so soon after an encounter with Avenazar. "How are you?"

"I'm fine."

He blurted it out right away, almost by rote, and only cried harder. Vellien gently extended a hand, palm up.

"You don't have to be. No one's asking you to hold it together, and you shouldn't ask it of yourself anymore."

Nevian dropped the tip of their fingers to the palm, a split-second touch from which he retracted quickly. "Can we leave? Varden said he only wanted a warm fire and the man he loved and—and I think he has the correct idea. I'd like to sit by the Shelter's fireplace with you then hide away in my room where no one but

Efua will find me."

Vellien's chest burst into a thousand fireflies as Nevian casually included them into the ones he loved. It had been a long, exhausting day, full of gruelling injuries and blood, but the joy washed away part of their fatigue.

"I'd love to. I can't heal anyone else today." Vellien moved to stand, but without feeling the ground under them, they lost their balance and fell down to their knees again. This might prove a challenge. "My body has forgotten a few important things, however."

Nevian's tears dried instantly and he frowned. "You said you were all right."

"I will be. I don't think this will last, and if it does… Arathiel has learned to walk again. I am certain I can, too. Until then…"

"I may have a solution." Nevian straightened back up. "Wait here."

He left Vellien, heading back towards the entrance flap with all his usual stubborn determination, and despite all the uncertainties about their health, Vellien could only grin like a fool and look forward to the future.

LONG before her allies had returned, Jilssan had stepped outside the medical tents as soon as her cut had been fixed, though none of the healers had had the skill to turn stone back into flesh. She had snaked her way to the edge of the tiny camp, to survey the Enclave.

Most of the battle had moved inside the walls, leaving a bloodied, trampled snow field behind, bodies and weapons strewn haphazardly around, intermingled with boulders from the destroyed wall. She'd left a sizeable hole in it, and staring at its width now, Jilssan understood better why her entire body ached from magic overuse.

More than anything, however, Jilssan scanned the sky. She had expected to find Isra at the camp, waiting for her, and after quick inquiries, it was obvious she'd never made it out. Panic slithered deeper into her with every new minute without the familiar shape of hawk wings against the pale sky, or even that of smaller, more common birds, swooping down towards her. What was taking so long? This infiltration had always been a risk, but Isra was quick on her feet and had grown tremendously over the last month. Something must have happened. Of course something had. What had Jilssan been thinking, sending her in alone like that? They should have hired Hasryan, should have kept Isra away from the battlefield, should—

A gust of wind lifted dust and snow near the breach, and through its cloud came a strange procession. Lady Amake Brasten led the way, maize-and-blue armour splattered with blood and a pronounced limp to her gait. Kellian Dathirii followed two steps behind, carrying Sora Sharpe in his arms—dead or alive, she couldn't tell at this distance. Last came Varden, heavily supported by Nevian, the pair of them dragging their feet as if the whole world weighed down their shoulders. But they were alive, which could only mean one thing: Avenazar was dead. Her relief was compounded by another: circling around the group was a great feline, its deadly grace a clear threat to any approaching, and it was so out of gloriously out of place, Jilssan recognized her apprentice immediately.

She rushed forward, a few spontaneous strides before she caught herself and slowed into a more dignified pace. Isra spotted her and split from the group, bounding forward in great leaps. Jilssan's heart thundered at the approach, but Isra began shifting as she neared, losing speed as she transformed into a teenager again and flung herself in Jilssan's arms. She sported a few tears and bruises but seemed mostly intact.

Jilssan squeezed her back. "You're safe."

Isra pulled back with a sheepish grin. "I might have taken a few risks? But I helped!"

The rest of the group joined them and Amake provided a quick summary of the situation. Both Master Avenazar and Master Hann were dead, the last pockets of resistance dwindled, and the Myrians had surrendered. Weapons were being confiscated, prisoners rounded up, and wounded tended to—Sora more urgently than many. It seemed Jilssan's instincts had been correct and Allastam soldiers had gone after not only her and Arathiel, but also Sora Sharpe. She had never made it to the office, but Varden, Nevian, and Isra had faced Avenazar within it and been able to retrieve the contract.

Amake held it now and her eyes met Jilssan's as she handed it over for inspection with a nonchalant 'this is it, isn't it?'. Jilssan gave it a cursory look, as if she hadn't recognized her own forgery and they weren't playacting this exchange for the crowd.

"Yes, milady. That'd be the fancy little paperwork you were looking for."

"Then I'll be on my way to the command tent. I suspect Diel Dathirii is dying from anxiety at this point."

After she left, Jilssan directed the rest of the group towards the healers' tent, and Isra stayed with her. They sat near a small fire, close to one another, to salvage what time they could of this chaotic day. Sooner or later, they'd request Jilssan's presence for negotiations surrounding the Enclave, as she was the highest-ranking officer left. She'd have to tread carefully, extorting enough resources to sate the Myrian Empire temporarily while she wove her own story of Master Avenazar's failures and how his leadership had doomed this mission. If she could negotiate a good deal, this might even garner significant political capital back home.

This, of course, presumed she wanted to head home. Climbing in Myrian society had been a tireless and deadly game, always trading influence, favours, or information ranging from gossip to magical techniques, all with no end in sight, no true ultimate goal. She'd thrived on it, hurtling up the ranks through charms and wits, carving either the path ahead or herself so they'd be a perfect fit, never noticing how it had hollowed her out until she'd stepped away. She'd thought of her years in Isandor as a necessary purgatory, a way to prove her political acumen, but now that they were drawing to an end … she did not want to return to Myria.

She rather enjoyed where she'd landed, the devious aid to a group of idealists striving to turn their city into a haven of justice. It was a different kind of challenge, entertaining in its own way, in a city far smaller and kinder than Myria would ever be—and it came with the best partner. Jilssan found herself daydreaming of days spent scheming with Amake—for the greater good, of course—and nights rewarding herself for her selflessness. A wide smile floated on her lips, but the real world was quick to call her back.

"You're not listening, are you?"

Isra pouted at her, arms crossed as if about to scold her. No sense pretending.

"I'm sorry, no," she said. "I was thinking of the future—our future, perhaps? What did you have in mind?"

Isra's face fell. "Oh. I … don't know. I miss Father, but he's all I miss from home. I don't feel ready to return like this."

She gestured at herself, and Jilssan needed a moment to remember what she meant. She'd grown completely used to Isra's real appearance and forgotten how recent the change, and how no one home except Master Enezi knew of it. No wonder the prospect of heading back to Myria felt daunting.

"I think I'm staying for a while, if they'll have me," she said. "Perhaps I ought to add a line in the first report about your considerable progress within this environment, and how I believe it best you continue by my side?"

Isra beamed at her. "I'd love that! It's a nice place, and I really want to start annoying Nevian again now that he won't be so busy creating entirely new magical techniques from scratch. He's really good with these rune things."

Jilssan suspected Nevian wouldn't be particularly pleased by these plans and might find brand new areas of magic to innovate just to keep Isra away. Before she could voice a kind warning, however, someone cleared their throat nearby.

"I will trade your two hours of free 'annoy Nevian' time if you help me out today."

Isra spun around, her grin somehow growing even wider as she found Nevian staring at her, brow pinched and arms crossed, the very picture of exasperation. Only the red rim of his eyes broke the effect.

"Of course, Nev Nev! What do you need?"

"A ride to Isandor's Lower City—not for myself. I'll walk along."

"Now?"

"The sooner, the better."

Isra turned to Jilssan, silently asking for permission. She was vibrating with excitement, and as much as Jilssan wished to spend more time with her apprentice, she didn't have the heart to deny her. Besides, her own return to serious and boring business couldn't be too far away.

"Of course. Enjoy yourself, and I'll see you at the Brasten Tower tonight."

Isra leaped to her feet and bounced towards Nevian, who stepped back with alarm.

"Tonight?" he repeated. "I only need the ride. I never said you were invited to *stay*!"

Isra only laughed. "Oh, but Nev Nev, wouldn't it be better with company? We have so much catching up to do!"

If Nevian noticed the teasing undertone in Isra's words, his frustrated sigh gave nothing away. They went off together, the ever-grumpy apprentice arguing that he already had company and only desired rest, and Jilssan watched them vanish between tents. She didn't understand why Isra bothered with him, but her giggles carried throughout the entire camp, sufficient reason for Jilssan to let it happen. Who knew what might happen? Nevian could mellow out before Isra got tired of trying and found new, local friends. Regardless, they would stay in Isandor, to see what life they could carve for themselves amidst the now familiar bridges and towers of the City of Spires.

Chapter Thirty-Seven

EVERY minute that passed after the initial assault grinded Diel's nerves until only raw anxiety remained. He paced in the command tent, unable to heed Jaeger's invitation to sit with him for more than a few seconds at a time. He had given everything to have Isandor united under a single banner, however briefly, and oust the Myrian Enclave. The path here felt long and torturous, the pretense for their assault almost absurd, but he reminded himself that only the result mattered. If Master Avenazar and his people left, they had won.

Only, the result was not guaranteed. Every time he stepped out to look towards the Enclave's walls, balls of flames and sparks of magic rose in the sky and the screams of dying soldiers rolled down the plains. Were any of them Kellian? Arathiel? Lady Brasten? Would Sora find her way to the office? And how were Varden and Nevian faring, on their own against the worst threat of them all?

The questions spun endlessly through his mind, dragging time down with their weight until word finally returned from the frontlines.

Lord William stepped into the tent, his armour bloodied with what he assured them was the blood of their enemies, and none of his own. Somehow his long dark hair had been dishevelled into a perfect scruffed look, as if he'd walked on stage in a play, pretending to be a great warrior.

"We are victorious," he declared, sweeping the air before him in a grand gesture. "Pockets of battle subsists, but after your fine captain of the guard slew Master Hann, most surrendered with haste. I've yet to hear from Master Avenazar, and so late into the day, that can only foretell good news."

His predictions were correct, as they learned when more and more fighters returned, including a very battered Varden and Nevian. Isandor's nobles had filtered into the command tent one by one, enough so that Diel stopped his pacing and hovered near Jaeger, trying and no doubt failing to conceal his anxiety. Confirmation that Master Avenazar was dead had brought huge relief and immediately freed his frenetic mind to turn to personal matters. They had yet to hear from Sora Sharpe.

When Lady Brasten entered the tent alone, even though they had gone into the Enclave together, his heart sank. She found his gaze and smiled, however, breathing back hope into his lungs. She extended a scroll to Lord William, its parchment rolled tight and held by a Myrian seal.

"My fellow nobles, I have important tidings," she said as William plucked it from her fingers. "Investigator Sora Sharpe is unable to attend this meeting and offer the result of her efforts, I am afraid, as she was ambushed before she could reach Master Avenazar's office. She has been hurried to our best healers, and I believe she will make a recovery in time. This, however, is the proof she sought."

"Preposterous," Lord Allastam growled.

Lady Brasten turned to him, her eyebrows arching in defiance. "Which part, milord? Her recovery, or the proof you tried to keep her from?"

The smattering of whispers around the tent died at Lady Brasten's implied accusation. Lord Allastam crossed his arms. "I never signed any contract."

No denial of a deal, Diel noted, only that a signed proof existed. The crack of a broken seal interrupted the conversation, and all turned towards Lord William, as if from a single body.

"Let us see, shall we?"

Lord William unfurled the parchment, slender fingers moving with excruciating slowness, and every crinkle sent a stab through his stomach. The preparations for this battle had siphoned the last of his mental strength, stealing sleep and diminishing even the comfort of Jaeger's renewed presence by his side.

Lord William cleared his throat and began reading the document, listing the components of the trade agreement in an overly solemn manner. A soft buzz started in Diel's ears, his apprehension growing as they approached the inevitable section about him. By the time they reached it, he struggled to keep steady on his feet, and Jaeger's hand on his lower back deserved most of the credit for anchoring him.

"And to deliver on the grounds of the Myrian Enclave, in the manner of his choosing, the person of Lord Diel Dathirii, bound and unable to resist. Upon the completion of such a delivery, all responsibility as to the fate of Lord Diel Dathirii passes away from Lord Allastam's hands, including but not limited to any successful attempts to retrieve him by allies or family members."

Vivid details of the ride to the enclave haunted Diel as Lord William's voice washed over him—the coldness of the shackles, the creak of the carriage with every bump, the crisp smell of winter all around him. He closed his eyes, dizzy.

Lord William paused, then rolled the document back up. "The rest is formalities. I don't think it's necessary to go any farther."

Diel breathed out, focusing on his body—Jaeger's hand at his back, the sharpness of the winter air, the flat anger filling that empty, defeated void he'd held within since that night. All this time, there had been something abstract about Lord Allastam's attempt, as if it had happened to someone else—as if it wasn't personal and he could distance himself from it. His indignation paled compared to the ire rising now, a pure bright flame burning until he trembled from it.

"You signed this," he said, his tone flat and hard.

"I did not." Lord Allastam leaned on the tip of his sword as he so often did his cane. His armour had acquired new chips and scratches in the fight, and dirt covered part of his greyed hair. "I will, of course, demand that this contract be examined for signs of forgery, as it is clearly fabricated."

"I'd expect any good investigation would carry that out," Lord William said. "It seems to me, however, that the conditions to allow Sora Sharpe to continue her work have been fulfilled."

"She'll certainly want to add to the accusations, as will I." Lady Brasten's tone took a turn to the sharp and dark, and the air around her buzzed with tension. "Tell me, milord, did you forget Lord Arathiel Brasten was a member of my House when you gave orders to kill him under the cover of battle?"

A tide of whispers rose from the gathered nobles, but Diel couldn't piece out their words or tones under the rumble in his own ears. Had something happened to Arathiel after they'd breached the walls?

"Is that your new lie?" Lord Allastam asked. "You know your contract's a scam, so you want to blame me for losing your freaky little ancestor?"

"I've lost no one." She leaned on her spear, bending forward with a dangerous gleam to her eyes. "My freaky little ancestor, as you've called him, has met Ezven and returned. You'll need more than a grunt to get him, but I don't think you understand the mistake you've just made. I've helped Diel Dathirii out of duty to Isandor's institutions, which you so clearly disdained, and as an extension of my welcome to Arathiel." She waved at the air, dismissing the reasons as insignificant. "I've never much liked you, milord, nor made any secrets of it, but you're about to find out what happens when I truly put my mind to ruining another. Sora Sharpe's investigation will be the least of your worries."

She gave him no opportunities for a reply, storming out of the tent. Lord Allastam sneered at her back.

"I love a good challenge," he said, and the sneer turned into a victorious smirk when his gaze found Diel. Somehow, despite the contract and his foiled assassination attempts, Lord Allastam still thought he had the upper hand. On a worse day, it might have pushed doubts in Diel's heart, but he reminded himself that the man's arrogance had no end. He wouldn't see or admit to the cliff's edge even as he walked right off it.

"My only regret is that I'll miss your downfall," Diel said. "Now if the illustrious nobles of the city will forgive me, I'd rather return to my family and spend the remainder of my time here with them."

One month felt suddenly far too short, and he didn't want to waste it on Isandor's politics. He'd given the city too much already. Jaeger fell in pace behind him, long fingers slipping into Diel's in a rare public show of affection.

"Home?" he asked. "Our family will be waiting."

"Not yet." Diel squeezed his hand. *Our* family, he'd said, not *your*. That, too, was new, and Diel wanted to soak in the soft warmth of Jaeger finally including himself. He had one last matter to attend to, however, and while it was not strictly pressing, it would gnaw at his mind until he did so. "If you could find me Sir Cal? I will need his guidance."

"Of course. I will meet you at the stable."

With a last discreet squeeze, Jaeger released his hand and left his side. Diel watched him slip between the milling soldiers and vanish around a tent, his heart fuller than it had been in a long time. He had one more loose end to tie, then it was time for him to look forward, to a long future with an ever-diligent, brilliant man and untold adventures.

HASRYAN received his news from the battlefront from an unexpected duo. Cal made sense; he had promised to come back as soon as possible, but he'd thought to do so alongside Arathiel. Instead, his friend hopped in, bowed deep down, and declared:

"His no-longer-lord, the great exile, Diel Dathirii."

And in came the elf, his golden hair contained by his thick scarf, the blush on his cheeks as likely to come from the outside chill than Cal's introduction. He began unrolling his scarf to remove it, but stopped halfway as Hasryan continued to stare.

"If I may?" he asked.

The question pulled Hasryan out of his surprised daze. "Yeah, sure, yeah! You're welcome here. Didn't expect it, is all."

"Good, good. My recent days have been a special kind of hectic, but I've meant to pay you a visit since the Golden Table."

"Why?"

Was he being rude? Hasryan wasn't certain he cared. He'd left his hideout twice today, armed and ready to infiltrate the Enclave, to do something—anything—to help everyone out. Inevitably, he turned back to sulk in the hideout. Isandor soldiers were as likely to attack him as they were to welcome his help, and direct battle wasn't his strong suit. The wait for news from the battlefront had turned his nerves raw, and Diel's presence only further flustered him. He had no idea how to deal with him after he'd defended Hasryan at the Golden Table.

"I owe you help, do I not?" The scarf gone, Diel Dathirii freed his hair with one shake of his head, causing the great wave of gold to roll down his shoulders. "My means are more limited than when I hired you alongside Arathiel, but I have an offer. I hear you'll be leaving, too?"

"It's either that or live in hiding all the time. Gotta get out until Allastam's done for, perhaps longer."

"But you'll be back, right?" Cal interrupted. "I can find you a new home while you're gone, and keep it warm until it's safer for you here."

"I… Yeah. I wanna come back." He had no idea when he could, or how to go about figuring it out. Probably he'd get tired of waiting in the outskirts, barred from the life he wanted, and just risk it all. It warmed him to know Cal wanted a place waiting for him and that his friends wouldn't forget him once he'd walked away.

"As for where you might go in the meantime," Diel said, sliding himself back into the conversation, "I have a friend in Mehr whom I believe could make great use of your skills and would be more than happy to house you or help you relocate. He's of a rather genial nature and I think you'd get along. I thought perhaps a referral letter would be of help? And you are, of course, welcome to use my departure with Jaeger as a convenient carriage to hide in and slip away. We'd love to have you."

Hasryan laughed—better that than to let them see the churning of his stomach. "Aren't you supposed to be honeymooning?"

Diel's smile widened, and it breathed new life into his expression, softening it. "Oh, we'll have plenty of time for that. I've waited decades for it; I can wait a few extra days. Especially if it gives us a chance to know you better, don't you think?"

No, he didn't think that. Not that he hated the idea, but he'd not expected Lord Dathirii to carve time and space to get to know him, not even after he'd so publicly defended him as a friend. They weren't friends; it had been a front, a tactic to salvage Sora's reputation. It seemed Diel wanted to turn it into reality, and a low, anxious thrill pinched Hasryan's stomach. He glanced at Cal and found him nodding with all the world's eagerness and none of its subtlety. Hasryan could only surrender.

"All right. Sounds like a deal. I'll take your referral and hop along for the ride. It's better than starting from scratch."

Hasryan had no idea what Mehr would hold for him, but he had a destination now, and it seemed a job might wait for him. Leaving Isandor didn't mean starting all over. The friends and allies he'd made here would carry him forward and wait for him here. The city was changing, and sooner or later, it'd be ready for his return.

Chapter Thirty-Eight

THREE days after the fall of the Myrian Enclave, Cal had successfully gathered enough gold to pay for decent decorations for the Big Dathirii Wedding incoming. After a rough day healing all the wounded soldiers, he'd been thrilled to have a chance to apply his skill and help another way. He'd lost track of the number of well-off merchants he'd wiped clean at cards over the last few nights, moving from one Upper City tavern to another, gathering coins and curses upon his names alike. All because of his last quick chat with Lord Dathirii—Diel—after they'd left Hasryan.

Cal had not been able to resist: he'd asked about the wedding. When was it? Were they having a big wedding with all the nobles? Only close family and friends? Did they have special traditions in mind? Secret hopes? The questions had tumbled out of his mouth one after the other, faster than Diel could even answer—not that

Diel even had answers to most of these. They'd had no time to give it any thoughts and Diel refused to burden Jaeger with the stressful task of organizing his own wedding on short notice and on a nearly non-existent budget. So *of course* Cal had jumped on the occasion and proposed his services as a very professional wedding planner.

Diel had laughed, then stopped walking to face him. "My dear Sir Cal, I could never ask something like that out of you. You've already been so generous to us all!"

"You make it sound like a burden!" Cal had clapped his gloved hands together, hopping from one foot to another. He'd wished they'd kept walking so he could spend his buzzing excitement. "This is what my talents are meant for. Healing wounded soldiers and infiltrating wizard enclaves aren't my cup of tea, but this? Cleaning out wealthy folks' purses with games to finance a beautiful, long-earned declaration of love? Shape a party around yours and Jaeger's tastes and history? Now we're talking! Don't worry, I'll talk to people who've known you longer. I hear you have an aunt that's great with tea."

Faced with his unbridled enthusiasm, Diel Dathirii had given in and placed him in charge of the preparations.

Ren must have loved the idea of this wedding as much as he did, because Cal's already legendary luck had grown even more ridiculous. He won every game he played, amassing a decent amount of funds, and he'd called in some favours from his extensive network. Over the years, Cal had shared his luck with a large number of artisans and craftsmen, giving them the boost they'd needed to get out of a pinch or find patronage, and most were thrilled to have a chance to return the help.

As enjoyable as the wedding resource gathering phase had been, however, Cal knew tonight's card games would be the best of them all: the Halfies Quartet had gathered at last. Larryn had prepared the Shelter's meal ahead of time, then asked trusted patrons to serve others for the night, promising a small pay for the effort, and Arathiel, arm still in a sling, had recovered enough to move about the city, so they had converged on Hasryan's hideout.

Cal had swept in with a huge grin on his face and the desire to shove all his apprehension about Larryn and potential awkwardness deep under a constant stream of bubbly joy. As the first to arrive, he got to ramble about his last days of Dathirii wedding planning without bringing up that particular slippery bridge with Larryn around, but even once they'd all arrived, conversations flowed with ease—no long pauses, no awkward glances, nothing but a back-and-forth of catch-up stories and friendly ribbing. They sat on the ground, gathered around the big pot Larryn had carried from the Shelter, and it wasn't long before they unanimously requested the great tale of Larryn's erstwhile posturing as a Sapphire Guard.

Red to the tip of his ears, Larryn started with his arrival in Sora's office, breakfast dumping included. Invectives peppered the tale, with a new one attributed to Lord Allastam every time his name turned up, and Cal almost choked on their delicious meal at the epitaphs. Larryn leaped to his feet as things got heated up and puffed his chest to imitate Sora whenever she did something grandiose. They teased him mercilessly about his disguise as a guard, Hasryan eagerly providing a detailed account of everything wrong with it from his perspective. They had fun, plain and simple, and before long, Cal's ribs hurt from laughing so much. Larryn mumbled something about needing new friends and cleared the plates away to make room for the cards. Arathiel retrieved the wooden tokens he'd brought to stand in for coins and split the pile in four.

Hasryan leaned forward, popped every knuckle, and snapped the deck of cards up. "All right. This might be my last chance to steal a victory from Cal in a long time. Let's get to it!"

The reminder of what the future held for them doused their collective bubble, but Larryn blazed right through the awkwardness. He sprang a familiar silver coin from his pocket and flipped it in the air. Cal's stomach flipped with it, and he barely resisted the urge to snatch his holy symbol. His palms itched with need. It had been far too long, and as much as he kept telling himself he wanted Larryn to be ready, he craved its return.

"You think it's your turn to grasp sweet victory?" Larryn asked, catching the coin before shaking it at Hasryan with a grin. "I hold the secret key right here."

"That's not fair!" Hasryan exclaimed, laughing. "Give that back to its proper owner and lose with pride like the rest of us."

"You wish," Larryn retorted.

Despite all the bluster, he did glance Cal's way, silently asking for permission. Cal grinned at him.

"Ren's blessing is more than a mere symbol," he declared, puffing out his chest in exaggerated pride—the last few days had proven that several times over. "Deal us a first hand, Hasryan. Let's see how you all fare."

Hasryan didn't need to be told again. He passed the cards in earnest and they began to play. Things returned to a delightful normal: Larryn followed one unwise bluff with another, Hasryan tried to play casual and cover his terrible hands with smirks, and Arathiel watched, mostly silent, difficult to read and deadly in his choices. Yet despite their best efforts, Cal's hands remained steadily better than theirs, and the pile of tokens before him grew.

With an overdramatic sigh, Hasryan set down his current draw. "I'm out. This isn't going to be my round either."

"Will any of them be?" Larryn asked, before pulling two cards from his hand and revealing them. "I'm getting rid of these two—an Allastam and a Lorn, can you believe?—and taking new cards."

"Revealing your hand, Larryn?" Arathiel leaned back and signalled that he was also folding. "I feel like Cal's holy symbol only makes you bolder, not luckier."

"Maybe it's like a ritual," Hasryan suggested. "Fortune favours the bold and whatnot."

A stream of giggles bubbled up to Cal's lips, and before long he was laughing heartily, garnering curious looks from his friends. Arathiel's guess might be accurate. Ren's blessing could have that effect, and perhaps more of the Luckbringer's magic stayed in the symbol than Cal had first guessed. A small boost of confidence in the future would absolutely push a hothead like Larryn towards recklessness and the predictability of it amused Cal more than he could explain. When his fit of laughter subsided, he wiped his eyes, panting.

"I love everyone so much," he said. "It's good to be back together."

"It is." Sadness softened Hasryan's voice. "I'll miss this more than anything else."

Part of Cal wanted to tell him he didn't need to miss it, that together they could figure out a way to keep him here and safe, but he was being selfish. He didn't want Hasryan gone—not for a day, and certainly not for a few years—but his friend knew best what path he preferred. He had promised to return, and that'd have to be enough.

"Think of all the incredible and silly tales we'll have for one another when you get back!" Cal said. "I'll make sure Larryn and Sora keep hanging out just so we get the juiciest bits possible."

A smile pulled at the corner of Larryn's lips, and he raised Cal's bet with a few tokens. "You're in for a surprise."

Cal stared at him. There was a strange glow about his friend that might be either Ren's twinkling love or his own joy. He matched the bet, and set his two pairs—House Carrington and House Balthazar—down with a raised eyebrow. Larryn set his cards down one by one, revealing a perfect Dathirii line. Everyone else gasped and choked.

"Can't believe you kept *that*!" Hasryan said, laughing.

"My hands are sullied forever, but if it gets me a win…" Larryn promptly raked in all the tokens, then added in the most casual of tones. "Also, Sora has a permanent welcome to the Shelter for as long as she intends to throw that fancy sapphire cape down the shitslides. We're on good terms, so you might not quite get you the juicy stories you're hoping for."

Perhaps not, but it sure filled Cal's tiny chest with a whole lot of warmth. Keeping the Dathirii card meant breaking a long-running tradition of always discarding them, no matter what it did to his winning chances, and the concession was no coincidence. But this developing friendship with Sora Sharpe was a thousand times better. If Larryn could keep calm enough for that, perhaps he'd get around to returning Cal's coin.

They continued their games late into the night, changing the rules at times to liven things up. Cal's luck never ran out, but he folded every now and then to let others have their chance—or, to be more exact, for the pleasure of watching Arathiel read his two adversaries like open books, calling their bluffs with ease and raking in all the coins. When Hasryan revealed a particularly bad hand after one such calls, Larryn ribbed him hard.

"Don't you ever know when to fold?"

"It wasn't against Cal! I thought I'd have a chance…"

"Learn to lie." Arathiel's teasing tone offered no warning for what followed. "I've long learned which of your smirk are genuine and which are shields."

Hasryan's mouth gaped and an awkward, laugh-like sound escaped him. The familiar smirk followed and Arathiel's eyebrows shot up, a silent pointer that this was exactly what he'd meant. Cal snorted, unable to help himself—there was something closed off in the way Hasryan held himself when he was trying to mask his feelings.

"Now we can all see through your bluffs!" Cal clapped his hands.

"Thanks, Ara."

Hasryan ran a hand through his hair. "Great. Maybe I do need new people to gamble with."

Larryn scoffed. "You like a challenge. Why else would you stubbornly take on Cal like that?"

Hasryan had to concede that point, and he was far more careful with his bluffs as the night went on. Larryn left them once, travelling to the Shelter in the dead of the night to acquire warmed drinks and a bag of dried apples to snack on. Too soon, the sun shone through the bright red curtains, and all the coin tokens had finally wound their way in front of him. Hasryan set his cards down and sighed.

"I guess this is it," he said.

No one replied. While others gathered the deck of cards, Cal fiddled with the wooden tokens in front of him. He wanted to give them all back, to just start the night over. All-nighters with great friends were all he'd ever asked of life, all he needed to relax and love the world at its fullest. Hasryan was stretching from the long night sitting on the ground, seemingly content.

"You'll write to us, won't you?" Cal asked.

"Sure, I can pen you some letters. Let you know how cold Mehr is, and how boringly horizontal. But you—" He waggled a finger at Cal with a smirk. "—you got to visit. Nothing ties you down here daily. Travel a little, come say hi! Imagine all the taverns full of unsuspecting victims you could gamble in."

"Oh, that sounds wonderful!"

Cal threw himself into Hasryan's legs, and his friend bent down to return the hug properly, his laughter music to Cal's ears. He'd miss it, could already feel its absence like a smouldering crack in his chest, but this talk of travel and small adventures in a foreign city helped dampen the impact.

Hasryan straightened back up, but his attempt to escape the hug was immediately thwarted by Arathiel sliding his healthy arm around his waist. Larryn joined a moment later, throwing his around Hasryan's shoulder, and for a few seconds they'd buried him in a pile of love. Hasryan laughed, but his voice had gone rough with emotion.

"All right, enough of this," he said, squirming out of their embrace. "Y'all should go, get some sleep, yes? And drop by whenever you get some spare time."

They all promised to, and they stored the rest of their things, putting on winter boots, scarves, coats, and mitts in the most complete silence. Hasryan was crying now, tears rolling down his cheeks. When Cal moved in for one last hug, he stalled him with a raised hand.

"No, I—Thank you, but no. I'm good."

He wiped the tears and smirked—the closed off, contained expression Arathiel had underscored earlier. This time, however, no one called his bluff.

"CAL, wait!"

Larryn's voice bounced around the tower walls on each side of them, crisp in the cold morning. Hope twisted Cal's insides as he stopped on the windswept bridge. They'd had a great evening, friendly and natural, but Cal had never quite forgotten that all was not fixed yet. It was time, wasn't it? Cal was ready—he'd been ready almost right away, ready to forgive and to love, even when Larryn had done nothing to deserve it.

His friend ran up to him, cheeks brightened red from the short run and prickly morning air. The rare sunlight filtering through towers creased the lines of exhaustion in Larryn's face, deepening them. He paused to catch his breath by Cal's side, then tugged his threadbare mitts off and reached into his pocket, retrieving Cal's holy silver coin. Sunlight glinted off Ren's relief as he extended it between them.

Cal stared at the coin, then back at Larryn. Was that it? No words, nothing? How was Cal supposed to take this?

"You have to take it back."

Larryn gave it an insistent shake. He kept his eyes on the towers behind Cal and balanced on his heels.

"I don't understand." As soon as Cal voiced them, the hurt and confusion surged through him, lodging themselves in his throat. Larryn was supposed to return the symbol when he felt ready to mend their friendship and build something better from it, but this didn't feel like a peace offering. It felt like he wanted to be rid of it—the symbol, the friendship, maybe even Cal himself. "You want to give up on us?"

"No, no! Except… I don't know, I—" Larryn's voice broke and he dropped to his knees, thin pants landing in the snow, and pinched his nose, eyes squeezed as he put together some words. "It's not that I want to give up. I just want to deserve that second chance, and I don't see how. You've always been there for me, but I've been too caught up in myself—too angry—to appreciate it." He sat back on his heels, finally meeting Cal's eyes, but the details of his expression were lost to a blur of tears. Larryn dropped the coin between them. "I'm sorry. I'm sorry I punched you, and I'm even more sorry you've always been my friend, but I was never yours."

Cal allowed every word uttered by Larryn to sink into his heart and soul. Finally—finally!—the words 'I'm sorry' had crossed his lips, and even though they were shaky, wrapped in guilt and confusion and a big mess of other emotions, Cal clung to them and their promise. He threw himself into Larryn's arms, sobbing as he hit the hard chest and wrapped his small arms around it. It took Larryn a few seconds to react and gingerly hug him back, as though afraid to touch him at all. Cal could feel his entire body shaking, though whether from cold, exhaustion, or emotion, he couldn't say. He squeezed tighter before stepping back.

"Silly you, I don't need a grand romantic gesture. Don't you even see how far you've come? Friends with Sora, and now an apology?"

He patted Larryn's leg, then picked up his silver coin. The cold metal warmed up at his touch, breathing courage into Cal. As much as he wanted to welcome Larryn in without another word, it'd be a disservice to their friendship not to lay down some rules.

"Here's what I want," he started, and the resolve in his voice melted halfway through, his courage faltering. What if he shattered the fragile understanding they were coming to? But no, this had to be a part of it, or they'd made no progress at all. "You can't redirect your anger on me anymore. You're right. Sometimes it felt like you didn't think I was a friend at all. I won't make excuses for it anymore."

"I don't want to be that person anymore." He tilted his head up, looking at the lightening sky, and sighed. "Only… I can't promise much. I don't think my anger will ever leave. It's rooted deep in me and everything I lived. I'm trying to harness it, put it to good use, but sometimes it feels so impossible. That's why I didn't want to keep the coin, y'know, or-or give it back properly? Felt like a promise I'd break."

"You're thinking about it like a promise of success. I want you to promise to try—and I think you already are. So maybe we can just do that? Try to build something new and better and beautiful, with a lot of laughter and a lot of good food."

A choked laugh escaped Larryn, then he wrapped an arm around Cal, pulling him close. They rested against each other, sitting on this cold bridge as morning crept on them, the city living on as they paused to savour this new invisible bridge between them. The contentment could almost make him forget Hasryan's inevitable departure, and the temporary loss of another dear friend.

"You hungry?" Larryn asked. "It's been an intense night, and you're a long way from home. People will be clamouring for their breakfast already, and I could fix you something hot while I do theirs."

Cal's stomach growled, accepting the request on his behalf. He meant to voice that properly, but divine inspiration struck Cal before a single word made it past his lips. An idea so simple yet so terrific it dizzied him with glee and fear. Cal grabbed Larryn's hand and tried to catch his breath. This would push at Larryn's most personal boundaries, trampling well-defined lines Cal had respected for years. Hadn't those already gotten muddled, though, with Vellien dropping by the Shelter so often?

"Ya know, if you're looking for big gestures, there is something you could do for me. You won't like it, though."

Larryn's face turned into an expectant frown, and he stopped his movement to rise. "What is it?"

Deep breaths. Larryn had just promised not to yell at him, and he wasn't forced to accept this. "I need someone to prepare a multi-course dinner for Lord Dathirii's wedding."

Larryn snatched his hand away and flopped backward on the bridge, arms spread out and gaze upon the sky above. "You're serious. I know you're serious, and I can't believe you're even asking."

Cal choked back a laugh—it wouldn't help to mock Larryn's dramatic misery, especially when part of the giggles bubbling upward were relief at his lack of anger. "You don't need to meet them," he said. "Just cook. And you'd have access to their full kitchens and everything you'd ever wanted. It could be fun."

Larryn pushed himself up, back into a seating position, to meet Cal's gaze. "That's where mom worked, Cal. The kitchens."

His voice shook, and although the cold had turned the tip of his nose red, the rest of his skin was pale. He set his forehead on his knees and Cal granted him the space to think it through. New relationship or not, he was asking a lot out of Larryn and he didn't want to pressure him. Finally, his friend lifted his head.

"I'll do it." His voice hitched and he forced a long breath in. "I'll do it—for you, and Vellien, and that old lady who saved Hasryan. I don't want any of them to know who prepared their meal. Especially not Yultes."

Joy coursed through Cal and he clenched his teeth to keep his squeal inside. Diel would have the best wedding ever. "Deal!"

At Cal's wide grin, a shy smile spread across Larryn's face. He looked strikingly young and uncertain, all of a sudden, so different than the wall of unshakeable fury he often projected—so much more like the wounded, vulnerable teenager Cal had first met. Larryn ran a hand through his hair, a habit he temporarily picked up whenever he was around Hasryan, then pushed himself to his feet.

"Let's go, before we freeze to death and your fancy noble friends are deprived of a delicious feast."

Anticipation fluttered in Cal's stomach as he fell in pace with Larryn. He hadn't lingered at the Shelter since their fight, and there were a dozen people he wanted to hear from. He couldn't wait to go about the tables, bring them a warm meal, and invite himself into the conversations long enough for a pinch of gossip. He must have missed so much! Together, he and Larryn would make sure all the patrons were happy, then they'd sit back to enjoy the meal, listen to the gorgeous music, and bask in the warmth of their strange, very public home, and a job well done between friends.

Cal pocketed his silver coin, thanking Ren for Xir never-ending blessings. "I would love to."

CHAPTER THIRTY-NINE

VARDEN searched Arathiel's chosen room for clues about the mysterious favour he meant to ask of him. They had snuck through the tower in the middle of the night, whispering like foolish teenagers, his heart as full of love as one but spared of all the fear that used to come with it. Nothing here struck him as unique or helpful for his guess, however. A handful of old chairs lined the walls and generic tapestries covered those not occupied by long, slim windows. Dust had gathered, and Varden wondered if the emptiness and disuse weren't the very pointers he was looking for. He flared the torches lining up the sconces, but no further detail revealed itself.

"No fireplace?" Varden asked.

The dancing torchlight helped, but the bright fires had become his refuge since their confrontation at the Myrian Enclave. He liked to keep them burning high, to keep Keroth's serene presence close at hand, a familiar warmth he could reach for whenever his mind wandered into darker corners. The last few days had been unexpectedly difficult, as if he was allowing himself to fall apart now that the threat was gone.

Arathiel clasped Varden's hand, drawing him out of his thoughts, and pulled him towards the centre of the room with his recently freed limb. His gaze drifted around the room, distant—filled with memories, Varden guessed. Arathiel perceived ghosts within the Brasten Tower only he had known, the past still alive before his eyes. In time, however, he snapped his attention back to the present and Varden.

"Here we are," he said. "Once upon a time, House Brasten was known for its love of the dance. Feet waltzed across the floor of this room at every hour of the day. We hosted classes and events for all of Isandor, and even at this hour, sleepless siblings would find their way here to spend extra energy. While Lindi was still healthy, she spent her entire days here, twirling. Even once her pain intensified, she'd come whenever possible—and when not, she'd use the support poles in her room to practise. She loved dancing."

He trailed off, his voice thick. Varden squeezed his hand as hard as he could, so that Arathiel would feel it, and waited. With this new context, he had a solid idea of Arathiel's coming request, but it only made the wait for it sweeter. Eventually, his partner looked up with a shy smile.

"With the wedding coming, I decided I ought to learn the steps again. My coordination and balance aren't what they used to be, of course, but..." He flipped his grip on Varden's hand then traced the back of it with his thumb. "If you would do me the favour?"

Varden clasped Arathiel's hand without hesitation, lacing their fingers together and stepping close.

"You should ask for more favours if they're all like this."

"We'll see if you still say that after I've stepped on your toes a dozen times."

A soft laugh hatched in Varden's chest, spreading its wings as he released it. He absolutely would. Few things instilled more joy in him than the prospect of spending hours with Arathiel, crushed toes or not. He wanted to learn the dances with him, and learn more about Arathiel himself, too. To uncover new layers of gentleness, of care, and fall in love ever more.

"Allow me," Varden said, before setting his hand on Arathiel's hip.

They didn't have musicians, so he hummed for them, choosing a soft melody Vellien had sung while they'd healed him, those first days out of the enclave, and which would always mark the start of a better future. Arathiel recognized it from his hours at Varden's bedside and picked up the pace. Neither of them was very good, especially compared to Vellien, but it had a heart of its own, their two voices stumbling through harmony as they began to move.

Varden led the way, guiding Arathiel at a slow pace, to give his body time to adapt to the movements and learn the shifts. Arathiel stared at his feet, his grip on Varden's tighter than necessary, concern and intense concentration lining his forehead. Minutes of deliberate dancing eroded his fears, however, and the more Arathiel met Varden's gaze and smiled, sending flutters through his chest, the faster he led them. They continued until the steps blurred into one another, their hummed melody picking up the pace alongside them. Now that he'd found his rhythm, Arathiel danced with an obvious ease born from hours of practice. They spun around the room, laughing almost as much as singing, giddy with excitement of the dance, the closeness of their bodies, the pure, undistilled joy of this moment. Varden caught Arathiel's gaze and read in it the same burning thrill now exploding in his chest.

"Spin me," Arathiel requested.

Varden grinned, his own head already spinning. He leaned forward first, stealing a kiss before he lifted his arm and initiated the twirl. Arathiel followed the impulse, and for an instant it was like he floated, hair whipping through the air—then his eyes widened, his foot hit the ground at a weird angle, and he tripped with a surprised exclamation. Varden tried to catch him only to stumble forward and be dragged down alongside Arathiel. They crashed together, laughing, arms and legs in a tangle. When he could catch his breath, Varden pushed himself on an elbow.

"See, I don't fall for you, I fall on you," he said.

Arathiel gave him a playful shove, then hooked his fingers into Varden's clothes, pulling him back into a long kiss. They stayed on the ground, their breaths short, Varden's heart hammering in his chest.

"As long as I'm always there to catch you."

"Please," Varden whispered.

After hours spent discussing potential wedding outfits with Branwen, romantic relationships had lingered in Varden's mind a lot. Jaeger and Diel had been together for decades, intimately at ease with one another's faults and marvels, pieces of a beautiful whole Varden envied. Could he and Arathiel build something this strong? What would they be like, far down the line, if they sanded each other's edges until they made a perfect fit? Even dreaming of it made him feel dizzy. Arathiel brushed Varden's cheek, meeting his gaze with reassuring calm, as if he could sense the racing of his thoughts.

"I want to find us a small house," Arathiel said. "Something quiet and made for us. I'm glad I have my family, but it has been … overwhelming to inhabit these halls again, and I do not think the memories will ever leave. Amake will understand."

Varden had always known he personally wouldn't stay in the Brasten Tower. He needed a space completely his own to rest and heal, a haven he could shape to his taste over the course of time. He hadn't dared to dream of inviting Arathiel, however, not when his homecoming had taken so long and been so fraught. The proposition left him speechless, quiet happiness warring with the idea he'd slowly cultivated over the last week: inviting Nevian to join him. He fretted over Nevian's recovery and found ways to check in on him often, and considering the young man had turned the Brasten's great brazier room into his favourite reading spot, Varden suspected the worry was reciprocal.

"Nevian is welcome along, if he wants," Arathiel said.

Varden jerked back, irrationally put off by Arathiel's read on him. "How did you know?"

Arathiel laughed, sat up, and reached for Varden's hand. The sound and touch calmed Varden's frenzied heart. "Vee, you've been hovering near him since he stepped into the Brasten Tower. You never left him alone with Brune, you've taken news every day since we fought at the enclave, and twice now, you've wondered aloud if he'd truly be comfortable surrounded by Dathirii elves. I made an educated guess."

Heat coloured Varden's cheeks. He hadn't realized he'd been so transparent. Had Nevian noticed? Did he think Varden overbearing? He used to spurn the slightest show of concern, but so much had changed since. If it bothered him now, he certainly hadn't said anything.

"It's … been on my mind," Varden said. "You wouldn't be disappointed?"

"Well, I admit he looks like the rowdy type…" Arathiel trailed off, unable to contain the laughter creeping into his voice, then pulled Varden closer to him. "I think it'd be good for you and him, and I'm sure we can find something that suits everyone's needs. House Brasten might be overwhelming, but I've always lived around many other people. So no, I don't mind, on the contrary."

Varden leaned his forehead against Arathiel's, breathing out slowly, letting the relief and thrill sink in. He wanted to enjoy it while he could, in case it didn't last. He hoped he never got used to this sense of freedom, yet sometimes he couldn't help but think bad luck always came around again, sooner or later. Arathiel's constant kindness shielded him against the brunt of that darkness.

"I love you."

He figured that was answer enough, and for a time they

remained still, forehead-to-forehead, simply enjoying the other's presence. Eventually, Arathiel pulled back and dropped a quick kiss on Varden's lips. Varden kissed his cheek in response, then struggled back to his feet and offered his hand. Arathiel allowed himself to be pulled up and immediately fell straight into Varden's arms—probably not an accident.

"Let's practice more," Varden said. Arathiel's idea had sparked a new desire in him, something he would never have been comfortable doing around Myrians. "There's a particular dance I'd like to share with you on the wedding's night. An Isbari dance. If you're up for learning it?"

Arathiel's face lit up, washing away Varden's fears that he'd be reluctant to learn new steps. "Absolutely."

"A few of our traditional rhythms share roots with southern Allorian music, so if you used to dance to those, you might pick it up quickly." He searched through his memories for the steps he'd learned as a teenager, when he left the temple to find street kids practising. He'd always watched from the sides, memorizing the lines and half-circles they formed as they hopped around, treasuring them to practise later, hidden in his room. "What matters here is your feet, and that they always remain timed with mine. You usually need more than two dancers, but it goes like this…"

He slid his fingers through Arathiel's and placed himself by his side, aligning in the shortest line possible. Anticipation nestled in his stomach. What if he'd forgotten? What if Arathiel hated it, or couldn't quite manage it with his current balance? He shoved the fears away and started. One hop, one clack of his heel on the ground, and the long-learned footwork flooded back in. His hips and shoulders only moved in occasional sharp movements, but his feet tapped rhythmically, slapping hard on the ground, creating echoes in the silent hall. Arathiel followed in silence, unmoving at first, but when Varden slowed down to better show him the pattern, he started imitating him. At first Varden had to pass an arm around him to keep Arathiel from falling off balance, but as time passed and they practised on, he needed less and less support. Soon they were only holding hands, dancing to imaginary music, switching between Isandor's local dances and the Isbari's stylish lines, any sense of time completely lost to their immediate pleasure.

Chapter Forty

DIEL Dathirii sat at his desk, in his office, in his home, and he felt like an outsider. Traces of Hellion's actions remained everywhere in the Dathirii Tower, small and big alike—banners with the Dathirii tree sigil hung in the corridors, wine stains on Diel's desk, Yultes' burned quarters, Hellion's clothes still in Diel's wardrobe and his perfume in the office. There was no point in pretending a return to normal with his imminent departure, but many tried anyway. Branwen had asked the banners to be returned to storage, found flowers to cover Hellion's perfume, and offered to put every outfit he'd left behind to good use. He let her; this was her home still, and she needed to reclaim it.

Unfortunately, Branwen was not the only Dathirii eager to erase recent events. He had barely returned home before Viranya, Iriel, and Enmaris had asked for an audience with him. They effusively welcomed him back to the Dathirii Tower and praised an inevitable return to unity. Diel allowed them a few minutes to believe they might get clemency before interrupting their charade.

"You're wasting your breath. I will leave the matter of your future within House Dathirii to my succession."

Lady Viranya had leaned forward, a sharp smile hiding her frustration. "Has that been decided, then?"

"Of course, but they will be the first to hear of it."

The audience had not lasted long after this, but Aunt Camilla had later told him she'd had quite the long afternoon tea with Viranya, and she'd rarely seen someone grind her teeth so often while maintaining a perfect smile. He wished he could have spied in for the simple pleasure of the incessant subtle verbal clash, all amplified by the sweet knowledge that Aunt Camilla was not, in fact, about to inherit House Dathirii's leadership.

That particular task would pass to a younger generation, and he ought to clean his office before they arrived, for his sake more than theirs. Hellion's continuous presence grated on his mood more than he cared to admit. His cousin was a ghost here, an inescapable reminder of his own family's betrayal and how close Diel had come to losing Jaeger. Thankfully, someone had left a morale boost on Jaeger's otherwise impeccably empty desk: a kettle and a cake, its golden glaze almost shining in the soft daylight, delicate flowers sprinkled over it. Camilla had taken full control of her small kitchen back, it seemed, and even lent him the self-heating kettle Branwen had gifted her years ago. Diel pushed his chair back, eager to cut himself a portion of the cake and replace haunting ghosts with the kindness of the living.

The cake was fruity, the white tea had a delightful hint of citrus, and the wonderful scent wafting off them covered Hellion's perfume. Diel set his plate over the wine stain on his desk, hiding it away, and set to work. Almost everything Hellion had ongoing would be burned, but he kept key information in case others needed it and set them in a different pile. Sometimes he had to read through the documents, and whenever Hellion's insufferable tone and words became too much, he returned to the kettle provided by his aunt.

By the time he heard voices in the corridor, he'd gone through all the tea and half the cake by himself. Should he hide his egoistical crime before his guests arrive? Camilla had most likely meant the cake for him, yet the half-empty plate instilled him with guilt.

"No, believe me, Branwen, 'I can introduce my fist to your face' was the sweetest thing I'd heard all evening," Garith exclaimed, warm laughter threaded through his voice. "Simple and to the point."

"That's only because you knew the banners were coming." Their footsteps stopped, then, and her voice dropped to the edge of Diel's hearing. "So, you're sure it's not Yultes who told him I'd be there?"

"Would have staked my life on it, Brannie. Kind of did, in fact, when I ran away and left them to burn the accounts and take all the risks."

Silence and shuffling followed. The familiarity of Garith's guilt struck Diel hard; it had weighed on him from the moment he'd sat in Cal's home, safe from the Myrians and Lord Allastam while Jaeger remained trapped in the Dathirii Tower, and it had interfered with his ability to do anything for days. He really should've kept tea for them—they both sounded like they needed it.

The door finally opened and Branwen strode in first, arms wide open and a grin plastered on her face. She bounced inside with so much energy Diel could only wonder how much of it was for his sake, and how much was her natural drive. Halfway through her greeting, she spotted the cake and her eyes widened.

"Camilla baked for you!" She changed trajectory for Jaeger's desk.

Garith followed more quietly, lines of exhaustion betraying his attempted smile. He laughed as his cousin hurriedly cut herself a chunk of cake, then raised his eyebrows as she prepared to leave the table without offering him any. Branwen had already taken a full bite when she caught his expression. She mumbled an apology through the food and prepared a proper slice for him.

"So little time apart and she already forgot how much she loves me." Garith sat in front of Diel's desk with a dramatic sigh.

"Impossible," Diel replied, barely keeping the laugh out of his voice.

Branwen plopped down on the second seat, offering the plate with a grand gesture. "Here you go, O Great Cousin. Stuff yourself."

Garith obliged, and Diel let the crunching, swallowing, and little satisfied hmms fill the silence. He'd spent a lot of time over the last few days going over this conversation, thinking of the best ways to explain his decision to them, yet now that the time had come, all those fancy words vanished and he dropped his decision on them without preamble.

"House Dathirii is yours."

They froze. Branwen swallowed her last bite and Garith slowly set his plate down on the desk. He wiped the corners of his mouth. "Ours?"

"Yes. Both of you."

"Not Aunt Camilla's?" Branwen asked.

Was that the agreed upon expectation, then? It hadn't surprised him from Viranya, who would see ancestry as a mark of leadership and a reason for respect, but he'd thought Branwen and Garith would know better. Aunt Camilla would always be happier in an advisor role.

"No. It's yours, as it was always meant to be."

They looked at each other, and it was easy to spot the doubts creeping into their minds.

"Uncle…" Garith trailed off, then his expression shifted into resolve and he straightened his back. "It'll be an honour to hold the fort until your return, however long that takes."

This time, Diel couldn't help but laugh, though not without a touch of sadness. Their loyalty was leading them astray. "The House is yours forever, Garith."

"You can't be serious!" Branwen pushed her chair back, jumping to her feet—to fight or flee, though, Diel couldn't tell. "This exile is nothing but a petty revenge ploy by Allastam, and you'll comply with it? This is your home and we're your family. You can't leave us forever." She slammed her hand on the table. "I won't have it. In a decade everyone will have forgotten or forgiven. I bet they'll even thank you!"

Diel gently set his hands over Branwen's. Waves of guilt had started building within him; perhaps his niece was right and he should have fought harder against this exile, but it had seemed a simple key to unravel everyone else's problems. Maybe he would, one day, but not now, when they had momentum against Lord Allastam.

"Branwen, we don't know where I'll be ten years from now, but I'm not abandoning you. I'll write, I might visit even eventually, but for House Dathirii? It's over. I am no longer its Head, and I will never be again."

His voice cracked towards the end. He had loved his time leading House Dathirii, and he struggled to define himself out of that role. Through decades negotiating with fellow nobles and merchants, pushing for better laws across the city and tying his fortune to local businesses, he had forged House Dathirii into a unique player with its own fiery spirit. Branwen and Garith would carry that flame perfectly. He squeezed his niece's hands, drawing courage from her.

"You're an incredible team and it's your turn now. Be bold. Define what you want us to be in the future, and shape this family towards that goal. Don't be afraid to shake things up, change the structure, and break with tradition—yes, even mine. I have no doubt I'll return to find the family better from all your hard work."

Branwen still stared at him, mouth slightly open and eyes wide, but she slowly regained her seat. He'd hoped to lift her spirit and rile her up, but instead he'd stunned her into silence. He remembered how she'd laughed, at Cal's house, when he'd first told her this had always been his plan. Perhaps she didn't want the position? He certainly hadn't, at first. Slowly, Diel pulled his hands away to give her space and glanced at Garith. He smiled when he noticed his nephew had slid his glasses on—that meant business.

"I'd say we're not ready, but I don't think I'd ever feel ready. We're … not you, Uncle, but if you believe we can do this…" He turned to Branwen and a wide grin eased the lines of fatigue around his eyes. "Nothing can resist Branwen's charms and my number magic. If she's with me, then I accept."

Branwen lifted her chin as she realized they all looked at her, waiting on her decision. A soft red coloured her cheeks, but she matched Garith's grin. "Of course I'm with you. Where else would I be?"

Relief washed over Diel and he leaned into his chair, basking in the appeasing knowledge that House Dathirii would remain in good hands. Branwen and Garith clasped hands and pulled their chairs slightly closer to one another.

"We'll miss you, Uncle," Branwen said, "but we'll make you proud."

Diel laughed and shook his head. He had no doubts they'd succeed, but he didn't need that to be proud. Ever since they were born, Branwen, Garith, and Vellien had brought him joy. He was curious to see where the two cousins would lead the family, but he wasn't worried he'd love it.

"You already do."

YULTES' body refused to stop aching. Vellien assured him only rest could truly heal and that he shouldn't worry about the throbbing pain in his midriff, but it was hard for Yultes not to think of it as a gaping wound through which his lifeforce escaped. He was exhausted all the time, too, and slept through most of his days. At least he had his plants surrounding him once more, embellishing his quarters with lively green and the occasional flower.

Despite his yearning for the quiet embrace of sleep, where the weight of his emptiness vanished for a time, Yultes dragged himself out of bed. He had one last important task, something no one cared about and that should be his duty. He searched his wardrobe for the dark green doublet and wreath of dried branches and flowers he'd first worn at the funerals for Diel's father, placed the urn with Hellion's ashes in a sturdy bag, and set off.

When he'd first mentioned Hellion's funerals to Diel, he had been met with resistance. He should rest, let others take care of this, shield himself from the emotional wounds. He didn't owe Hellion anything, not even in death. These were all perfectly logical reasons, but they didn't change the gut-churning inside Yultes, this overwhelming feeling that he had to do this, to go all the way and give Hellion proper rites.

"It's not for him," he'd said, the words a whisper in the wide room, small and shy.

But Jaeger had heard them, and he'd known what they'd meant. "No one would think less of you for not tending to Hellion's remains, Yultes, but if such is your wish, then I humbly ask to be by your side."

The request had surprised Yultes, but he hadn't asked for Jaeger's reasons—not then, and not now, on the fateful day, as they climbed down Isandor's many staircases, to the docks below, then past them into the small neighbouring forest. He was glad for the steward's presence as they walked along the Reonne's shore, the packed snow crunching beneath their feet and naked tree branches wincing in the winds above their heads. The occasional bird chirped, and squirrels scuttled across the snow-laden floor. When they reached the Reonne's first affluent, Yultes stopped and stared at its surface.

Here was good, he told himself. Here was where his brother had stepped into the river after one final goodbye and let the currents rise to take him. Towards the ocean, Lehran had declared—never mind that Diel's sister had been waiting for him on a boat at the river's mouth, where it threw itself into the Reonne. Lehran had always loved the symbolic and the dramatic. Perhaps he wouldn't mind if Yultes repurposed this very place for a similar gesture.

Now that the time had come, however, he felt awkward and lost, a pathetic adult playacting mourning—more a liar now than when he cajoled Hellion and misled him, betraying his trust. Were these rites he had in mind an acknowledgement of decades of friendship, however twisted, or were they a final insult? Perhaps it didn't matter.

Yultes removed his boots and socks despite the cold day, retrieved Hellion's urn from his sack, and stepped into the freezing water. He gritted his teeth against the burning cold and upended the urn over the currents. The ashes darkened as they touched water then vanished from view, taken by the river.

"Hellion often spoke of upholding ancient elven values, but in the end, he knew little of them. He had constructed a version of it in his mind, one to justify his path." Yultes wasn't sure who he was talking to: himself, Jaeger, or the river. He ached for his lost friend, his decades of foolishness, and his growing bereavement. The cold numbed his feet and the water grew more comfortable, more comforting. "I forgot, too—buried it, far from my mind. But it never truly left, water ready to well back to the surface."

No doubts there were other elven traditions in the world than his. After all, the isolated community he'd come from had not worshipped Alluma, who guided elves down endless paths and along the cycles of life, but Meltara, They who trod water and poured from the sky, who lived in the depths of ocean and the smallest rivulets. Yultes intoned the final rites that had marked his youth.

"The river flows in a single direction, but water cycles. A death is but the start of a new cycle, here by the guiding flow of the Water Dancer. May life spring in your depths, unseen but not unknown." He reached into his pocket and retrieved a single, large tulip bulb, then flung it into the river. The rest of the Meltara's funeral rite was closely tied to his hometown of Lelli, their frays of fish and the sacred shrine at its heart, and he did not want to share it with Hellion. Instead, Yultes added, "May Alluma never abandon Their children, be they traders, servants, nobles, or peasants, as their lives ebb and flow under the grace of all deities."

He watched the seed as it bobbed for a moment, then sank. When elders performed this ritual in Lelli, it shimmered a soft blue before vanishing underwater. They did not use a tulip bulb, however, but the seed to Meltera's Treat, a gorgeous waterborne flower he'd never seen outside of Lelli's forest. With a sigh, Yultes stepped out of the river. The winter cold slammed into him, sending his teeth chattering. He didn't feel any better, and apart from freezing every single one of his toes, he wondered if he'd accomplished anything. Yultes pulled on his socks and boots in a hurry, his mood worsening.

"It has been a long time since you've spoken of Lelli and Meltara," Jaeger remarked.

"It has."

He'd always kept stories of his past to himself, afraid to remind others that he didn't belong. He had wanted to be a Dathirii noble, to become part of their history, and Hellion had always made it clear that this didn't include remote villages with strange Meltara-worshipping customs. Was he returning to them now because of his abject failure at fitting in? It felt unkind to himself, such a conclusion. He had fit in and it had made him miserable. Yultes didn't know who or what he wanted to be now, and he didn't particularly care to find out, but the river comforted him, made him feel less empty, less exhausted. Colder, though—his feet had frozen until they burned, and now every step was a hardship.

"A new cycle with very old habits, you could say," he added.

"Forgive the evident bias, but I daresay these are much better than what you had developed under Hellion." Jaeger clasped his hands behind his back, the hint of a smile curving his lips. "I believe I owe you an apology, too."

"An apology?" What could that even be about? He and Jaeger had certainly been at each other's throat for decades, but Yultes had a hard time believing Jaeger regretted any sharp words or hindrance during those years. They had all been well deserved, a justified counter to Yultes' destructive jealousy.

"I may have volunteered your name for a rather ungrateful task."

Yultes' strides faltered, and he turned fully to Jaeger, his grip tightening over the empty urn. He did not feel up to any task. He'd thought that perhaps he'd feel better after these rites, that they would unlock a part of him that was trapped, but the emptiness remained, eating away at his desire to do anything. He'd closed a cycle but did not want to start the next. Perhaps he'd benefit from someone else pushing him forward.

"Do tell."

"Diel is passing leadership of the House to Branwen and Garith. As much as I approve of the idea, however, I daresay I trust them even less around paperwork and logistics than I did Diel."

A sharp laugh escaped Yultes. Individually, they might manage the boring tasks, but together? These two were a dangerous pair, operating at constant high energy. Yultes guessed what role his name had been volunteered for: House Dathirii's steward. Why else would Jaeger be the one bringing it up?

He did not know if he could.

This felt like something that should have ended with Hellion, a position that had not been rightfully his, despite what he'd told himself through the decades. Shouldn't he let go of this, too, if he wanted to extricate himself from the person Hellion had wanted him to be? But he had longed for this role before he'd even met Hellion; his bitterness at losing it to Jaeger is what had first brought them together.

"I understand the position may carry its share of bad memories, and no one will blame you if you feel it's better to keep a distance. If I may be honest?"

Yultes almost laughed. Had Jaeger ever been anything but honest, whether or not he couched his meaning under the guise of politeness? Decades of enmity had taught Yultes all he'd needed to know about reading between the lines, and it felt absurd for Jaeger to ask permission. A lot had changed between them, however, and Yultes no longer knew where they stood. Jaeger, it seemed, had garnered enough respect for him to ask permission before offering his sharpest words—and Yultes found that he cared and feared it in a way he never had before. Trepidation drummed under his skin.

"Let's not waste what time we have together with half-truths and careful edging."

Jaeger welcomed his reply with a small, satisfied *hm*. "Well, then. I owe you my life, and asking this of you as a favour seems an unfair demand. Then I remember our past, and all you put me through, and it transforms into a just purgatory. I can't decide which it is." He shrugged and started back towards the city. Yultes fell into step behind him. "What I do know, Yultes, is that your synergy with Garith is unparalleled. You have an easy grasp of how small details affect the wide picture, and vice versa, and, for better or for worse, you know how the most arrogant elements of the family think. My conflicted feelings aside, you are the best person for the task. The only question that remains is whether or not you want it."

Yultes wished someone would answer the question for him. What *did* he want? The life he'd spent so long building had crumbled, its shaky foundations finally given in, and he was left standing in its ruins, wondering what to make of himself. He'd avoided thinking of his future until now. It had seemed too enormous a decision, all paths forward too overwhelming to consider on his own.

But he wasn't alone, was he? Jaeger had just shared his own thoughts on the subject, and Garith couldn't keep an opinion to himself. Yultes needed only to ask, if he wanted. Garith had opened that door wide once, for far more personal issues. He had told Yultes in no uncertain terms he wanted him on his team. His sharp anger at the others' mistreatment floated back to Yultes' memory. *On my team, everyone matters.* At the time, the affirmation had sunk into Yultes, settling down like an anchor in his internal storm. It did so again now, clearing enough of the confusion to leave one simple truth behind. He trusted Garith. He enjoyed working with him. The rest of his future might seem unfathomable, but he knew that one small thing, and he'd use it as his guiding light.

Yultes closed his eyes, even at the risk of catching his numb feet in a root. None of today felt real—not the grey sky, not the warmer, sticky weather, not the improvised funerals, and certainly not this turn of events.

"I'll do it," he said, tongue thick from the enormity of it. "Let them know that whatever mad plan they're already building, I'll make it reality for them."

Jaeger turned to smile at him. "Very good. I'm certain Branwen will be quite pleased she has a new miracle working uncle to harass once Diel and I have left."

To his surprise, the idea did not terrify Yultes. He had always loved problem solving, and his brief letter exchanges with Branwen had brought their share of laughter and good surprises. He could envision more of that as a piece of his future—it even sparked a hint of excitement, a miracle of its own in the slow dregs of the last days. Perhaps this was how he figured out who he was now and what he wanted. He started with Branwen and Garith—with family who had seen the worst of him and still hoped the best might emerged from it—until he found new goals, new ways of being that brought him joy and let him build something worthwhile from decades of mistakes.

Chapter Forty-One

MIA braced herself as the door to her father's prison quarters opened—the rooms he had been moved to could not rightly be called a cell, not when it held a lounge area, a crackling fireplace, and a small desk, all in tasteful and near pristine furniture. Only the bed was missing, but that mystery was easily solved by the door leading to a second room. The bars in the windows and the lack of personal belongings, however, dismissed any idea that these were Lord Allastam's dwellings of choice.

No candles had been lit to battle the evening's darkness, transforming the comfortable space in a foreboding lair. Lord Allastam himself sat by the fireplace, his face bathed by the changing light while the rest of him was lost to the shadows clinging around the room. Even after Mia slipped in, he did not turn in her direction. She gripped her cane tighter and studied him;

studied the angry turn of his mouth, the hunch in his shoulders, the slow tap of his fingers on the couch's leather. He was in a bad mood. He had summoned her here, and he was in a bad mood.

This did not bode well for her.

After the new accusations of attempted murder during the Enclave battle, he had been confined to a cell in the Sapphire Guards Headquarters and been granted limited visitation time—a precious resource every Allastam of middling importance fought over. Her father was the only authority her aunts, uncles, and cousins recognized, even if Drake had always been the designated heir, and all acted as if the longer they spent with him, the more legitimate they became. It would have been amusing if it didn't paint a bleak picture of her own future, if she attempted to take over the House.

Not if, she reminded herself. When.

Ironically, Drake was the only one she was truly concerned with. Always, Mia returned to this one question, this crucial flaw in her ambitions. She balked at the idea of hurting her tumultuous, arrogant brother, the seed of love she still held for him refusing to wither under his dismissals. It was easier with her father, who held the power and influence over her, whom she could blame for the isolation and dismissal, who had scolded Drake for playing rough with her or bringing her along wilderness outings with other noble friends. When Drake was mean or difficult with her, she always heard her father's words.

Perhaps her brother's tune would change if it was just the two of them. For now, however, she had to face the one figure who dominated their lives.

"Father," she greeted, snagging his attention.

He shook himself out of his contemplative daze, turning in her direction. The grimace softened into a smile and he straightened. "Mia. My sweet girl, you are a sight for sore eyes. Come sit."

He patted the seat next to him and Mia moved across the room, her grip tight on her cane, each step deliberate. She needed time to sort through the flip-flop of her feelings; the surge of warmth at his smile, the frenzied staccato of her heart at his inevitable judgment. He would know by now that she had met Hellion in his stead and that she had entered the Dathirii Tower the night his puppet had died. What else might he have found out or surmised? Did he understand she'd worked against him? She feared his anger—of course she did; who wouldn't?—but under it all remained the uncrushable hope he might approve of her cunning and see what she had to offer. She settled by his side and cast her eyes into the fire.

"You ought to light more candles," she said. "Gloominess does not suit you."

He huffed and waved dismissively towards the closest set of candles. "Why bother? I will not endure this place for long."

His conviction should not have surprised her. He'd never been one to admit defeat. He couldn't conceive such a thing for himself.

"How long?" she asked.

"That depends on your aunts and uncles."

Mia heard the smirk in his tone. He had set a scheme in motion, then, something he expected could overcome even his hired swords being caught red-handed, trying to kill Sora Sharpe and Arathiel Brasten on the battlefield. She doubted the new plan was any less violent, but at this point even Sora's death wouldn't stop an investigation. Too many important houses had approved of it and would benefit from their House's downfall.

Mia would need more information to foil this plan, but the last thing she wanted was for her father to guess she was fishing for it. She kept her hands on her lap and her gaze firmly on them, then affected a small, anxious tone. "Is … is it violent?"

He laughed—a single chuckle soaked in wrath. That was all the answer she needed.

"Don't fret over it, dear. You're safe in House Allastam, and you will always be."

"I am not worried. I—"

She cut herself short as he turned on her, his eyes gleaming in the dim light, and lifted her chin with a thumb. His grip was firm but not tight; it didn't hurt but it commanded attention. Mia knew better than to forge ahead. She stilled, letting his fingers run along her jaw then stroke her cheek, his beautiful, meek doll. Knots lined her stomach. If she knew her father well, this was the dramatic moment of tenderness before he said whatever he'd called her here for.

"I would like to apologize."

Mia stiffened, uncertain where he was going with this. Father only ever apologized to her, but never for what he ought to, only for failures he imagined for himself. Failures to contain her—protect her, as he would put it. And indeed, today was no different.

"When we lost your mother, I vowed to myself I'd always be by your side, always there to protect you. My disappearance must have shocked you. So little of the outside world touches your life."

Twice, Mia opened her mouth to reply. Twice, he shushed her, begging her to 'let him finish' even though he wouldn't allow her a single word.

"I failed you," he said, "and as such, I accept responsibility for your mistakes. I've told everyone as much, but I wanted to tell you most of all. House Allastam will always be there for you, Mia, and I'm sorry I led you to think otherwise."

His words burned as she swallowed them, acid down her throat, sizzling in her stomach. It brought tears of frustration to her eyes and they spilled before she could think better of it. She would always be a piece of his story, an object with no agency to her name, to fit whatever narrative he created. There existed no universe in his mind in which she'd conspired against him and successfully snapped his alliance with Hellion Dathirii. Just as there was none where she'd want him gone.

Rough, wrinkled hands caught her tears, her father's thumb brushing her cheek while he squeezed her leg. She let him. Let him have his moment and lose himself in his illusions. Hadn't she crafted those too, offering him only what he wanted to see as cover for who she really was? It shouldn't be so infuriating to be dismissed again when that was integral to her strategy and essential to survival. But she was tired of surviving this House.

When Mia had been younger, she'd often dreamed of escaping. She could do so any time now. Alton would sneak her out and she could petition House Brasten for protection. She would be safe there—happier, even—but if she went down that path her story would be that of the sick bird who had escaped her father's gilded cage.

She did not want that story.

She was Lord Allastam's daughter, and she had inherited his ambition. She wanted House Allastam—its prestige, its wealth, and its power to change the world.

Mia would not wait for his death to have her turn. Today, she could still endure her father's apologies, even smile at him meekly and accept them, but it wouldn't last. She could not go back to that dance, lying about herself, not after she'd let so many see what lay beneath the masks. If she had her way—and she would put every ounce of cunning and resources into it—Lord Allastam would never recover from the accusations levied against him.

It was time for Mia Allastam to tell her own story.

Chapter Forty-Two

T HE Dathirii's great tree home towered over Larryn, its bark walls rich brown in the sun. The kitchens' entrance was nestled between two root-like protuberance, one of which wrapped under the bridge and seemed to support it. Larryn stood before the massive structure, small and insignificant and unwelcome. He regretted agreeing to Cal's plan. What did he think he was doing? He hated these people—hated their name, their wealth, their arrogance, everything they represented. It was bile in his stomach, a lifetime of pain with a single cause. He hadn't come for himself, though, had he? Larryn loved Cal, and this was a favour to him, a seal on their new friendship. He could cook here, just this once.

He ran a shaky hand through his hair and tried to recover his determination of the last days, while he was planning the meal and dictating shopping lists to Nevian. He'd riled himself up, building his righteous fury as a shield, promising himself he wouldn't let anyone ridicule him for where he was from. He'd prepare them a feast unlike anything they'd ever tasted, and which they would remember for years to come, then he'd vanish back to the Lower City. No need to meet a single one of them. Larryn would give them nothing he didn't want to—not even the focus of his anger.

He wrapped his fingers around the doorknob, braced himself for a long evening clinging to his pride, and pushed the door open.

Warmth blew at his face the moment he stepped in, the heat of half a dozen fires and thrice as many workers washing over him. Shouts and conversations bounced around the massive and cluttered space, but they all died when the door clicked behind him. Larryn's insides shrivelled as more and more of the staff turned to stare at him, faces ranging from a sneer to slight confusion. Without a word, he slid off his leather coat, hung it on the wall atop several thicker, fancier ones, and blew on his freezing hands.

An imposing woman stepped out of the rows of work benches, her apron stained with countless specks of sauce. Larryn didn't even have one of those. He'd picked his cleanest clothes for the occasion—which didn't mean much, they still sported stains and tears all over. This had always been a terrible idea, but as the head cook detailed him from head to toe, Larryn felt the full extent of his mistake. It crushed his stomach and tightened his throat, reeling up long buried feelings of inadequacy. She was everything he wasn't: fat where he was scrawny, blonde and pale where he was brown-haired and darker, professional when he was a fraud. She belonged here, and he was an intruder.

"You're the cook?"

Her voice was deep and authoritarian. Larryn's gaze snapped up at the doubt saddled within her words, and he fought his own with hard-earned pride and stubbornness. He might feel like an imposter, but he wouldn't let them treat him as one.

"S'that a problem?"

"No, I don't think problem is the right word," the Dathirii cook said, her voice much softer. There was something strange to her tone, something he couldn't explain but that riled him up nonetheless. "Surprise is more accurate. I'm Nicole. I've been in these kitchens for decades. I'll … assist you today."

She extended a hand, he reminded himself he couldn't ruin this, if only for Cal's sake. "Larryn."

Nicole drew a sharp breath, then held Larryn's hand tight in her own, crushing his fragile bone for far longer than necessary. Larryn grimaced, unable to hide the pain. What was up with her?

"Let me show you around," Nicole said, releasing his hand. "Starting with the pantry."

After a quick stammer, he managed a 'right' and followed Nicole through the kitchens. She didn't explain anything on the way, and he had a growing feeling the pantry was an excuse. He was going to get his fight, but in private.

They entered a colder chamber, with rows and rows of stored food. Larryn's eyes widened as he stared at everything, calculating how long he could feed the Shelter with all of this. He prepared two hearty meals a day and tried to feed a great many different people on each occasion. The Dathirii's pantry had enough for perhaps two weeks at that pace, but he doubted they fed quite so many. Yet they had almost twenty cooks! Larryn's grin grew as pride swelled within him. He might spend his time cutting, frying, and stirring until his back hurt and his legs refused to support his weight, but he was worth a dozen regular cooks. Even more, if he could steal their spices. Larryn reached for the small bags and pots with envy when Nicole closed the door.

"Did your mother ever tell you why you're called Larryn?"

Larryn's breath abandoned him, slipping out of his lungs with such force it left him light-headed. His vision blurred as he struggled with the question's implications, shock spreading through him. He leaned against the shelves, fingers wrapping around one of its vertical bars.

Of course she'd know. She'd been here for decades, she'd said, so she'd been around when his mother was. It wasn't his downtrodden clothes, the grease in his hair, or the bony thinness of those used to starve that had surprised her: it was his high cheekbones and thin nose, so similar to his father's, the point in his ears, the undeniable proximity of their appearances. She'd recognized him, as Vellien had in the Shelter.

"I don't care."

He forced the words out, pushing them past his frantic heart and growing curiosity. He'd had a few, precious years with his mother, enough to remember how she'd adored cooking, how often she'd mention these specific kitchens. He'd longed to know more for years, only to eventually accept it wouldn't happen and to build his life without the information.

Nicole's eyebrows shot up. "But your mother—"

"I said I don't care!"

Larryn slapped the nearby shelf so hard it sent pain coursing through his palm. Only his sharp breaths filled the subsequent silence, rattling gasps Larryn wished he could better control. Nicole waited without commenting on his outburst and the clamp around his throat and heart eventually lessened.

"My name is Larryn. I own a small place down in the Lower City, where I cook for the homeless, the erased, the persecuted. I provide food in memory of my mother's dedication to good meals no matter the circumstances. I provide shelter in memory of my father's dedication to his peers, whom he protected to his last breath. *That* is my history. I don't need to know more."

A soft euphoria coursed through him. He'd spent so much of his life wishing he'd known his mother more, then wishing Jim hadn't died. Wishing he could be someone else, born under different circumstances, only making the best of his lot in life to spite others. But not anymore. He loved his Shelter and his work, loved so much of who he'd grown into—and now he was working to fix what he didn't love. Larryn lifted his chin and met Nicole's gaze.

"I came here to settle a debt and help a friend," he said, "not to learn about my mother's history. It doesn't change who I am."

Nicole tilted her head to the side, pensive, but a smile soon followed. "I like you. If you ever change your mind, let me know." She clapped his shoulder hard and gestured at the pantry. "In the meantime, you're here for a wedding meal, aren't you? Let's get on with that. We should have everything on that list you sent ahead, and most of the prep's well underway. You can look around for anything missing, get a feel of our stock. I'll go make sure absolutely everyone here obeys you without hesitation."

Light spilled back inside the pantry as she exited, leaving Larryn alone with the food. He didn't move to inspect the shelves, only closed his eyes and breathed in deeply. He'd expected the Dathirii kitchens to shake him harder, yet any sadness and anger had given way to a strange feeling of displacement, tangled with renewed confidence in himself. Larryn ran a hand along the many seams of his oft-repaired clothes, the tangible reminder of his origins. The Shelter would always matter more than this place, this past. And only one thing mattered more than the Shelter: his friends.

One of them was counting on him to stun a bunch of nobles into reverent awe through the magic of a long, delightful meal. He wouldn't want to disappoint, would he? Not even for the petty pleasure of so many Dathirii choking on awful food. With a determined smile, Larryn set to exploring the pantry—and if the occasional bit of spice vanished from the shelves and landed in his pocket, well, surely one would blame the chaos of the momentous evening, yes? After all, it'd be a shame for him to step back into the Dathirii Tower and not honour his age-old tradition of reclaiming some of their wealth. Not everything needed to change in this bright new future.

Chapter Forty-three

C AL set his hands on his hips and surveyed his handiwork. Tables had been arranged in the Dathirii reception hall to form an immense circle to seat everybody. In the space at the centre stretched a majestic tree, its branches reaching high before spiralling back towards one another, forming a huge sphere of leaves through which golden fairy lights had been sprinkled. Above everyone's head, glowing buds flew in circular patterns like so many fireflies, casting a soft light that shifted in colour from gold to green to night-blue. The finished decor sent shivers of joy across his forearm. He'd needed to call on every favour owed to him, but he regretted none of it.

The first step had been research, but he'd had the perfect collaborators for that. Nevian had welcomed the opportunity to spend days sifting through mountains of books looking for elements about elven culture, the worship of Alluma, and any wedding-like rituals. Vellien guided him, discarding books full of incorrect information or exotifying exaggerations. They roamed both the Dathirii and Brasten libraries together, never far from one another, and every time Cal joined them for a brainstorming session, the two teenagers beamed with soft, loving energy.

Cal's most eager helper, however, was undoubtedly Efua. Vellien had found her a treaty on elven rituals meant to educate teenagers, and although it was above her current reading level, Nevian helped her through it. From that point onward, her bubbling imagination provided a constant stream of new ideas, which she happily shared with Cal every time they crossed paths, either at the library or the Shelter. The magical fireflies had been her idea, and she'd also delivered all the official invitations to the wedding. Cal was infinitely thankful for all of that, of course, but more than anything, he was glad Efua had solved his conundrum around who would officiate the wedding. He'd wanted Vellien to do it, but he had no idea how to ask the anxious elf to put themself in front of everyone.

She had simply turned her big brown eyes on them, all eager innocence, and shown them the beautiful flowing robes of a priest in one of the books. "Is that what you'll wear when you wed them? They look so pretty!"

Vellien had stammered their way through a denial, but that had only confused her.

"But you're a priest of Alluma, and you love them, and you sing very well. Why would anyone else do this?"

That had been the end of it. Vellien, cheeks flushed a deep red, had simply taken on the role. When Cal had asked again later, to make sure they would be truly fine with it, the idea had settled in them enough for an enthusiastic confirmation.

Cal wondered how Vellien fared now that the big day had arrived. If his own trepidation was anything to go by, they might be in quite a state. They had no space for practice and change of plans, however. The time had come to stun everyone with a gorgeous ceremony and an even finer meal. Cal surveyed the grand room one last time, then turned towards the two great doors behind which emerged the murmur of their guests' conversations. Cal stretched upward, grabbed the handles, and pulled the doors open.

VELLIEN'S stomach threatened to betray them at any moment now. They were more anxious than on the day of their first concert and regretted their decision to officiate. It made sense, yes, but the pressure was sending their mind in a spiral. What if they stumbled through the words? Said the wrong thing, or the right things in the wrong order? Singing was easy in comparison. Once Vellien started, they could let the world fall back and focus on the notes. It wouldn't be an option today.

Not that they could back out. Vellien stood in the tight, dark space in the centre of the tree's trunk, flanked by the two men they would bless in Alluma's name today. They both had been blindfolded and held hands in the darkness, waiting for the start of the ceremony. Jaeger remained perfectly still, a slight smile on his lips as Diel bounced on his heels. Twice already, their uncle had asked Vellien if it'd take much longer before they began.

The stomping of feet and rattling of chairs all around them eventually answered his question. People had arrived and were filtering through the great hall, around the tree and towards their seats. Garith and Branwen spoke louder than everyone, speculating on every element of decor in great details.

Diel's eyebrows shot up from under his blindfold and he whispered "Can't wait to see that."

"Be patient," Jaeger scolded him, his tone dripping with fondness.

Vellien swallowed hard. The guests' excited chatter did nothing to calm their nerves, but it was better than the near silence that followed as chairs stopped rattling. Everyone must have reached their seats, then. Cal would have told them to wait for Vellien to begin. It was their turn now. Ready or not, they had to do it.

They spread their arms, placing their palms firmly against the surrounding wood. Soft, quiet power flowed through it, a blessing Vellien had placed there earlier with Nevian's help. They drew upon it now, activating the spell embedded within, and vine-like tendrils of light wrapped around Vellien's arms as the magic took effect.

Vellien's mind expanded, reaching into the tree's canals, allowing them to feel the slow crawl of sap and the life throbbing through branches and leaves. The sensation reminded them of blood pounding through a human's veins, except slower, sturdier, more eternal. They let themself sink into the feeling, then raised their voice in a low hymn, calling upon Alluma through their chant and pushing at the magical tree's form.

The ground rumbled under their feet, then wood popped and cracked as the platform on which they stood moved upward, sliding alongside the trunk's inner walls. Above their head, the sphere of branches opened outward, like a flower blooming in the morning's sun. Light cracked through it, flooding them. It shone golden into Diel's hair, glittering across the beads braided into it like a thousand sparkling crystals. Vellien grinned through their song and lifted their voice higher as they continued to rise, their wooden platform cradled by the branches of the tree. The thirty-or-so guests sat in a wide circle around them, staring at the two blindfolded elves in a respectful hush. Diel no longer fidgeted, instead holding tight to Jaeger's hands, his jaw trembling from emotion. Branwen had wanted to wager on him crying before the ceremony was over, but no one had wanted to bet against her. Watching him now, Vellien knew with absolute certainty that had been wise.

Their song drifted to a slow end as Vellien cast out the last spiral of notes, fighting against the lump in their own throat, a knot of fondness for their uncle and anxiety at doing right by him. Excitement filled the air, weighing heavily on them, and they forced their throat clear with a small cough.

"You may remove the blindfolds," Vellien declared.

Jaeger stepped forward—and in doing so immediately broke with tradition—then ran his fingers along Diel's sleeves, up his arms and shoulders and to his face, until he touched the other elf's blindfold and could reach out to slowly undo the knot. Diel's initial surprised laugh caught into his throat and he waited, vibrating and grinning, until the fabric fell. Then, keeping his eyes squeezed shut, he sought Jaeger's blindfold and returned the favour. Their barely constrained laughter echoed in the thick silence.

"Ready?" Diel whispered.

"My ability to wait is rapidly approaching its end, yes."

They pulled apart, clasped hands together once more, then turned towards Vellien, eyes still closed. This hadn't been part of the plan and their heart hammered hard and fast, but Vellien managed to keep their voice steady.

"You may open your eyes."

Diel and Jaeger obeyed with perfect synchronism, and their faces lit up as they finally saw their partner and the detailed, beautiful outfits Branwen had put together for them. The Dathirii family tree was woven in gorgeous golden thread upon Diel's chest, shining against the forest green background, and its branches stretched across his shoulders and on his arms, wrapping up around his wrist to become golden cuffs. The end result was breathtakingly elaborate. Diel's hair had been braided with emerald and gold, the jewels shining bright in the surrounding lights, though not quite as bright as his eyes as he stared at Jaeger.

By comparison, the steward's garments shone in their simplicity. Branwen had stayed with the dark blue and silver tones Jaeger always preferred, creating a suit reminiscent of his favourite garb, but heightened by echoes of Diel's outfit, such as the tree pattern imprinted in a darker shade of blue on the doublet and woven clearly on the cuffs. His buttons mimicked the Dathirii brooch, and a bigger version tied his long braid—the only change from its usual style. Vellien appreciated the notes of stability. So much was about to change, it felt right for Jaeger to be a rock amidst it all.

The two of them were so absorbed with each other, Vellien paused to stretch the moment. They struggled to muster the courage to break their bubble and move the ceremony forward, but after a near minute of loving stares, they felt obligated to do so. They extended their hands out, palms upward.

"I-I won't be long," they said apologetically.

Diel's soft chuckle put a reassuring balm on Vellien's growing anxiety, loosening the painful knots in their stomach. He settled his hand in Vellien's and squeezed it. "Take all the time you need."

Opposite of him, Jaeger took the second hand. The vines of light curled around Vellien's arms slithered outward, wrapping themselves around the two older elves' wrists, their pale white colour shifting—green around Diel, gold around Jaeger. Their bright shine lit their smiles from below.

"I won't be long," Vellien repeated with more force, "because there is only so much words can convey. What could I say that decades of love have not already made obvious?" This wasn't the planned speech, but Vellien's carefully prepared words flew out of their mind. So much for hours spent crafting it, writing and rewriting, consulting Camilla and agonizing over every comma. "You stand here before me, before Alluma, seeking the Elven Shepherd's blessing, but They have been with you on every step of the road. Uncle Diel… Jaeger … your unshakeable, long-lasting love *is* a blessing—to us, who have known you for so long and learned so much from you, to Alluma, who guides all elves down

Their winding road, to Isandor, which you've constantly striven to make better. We have gathered here to honour this: *you* are our blessing. Thank you, and blessed be your cycles."

Vellien swallowed hard. They had meant to speak of cycles together, of love as mutual respect, of the lessons Jaeger and Diel had imparted on everyone around them through their bond. This was why Vellien shouldn't make speeches. They weren't good with words that weren't lyrics. That was fine, though. Judging by the dazed happy smile curving Diel's and Jaeger's lips, Vellien could have said nearly anything without ruining the moment. Besides, they might struggle with words, but they excelled with songs. With a grin, they let the notes bubble up once more and allowed their voice to carry the full depth of their—and everyone's—love.

> *The world is a circle made of many*
> *Sun and moon forever turning*
> *Wheels above us as below*
> *The seasons change, to start anew*
> *The Shepherd leads us around again*

With the very first note, the vines around the elves' wrists shone brighter. They slithered across the gap between Diel's and Jaeger's hands, green reaching for gold, gold reaching for green, until they met and entwined with one another. Warm energy pulsed through Vellien as they released the two hands, allowing Jaeger and Diel to be tied to no one but each other. They kept singing, their crystalline voice carrying the elven cycle celebration hymn clearly in the hushed room.

Alluma's road is ever winding
Following Their shadow towards the sun
That sets and rises to follow us
There is no end
And always we return to where we began:
How blessed we are
To turn together

And then, because this *was* a wedding celebration, Vellien broke from the traditional song and added,

How blessed you are
To turn together

Silence wrapped around their last note, cushioning it as it trailed up in the great hall. Vellien's ears buzzed—or perhaps those were the fireflies drawing circles above everyone's heads. They allowed themself time to breathe in and out deeply, to feel the ground under their feet, the hammering of their heart, the coolness of the surrounding air on their flushed cheeks. Songs had a way of carrying them away, out of their body, and the return to a crushing weight on their lungs and the never-ending sense of impending catastrophe could be brutal. They'd learned to get reacquainted with them without giving them too much room. Once the ceremony was over, though, they would be heading straight to a quiet, private room.

"If you have any words for each other…"

A small chuckle escaped Diel. "I always have words. Jaeger … the first thing you ever said to me mocked my inability to read a map. Since then, you've guided me at every turn, tracing my path and preventing me from getting stranded in mazes of my own making. The truth is, when Lord Allastam sold me out, I thought we would never see each other again. So I said to you everything that needed to be said, everything I could remotely express with words, and I hope they are forever lodged into your heart."

Jaeger's eyes shone, yet the rest of his expression remained surprisingly neutral—solemn, even. He replied to Diel with a curt nod. "Ten days ago, you told me everything you needed to, yet I had no words with which to reply, so I kissed you instead. For today, however, I had time to prepare." He reached inside his doublet and withdrew a folded piece of parchment, sealed with dark blue wax. Jaeger offered it to Diel, who accepted the envelope with reverence. "These are for you, Diel, and you alone. I am by nature a rather private person and some things I feel should remain between you, me, and Alluma. I will say this, however: I love you. With every inch of my body, every part of my mind, every fibre of my soul. And I am at ease with the whole world possessing this knowledge."

A loud sniff and an ill-concealed sob from the crowd shattered the following silence. Vellien risked a quick glance in its direction and found Camilla dabbing at her eyes with a handkerchief, struggling to control the flow of tears. It was enough to constrict Vellien's own throat, and they decided to move the ceremony along.

"And thus Alluma blesses this union. May you remain forever linked through happiness, turning together in the cycles of life." Vellien's voice ran across the hall with surprising strength, considering how close to tears they felt, both from the exchanged vows and from their own, prolonged presence at the centre of attention. It was almost over now—just a few more words, and the attention could shift away from them for good. They cleared their throat. "Many traditions seal these things with a kiss, if you—"

Vellien never finished their suggestion. Jaeger leaned forward and Diel met him halfway, placing his hands around Jaeger's shoulders even as Jaeger reached for his neck. They shared a long, intense kiss, illuminated from below by the magical bond around their wrists. After a few seconds of respectful silence, Branwen whooped and jumped to her feet, clapping loudly. Garith whistled, and Kellian started scolding them, but his voice was buried under the other guests' applause. From up close, Vellien could see the smile spreading across Diel's lips as he reluctantly pulled away.

"I don't remember ever kissing in front of such a crowd," he whispered.

Jaeger flushed a deep, embarrassed red, but his eyebrows shot up. "Perhaps it's because you kiss better when you pay attention to me rather than who is cheering you on."

Diel laughed, pushed Jaeger's shoulder a bit. "Let's delay any further kissing until later, then."

"If you can hold for that long."

Jaeger clasped their hands behind their back with a soft smirk. Warmth blossomed in Vellien's chest, temporarily loosening the pressure upon it. No one else was privy to their easy teasing, and Vellien clung to that privilege as proof they hadn't messed anything up. As the sign of Alluma's favour around their wrists slowly dissipated, Vellien took pride in their work today and allowed themself to dream of a quiet, solitary place to recover.

BRANWEN stared at Yultes, who was staring at his plate. She'd requested a seat next to him, hoping to get a better sense of the person Garith saw, but they'd barely exchanged ten words for most of the meal. In his defence, he'd not talked a lot to Aunt Camilla either, right on the other side of him. It seemed like his mind was elsewhere—a common occurrence for Yultes, these days, and she couldn't blame him for it, not even at Diel's wedding. Perhaps especially not here, considering it marked the official end of Diel and Jaeger as the leading pair of House Dathirii, opening the door for Branwen, Garith, and Yultes to step into their role.

They'd had a first meeting about it, and Branwen had resolved to reinstate the strange but hilarious dynamic she'd built with him through their secret messages. They had handed him a thin manuscript, worn paper bound in leather that had cracked over time, the ink pale from age in places, and asked him to read it aloud. Yultes' gaze had flicked between Branwen and Garith, both sitting all-too-innocently in Garith's open quarters, and he'd rolled his eyes.

"I have a feeling I know what sort of words awaits me," he'd said.

His prediction had been correct, but that had not stopped the flush in his cheeks as he reached the descriptive sequence between the elven heroine who'd plunged into the Reonne and the enthralling creature living within its choppy, cold water, and all the tricks they had to keep her warm and thrumming with life. Branwen and Garith had been giggling long before he'd reached the climax, and he'd snapped the book shut with a dramatic sigh.

"If you're going to behave like children, perhaps you're too young for this sort of content."

"Oh, come now," Garith had protested, "we've read it a hundred times over. It's one of our favourites!"

"It is, in fact, our very first," Branwen had added. "That's why it was so important you read it, too. No one is truly an associate of ours without sharing in *As The River Pulses Through Me*."

It had earned them another eye roll, then Yultes had cracked the manuscript open. He'd tapped the pages, lips pursed. "I cannot help but think that there's something very familiar about the calligraphy. It isn't Garith's, however; I'd recognize that, even without the numbers."

His gaze had slid towards Branwen, and she'd laughed. "Are you implying I wrote this?"

"It has stylistic elements in common with what you've provided me in the past, yes, and I would not trust myself to recognize your handwriting without fail. My precise thought, however, was that while you'd put the words to the page, Garith might be as responsible for their existence as you are."

"Well! I'll take that as a compliment, but I'm afraid similarities are but the imitations of a long-time fan. You should know Alayna Whitewool was a legend long before I was even born. The folks of Isandor have passed and copied tales from her for so long, she ought to have a park named after her. Some say she is actually a wide array of authors, all sharing the pen name without ever knowing one another. It makes sense, considering some of these existed two hundred years ago, and the latest is but four months old."

She hadn't even finished sharing the rumours before Yultes' eyes widened and the corners of his mouth lifted in a knowing smirk. He'd flipped through a few pages then snapped the book shut.

"Which one of you found Aunt Camilla's original manuscripts while snooping around her quarters?"

Branwen had proudly raised her hand while Garith laughed, and she'd resented the hint of victory in his tone.

"Told you he'd know right away."

And he had. He'd known Yultes would piece together the mystery, and Branwen had only half believed him. She had certainly not expected him to not only guess that Aunt Camilla was behind Alayna Whitewool, but also that they'd uncovered that particular secret on their own, behind her back. Garith had served as a distraction, dragging Aunt Camilla all the way to the park while Branwen had snuck in to look through those forbidden rooms. They'd huddled in Branwen's not-so-full-yet walk-in, palms protecting the flames of candles, reading the words to one another, thrilled by their transgressions.

"If you want to finish the story, Uncle Yultes, you can keep it until Diel's wedding. We do need it back before then."

"I'll be good, thanks."

He had handed it back to Branwen, who had since gone to Aunt Camilla, told her she had 'this nice gift to keep Hasryan busy on his long trip' and given the long-lost manuscript back to her aunt, looking her directly in the eyes. Camilla had only laughed, but Branwen knew the twinkle of mischief in her eyes. Sooner or later, she'd hear from it again.

Aunt Camilla's secret erotica writing had not been the only topic of their meeting, of course, and they had eventually drifted back to the more serious matter of House Dathirii's future and their ideas about it. Neither Garith nor Branwen had much to offer except to repair the damage done by Hellion, including the staff they'd had to let go, but Yultes had said a few, more radical things that still stayed with her. She leaned towards him now, his words on her mind.

"I've been thinking about what you said, when we had that little meeting. How House Dathirii is dying and we should take cuttings and start new roots and what not. Very dramatic, but you never really explained what those cuttings were for you."

He hesitated again, the same fear rustling over his face, tightening his mouth and pinching his nose that had stopped him then. Branwen huffed.

"Are you afraid I'll laugh or something? I spend half my time with Garith. You can't get more ridiculous than that."

He closed his eyes, and each of his subsequent breaths felt like a gathering of courage. Branwen waited, clinging to her thin patience, reminding herself he'd had a rough time and hadn't bounced back, that she might not laugh at his ideas but Hellion likely did.

"It's many things. You and me and Garith, if-if we were to do this. But I think… I think one of these cuttings is the household staff, that it should root—that is, make decisions—with us. The House doesn't live without them and they pay for our mistakes. We're already one organism. They should have the power to choose how we grow, too."

His early hesitation melted away as he explained, passion creeping into his tone. Branwen barely recognized the Yultes she'd known most of her life—measured, arrogant, and cold. She saw what Garith meant now, why he'd vouch for the asshole they'd spent decades antagonizing.

"Oh, I like it. Get them in on the coinage too, I imagine?"

"And the lodgings, if they want. We have some extra space."

The darker inflection in his tone told her he was not strictly speaking of those quarters long empty, but of the rooms recently liberated—though whether he was most bothered by Diel's and Jaeger's or Hellion's, she'd be hard pressed to say.

"We might get more soon. This will be a hard one to swallow for some, and I intend to extend them Hellion's considerate offer: they can leave if they don't like it. You don't keep dead leaves on a plant, do you?"

"No, you don't…"

Gloom had snuck back in Yultes' countenance, and Branwen didn't think she could fight it off. They'd need to face Viranya and her cronies before they could push any change in this House, but

Branwen didn't intend to give her an inch. She was toying with the idea of exiling her before they did anything else; excise the rotten elements immediately, before any more damage occurred. It didn't feel real—or right—that she had this power now, and perhaps that was why Yultes' idea appealed to her so much. But those were serious thoughts, for another night than her radiant Uncle's wedding. She glanced at Diel, cheeks reddened by the warm wine and the love surrounding him, his laughter constant music in the background.

"You know who I'd love to rope into your whole collective business deal?" Branwen asked, guiding them back towards better topics. When Yultes arched his eyebrows questioningly, she tapped her long-empty plate. "Tonight's fabulous and mysterious guest cook! Tried to go give my compliments earlier and got told none of us are allowed in the kitchens today, can you believe?"

Yultes choked, and instead of leaning in for the bit of juicy gossip she was obviously offering, he smacked his chest to clear his throat and set his fork down. She peered at him, trying to figure out what had provoked such a reaction, but all his earlier expressiveness had vanished.

"Didn't you like it?"

"No, yes! Of course I did." He laughed, an edge slipping into his voice. "Has anything ever tasted so uniquely delicious, truly?"

"Oh yes. Once, actually." Branwen brandished her spoon, victorious. "No mystery is safe from me, Uncle, and as you've said, this is uniquely delicious. I think I know this cook—we had a meal from him, once, the first night we hid at Cal's place, after we saved Diel from the Enclave. It sounded like he had quite the history with us. A bad one, at that, so you can imagine how surprised I am to find his food here."

"I can," Yultes said, and curse him, his voice was exceedingly measured and flat. "Are you certain it's him?"

"Has to be. Cal organized this wedding. He told us he'd pulled every favour owed to him. And we're not allowed? It all adds up, I tell you." She pointed at her temple and smirked, hoping to get at least a thin smile out of him. His lips did twitch, but that was as far as it got. She pouted. "Regardless. It'd be grand, no? You serve this food to people, you can get them to agree to anything!"

That did get a smile out of him, soft and dreamy and utterly unexpected after the last few minutes of stone face. "Yes," he said, "that would indeed be grand."

For the hundredth time tonight, Branwen wondered what went on in his head. It was impossible to find her bearings around this new Yultes, so different and unpredictable, sometimes aloof and lost, sometimes intensely present and impassioned. For years, she'd cultivated her ability to read others, grasp their goals and ethics and half-truths, yet none of these skills helped here. Yultes remained a mystery—for now. After all, no mystery was safe from Branwen, and this was one she was eager to solve.

DESPITE the rich, multi-course meal weighing in his stomach, Jaeger was floating. From the moment he had first laid eyes on Diel, a river of gems braided into his flowing hair, his smile dazzling, to the last bite of the dessert's caramelized apples, Jaeger had lived in a dream. Everything was *perfect*: the fireflies floating above his head, the gorgeous tree on which he had sealed his union, Vellien's crystalline voice, the delicious and rich coarse stew of bell peppers, zucchinis, eggplants, and various other vegetables in a tomato and garlic sauce, the flowing wine, and the joyous company. Diel had spent most of the dinner eagerly chatting with Varden, getting to know him better now that the threat of Avenazar no longer hung overhead and, amusingly, he had been flirting shamelessly for at least two courses now. Varden's cheeks were flushed, though whether it was Diel's attention or the copious wine he'd drunk, Jaeger couldn't tell. Varden didn't seem to mind, but he'd been gently letting Diel down for a while now, to Arathiel's obvious amusement. Jaeger could see the strands of a polycule dynamic there, and a wave of sadness washed over him as he remembered they'd be leaving soon and would never get to prod at these relationships and watch them evolve. Surely in the coming years or decades of travelling with Diel, there would be plenty of other opportunities.

Jaeger fought off the bout of sadness by turning to Camilla. She'd been suspiciously quiet through dinner, her occasional discussions with Yultes falling short. Yultes himself didn't seem in a great celebratory mood, but that wasn't a surprise: very little shifted his mood since he'd killed Hellion. Camilla, though… Jaeger leaned towards her, touching her wrinkled hand to catch her attention.

"I expected to hear your delightful laughter a lot more tonight," he whispered.

Her face lit up with a smile—one soft and sad and apologetic.

She squeezed his hand and shook her head. "Ah, dear, please don't let it trouble you. It seems I cannot stop thinking of the one ally missing from this table, despite everything he did."

Hasryan Fel'ethier. The young assassin she had sheltered for ten days, and who in turn had done so much for them, from rescuing Varden and Diel to protecting Camilla, even at the risk of capture by Drake Allastam and his goons. Jaeger's gaze swept the gathered crowd, among which most of their key allies sat, celebrating their victory alongside the wedding.

"I'm sorry," he said. "I do wish I'd had more opportunities to know him. Our brief meeting was quite enlightening and I look forward to our travel together."

"I can guarantee it won't be boring."

Jaeger laughed. "I never expected it to be."

He wanted to ask Camilla for her stories about Hasryan, but a few notes floated through the room. A small orchestra had made its way upon the tree's platform and were now tuning their instruments. The circle of tables had been broken on the other side, the seats moved out of the way to create a large dancing area. Diel set a hand on Jaeger's shoulder and grinned.

"Will you do me the honour of first dance?"

"I would have it no other way."

Chairs rattled as the gathered guests left their tables behind to form another circle around the dance floor. Diel led Jaeger, fingers linked in his, to the very centre of their friends and family. It had been a very long time since they had danced together, let alone in a formal fashion and in front of so many eyes. Jaeger could feel the flush creeping up the back of his neck. He tapped his feet to the floor, praying he wasn't too out of practice.

Diel leaned forward and whispered into his ear. "They're not watching and waiting for you to fail. There is no amount of feet-tripping in which you would shame me."

Jaeger's flush intensified. Sometimes it felt like Diel could snag his thoughts before they even became fully formed and conscious. The first time he had danced at a formal event with Diel, there had been many Dathirii eager to watch him stumble and deride him as lesser. Behind Diel's knowing grin was a hint of concern, born from shared experience and past fears. Jaeger replied to it with a small smile of his own.

"I daresay *my* feet won't be the problem."

In truth, neither of them had ever particularly struggled with dancing, and when the music started, they quickly fell back into old rhythms. The stress had been there nonetheless, and so focused was Jaeger on getting the steps right that he didn't immediately recognize the composition picked by the orchestra. *The Shepherd's Path* had been the first formal song he'd ever danced to with Diel, decades ago in the privacy of his quarters, when Jaeger still had no idea how to dance to classic elven compositions and had needed private classes to learn.

He leaned forward, his lips near Diel's ears. "You asked for this first song, did you not?"

Diel continued moving to the music, leading Jaeger across the floor, a warm hand on his hip. "Cal impressed upon me the importance of choosing the most romantic song. Something that symbolized our entire relationship, he said."

"A tall order."

"Was it?" Diel leaned in and rested his cheek against Jaeger's. "From the moment we met, we've walked together on this path. Now we head onto another road, hand in hand, mutual dedication unbroken. I can think of nothing better."

Jaeger squeezed Diel's hand, the growing warmth in his chest stealing his words as they waltzed across the floor. A month had passed since he had been reunited with him, and still he could not get enough of him, all sweet words and easy humour, open-hearted and truthful to the end. Trapped in Yultes' quarters, under a constant, unspoken threat, he'd not had much time to contemplate the depths of the hole Diel had left behind. Not until he had seen him again, by Yultes' bedside, and it had felt like the entire world righted itself once more.

Jaeger didn't know what the future held for them, but as long as Diel stayed by his side, his world could not shift out of balance.

"MAY I sit?"

Varden's question broke through Nevian's bubble. He'd been tracking Vellien on the dance floor, watching them spin with their cousins and laugh, his mind wandering far away from the wedding itself. It did that a lot, these days, his concentration melting like snow on warm skin. Nevian suspected it would never return, that Avenazar had forever left his mark, and he tried not to mind. Better this than the oppressive certainty his life could end at any moment and he shouldn't count on any reprieve. It was over now. He was free. He might not know how heavy the cost yet, but it'd have been worth paying. Nevian looked up at Varden, who had done so much to get him there, and smiled.

"Of course."

Varden grabbed one of the many chairs provided around the dance floor and slid it closer. He looked splendid in his new outfit, elegant and powerful without being intimidating. Branwen had insisted on providing everyone with specially designed and tailored clothes, but it was obvious she'd put extra care into Varden's. Every time Nevian looked, he found new ways the flowing fabric reminded him of flames.

"How are you feeling?"

Varden had asked that every day since they'd confronted Avenazar.

"Fine," Nevian answered, as he always did, even though Varden must've known it was only technically true, an obfuscation of the unsettling ways in which he'd changed. "Larryn's meal was delicious. I don't think I can last the night."

Varden laughed—a gentle sound that had grown far more frequent since they'd defeated Avenazar. "No one expects you to, Nevian. Did they provide you with rooms here?"

"A whole set of them. It's … a lot of space. The tower is very big." He clasped his hands on his lap and looked down. He appreciated the gesture, but he had no idea what to do with his quarters. His room in the enclave had almost been a cupboard; the one at the Shelter barely any bigger. "They do have an enormous library, though. Bigger than anything we had at the enclave."

"They didn't have to lug every book across countless miles," Varden pointed out. "I'm glad you have somewhere to stay now that everyone is moving out of the Brasten Tower. I thought you'd return to the Shelter?"

Nevian frowned. A part of him had wanted to. He'd be close to Efua for their lessons, and he'd learned to enjoy the ambient noise from the common room, even if he avoided the crowd itself. Larryn had subtly implied he could return, if he wanted, but Nevian knew those rooms were meant to be rented or to accommodate disabled patrons who had no other options. He did, now. Taking the space would feel wrong.

"It wouldn't be right. I'll miss it, though."

They lapsed into a comfortable silence. Varden traced dancers with his eyes, and Nevian wondered if he imagined a sketch there, if the rhythm made him want to draw. Perhaps that was why Varden's fingers twitched, playing with the edge of his sleeves. Almost like he was nervous about something.

"Nevian…" Varden started, and Nevian's own heart sped up at the tightness in his voice. Varden *was* nervous! What was going on? The priest ran a hand through his curls then shook himself, as if to shed off his anxiousness. "Arathiel and I have decided to move in together. I need my own space, and the Brasten Tower stirs too many memories for him. I thought… I thought perhaps you'd appreciate having your own room and office, somewhere quiet and out of the way of the city's politics."

"You mean… live with you? You and Arathiel?"

"Yes." Varden looked away quickly, a shy smile dancing on his lips. "Our library could never compare to the Dathirii's, however, so I understand if you'd rather stay here."

"I…" Nevian trailed off. Shock had stolen his words and the pleasant buzz in his skull didn't help. Vellien's gifted quarters had pleased him, but he'd known it was not a major drain on House Dathirii's resources. They had space in their tower home and he had an entire set of rooms just for him, where he wouldn't bother anyone. Varden, on the other hand, was inviting him to share a much smaller—much more intimate—space. They would be an inevitable part of each other's everyday life. "Won't I … won't I be in the way? Of Arathiel and you, and, hum—"

He gestured vaguely, flushing a deep red as he stopped short of mentioning sex. Varden pressed his lips together; he was obviously trying not to laugh. "We've discussed it at length and are both convinced it wouldn't be an issue. I know this is a strange offer, Nevian, and you don't have to answer now. But it's been an honour to watch you grow and to fight alongside you. I would feel blessed to share my house and a quieter life than what we have dealt with so far."

Before he understood what happened, tears filled Nevian's eyes and streamed down. He wiped them out in a frustrated gesture, desperate to get himself under control, to stem the surge of dizzying warmth and joy. Sharing a house had always been a sharing of resources, a practicality—from his parents, struggling to get everyone fed, to the students sharing dorms and his brief life with

Master Sauria, before the enclave. Nevian had lived where it made sense, but never where he had been invited. He had never been wanted like that, just for himself.

"I–I think I'd like that."

Nevian cringed at the inadequacy of his words, but better ones refused to come. He did not know how to tell Varden how important he'd become to him. Few adults treated him like Varden, who had *always* granted him the space he desired while materializing the moment Nevian needed help.

Varden's eyes also shone, but an eager smile spread across his lips. "I'm glad," he said, and although these were two simple words, they emerged from a layer deep within him, thick with solemn feelings. Then his demeanour changed—his smile widened, and he clapped his hands. "Imagine, we'll get to *choose* a home we love, something ideal for us?"

Nevian hadn't realized how much this counted for Varden, too. It made sense. He must have always lived in temples alongside other priests. His excitement was both strange and comforting, and Nevian found himself increasingly eager for this future. He hadn't given a lot of thought to his life in Isandor—it had been so pointless, before Avenazar was gone—but now the world opened before him. He could teach Efua, and explore his love for Vellien, and pursue magical studies. He could do anything, really, and he couldn't wait to shape this new life.

Chapter Forty-four

INSTEAD of great friends and a wedding to fill his evening, Hasryan found himself in the company of horses. He had no doubts many would love to be in the stables with the two magnificent beasts, but he hated it. He hated the reason it had to be this way even more. Even now, after most was said and done and Isandor was finally settling down into a calmer state, he couldn't be seen around Diel, least of all as a trusted friend at his small wedding. If he'd been waiting here by choice, it would have been a whole different story. Not that he'd have chosen horses, ever.

The truth was, the beasts scared him a little. Or, well, more than a little. He'd spent most of his life in one of two cities in which horses were a hindrance more than anything. They didn't deal well with Isandor's narrow bridges and heights, and in Nal-Gresh people either used systems of levers and pulleys or domesticated goats to move goods upwards. He hadn't been in contact with horses a lot, which had given him next to no chances to get over his childhood fear from that one beast almost running him over. Why not now, then? He had hours ahead of him.

Hasryan inched closer, his heart hammering as he contemplated the huge animal, then he approached his hand. It took him ages to get close, but eventually the horse sniffed at his hand and Hasryan dared to caress him. The horse leaned his head into Hasryan's hand, making him freeze in surprise. Why was it doing that?

Heat rushed to his head, but after a moment he laughed at himself. It was only a horse. Sure, it was huge, but this one was used to people.

"Don't bite my hand off and I won't be an asshole later."

"Why would you be an asshole to the poor horse?"

Hasryan jumped at Camilla's voice and spun on his heels, heart speeding up. She stood at the entrance of the stables, her gorgeous wedding dress flaring out on each side of her, the flowery white pattern on its lilac velvet only partly hidden under a warm winter cloak. She smiled at him and lifted a small sack, from which a deep red scarf emerged. The sight was a punch to his guts, and it was all he could do to get a few words out.

"Don't you have a wedding to attend?"

The question turned harsher than he'd intended, but he couldn't shake his anger at being here, waiting for the newly-wed to hop into their carriage so they could all leave together on their fancy exile.

"As a matter of fact, I do." Camilla strode to him, her smile never faltering. "But the ceremony is over, the first dance was had, and frankly I could no longer bear the obvious hole of your absence. Arathiel will not be far behind, I suspect, but I demanded he enjoyed the dance floor longer. I don't think there will be many opportunities for him to sweep around with Varden as he does now, and it obviously brought him great joy."

Halfway through her answer, Hasryan looked away and leaned back on his railing, fighting against the tightening in his throat. "I wish I could see that."

He'd wanted to see all of it. Not because he had a profound attachment to Diel and Jaeger—he liked them well enough, but in the end, they'd never spent an inordinate amount of time together—but on principle, to be with everyone he'd helped and who had helped him, to discover the results of Cal's frantic handiwork and dance and sing in public, like he belonged there.

"I'm sorry we never cleared your name," Camilla said, setting a gentle hand on his forearm. "I know it isn't the same as being at the wedding, but I brought you portions of the incredible meal we had. I'd never tasted anything like it. Sir Cal has quite the network of friends, I daresay."

She retrieved a bowl wrapped in a thick cloth, and Hasryan's mouth watered at the rich aroma that wafted from it. He reached for the bowl immediately and Camilla handed him a fork with a laugh.

"Little bastard knows how to be convincing, too," Hasryan agreed, before uncovering his meal. He'd snacked on dried fruits and old bread earlier, forcing himself to eat despite the knots in his stomach. Hunger always returned for Larryn's food, though, and he planted his fork in a beautiful roasted piece of eggplant and shoved it in his mouth. "Delicious as always. Gonna miss Larryn's food once I'm gone."

"Larryn's?" Camilla repeated. "This is from your friend down at the Shelter. The one Vellien helps?"

"The one and only. But I don't think people are supposed to know, so … secret?"

"Of course," Camilla said smoothly, and he knew without a doubt she would keep the information to herself. He trusted few people as much as he did her.

She let him eat in silence, and he returned his full attention to Larryn's delicious stew. Hasryan leaned on the stall while he chomped down on the various vegetables with increasing speed. When most of it was gone, he ran his fingers along the bowl and licked them clean of the sauce. Camilla laughed at this, then offered a skin.

"Wine to wash it down."

Hasryan accepted with great joy, and as the slightly spicy wine joined the tangle of savours in his mouth, he regretted not having it right from the start. He wasn't a very knowledgeable about fancy alcohols, but whoever had picked this clearly knew their business— and likely wasn't Larryn.

"Thank you," Hasryan said, then they fell into a companionable silence. These often happened with Camilla and after days living with her, Hasryan had gotten used to it, but usually tea was involved, and the absence of clinking cups felt strange. Camilla must have sensed it, too: she repeatedly rearranged her fur cloak before fetching into her sack and withdrawing a long, red scarf.

"You left this behind." She extended it to Hasryan, who still wore Garith's old winter coat under his cloak and had Esmera's mitts. If this kept up, she'd have dressed him entirely for winter. Camilla smiled as he wrapped it around his neck and nestled in the sudden warmth. "I told Esmera you were leaving. She said everyone does, eventually. Then she asked me to fetch her red wool and…" Once again, Camilla searched through the sack. This time, she retrieved a tuque. "She says it'd be a shame for winter to kill you before you give her the stories you promised."

Hasryan stared at it, his mouth dry. Then he ran a quick hand through his white hair. "I'm not putting that on my head. Oh gosh, are those to cover the ears?" The tuque had small triangles on each side, and Hasryan was certain he was right. "Big no."

Camilla laughed, opened the bottom of tuque, and gestured for him to ready his head to receive it. "You'd deny two old ladies this pleasure? I promised a comprehensive description."

Hasryan huffed, then cast his gaze around. No one but the horses to witness this. He crossed his arms, then bent his head forward, allowing Camilla to set the tuque firmly on his head. The wool espoused his skull and warmed his ears immediately, making their tip tingle. Camilla offered him the mitts, and he slipped them on, mumbling.

"I bet I look ridiculous."

"You look warm. Cozy."

She stepped back to admire him. Heat burned his cheeks and he balanced on his heels, at a loss for words. Along with Garith's old coat, Esmera and Camilla had completely equipped him for winter. It was late in the season, but they still had many cold nights to go, even more so since he was heading north. He patted at the tuque, a strange pain constricting his heart. From anyone else, gifts like these would have felt patronizing, but Hasryan didn't mind Camilla's doting. It felt reassuring to know someone would always treat him with a surplus of love, his own personal pride be damned.

When he returned his attention to Camilla, he immediately noticed her smile had turned more serious. He frowned, but she didn't give him time to ask what was wrong.

"I know you've faced Brune again and … if you need to talk about it—or anything, really—I'm here."

Hasryan's hands dropped by his sides. Did he want to talk? He'd told Brune everything he needed to, had hoped to slam the door on that part of his life. Yet every day since then, he'd thought of what she'd done for him in the past, of her apology and subsequent help with Nevian's spell, of how he could stay here, in Isandor, protected by her divination shields, if only he forgave her. Worse, he'd thought of their quiet, pleasant moments together, both in Nal-Gresh and Isandor, and how she had made room for him in her life. To use him, he reminded himself, yet that never washed away his sadness.

"I miss her," he admitted, his voice a low husk. "I hate her, but I miss her, and I feel silly about it. It's like a part of me won't accept I did the right thing, and having to leave Isandor really isn't helping."

A light hand touched his shoulder, and Hasryan leaned forward, into Camilla's open arms. He drew upon her warmth and comforting presence, calming his turmoil.

"Let yourself mourn, Hasryan. She has been a part of your life too long to disappear without pain. Some people stay with us through our entire lives, imprinted in our memories and easily called forth by small reminders. That's true whether or not we were right to cut them off." She pulled back and gently cupped his cheek, raising his head. "Don't beat yourself over it. If Brune is an indelible part of you, it only means she at least did one good thing in this world."

Hasryan blinked, struggling for an appropriate answer. Camilla's soft compliments whammed into him, always unexpected. Perhaps one day he'd learn to accept them, but right now, all he managed was a confused stammering and an awkward laugh. Then Arathiel appeared, saving him from further embarrassment. He was striking, the light-blue doublet in Brasten colours perfectly fit for him, and his locs had been redone, replaced by feed-in braids held in a tight bun.

"What a beautiful winter hat," Arathiel said with a wide grin. "Makes your red eyes even more striking."

Hasryan choked, then swiped the hat off his head in one smooth motion. "Don't you have a boyfriend to spend the evening with?"

"I'm afraid I had someone more important and urgent to see. Besides, Varden and I will have ample time together while we look for a new home."

More important. Hasryan had no answer to that, either. What was up with these two tonight? Every word they said made the thought of leaving harder to bear with.

"Oh, you decided to move in together?" Camilla asked.

"With Nevian, if he agrees. We could all use the quiet."

"Wonderful." Camilla picked up her now-empty sack and readjusted her fur cloak. "I will leave you two together, then. Lord Arathiel, it will be a pleasure to share tea again in this new home of yours once you have it. Hasryan…" She stepped to him, lightning-quick, and set a kiss on his forehead. "Take care. It was an honour to share my quarters with you, and I hope you'll send an old lady some letters about your travels."

"More letters?" Hasryan blurted out, because it was easier to latch on that than everything else she'd said. "I'll spend my entire life writing them, if this keeps up!"

Arathiel's eyebrows shot up. "Would that, perhaps, be a sign that you finally have too many friends? What a tragedy, all these people who care about you."

Hasryan laughed. It was true, in a way. He'd met so many people here who loved him, and whom he loved back. Yet it hadn't been enough to carve a place for him here—all it had taken to rip him from his space was Brune's betrayal and a city's hatred. Hasryan's fingers tightened around the tuque as he fought a rising wave of bitterness.

"I'm not complaining," he said. "But letters aren't the same."

"I know," Arathiel replied, his playful tone gone. "We all do. We'll miss you. But you're here now, and I want to enjoy that while I still can."

"You should take a walk," Camilla suggested. "It's a warm evening, perfect for long talks and testing out Hasryan's new winter gear."

Hasryan's gaze darted to his tuque and he sighed before obliging Camilla and shoving it back onto is head. It made him immediately warmer, not that he'd dare admit that. Still, he turned to face her, knowing he wouldn't have an opportunity to see her again for a long time.

"Thank you for everything. I promise I'll write."

Camilla nodded to him, then strode out of the stable without looking back. Hasryan thought he heard a sniffle, but she was gone too fast for him to confirm, and he wasn't sure he wanted to know. Something about the idea of Camilla crying for him unsettled him more than he could explain. When she was gone, he turned to Arathiel.

"So. Camilla came bearing gifts. What do you have to offer?"

He laughed and spread out empty arms. "Nothing but my company, I'm afraid. Was there ever anything else, however?"

"Nothing else is needed."

Hasryan lead the way out of the stables, and they walked together for hours, talking about everything and nothing all at once, starting with the wedding and moving out from there, to Arathiel's difficulty staying in the Brasten Tower and his plans for the future, his dream home. Hasryan had never chosen where he lived in such a fashion, instead moving from one Crescent Moon hideout to another, with a room in their headquarters to land back in every now and then. It hadn't been home the way Arathiel described it now: comfortable, intimate, safe.

No, that had been the Shelter, its music, and its people—Larryn and Cal especially. Hasryan wished he could soak in the sounds of the common room one last time before leaving. Brune wasn't the only part of his recent life to have left indelible marks on him. It didn't matter how far he travelled or how long he left: Isandor and its people, the friends he made here, would always stay with him. One day, whether the city wanted him to or not, he would return.

Character Guide

THE following is a list of characters featured in *City of Exile* with short descriptions to help readers navigate the story. The "titles" assigned to each character are meant to poke fun at them—don't take them too seriously.

House Dathirii

<u>Diel Dathirii (Lord Dathirii), Eternal Idealist, he/him</u>
Head of the Dathirii House, loves political fights and people, but none more than Jaeger.

<u>Jaeger, Stalwart Steward, he/him</u>
Diel's personal steward, the logistics behind the passion, a stickler for titles even for his long-time love.

<u>Branwen Dathirii, Master of Disguises, she/her</u>
Dathirii spymaster, her heart is as big as her multi-gender wardrobe.

<u>Garith Dathirii, Number One Flirt, he/him</u>
Dathirii coinmaster. Has ladies over at irregular hours, beware.

Vellien Dathirii, Anxious Healer, they/them
Dathirii priest of Alluma, youngest cousin. Would sing more if it didn't focus everyone's attention on them.

Camilla Dathirii, Tea of Kindness, she/her
Diel's aunt, has retired from wilder years to grant tea, cookies, and wisdom to those in need.

Kellian Dathirii, Stiff Guard, he/him
Captain of the Dathirii Guards, spends many hours wishing people would stop taking huge risks. Vanished.

Yultes Dathirii, Professional Impostor, he/him
Once main Dathirii liaison to House Allastam, now Hellion's steward. Diel's step-brother and Larryn's father. Is great at lying to himself and others.

Hellion Dathirii, 'Cunning' Shitlord, he/him
Yultes's "best friend", Lord Allastam's underling. Took over the Dathirii Tower to prove elves and nobles are superior.

House Allastam

Lord Allastam, Bitter Crusader, he/him
Head of House Allastam. Would watch the world burn to get his way and avenge his murdered wife.

<u>Drake Allastam, High on Privilege, he/him</u>
Lord Allastam's son, heir to the house leadership, typically responds to 'no' with violence. Long history of harassing Larryn.

<u>Mia Allastam, the Discreet Daughter, she/her</u>
Lord Allastam's daughter, equally ambitious. Neither chronic pain or a family's overbearing protectiveness can stop her.

House Brasten

<u>Amake Brasten (Lady Brasten), Slicing Politician, she/her</u>
Head of House Brasten, ready to own the Golden Table on her own if needed.

<u>Arathiel Brasten, Drifter from the Past, he/him</u>
Stayed trapped for a hundred and thirty years in a mysterious Well that drained his senses, but has found home once again in Isandor and its people. Member of the Halfies Quartet.

<u>Oloan Brasten, Twin Coinmaster, he/him</u>
One of House Brasten's twin coinmaster.

<u>Lindi Brasten, Afflicted Dancer, she/her</u>
Arathiel's sister, sick when he left for the Well. Dead.

The Shelter

Larryn, Anger Stew, he/him

Owner of and cook at the Shelter. Rages against the machine (and everyone else, really). Member of the Halfies Quartet.

Hasryan, Assassin Seeks Friends, he/him

Once Brune's favourite assassin, now helps House Dathirii. His sass is as deadly as his blades. Member of the Halfies Quartet.

Cal, Luck's Generous Hand, he/him

Priest of Ren, the luck deity. Lover of cheese, quick to develop friend crushes and act on them. Member of the Halfies Quartet.

Nevian, Stubborn Pupil, he/him

Avenazar's old apprentice, now hiding at the Shelter. Still determined to learn magic—and now, to teach it to Efua.

Efua, Genius Letter Girl, she/her

Orphan living at the Shelter. Larryn's unofficial little sister. Works as a letter delivery girl.

Jim, Hard-Working Father, he/him

First owner of the shelter. Adoptive father for Larryn and Efua. Dead.

The Myrian Enclave

<u>Master Avenazar, Destructive Ego, he/him</u>
Head of the Myrian enclave. Ruthless and powerful mage who avenges every slight. Grievously wounded (for now).

<u>Master Jilssan, Ambitious Pragmatic, she/her</u>
Transmutation specialist and Isra's master. Always ready to do what it takes to survive.

<u>Isra, Conflicted Princess, she/her</u>
Jilssan's apprentice. Is learning to untangle herself and be a better person, one clumsy step at a time.

Other Figures of Note

<u>Varden Daramond, Gentle Flames, he/him</u>
High Priest of Keroth, imprisoned for treason. Talented artist, loving soul, powerful fire-wielder.

<u>Sora Sharpe, Unapologetic Law Enforcer, she/her</u>
Investigator for Isandor's Sapphire Guards who first arrested Hasryan. Hates political games and has had quite the change of heart.

<u>Lai, Confident Informant, ne/ner</u>
An informant for Sora Sharpe. In a queerplatonic relationship with one of House Dathirii's kitchen boys.

Brune, Ruthless Mercenary Leader, she/her

Leader of the Crescent Moon mercenary, powerful mage, Hasryan's old boss. Has hands in every pockets. Loves the colour brown.

Nicole, Iron-Grip Cook, she/her

In charge of the Dathirii's kitchens. Knew Larryn's mother. Don't mention Yultes to her.

Alton, Considerate Spy, he/him

Serves House Allastam. Part of Branwen's network of spies and friends. They disagree on fashion, though.

Lord William, Single Noble, he/him

Presides the Golden Table but has no House. Loves drama in many shapes.

Noble Families of Isandor

House Lorn

Founding family, and currently the biggest family in Isandor. Holds more seats on the Golden Table than any other House.

House Allastam

Second biggest family in Isandor. Its rise to power can be attributed almost entirely to the current Lord Allastam.

House Balthazar

A rising star in Isandor politics. Its wealth increase is recent but, speculation says, unlikely to last. Third biggest house.

House Dathirii

Founding family and the only elven noble house.

House Brasten

House of medium importance. Has managed to retain a seat on the Golden Table despite the family's often deadly hereditary illness.

House Carrington

Founding family that fell from power after a botanical spell gone wrong infected and killed half their family. Still sits at the Golden Table.

House Serringer

Small house that has a fur monopoly. One seat at the Golden Table.

House Almanza

Minor Isandor house. One seat at the Golden Table.

A Friendship Bargain

An Isandor Short Story

Lively bell welcomed Cal into the shop, followed by a burst of rainbow lights. He grinned—those were new, but unsurprising. André loved customizing his door's welcome reaction, and these matched his personality to a T.

"Trying to lure back the sun?" he called.

It had rained almost without stop for the last two weeks, leaving Isandor's bridges and stairs slick and slippery, and everyone's mood on edge. Thankfully, only a few warehouses close to the water's edge had flooded; almost everyone lived either far enough not to be affected by the rising water level or several floors high in Isandor's towers. Larryn had changed the configuration of the tables in the Shelter to accommodate even more folks than usual, both during the day and night, and Cal had welcomed a few regular patrons into his home on nights the constant drizzle became a heavy downpour. Faced with the depressing weather, André had apparently upgraded his entrance bell into a full-blown magical light show.

Cal's question drew a pleased exclamation from the back store, immediately followed by the crash of several boxes and a yelp of pain. Cal stifled a laugh and hurried across the tiny shop, past rows of heterogeneous objects, and to the miniscule room in which André stored what he couldn't cram on a shelf upfront. André had a shock of bright orange hair and a constellation of freckles spread over his cheeks and arms. He always picked extravagant clothes, and today's cat-patterned shirt was no exception. Cal grinned at its intense green colour, on which the black and white cat stood out. The bookseller was sitting on the floor amidst trinkets of all sorts— magical bottle openers, cat toys of all shapes and sizes, and, to Cal's great pleasure, a handful of religious statuettes.

"Good afternoon." Cal greeted him as if this fall and the chaos was the most normal occurrences in the world—and in truth, where André was concerned, they were. "Did you get hurt?"

"Not in the least!" André sprang to his feet, inadvertently throwing a stuffed mouse to the ground. He dusted off his hair, messing it further in the process, and then he was off. "I'm so sorry for the mess! You surprised me, you see—didn't expect any customers today, not with the rain. It's been a dull few weeks, let me tell you, and I'm really happy you dropped by, Cal. You always liven things up!"

"I brought gifts!" Cal confirmed, knowing full well nothing would excite André more than new trinkets to sell. The shopkeeper must have known, deep down. Cal rarely arrived empty-handed.

They had known each other for as long as Cal had lived in Isandor, and most of the statuettes lining up the shelves of Cal's home had come from André's shop. Conversely, a significant number of the objects on sales had been provided by the halfling. Cal's gambling habits meant he'd played with hundreds of people through the Lower and Middle Cities of Isandor. He'd won almost every single time. Instead of hoarding other people's money, however, he often called in favours: repairs at his house, cooked meals he could warm, strong arms to help other friends in needs. And with richer players, Cal asked them if they could clean their houses of odds and ends gathering dust, especially if they had minor enchantments. Most people were thrilled to get rid of their 'junk', and Cal knew André would call them 'treasures'.

At the mention of gifts, André let out a happy squeal. "Of course you did! I can't wait to discover what you found this time—getting goosebumps just thinking about it!" He dragged Cal out of the back store and to the main counter, buried under a huge pile of cups, waterskins, and other liquid containers. "Don't mind these. I had a wine-seller earlier looking for something to hold her products at just the right temperature, or even just inspiration for spells she could buy directly. She wants a stand at the next Festival! All day, in the sun. Or, well, rain if it rains, but you get my meaning." He shoved it all to the side to make room for the new stuff, and Cal cringed at the clattering cacophony. Hopefully nothing had broken in there. It obviously hadn't crossed André's mind, or the shopkeeper didn't care. He spread his arms out. "Show me the beauties!"

Cal laughed and rose to the tip of his toes, stretching up to set his bag on the counter. At the sight of him stretching, André gasped and dashed for his back store. He returned with a small stepladder, enchanted to respond to verbal command and move around. Cal climbed on it with a grin; he loved the human-sized vantage point. "You rummage through the bag, and I'll check out your stock. Did you move the statuettes again?"

André had opened Cal's sack and dove an arm into it long before the halfling finished his sentence. He looked up at Cal's question, a hint of confusion in his usual smile. "I did not? Though I will admit, I thought about it last week! I had this huge collection of handkerchiefs come in, and they would have looked just *perfect* on that shelf, with the outside light shining down on them. A real prize, I tell you. I was still considering it when a schoolmistress visited the shop—a really beautiful lady, with the longest twists I've ever seen—and anyway, she had this whole class of kids who had caught a bug and were in urgent need of something to wipe their noses, you see, so I sold those handkerchiefs within two days. I guess the rain does have some blessing."

"That's good. I'm glad your business isn't suffering because of the weather." Cal suspected it still did to some extent. A lot of people preferred not to risk Isandor's slippery bridges when it rained, or only stayed on plazas or streets with railings. André's shop was located in the Middle City, where half the stairs and bridges no longer had protection, and his tower was a little way off the main travel paths. You had to know where to find it, but after a few years, word had gone around the neighbourhood that you could find a great many things in *André's Little Cove*, provided you had the patience to listen to a story or two.

Cal secured his feet into the stepladder's little straps and whispered for it to head down the leftmost row. It lurched forward as it moved, emitting a low whizzing sound despite the slow speed.

They travelled past bright-coloured inks, fancy quills, and leather notebooks, past hammers of various sizes and scissors with special shapes embedded in them, past mugs and tankards of wood and metal and even glass, and past weird apparatus Cal couldn't identify for the life of him. And all of it was *gloriously* eye-level.

The short ride to the statuettes left a wide grin on Cal's face. André muttered to himself at the counter, taking objects one by one out of the bag and examining them. No doubt if Cal had stuck closer, he would have gotten one anecdote by André for each of them. While he didn't mind the long conversations this entailed, he hoped to be back to the Shelter in time for the evening rush. He couldn't linger forever.

Cal turned his attention to the statuettes, and for once wasn't overwhelmed by the sheer number of options. André often had over twenty of them lined up on the shelves, with a variety of sizes and material and colours that made Cal's head spin. Today, only four were left—much more manageable. Perhaps he wouldn't spend hours tethering on the edge of a decision this time!

Cal started with the smallest statuette of all: a depiction of Thanh, Mapper of the Stars, a wiry halfling from the Phong peninsula. Unlike with many other demigods, people had an excellent idea of Thanh's appearance: He had recorded shifts in appearance and gender as thoroughly as He had star positions or magical discoveries. Short hair and deep-set eyes had been carved in great details into the tiny figure, and when Cal brought it closer, he discovered the scroll in Thanh's hands had stars etched into it, too. How the artist had managed such a precise feat was beyond Cal's imagination.

Towering over Thanh's tiny figure was a massive black representation of Gresh. The sculpture almost reached two feet and represented a common depiction of the Earth Shaper in Alloria: a barrel-chested and brown-skinned masculine God, with flowing dark hair down to the small of Their back. They held an egg-shaped stone, opened at the top, and Cal peered in with a grin. Sure enough, the inside had been roughly sculpted like a city—Nal-Gresh, the thriving port at the end of the Reonne, with which so much of Isandor's trading happened. Cal already owned an even bigger version of this particular image of Gresh, however. He wished he could find the fat and feminine elf with bark-like skin that widespread around Aberah Lake and which had populated his youth.

The third was Ren, and despite owning over a dozen variants of his chosen patron, Cal almost chose this one right away. How could he not, considering its blindingly bright colours? Two Rens stood back-to-back in the statue. One, lime green, had hair hidden under a cap, a fit jacket and puffy pants, along with a mischievous grin. The other, a deep blue, sported wide skirts and a flowery hat, and was blowing a kiss at someone in the distance. Cal loved how alive Xe felt, and how the carving captured different facets of Xir gender and playfulness. This piece called to Cal's heart the way Ren always had—it would fit so well with his living room!—and it took great effort for him to put it down once more.

He regretted it when he turned his full attention to the last sculpture—a prime example of racist propaganda on dark elves. Much like Ren's, this statuette featured two figures, Sellar and Lanne, the twin deities of Creation and Destruction, which had long ago been associated with Light and Darkness, Good and Evil. Here, the artist had carved Sellar in ivory, as a delicate white elf, clearly feminine, while Lanne towered over her, a dark and muscled dark elf with a hand twisted into Their hair. Sellar's fingers stretched towards a sword thrust in the ground—the Halkaar, no doubts, the Holy Blade used by the four elemental deities to split Sellane, the Creator, into twins. The whole piece had undertones of sexual assault which twisted Cal's stomach. Always, dark elves played the role of attackers in stories—evil men stealing a pure white elf's virtue or women seducing innocent heroes. It didn't matter that dark elven communities lived isolated behind their walls, minding their business and barely ever leaving their territory: if a tale needed corruption or destruction, dark elves were the chosen targets.

If Hasryan saw the sculpture, he would crack jokes about it—cast his voice in a fake narration of evil dark elves overtaking the world or suggest Larryn expose it on the mantel above the Shelter's fireplace, so that all could remember the dangers of crossing their resident half-elf. But under all the smirks and bravado hid a wound, one constantly poked at, and Cal had no desire to reopen it. Someone else would fast enough; why would he remind his friend the world hated him? Cal promised himself once more to keep an eye for histories written by dark elves. One day, luck would bring one to his door despite their rareness, and he could learn more about this mess.

For now, he needed to pick his statuette. His gaze turned to Ren's glorious rendering of Xir bigenderness, and his heart longed to leave with it. His hand hovered nearby, chubby fingers ready to claim the deity of his soul, but then—on impulse, both whim and divine inspiration—he changed his mind and grabbed Thanh's. Before he could regret his decision, Cal whispered instructions to his stepladder. It jerked as it turned away and rolled away from André's religious treasures.

When Cal reached André again, the shopkeeper had separated everything into two piles: one for objects he wanted to keep, and one for the rest. Almost everything Cal had brought had stayed into the 'want' pile—a heartwarming sight, as far as Cal was concerned. André's talent resided in breathing new life into dusty objects, whether through small enchantments or by selling their merits one meaningful tale at a time. He might have trouble finding space in his back store for everything, but he would try. And in exchange for providing this new stock, Cal could take his pick of statuettes.

"Looks like you love my haul," he commented as the stepladder stopped at the counter.

André lowered the letter opener he was examining. "Don't I always?" When he noticed the little Thanh in Cal's hands, his eyes widened. He set his letter opener down then spread his hands on the counter, as if in need of support. "Don't you want the Ren one?"

Genuine worry filled his voice, and it was all Cal could do not to laugh. "I got thousands—you know that, I almost got them all here! But I'll admit, I almost picked it up anyway. It's so beautiful." Even now, Cal longed to return to the shelf and exchange. He glanced back before forcing himself not to look or rethink his choice. "I don't have Thahn. It'll be good to have a halfling on the shelf. There's so few of us this far north, it feels lonely sometimes."

"Oh. That's a good reason! But why not both?" André grinned and spread his arms, a wide gesture at the significant pile in front of him. "A single statuette doesn't feel like a fair trade for everything you brought me, and for the continuous support. You have to take Ren's, Cal! I haggled over it for ages with the merchant who brought it. Ne was also bigender and had me promise I would guide this particular piece into the hands of someone who would appreciate it fully. I put it on the shelf for show, but it was always meant to be yours, and if you don't take it then I'll have to find someone else even more perfect! But I think you should have it, really."

Without waiting for Cal's answer, André strode around the counter and down the rows of shelves, obviously heading for Ren's sculpture. Cal stared at his back, taken aback by André's insistence, and when words stumbled past his stunned tongue, André was well on his way.

"That's a really bad business model, André! You can't purchase things at high price to just give them away."

André laughed, the high-pitched and repetitive chuckle strangely reminiscent of his doorbell. "You're the expert, Cal," he said. "But tell me, is it a good friendship model?"

A delighted squeal escaped Cal's lips and he knew right that instant he could no longer refuse the gift. André's question had shot straight to his heart, spread happy warmth through his stomach, and slapped a grin on his face. While André sought his gift, Cal recovered his bag and put his Thanh sculpture in it. When the shopkeeper returned with Ren's statuette, Cal extended his hands as if to accept an offering. André blushed, his bright freckles making him seem even younger—as if his round face and chirpy energy didn't already incite people to underestimate his age. Cal wrapped his fingers around the statuette, making sure to catch André's hand and squeeze it briefly as thanks.

"You are too kind," he said, before climbing down his stepladder. The world immediately seemed to grow taller, familiar and comforting. For all that Cal loved the temporary height boost, he preferred his close-to-the-ground station. "If I may offer more advice? Throw the Sellane one into the Reonne River. Selling racist shit isn't a great business model either. I'll pay you if you want."

Confusion hovered on André's face as he worked through Cal's words. His frown increasingly deepened, until he shrugged. "Makes sense. Do you want to be there? Do it yourself?"

This time, Cal laughed. "Why not? And after that, I can show you how my house looks with your pillows! You ought to witness the glorious living room you contributed to."

"I would love to!" They headed together towards the entrance, Cal clinging his bag and statuette while André stopped to rearrange objects on the shelves every step or so. "I'm glad they make you happy. Devising that colouring spell was harder than I thought it would be but so worth it! I should practise my magic more often, but theory books and I just don't agree. The headaches they give me, you wouldn't believe! But everyone is always obsessed with big magics and fancy alchemical gardens when they could take ordinary objects and introduce magic in their daily lives! Imagine how the people we could help if I was more skilled!" He threw his arms up in exasperation. They had reached the door, and he stopped with a sigh. "I'm rambling again, and I'm sure you have a busy day. It's always a pleasure to have you here."

Cal pushed the door half opened, then stopped and looked up to

André. "I love coming. See you next time for a majestic statuette send off, and your first tour of my home!"

In his first visits at *André's Little Cove*, Cal had often stayed at the door for over an hour, chatting with André while customers browsed or to pass time until someone entered. Cal had learned his lesson since: if he wanted to leave, he needed to be expeditive about it, and even a little rude. Reminding himself André wouldn't be hurt and that the Shelter's rush hour would start soon, Cal waved at his friend and slipped out of the shop before André could prolong the goodbyes.

ACKNOWLEDGEMENTS
REMERCIEMENTS

HERE we are, at the end of a long journey. A temporary end, most likely, but an end nonetheless. So many people have left an imprint on these books since I first imagined these characters, it'd be impossible to name them all—even to *remember* them all.

But it has been a good fifteen years, if not a bit more, since I first imagined Cal and Larryn (the original pair!) and a whole universe emerged from it. Isandor will always be special to me; I wouldn't be writing without it. So everyone that touched this—every friend and family that has listened to me ramble and scream and rant, that has watched me unravel plotlines or bounce ideas, that has squealed in joy at a juicy lines or roleplayed on of the countless iterations of these characters; everyone, also, who has brought me coffee and wine, cooked me food or cleaned the house, cheered me on during drafts or revisions … you've all made this happen. There have been times, especially with the last two books, when I could barely look at this series anymore, and the support has been essential to my ability to pull through.

In particular, I owe so many thanks to Lynn and Cedar for the support and feedback, along with my little self-pub discord and the Kraken Collective members. All my close friends at home, my partner and his endless puns, my family—my twin, in particular, who keeps giving me these amazing covers.

And finally, perhaps more than anything, thank you so much for reading. Every single one of you enjoying these characters, tweeting or emailing me. Your love for these characters and their story has meant the world.

WANT MORE?

At The Kraken Collective, we know how frustrating it can be to reach the end of a book and want more. Within the following pages, you'll find books with a similar feel to help you scratch that reading itch and why we're recommending them.

We hope our suggestions will help you find your next favourite read!

Odder Still
by **D.N. Bryn**

Looking for more speculative queer stories with fantastical cities and complex politics? Odder Still by D.N. Bryn is an achillean romance with a trans LI, a venom-style parasite arc, and an incredible underwater city full of selkies. Highly recommend this fast paced adventures if you enjoyed Isandor.

The Ice Princess's Fair Illusion
by Dove Cooper

City of Exile gives a lot of room to exploring aromantic identities, but if you're looking for more, check out *The Ice Princess's Fair Illusion*, by Dove Cooper. A sapphic, queerplatonic retelling of King Thrushbeard told in free verse, *Ice Princess's* touches on many facets of asexuality and aromanticism, from compulsory heterosexuality to the choosing (or eschewing) of labels. Truly a gem of a story.

Learn more about these and other titles at
www.krakencollectivebooks.com

About the Author

Claudie Arseneault is an asexual and aromantic-spectrum writer hailing from the very-French Quebec City. Her long studies in biochemistry and immunology often sneak back into her science-fiction, and her love for sprawling casts invariably turns her novels into multi-storylined wonders. Claudie is a founding member of The Kraken Collective and is well-known for her involvement in solarpunk, her database of aro and ace characters in speculative fiction, and her unending love of squids.

You can also always find all of her books at
claudiearseneault.com